SAVAGE LITTLE LIES

SAVAGE LITTLE LIES

COURT LEGACY: BOOK TWO

EDEN O'NEILL

PROLOGUE

The Summer Before Senior Year

Dorian

Old fucker: Feel free to let yourself in, son. I'll be in the parlor.

My thumb closed out the text, countless others above it.

They'd been what led me here today.

I'd driven over two hours to see this fucker, tell this fucker what was what. I didn't need his old ass anymore.

Today was the day I told him.

I'd admit, the ruse had to go on longer than I had anticipated. I couldn't come right out with asking the old man what I needed from him. I had to lean into things a bit and pretend like I wanted to get to know him.

I got out of my car, parked in front of a manor the size of a city block. The old fucker had done well in his reclusion. He was an outcast from our town. At least, when it came to me and mine. He wasn't wanted, and after he got out of prison, he'd made a new home for himself far away from my family and me.

Dad had kept watch on him the first few years he'd been out, from what I understood. He hadn't wanted the old man to have anything to do with us, with me. Apparently, the old fart upstate didn't pose much of a threat because eventually I no longer heard whispers of Dad utilizing his monitoring team upstate. He used to often talk about the details with my mother, but that stopped.

"He's dead to me. Dead to this family," I'd heard my father say. He'd sighed. "Might as well make it official. I won't grant any more resources to him."

But Dad did still keep tabs, and I knew that because, on occasion, he did have his PI come in with a report for him. Dad had many contacts, things he used for various reasons. He ran many successful businesses and worked with many people. With the high-stakes clientele he worked with, he often had to find out if those people were on the up-and-up.

His PI, Marshall, usually came through around once a year, and I knew the guy, knew what he did. Dad claimed he was a friend, but I had my best friend, Thatcher, look the guy up one day. Marshall was my dad's way of dealing with the fact that his fucked-up kin was currently out in the real world. It was Dad's way of functioning.

What I'd been doing recently was mine.

Since Charlie had died, I'd needed help. I hadn't wanted to stress my father out or my mother. Coming to see this old fuck weekly all summer had been my way to get what I needed. He'd helped me find the woman responsible for Charlie's death, and according to Thatcher, she was returning to her position as headmaster of my school this upcoming term.

Things were finally coming full circle, and I didn't need to go on with the ruse. I didn't have to take the old man's phone calls or worry about his texts being seen by my mother or father. I didn't have to *pretend* anymore. I was ending this with my grandfather today.

And it'd be oh so sweet.

I slammed the car door behind me, my grandfather's manservant Samuel meeting me out on the cobblestone walkway. He offered to take my keys from me and drive my car around to my grandfather's garages.

I told him no need.

I wouldn't be long and met my grandfather in his parlor. He had a fine mansion, opulent with all the bells and whistles. He had more rooms in it than his old-ass knees could even take him into. Same with the stairs. I was quite sure he hadn't seen a quarter of this house that looked like something out of some old-ass European flick.

My feet creaked on the polished hardwood, my grandfather sitting in front of a chess set. We had a routine during these visits, and I forced down the bile in my throat every time. I had to sip tea with him like some uppity-ass prick, moving chess pieces around with him while he spoke to me about my dad, old stories he had about my father in his youth. I listened to this while trying not to choke on the fucker's cigar smoke. He'd also offered me a puff on the thing more than once.

He'd offered me alcohol too, like a good and responsible grandfather. He *claimed* norms imposed on regular society were for the normal.

We weren't normal.

We were elite. We were above, and this was something he never failed to remind me. He never asked about current details regarding my father or mother. I didn't think he cared.

He was too busy working on me.

His eyes lifted from his chess set, our tea already out and ready. He also had that cigar smoking in his fingers. He waved a hand. "Take a seat, son."

I wouldn't, no longer fighting the sneer at being referred to by a title *only my father* was able to use. I wasn't his son, and I may be blood-related to this man, but as far as I was concerned that didn't mean much.

Grandfather noticed me standing there, the man aged but not as old-looking as what I'd hoped. He was in his seventies, but took very good care of himself. He appeared at least a full decade younger, his graying blond more pepper than salt. He appeared distinguished in his smoking jacket and was probably the only old man I'd ever seen that might actually pack a punch if he ever decided to throw down. My grandfather was a large man, and I knew he had used those fists in the past. He'd done so on my father. I'd heard the stories.

I stayed by the door, clenching my own fists, and I'd give it to my grandfather. He pretended not to notice. Instead, he angled his gaze down to the chessboard.

"You have words for me," he said, moving a pawn. These were always sacrificed first. He sat back in his chair. "Be a man and say them, son."

Be a man.

I smirked. The toxicity that emanated off this fucker could be bottled. It reeked of privilege and old values. I wet my lips. "I'm not your son, old man." Shit, did that feel fucking good. I'd been holding back my taunts, my own jabs. I forced a finger in his direction. "Never fucking call me *son*. Ever."

I honestly had no idea how I'd been able to hold off on this day for so long. The words itched on my tongue every sip of tea I took and during each piece of bullshit I did have to tell him about my life. I never told him the truth. I made shit up about me and what I was into. I never did speak a word about my family. This was all a lie with him and had been from the beginning.

Grandfather tapped his cigar on an ashtray, not phased in the slightest by what I said. "I see."

"No, you don't actually." I went over and placed my hands on the chess set.

I tossed it.

The pieces flew everywhere, all over the floor, and scattered. I didn't bother to watch them roll before I was in this old fuck's face.

"I don't want anything to do with you," I said calmly, strategically. Grandfather hadn't moved an inch, only watching me. He appeared nothing if not intrigued by my rant, and that only made me want to punch his old ass more. "I never did. This was a lie."

His blink was rather slow. "A lie?"

"Yes." I pushed off the table. "I used your ass, old man. I did, and now that I got what I needed regarding my uncle, I don't want anything to do with you."

I watched the words play on my grandfather's face. His poker face was a good one. I couldn't tell if anything I said meant anything to him.

At least, at first.

Sitting up, he tapped the chess-free table. He nodded. "I know."

"You know?"

He nodded again. "I know you haven't been coming here because you particularly liked me, *son*—"

My teeth gnashed.

His head bobbed once more. "Dorian. I know you don't want to be here and only came here because you did need help with your little problem."

My heart raced, my vision red. He called my uncle's death a *little problem*, and it was only the man my mother raised who kept me from punching a seventy-year-old man.

My nails dug into my palms, probably enough to draw

blood, but it was all I could do in order to stand there when my grandfather got up.

He placed his back to me, going to the roaring fireplace. He took the poker, tending to the fire.

"You needed me for something," he said, tossing the embers. "You did, and it brought you to me. I didn't care your reason. It brought you here. Got you to get to know me."

"I don't want to fucking know you." My fists unclenched, and only then did he turn around. He had his cigar still in his hand, puffing out thick smoke.

"I think you know more about me than you think," he said, studying my hands clenching and unclenching. Thick smoke clouded around him. "We had a mutual exchange, and I forgive you for taking advantage of the situation."

I smirked again, coming over. I shot a finger in his direction. "This ends today. I won't be coming up here anymore. Playing chess or smelling your funky-as-shit-smelling cigars."

To prove that, I took it from him. I broke it in two, then tossed it into the fire, the thing going up in flames.

Grandfather did nothing. He said nothing when I got in his face again.

"I hated you from the moment I found out you existed," I said, my throat working. "You're a monster and an abuser. The only thing keeping you from the title *murderer* is because you didn't technically kill my aunt Paige." He'd covered it up, which was as good as him being one as far as I was concerned. "You stay away from me, and you stay away from my family."

Grandfather studied me as if I was a child, and he was merely entertaining my presence. Without missing a beat, he pulled another cigar out of his jacket.

He lit it up in my face.

"Now that you've proposed your terms, I'll state mine," he said, blowing smoke in my face now. He smiled like an arrogant fuck. "Only fair, correct?"

What the fuck did I give about being fair when it came to him? Even still, he continued on, placing his back to me again. He walked over to the window our chess set had faced, a perfect view of his gardens and fountains. In fact, it looked so much like our property back home in the backyard it made me sick.

What he had out here was about three times larger. Like he was trying to outdo my father's childhood home and the gardens my biological grandmother planted. Grandpa Prinze soiled her name with this whole phony-ass display.

Probably on purpose.

"You know, you're so much more like me than he ever was," Grandfather said. He grinned. "Your father? What you call abuse, I call toughening him up, making him a man."

I saw red, seething, shaking. I almost couldn't see through the haze of red.

He faced me. "I'm sure he never used my tactics, but you still managed to be stronger than he ever was."

"Fuck you," I growled, and in my haze, I approached him. I raised a fist.

He caught it. He did by the wrist, but he only stopped me from hitting him, *made me hesitate*, because of the look in his eyes.

There was madness there.

Horrifying, it stared back at me, a warning in the old man's gaze.

The smile with it only made it appear more warped.

"My new proposal is that you do what I say," he said, his head tilted. "You continue to come here and do what this old man says. You visit me and humor your grandfather."

"You're fucking crazy—"

"Because otherwise, things can happen," he stated, making my blink. "Terrible things can happen, and I'm sure you wouldn't want your parents knowing about these visits.

They'd be pretty upset, their lives disrupted. And how is your mother these days? She still work for the city?"

I twitched.

His grin widened. "Surely, you'd know I'd keep tabs on my son and his family. I mean, where do you think he learned it?"

He lowered my fist slowly, so chillingly calm my stomach clenched. He puffed his cigar again, wetting his lips after. He directed his cigar at me. "You'll continue to come see me. You will until I see fit." He leaned in. "After all, we wouldn't want another accident. What happened to your aunt Paige was so tragic." He made direct eye contact. "Wouldn't want your mother having any bad luck."

He tapped my face, making me twitch again.

He sat at the table, picking his ashtray up off the floor. He knocked some ashes into it. "You're dismissed for today. I'm sure you have a lot to think about."

He said it so coolly, so coldly. Like he hadn't just threatened my mother's life.

Like it meant nothing.

Such words probably didn't to this man, this monster.

Turning, I left, but his words stopped me at the door. He said my name, and when I turned, he was smoking his cigar again.

He blew smoke from his lips. "How's the weather in Maywood Heights this time of year?" he asked, casually. He shrugged. "I might be thinking about making a visit. Excellent fishing out there. At least from what I can remember."

Shock kept me silent, but strength kept me standing.

Grandfather grinned. "You think about that too," he said, then stared at the window. That was the last thing I saw before I closed the door. I strode with unsteady footing all the way to my car.

I had a lot of time to think during my drive home that night, but my last thought sobered me. He said I was more like him than my father, and he may be right. There was only one way to fix what I'd done. I'd opened Pandora's box, and there would ultimately be only one way to close it, *end it*. My grandfather couldn't be on this earth if I wanted my family safe.

I'd have to take care of him.

CHAPTER
ONE

Dorian

"Bru? Hold on. It's so loud." Sloane covered her phone after what she'd said, smiling at me. "It's Bru. I'm assuming he wants an update. About you?" Her grin widened. "I'm just going to tell him how things turned out. That we got you out okay."

Her reference, of course, was to my grandfather *getting me out.* He'd handled my bail, in the police precinct with us now.

His attention never left me.

And what a sight to be had, the old man with his mother-fucking jewel-top cane. He stood in a crisp suit, mingling amongst Maywood Heights's scum. The police were bringing people in and out of county lockup, but even with all the traffic, my grandfather's attention stayed pointed on me.

As stated, it never left.

I watched, a twitch in my eye as *my grandfather* hovered a hand behind my girl's back. *My girl* who looked cheesed to the fucking nines to be in his presence. Grandpa Prinze smiled at her. "Yes, tell him everything worked out." He placed that smile on me. "He was quite worried once I told him everything. I was at the house with him when Sloane and I spoke on the phone."

I swallowed, saying nothing.

Grandpa Prinze nodded at Sloane. "Don't worry about Dorian and myself. I'm sure we'll find something to talk about while you're gone."

I was sure we would, my body stiff as a goddamn board in the old man's presence.

I suddenly found myself very relieved to be in a police station. There were at least a dozen cops here, all fucking strapped.

Not that it would matter.

My grandfather stood in front of me *resurrected*, alive when he shouldn't be.

I knew because I had stood over the body.

I'd been the grim reaper not long ago, and apparently, this old fuck had nine lives. Sloane touched my arm before she left, and it took all I had in me to not react to anything happening to me at the present. I didn't want to show that I was thoroughly shaken, especially in front of the man I'd attempted to kill.

I couldn't show my cards.

If Grandfather could tell I was thrown by his presence, he didn't act like it. He simply watched Sloane go, as I did. She took a corner of the police station to continue with her call, one away from the doors and cops moving in and out of them with perps. Once there, she proceeded to take her call with her brother, and that was when my grandfather turned in my direction. His jeweled cane shifted under his hand, and when he made a step in my direction, I flinched.

The corners of his lips lifted, his smile a small one. It was almost coy as he lifted his chin. "Are you all right, son?" he questioned, his poker face a good one. He was acting as if him standing here was the most normal of occurrences. His head lowered. "You seem to have some nerves going about you."

Well, that happened when one saw a fucking ghost.

I eyed the area, studied Sloane. She was waving at me now, grinning, but my reaction to that wasn't much.

I was in too much fucking shock.

In any case, she went back to her call, and I faced the old man who'd called me *son* again. I pocketed my hands, my throat tight. "Nerves happen when you see ghosts."

This man should be *dead*, point-blank, and though it shouldn't have been, offing the fucker had been the hardest thing I'd had to do. I wasn't a killer. I was a good son, an honorable one my father and mother raised, and as dark as some shit had been in my life, it'd never crossed my mind to kill someone. Even my worst enemies.

The old man had brought the devil out of me, the monster within. I'd done what needed to happen. I had to in order to protect my family.

He'd threatened my mother.

That very fact lingered between us now as we stood here today. The old man drew his fingers down a smooth jawline.

"Yes, well." His hand returned to his cane. "My doctors assure me I have a clean bill of health." His head tilted. "If anything, they tell me I've never been stronger after more *recent* events in my life. I am stronger, and you'd best know that, understand it."

A threat laced there beyond his words, and not on the subtle side.

How was he alive?

I'd poisoned the old man's tea in the end, a bitch move, but I'd never had to consider doing such a thing before.

Murder and darkness were only reserved for the most vile monsters in my world, ones like this man who stood before me today. In a single act, he'd made me a monster too, but I obviously hadn't done the job well enough. Someone must have found him after I'd watched him choke on his own bile. He'd had another one of those funky-ass cigars in his hand when he'd fallen off his chair.

I'd left after he'd hit the floor, not staying for the final result. I'd just wanted to get the fuck out of there. His servants had had the day off that morning, a big reason I'd chosen it. I hadn't needed anyone knowing what I was doing.

I'd even wiped the security cameras.

Upon leaving, I recalled wishing that cigar in his hand would burn down the house with him inside, and I wished I could say it was because I wanted him and the evidence of my presence in his home burned. That'd been far from the reason.

I'd wanted *him* to burn, and that was when I knew something had changed in me. I'd come full circle. I had crossed a line I couldn't come back from when it came to my life. My grandfather had made me a murderer, as deep and as dark as some of the shit I'd heard he'd done in the past. The difference was I'd done what I had beyond purely selfish reasons.

At least, that was what I told myself.

In any case, I hadn't even been able to do that fucking right, my grandfather standing here today.

He watched me watching him, and I bet if he had a cigar now, he'd be studying me from behind the thick smoke. He liked to do that, watch me during our time together. Like it gave him joy or contentment just to be in my presence.

Like he cared and had a soul.

Grandfather's head lifted again, but soon he was passing his attention over to that corner again. The one with Sloane, my girl still on her phone.

My girl.

How did she know this *fucker*? None of this made sense.

"What is she to you?" Grandfather Prinze asked me, causing me to blink. I should be asking him that fucking question. His eyes narrowed. "Son?"

I was *not* this man's son. I stayed silent, and his hand moved on his cane.

"You're lucky, you know," he said. "That I happened to call and she mentioned your situation? You were so sloppy, Dorian."

I twitched.

His eyes narrowed. "Multiple witnesses saw you fleeing the very scene where the Mayberry woman's body was ultimately recovered." He tsked. "They found her in a warehouse and *your car* had been leaving the area. Like I said, spotted by multiple people, farmers who were up and doing their morning work."

That was because I'd stayed longer than I should have, too long after my friends had already left.

I honestly didn't know why really. The guys had all peeled off, but for some reason, I'd stayed by the door on my way out. I'd been angry, frustrated after we recorded Mayberry's confession.

So much darkness.

I didn't think I'd hurt our headmaster after my friends left, but what she'd said about her, *about her and Charlie*, had been so fresh. I'd also just come off the week from hell regarding what I'd done to my grandfather. I'd been in a really dark place.

I wouldn't have hurt her. I wouldn't have hurt her.

I believed I wouldn't have. But it had taken a lot for me to leave after having an opportunity. I had left in the end, though. I had. I'd left.

I'm a good person. I'm not a monster.

My fist clenched, and my grandfather noticed.

His attention in my direction didn't waver. "Like I said, you were sloppy." He straightened. "It was a good thing I was around to get you out of that situation."

My head shot up, my mouth dry.

And my grandfather didn't even miss a beat.

"When Miss Sloane told me about your situation... told me about my grandson of all people, I was quite disappointed." He passed a look around the area before finding me again. "Fortunately for you, your uncle's old girlfriend can't seem to stay out of trouble."

What the fuck?

"What..." I started, then swallowed. "You?"

Him.

It'd all make sense, though, *him*. I shook my head. "It was you? *This* was you?"

My grandfather's laughter was light, laughing like there was anything to fucking laugh about.

He straightened. "Actually, it was one of the woman's debt collectors. It seems her particular *habits* didn't die just because she was back in town." He shrugged. "I guess her being out in the warehouse just gave someone the opportunity."

Just someone, huh?

And how convenient. How *obvious* that she'd happened to be there in a place of vulnerability for something to happen to her. My friends and I had left her in an *abandoned* factory, one of my father's old businesses.

A business my grandfather used to own before that.

So much was convenient about all of this. The debt collector had just happened to know where Mayberry was.

Then Sloane talking to my grandfather to fix the situation...

My grandpa definitely looked like the hero today. He looked like a hero because *she* talked to him.

The fuck...

My attention redirected to Sloane in that moment, my grandfather coming closer. Sloane was still on her call, but I didn't move when my grandfather was in the same breath as me.

I was too busy looking at her.

I was too busy trying *not* to think shit and go to an even darker place, one of madness.

One of betrayal.

"What is she to you?" It was me to speak the words this time. I studied my grandfather. "What is all this?"

I didn't think I needed to elaborate. There were just… too many convenient things. Not to mention the cops had known where to find me in the first place. Sloane had said up and down she hadn't said anything.

I believed her.

I honest to fucking God did, even though everything within me told me I was naive.

I was going on faith.

I *wanted* to believe her. Still did.

Sloane had her back pressed against the wall now, and she was the only soft thing in his place, the only delicate thing. She had her hand all wrapped up in her dark hair, her body thick in all its perfect places. I'd wanted to shove my cock in her the moment I saw her after getting out. I'd wanted to take her out of his place and wrap myself up in her. I'd wanted to *feel* the security of her, and I was man enough to admit she'd been doing that for me.

That was why I'd called her in the first place today.

She'd been the first one I thought of when I'd been alone in that cabin, aching about all the shit with Charlie like a little bitch. I hadn't even called my boys.

I'd just called her.

I shot in my grandfather's direction, really happy I was in a police station now. If I had things my way, I'd have taken his cane and shattered his old fucking legs.

"What *is she to you*?" I gritted, needing some fucking answers. "What's going on, and why do she and her brother call you by the name Montgomery?"

Callum was his first name. I knew that, but obviously not his last.

My grandfather's blink was subtle, his attention focused. "You wouldn't know, would you? The name Montgomery?"

My mouth dried as I watched him look at her again, *my girl*. Mine.

Grandfather stood tall. "As far as who I am to her, why don't you ask Sloane herself? You two seem pretty close. Have to be since she pleaded to me about you. To fix things *for you*." He smiled. "But then again, how close are you really?"

I blinked, my gut turning. Few people had known where I was today at that cabin, and she'd been one of them. She and my grandpa getting me out of jail together could have just been an act, this whole bailing-me-out thing *a lie*.

Sloane happened to choose that precise time to come back, and I must have looked fucking ghost white.

She had my arm, making me face her, and basically assaulted me with that softer-than-shit scent I'd wanted to drown in on more than one occasion.

Now, I just felt like I was drowning.

"Dorian?" She squeezed my arm, her lips parting. She pulled her hair out of her face. "Do you need to sit?"

I didn't need to sit.

I needed to fucking run.

My grandfather's hand on me kept me from going anywhere. He smiled. "I was just telling him how lucky he is." He squeezed my shoulder. "The true assailant was apprehended before Sloane and I arrived at the precinct." His smile stretched. "Your bail didn't even have to be paid in the end."

And how lucky for that.

I definitely noticed my grandfather's hand didn't loosen, Sloane smiling too.

"He is lucky," she said, but then faced my grandpa. "And, Dorian, Callum was able to reach out to the right people." Her eyes warmed in my direction. "Get you out quicker."

"I simply made a few calls." My grandpa's hand left my

shoulder, returning to his cane. "I lived here for a time. It's been a while, but I'm still able to move things along. The right pieces and the *people* if I need to."

I glanced between the pair of them, my back more than up.

My phone buzzed.

It quite possibly might have been doing that the whole time, but I hadn't been paying attention.

Maybe in more than one way.

Wolf: Where are you? You need to come home. NOW.
NOW.

My phone had been going off before I'd been arrested, Wolf trying to get to me. My parents had been blowing up my phone before that.

Wolf wasn't the only one to text.

I had missed messages from Thatcher and Wells too, and of course, my parents. They'd been trying to get to me before all this, but I also had missed messages and phone calls from my god dads.

In fact, they had *all* called.

I lifted my phone, answering one. It was from Ramses, Wolf's dad.

"Where are you, kid?" he asked, sounding like he was moving. "We're all out looking for you."

What the fuck?

I ended the voicemail, and when I looked up, Sloane wasn't where I'd left her.

In fact, she'd been hovering over me, close.

Too close.

I found myself stiffening in her presence, and when I did, she blinked.

"Hey, what's going on?" she asked.

What *was* going on?

I exchanged a look between my grandfather and her again, my mouth dry. I looked at her. "I need to leave."

I angled around them, not knowing what she was fucking playing.

It was all a lie, *a lie*, and I needed to get the fuck out of there.

I ended up outside, straight walking. I was aware of steps behind me, and considering how light they were, they had to be Sloane's.

"Dorian, wait!"

She'd obviously just confirmed that, but I wasn't turning around. The parking lot was a clusterfuck of cops and traffic, a great place to be. My grandfather wouldn't be able to try anything here.

"Dorian, please wait. Your car?" She sounded like she'd stopped, her voice farther away. "It's at the cabin, remember?"

She was right, of course. It'd been left at the cabin because I'd been arrested.

And you're a fucking idiot.

I was at a standstill, completely giving Sloane an opportunity to come around me. She stood there in her high-top shoes and the shorts that gave me nothing but her ass cheeks when she flashed it at me. I was still drawn to her.

And I hated myself for it.

I'd been a complete dumbass to be fooled by her, and when she stopped in front of me, she had her hands up. Cheeks flushed, she appeared to be more panicked than winded.

As if she cared.

As if all of this shit wasn't a fucking lie and presented by the devil himself, my grandfather.

It took all I had not to bowl through her at that moment, and it was a good thing she kept her distance. I didn't want to do the opposite of what my father and mother had taught me.

Even if she had played my ass.

"Let Callum take you home," she pleaded, and I winced at

her referring to my grandpa in such a way. She said it so inno-
cently. As if she didn't know at all what my grandpa was to
me. She raised a hand. "He can take you. You don't
have to…"

"She's right, son."

I swiveled around, my grandfather still on the steps of the
precinct. He had his cane still in hand, his chin lifted. He
appeared as nothing but the savior he'd clearly wanted to
come across as.

He gestured to a man who came out of nowhere, right
near Sloane and me. This was a big guy, wearing all black
down to his gloves. He came off as nothing but a hit man, but
the billed hat gave me an indication.

"My driver, Lucas," Grandpa Prinze said to me, coming
forward. "Just tell him where you want to go. He can take
you anywhere."

Lucas took off his hat, and I noticed right away where his
hand went.

It settled right on his jacket.

"Is it home for you, then, sir?" he said to me, but his hand
didn't leave that area. The gesture was more than telling. This
guy wasn't merely a driver.

He was a fucking goon.

Odds were my grandpa wasn't trying to tango with me,
not after I'd tried to off his ass. This guy Lucas was no doubt
strapped to the nines.

"Dorian."

I fought myself from jumping, *cringing* when Sloane's
hand touched my shoulder. How crazy that earlier all I'd
wanted to do was to hold her and just get a feel of her after
being in this place. I thought she'd been my saving grace.

But as it turned out, the girl couldn't be farther from my
fucking salvation.

CHAPTER
TWO

Sloane

Dorian was tense for some reason.

It made me sad.

I mean, I got it really. He'd just been arrested, but as I watched him clamp up in the back seat of Callum's car, I felt bad *for him*. It'd been a shit day. Hell, he'd had more shit than anyone should ever deal with. This morning should have been a victory for him. He'd gotten Principal Mayberry to confess to her place in his uncle's murder.

It had been a victory in regards to that, but obviously things had gone sour. Mayberry wasn't supposed to turn up dead, and Dorian had led on that was the opposite of what he wanted. He hated the woman, yeah, but he also wanted her to live with what she'd done.

No, things weren't supposed to turn out like this.

Things were quiet in the car, so quiet. Dorian's reaction at the precinct had been so unsettling. He was jumpy, and I wanted to help him.

He wouldn't even look at me.

He was in his head, thick fingers flying through his blond locks, and as happy as I was Callum had been there to help us, I think his presence wasn't helping in that moment. Callum was acquainted with me as my brother's and my guardian, yes, but he was a virtual stranger to Dorian. He had helped Dorian, which was good, but I couldn't be open with Dorian with him here.

And I wanted to be.

I just wanted to talk to him. Things had been so different when he *just* saw me at the precinct. He'd been relieved. I know he had. At least, it had felt that way.

"You sure you don't want us to take you home, Dorian?" Callum stated, up front with his driver, Lucas. The black sedan was spacious, but not enough room for him to ride in the back as well. Hell, Dorian took up two seats on his own with his size. The large boy was like a sardine in the cabin. Callum's eyes directed to the rearview mirror. "I'm sure you'd like to see your family right away after being where you were. Go home?"

Callum was referring to the fact that Dorian wanted to go back to the cabin and get his car. He'd been adamant about making his own way after that, and even I told him I'd take him back to the cabin later if he wanted to get his Audi. Ares, his friend, had been blowing up his phone before he'd gotten arrested and his parents had too. The news had just broken about Mayberry and her affair with Dorian's uncle.

Dorian winced, like actually winced, in the back seat. He was *so* jumpy, and it hurt my heart. He wasn't like that before at all, not before his arrest, even after everything that happened today. His lips parted. "I need to get my car."

And that was it before he faced the window. Callum hadn't tried to make small talk with him, but I had. Again, he hadn't looked at me.

I wanted to try again, but not here. We needed to be alone. It might make him more comfortable.

The cabin wasn't far, but far enough that we had to drive. Things were starting to get a bit more scenic, and after a few moments, I spotted Callum's eyes again in the mirror.

"I don't know if Sloane told you, but her father was an old friend of mine," he said, clearly trying here with Dorian. Anyone in the car could see he was so tense right now. Callum smiled a little. "He used to work for me actually. Did I tell you that, Sloane?"

He hadn't, my head shaking. This did raise Dorian's head, though, his sight in that direction.

Callum nodded. "We go way back. He was a very good man. I was very sad to hear what happened to him."

My father was a good man. Though troubled. He had struggled with mental health long before the end of his life.

"I was glad I was able to be there for the children," Callum continued on with. "Sloane and her brother."

Dorian raised his head again, his eyes narrowed. He exchanged a glance between Callum and me before facing the window again.

"Going to be in town long, Callum?" Dorian asked, surprising me. He continued to stare out of the window. "This is a pretty moderately sized town, but small, which means basically everyone knows everyone." He glanced at him. "You're not from here, right? I don't believe I know your family."

Callum's head tilted up front. "I'm visiting town, yes." He lifted a hand. "I came to visit the children."

"Long visit?" Dorian continued. "Short?"

Dorian sounded short, again tense.

Callum acknowledged what Dorian said with another nod. "A few days, and I'm glad I came when I did."

"I'm glad too," I said, trying to get Dorian's attention. "Really glad."

Callum played it off like he hadn't done much earlier, but he'd been around to get answers when I had no means to get them. He'd been ready and willing to pay Dorian's bail. Something he would have had to do had Dorian not been released when the real murderer came forward.

Dorian swallowed at me. "Yeah," he said, his eyes flicking forward. "I'm real lucky you came. Don't know what I would have done."

He sounded so off, weird.

And he faced the window again.

We drove in silence for another few moments before something on the radio took my attention. My head shot forward, and Dorian's did too.

"Officials say the woman found at the old Prinze textile factory on Glen has been identified as Elaine Mayberry," the radio said. *"As this community knows, Mayberry was the headmaster of the prestigious Windsor Preparatory Academy."*

They were talking about our principal, the woman Dorian had been accused of murdering only moments before.

Dorian looked sheet white, and Callum asked Lucas to turn up the radio. He obviously recognized the name too. I'd told him all about the situation with Dorian.

"Officials also say a suspect surrounding her death has not only been apprehended, but they have an active confession on the record as well. Douglas Abernathy admitted to strangling and bludgeoning the woman following a recent debt she had to him surrounding illegal substances."

"Oh my God." The words fell from my lips. I'd known she died, but I hadn't known the details. My attention shifted to Dorian. "Callum, maybe we shouldn't be listening to this..."

It was probably hard for Dorian to hear anything about that woman. This was too close to home.

Dorian raised a hand.

"I want to hear it," Dorian said, his voice quiet. He appeared haunted. "Keep it playing."

The news broadcast continued on, but gratefully didn't

say any more details surrounding the murder itself. This was all completely messed up, fucked up.

"This news comes as a surprise," the broadcast stated, *"especially surrounding the recent controversy and confession surrounding Maywood Heights's star quarterback Charlie Lindquist and a shocking affair he had with Mayberry herself. An affair that Mayberry admitted to in a video that went viral this morning after being posted anonymously to the Windsor Preparatory Academy's academic website."*

I waited a second before looking at Dorian, not wanting to make a huge declaration about the video. Callum didn't know about that, and I didn't want to make it seem any of us knew the details about it.

Dorian wasn't even breathing, let alone moving. He simply stared ahead, his fingers to his lips.

"As our listeners and the entire Maywood Heights community knows, Charlie was involved in an unfortunate shooting just last year in Mayberry's home, in which her husband shot the young man before pulling the gun on himself. After this morning's anonymously posted video, there are definitely some holes that have been filled in there. As the community also knows, Charlie was a well-loved member of the Maywood Heights community. His family, the respected and esteemed Prinzes, have helped to lay the foundations of this town, and our hearts go out to the family once again. The station is currently attempting to get a statement from the Prinze family surrounding today's events. The family has expressed no comment at this time, but we hope to hear something soon. We will wait on your behalf, dear listeners, and worry not, you'll be the first to know when we know."

"Those fuckers are probably parked out in my neighborhood," Dorian gritted. Though I believed mostly to himself. He scrubbed his face. "That's probably why everyone was blowing up my phone earlier."

Shit.

The "news" kept going on with their drivel, talking about

Dorian's family like they were simply a news story and not real people. Eventually, I asked Callum if he could shut it off, and he did, quickly.

"Very unfortunate," my guardian said from up front. "My heart goes out to you and your family, Dorian."

Dorian's head shot up, his eyes narrowed.

Callum nodded, his eyes direct in the mirror. "I can't imagine what you're going through. This must be so hard for your family." His head lifted. "It's a good thing everything worked out today for you. I can imagine your family wouldn't want to deal with another thing. Your parents especially."

A tight muscle feathered in Dorian's jaw, all this obviously too much.

The car was slowing.

We'd returned to the cabin, both Dorian's car and my brother's Audi (the car I'd driven here) in sight and at not a moment too soon. Dorian obviously had to leave.

And he was so pale. He honest to God looked like he'd be sick.

"Thanks for the ride," he ground out, trying to *get out*. He clicked open the door, then pushed himself through, the door slamming behind him. He stalked his way over to his car, and I unstrapped myself from the seat.

"Thanks for helping him," I said to Callum on my way out too, stopping long enough to do that. The man had done so much, and really, he hadn't had to at all. He just kept doing favors for me, for me and my brother and taking care of us.

Shifting around, Callum's smile was small. "Of course. I hope things work out for your friend."

I hoped so too.

After telling Callum I'd drive my brother's car home, the wheels of Callum's sedan pulled away, and I raced to catch up to Dorian. "Dorian!"

He was already in his car, the engine running. He was

attempting to get the fuck out of here and quick. I waved my arms, but he didn't see me until I got behind his car.

The wheels of his Audi burned to stop, and the next thing *I knew*, he was out of the car.

And pressing me against it.

He literally picked me up from behind his ride, pinning me to the back passenger's side. His breath expelled, harsh and heated over my face and mouth.

"Don't be stupid," he growled, and I assumed referring to the fact that I got behind his car. He was angry, his eyes wild. He started to move away, but I wouldn't let him, cutting him off.

"I know you have to go, but—"

"Then let me." Our chests collided, the large boy looming over me. His eyes darkened. "And if you stand in my way again, I'll go right through you. I swear to fucking *God*, little fighter."

I blinked, not expecting this. My mouth opening and closing, I didn't understand. "Dorian, what—"

"Don't." He put a finger in my face, actually shaking in front of me. He winced. "Just fucking don't."

Don't what... exactly? My lips parted. "I understand you're upset about everything today."

"You do, huh?" His voice cracked, strained like it was laced with emotion. He got in my face. "How much do you know and how much do you think *I'd* be a fucking idiot?"

I twitched.

"Too convenient," he gritted, and out of nowhere, his hand encased my neck. He squeezed, my breath catching. "Too fucking convenient, Sloane."

I gasped. "What?"

He looked like he wanted to punch me, like he was straddling a line between doing that and squeezing harder.

He chose to squeeze, and the air stopped, my hands to my neck. I had no idea why he was so upset and why that rage, *that anger*, seemed to somehow be channeled at me. I gagged. "Dorian..."

"Don't *say* my fucking name. Don't—" His voice cracked again when he physically forced his face to mine.

He didn't do it to kiss me.

His warm mouth hovered over my face, nose pressed to nose, mouth above mouth. I gasped.

He squeezed harder.

I couldn't breathe, let alone think.

"What did I do?" I breathed out, but he blinked down.

"Get out of my sight," he gritted, letting go, and I finally got to draw in air. I coughed, the harsh press of his fingers still felt in my neck. His gaze bored down on me. "Too convenient, and I'm not fucking stupid." He shook his head. "Anyway, thanks for getting me out of jail." He frowned. "Even if you're the reason I got put in there."

What...

He thought...

He thought it was me? He thought *I* got him locked up. "Dorian, I—"

"Don't." He physically cringed, like the words or whatever I was going to say pained him.

Maybe it did.

"No more," he said instead, shaking his head. He left me basically on the ground, and this time when he got in his car, I got out of his way.

He peeled off, leaving a cloud of dust in his wake. He *blamed me* for this, his arrest. He'd accused me of such when it all happened, but I'd told him I hadn't tipped the cops off about where he'd been. I'd pleaded with him. Begged.

I thought he'd believed me.

He obviously hadn't, and his tension in the car made sense. He hadn't just been upset about everything today, the situation. He'd also been upset with me.

He thought I betrayed him.

CHAPTER
THREE

Dorian

She'd fucking played me, but what was worse was how I'd let her.

I've been so fucking stupid.

I only wished I had time to deal with it, but the moment I turned into my neighborhood, my window filled with news vans and reporters. My normally quiet neighborhood was a clusterfuck of activity, and it didn't take a scientist to figure out where all the activity led to.

Shit.

The radio had said the reporters were trying to get a statement from my family, and the chaos I drove through chillingly resembled the past. My neighborhood had held a similar look when Charlie had been first murdered, and that was only partially because of the fact that my uncle had been a golden boy in my town.

We were Prinzes, *the* Prinzes. Anything we fucking did required an audience, and the air horn only sounded louder when scandal surrounded us. People wanted in our business, point-blank, and I could only hope to God none of these people knew, in addition of my uncle being connected to Mayberry, that it'd been me to shoot that video of the headmaster. My grandfather had been right about one thing in regards to me. I had been sloppy, at least when it came to that situation. I definitely had my voice on the footage.

I'd lost control.

I'd been *weak* and in so many ways. Who knew how long he and Sloane had been working together?

Sloane...

I couldn't think about her now, *my family* priority. I didn't know what my grandfather was up to, but he had let me leave today. He'd let me go home, and if my rearview mirror told me anything, he hadn't followed me. He may be just trying to play with me and let me know he was around. For all I knew, he really only would be here a few days.

I honked, the fuckers surrounding my car. They could only get to my street so close before the gates kept them back, but that didn't stop them from trying. My family and I lived in a gated community.

"It's Dorian Prinze," one of the reporters said, and next thing I knew, my car was crowded on. One patted on my window. "Do you have a statement, son? For the press?"

"How is your family handling this?" another said. "This must be hard for everyone."

"Did you hear about the murder, Dorian?" That woman who hit my car caused me to blink. "Do you feel Mayberry got what was coming to her? Revenge for your uncle?"

So they didn't know about my arrest in connection to it... that was good, but still.

"Do you have comments about the viral video that was posted," a man said, his big camera right in my face, and that was when I rolled forward. We had security at the gate, and the attendant let me in, saving me from doing it myself. I normally had to enter a code.

People backed off as I peeled down my street, and more than a little sweat bulleted my brow. Could I be lucky enough no one had put two and two together that'd been me on the video with Mayberry, I didn't know. But I wasn't sticking around to find out.

Everyone was here.

Like, legit, *all* my friends' cars were here and even my god dad LJ's car. They'd called him into town? I didn't notice my other god dads' cars, but Ramses's message earlier had said that he was out looking for me.

Maybe the others were too.

This isn't fucking good.

I buzzed the garage open to get inside, turning off my car immediately. I pushed myself inside and nearly ran into Wolf.

"The fuck, kid?" He had his phone to his ear, his eyes wild and his curly hair all over the fucking place. His face was bruised and battered from the job I'd recently done on him. I'd done it over a girl.

A girl.

I was stiff when my buddy hugged me, nearly dropping his phone. From what I wagered, he'd been trying to call me on it.

"D!"

Wells and Thatcher weren't far behind, literally crowding into the hallway, and when I say all my friends crowded around me...

They hugged the shit out of me, a group fucking huddle like when we were on the field. This was different, though. This was intense, and I felt them all grab for each other. I felt them grab *me.*

I grabbed right back.

I was fucking shaking, and I didn't realize why until, well, I did. A lot of intense shit just happened. A lot of overwhelming shit. My grandfather was back. He was *here* in town, and I didn't know what that meant for me. It took a lot to shake me.

This fucking shook me.

"We didn't know where you *were*, kid. Where were you?"

That was Wolf, the one who looked just as shaken as I felt when I pulled away. He started to say something, but Thatcher grabbed my shoulders. His face was red, like legit red like a goddamn tomato.

"You don't go off the grid. You don't not fucking answer calls." He shot a finger at me, his earring dangling. "You don't do that to your boys. We didn't know what to fucking think."

He'd been worried.

They'd all been.

Wells wasn't even saying anything, squeezing his mouth. He forced a hand over his platinum-blond hair. "We thought you *ran*, but you didn't have to. Our parents took care of—"

"Is that my son?"

Dad.

I shot in his direction, my father behind my buddies. He had his phone to his ear, his eyes twitching wide.

He looked like he'd seen a ghost.

Worse, he looked like I'd *scared* him, and I didn't think I'd ever seen my father frightened. He was so strong, never scared.

"It's him, Ramses," he murmured into the line, and it appeared as if on autopilot. He blinked. "He's back. No. No. He seems fine. You can call the others to come back. Knight, Jax, and the girls?"

Fuck, they really were out looking for me.

And my dad was coming over, my friends immediately parting for him. He grabbed me, headfirst, and my dad wasn't really a hugger.

He seemed to be today.

He held me so tight I thought he'd break me, and I didn't

know how I kept standing there in one fucking piece. I *wanted* to break. I felt like I was going to break.

"Why would you leave, boy? *Why*?" he gritted, shaking his head. "You come to me when you need something. You hear me? That goddamn video? What the hell were you thinking?"

I didn't know. I thought I was helping.

And he obviously knew about that.

For all I knew, my friends could have told them everything. Or maybe, after the video had dropped, he'd just known. I mean, that was my voice in it.

"I'm sorry," I said, and all he did was shake me, pulling back. His hands held my face.

"You don't *run*. You hear me?" His face was serious, words serious. "If you feel like you're in trouble, you don't go AWOL."

His throat moved after he said that, and I realized something.

He thought I'd run.

They *all* thought I'd run. Even my friends.

Their reactions to my arrival definitely said that.

They believed I'd dropped that video, then gone off the grid like Thatcher said. My mouth parted. "I'm so sorry, Dad."

"Don't apologize to me." He took me by the back of the head, guiding me alongside him. I stood shoulder to shoulder with my father, but even with my size, he was bigger than me. "Your mother is worried sick."

Mom.

She was in the living room, Bow, Thatcher's sister, right next to her. She sat smooshed between her and Brielle, Wolf's mom. Wolf looked a lot like his mom besides her lack of curly hair. Hers was nearly raven black it was so umber-toned, a single gray streak on the side of it like Rogue from my old comic books. Honestly, outside of that, no one would have guessed his mom was over a decade older than Wolf's dad. The woman appeared to be in her early forties like my mother.

"December." Brielle rubbed my mom's back, and Mom's head popped up. I didn't know what to expect about her reaction. I mean, my dad looked about a half a second away from blowing a gasket, his reaction fear-based. My mom typically wore her emotion in a different way, but anger never had been it.

But that's what I got today.

A clear anger laced her features as she got up, and when she raised her hands and left the room, I flinched.

Fuck.

I started to go after her, but Dad pulled me back.

He directed a finger toward the couch. "You sit and *don't move,*" he said before leaving the room, and I did exactly that.

My friends joined me.

They crowded around on the other couches, Brielle making space for Wolf. She actually made him sit next to her, me on her other side. "What were you boys thinking with that video?" she asked, exchanging a glance between her son and the rest of the room. She landed on me. "And your mother was worried sick about you. We *all* were. How could you do that to us? Your parents?"

Only one person could intimidate me nearly as much as my father, and that was Brielle Mallick. She didn't put up with any shit, and my god dad Ramses was definitely the one Wolf went to whenever he wanted something. Brielle didn't play the fuck around.

But she loved just as hard, loved me. She brought her arm around me, really my second mom. All my buddies' mothers had a place in my life, but with Wolf's parents, it was different. It was like another layer, and considering Ramses was my mom's best friend, that made sense. Ramses and Brielle were just closer, always checking in with me and making sure things were okay.

Out of all my friends, Wolf and I did spend the most time together. A lot of that had to do with our ages, yeah, but something about us had just always been in sync.

My buddy stared at me now, long and hard. He also rocked back and forth, his hands rubbing like his insides were spinning. He looked like he wanted to talk.

I wanted to talk too.

I needed to, but now especially wasn't the time.

"Where were you?" Bow asked me from my other side. She hugged her arms. "We were all so worried."

I was too, and had they all known where I'd been, they would be as well.

I obviously couldn't say anything now with Brielle here, and I watched my mother return to the room. She was under my father's arm.

But that didn't mean he was the one to speak.

"Where were you today, Dorian?" she asked, her chin up. "The boys said you were going to our family cabin, and though your car was there, you weren't. We know because we checked, and your phone was shut off, so we couldn't even track that."

My parents had access to my whereabouts through my phone, my friends too.

The police must have shut it off.

"Where were you—"

Mom started to come forward, but LJ appeared in the room. He came from the direction of Dad's study, his hair up and his tie loose like he'd been here for a while.

He also had his phone in his hand, one he pocketed when he faced the room.

"Your son was apparently at Maywood Heights's county lockup," he said, bracing his big arms. The dude towered. There were vaulted ceilings in this room, and the guy could probably touch the point with a slight jump. He frowned. "My guy at the force tells me he was arrested."

Dad's gaze shot in my direction. "Arrested?"

"Dorian?" The shocked reaction was my mother *and* Brielle, and their responses matching didn't surprise me. Like stated, Wolf's mom was pretty much mine too.

LJ nodded. "Arrested in relation to the murder of the same woman who happened to be the subject of you boys' video." LJ directed a hand toward the room. "He was released because *the actual murderer* was arrested around the same time."

"Dorian." My mother had her hands together, touching her lips with her eyes closed. It was like she was doing all she could not to freak out on me and the situation. She pulled her hands away. "Tell me you had nothing to do with what happened to that woman like you did with the video."

Wait. She thought…

I shot up. "No, Mom." I had nothing to say. She thought I *killed* that bitch? Or at least hired someone to do it.

But is that so far-fetched?

I shut down the thoughts, swallowing. "I had nothing to do with what happened to Mayberry. The murder, I mean."

"No, you only kidnapped her, Dorian," she whisper-shouted, causing me to blink. She directed a finger. "How would you not think your voice couldn't be recognized?"

I said nothing, and Wolf leaned forward. He nodded. "We told her what we did, D. We had to when our parents all asked us."

The rest of my friends nodded too, Thatcher's and Wells's gazes escaping. They hadn't had a choice but to admit what we'd done, and I got that. Bow was the only one not involved in all this.

"As if it wasn't obvious," my dad barked, then pinched the bridge of his nose. He rubbed my mom's shoulders. "You're only lucky the press hasn't picked up on the fact."

"No, they're too busy talking about the woman's early demise." This came from LJ, his face nearly as red as my buddy Thatcher's before. "And that was a nice little fire I got to tame for you, Dorian. To keep your *arrest* in relation to the murder from being found out by the press." He placed a hand toward my dad. "I took care of it, brother. My guy at the precinct's got my back. As far as anyone at the precinct knows, your son never set foot in the place."

He'd wiped it away, shielded me.

Though I was sure that wasn't without cost. Financial if anything else.

I admit I'd been arrogant, and maybe that was why I'd gotten so sloppy when it came to that video. I knew my family and the people in my life would take care of me. I did what I wanted to do.

"I guess we all just got lucky the cops found the guy who the woman got wrapped up with. Some kind of drug dealer, I guess," LJ continued. He faced me. "So the police just let you out after they brought the perp in? Didn't give you any trouble after that?"

Everyone in the room faced me, and I realized something else, something *big.*

He didn't know about my grandpa's place in all this. Either his guy hadn't mentioned it, or the dude hadn't thought to.

And why did that relieve me?

After all that had happened with my grandpa, I thought the next thing I would be doing was blowing the horn on his ass and outing his place in whatever happened to me today.

But as I watched my parents, *my mother* sitting there awaiting my next words...

I wet my lips. "No problems."

"Good." LJ stood tall. "I'm going to go make a few more calls. Make sure this thing all stays controlled, and the narrative continues to go in our favor. I also got to call Billie." His eyebrows narrowed. "She was trying to find flights to come into town too. She was worried."

I didn't know where he and his wife had been, but obviously not in town. They did like to travel a lot.

And I definitely had everyone's eyes now.

LJ left the room, and I wasn't surprised he was the one doing damage control. He had many contacts and was the only one of my dad's friends who built his wealth from the ground up. He wasn't born into it like the rest of us, and since he didn't have kids, he probably wanted to do the grunt work for the rest of the parents.

Of course, that was just a theory, and I heard his voice right after he disappeared into the hall.

"Yeah, he's back," he said, his voice drifting into the room. "He's in the living room with the others, and I'm sure very happy with himself."

Shit, he was pissed. Everyone was pissed, and the next thing I knew, my parents' living room filled with more annoyed parents.

They all really were here now, the closest people in my life. Well, all but my great-aunt Celeste. She'd moved out of state when Grandfather Lindquist died. She'd just wanted a change in scenery after all that, so much pain that day.

Thatcher and Bow's parents, Knight and Greer, arrived in the room first. Their father married a short (little) blonde, and little was about the only thing that could explain, well, Bow. The timid thing was an anomaly in our group, but the outward perception of her could definitely fool. Thatcher's little sister had some fight in her. She may even have gotten that from her mom.

The small woman did nothing but mean mug me the moment she graced the room, her arms crossed. Jax and Cleo, Wells's parents, were behind her and Knight.

A weird story about Wells's parents was that they were stepbrother and stepsister. Though, they hadn't grown up together. They met later in life, I guess, but still, all us kids thought that was… different.

Let's just say, it wasn't something Wells preached from the rafters, and he wasn't a thing like either of them. My god dad Jaxen was basically that corny uncle with all the fucking fart jokes. He had my buddies and me roaring during the holidays, and Cleo couldn't be any different. She didn't talk a lot and was pretty shy.

"Oh my God," she said, seeing me. She had her hand on her chest. "Thank God."

"Damn fucking right." Jax said that, two faces to him. He had his funny side, then the don't-mess-with-me fucking side. He propped his hands on his hips. "You got a lot of explaining to do, boy."

"He does."

I missed Ramses, Wolf's dad, behind the group. Though, I had no idea how.

He was taller than everyone.

Wolf definitely got that from his dad. In fact, my god dad daunted with his size. He was just as beast-like as my buddy but was incredibly laid-back. The two were basically yin and yang, his son the crazier-than-shit version of him.

His dad didn't come closer.

Actually, Ramses kept his distance, his hands cuffing his big arms. The guy wore a trench coat over his suit, his tie undone like he too had been at the office, which caused me to wonder how many lives I had disrupted today. Ramses looked *pissed*, and he had to have been because Brielle left my side and went to her husband. Let's just say, normally he calmed her down.

So yeah, this wasn't good.

She pressed a hand to his chest, rubbing, and he shook his head, parting his attention from me. It was like he couldn't deal.

"Who wants to go first?"

My dad said the words, and I realized my mom wasn't looking at me either. She was holding my father's hand, her face turned toward him. He still stood behind her chair, his other hand rubbing her shoulder.

"I'm sorry, but that Mayberry bitch had what was coming to her after how she did Charlie." Thatcher, surprisingly, was bold enough to make the statement.

He regretted it immediately.

His dad's eyes expanding in his direction told the room that. Thatcher's dad was already fucking big, but he seemed to grow three sizes in the few words his son voiced. Knight shot a finger that way. "Your first warning, boy. You talk, then talk some *goddamn* sense."

Thatcher shrunk a little, shifting in his seat. He tried to hide behind his hand like that fucker could. He was big enough and barely fit in my mom's easy chair.

Wolf raised his head. "We did what we had to do."

"What you had to do, huh?" Ramses brought his arm around his wife. She was still holding him, the man's jaw tight. "So you kids really feel you're equipped to take things into your own hands?" His eyes narrowed. "The same kids who are roughing the hell out of each other?"

Ramses directed a finger between Wolf and me, the evidence of our fight still on his face.

And my knuckles.

They were still split and roughed up. I tried to hide them, but not fast enough.

The room saw, *my mom* saw. She covered her face, and my teeth dug into my lip.

"That was a misunderstanding." I hadn't felt it at the time, and though no one should be doing hazes, there were bigger factors going on here. I had new information.

There were things I couldn't say in this moment now, my throat tight and constricted.

Greer, Thatcher's mom, eyed in my direction. "And, Bow, you had nothing to do with this?"

She shook her head quick, and I didn't blame her.

I almost wished I could shake my head.

I stood by what I'd done, though, but I hated it was hurting the people I cared about the most.

Thatcher came from behind his hand. "I told you, Ma. Bow had nothing to do with it. It was just the guys and me."

Knight raised his fingers. "How about you *not* until we leave."

"It's true, though, sir." Wells was brave enough to speak, which got more than an eye from his parents, his dad. "It is true. She didn't do anything."

Bow's head turned in his direction, but Wells wasn't trying to make eye contact with her. He broke it just as quick as he had it.

Jax braced his arms. "You kids are something else."

I was happy LJ chose to come back in the room at that point. He broke up the tension a bit. He still had his phone in his hand, but it wasn't to his ear.

"You're all good," he told the room. "Your children have managed to avoid scandal. The woman's murder has basically covered this whole kidnapping thing up from the press, the police, and thank God for that. I'm glad you kids at least had the sense to not put any of your faces on camera."

Yeah, sense.

Our parents didn't look relieved at all. Just disappointed.

Especially mine.

My own mother couldn't even look at me, my father's gaze heated in my direction. He may have been worried that I might have run earlier, but that was all in the past. There was nothing but anger in his eyes now.

LJ pocketed his phone. "But with the press at your house here, buddy," he said, causing my dad to face him. "You might want to get yourself and your family out of town for a little while. It'll probably be unbearable here, and…" He sighed. "It'll probably be like it was the first time. You know how those people are leeches."

They were, point-blank. They'd harassed my family and me after Charlie died, stalking us for a news piece. They didn't care about us. They just wanted the story.

And I noticed he said the first time.

LJ spoke of *a time* that I barely remembered.

I'd been too young.

Charlie's murder hadn't been the first time my family had gotten wrapped up in the press and scandal, and as bad as the media had been following what happened, my dad hadn't been advised to leave town. No, only one event had caused my dad to actually uproot his family to relieve us from the burden of the press. Only *one man* had caused that.

This family still felt the burdens of my grandfather's dirty deeds. His release from prison had caused a similar uproar, one I gratefully hardly remembered. I'd been spared.

I swallowed hard, then again when my mom left her chair. "Mom?"

It was obviously too much, us having to leave again too much. The room watched her leave, and my dad and I followed her. He was too busy going after her to stop me this time.

The staff had to have been dismissed because normally, this room was filled with smells. The air was constantly warm with home cooking, but not now. Our family was dealing with a crisis, and when my dad and I arrived in the kitchen, we came to find my mom with her arms folded, her back to us.

"Em?" Dad brought her in, coming around her. He called her Em, his nickname for her.

He soothed her once he got to her, his hands down her arms, and I swallowed, feeling the guilt that he had to soothe her. They took a moment, several like this, and I continued to be blown away by the type of man my father was. He also had two faces, one that was completely different in the outside world.

But when he came home, he was this, a father, a husband. He was a provider in every way he needed to be for me, my mother, or Charlie. He'd been this way for my uncle too, even though Charlie wasn't his son.

I stood quietly, waiting. Some steps came into the kitchen, and when our family's Labrador, Chestnut, arrived, I realized she must have gotten out. Mom and Dad tended to put her in their room when they knew people were coming by the house. She could be shy.

Chestnut was basically my mom's dog, and the dog rubbed at my mother's ankles for her attention. I called her over, and she came to me.

"How long did you know about all this?" my mother asked me, turning around in my father's hands. She had her fingers to her lips. "How long did you know about what really happened to my brother?"

My throat tightened, the guilt extremely heavy at this point. Standing up from Chestnut, I pocketed my hands. "Since it happened."

"What?" My dad shot the words, his eyes emerald fire.

I cringed. "I didn't know the details, which was why I had her do the confession. I didn't know what she'd say. I just had a feeling something more happened that night."

"Why?" Dad asked.

I swallowed. "I knew Charlie was seeing her." At this point, my parents wouldn't even look at me. I continued on. "I caught them together my sophomore year."

"You what?" Mom approached me, her eyes expanded. "You've known about it for that long and said nothing?"

"I thought I was protecting him." I felt stupid about that now, and none of this would have happened had I said something.

I think they saw that, that all of this could have been prevented had I made different choices. Better ones. I was still messing up today.

The thought sobered me where I stood.

I definitely couldn't say anything about my grandfather now, and at this point, my mom turned away from me. I started to move toward her, but Dad halted my attempt with a raised hand.

"Go to your room, son," he said. "Don't say goodbye to your friends. Don't say a goddamn word. Just go. To. Your. *Room*. While we all figure out what to do next."

I blinked, nothing more than that. I left the room.

I didn't need to be told twice.

CHAPTER
FOUR

Dorian

Wolf climbed through my window later that night.

It was late as fuck.

He arrived around three, us climbing through each other's windows not a thing. Wolf even had the key code into my neighborhood.

I got up, meeting him, and the first thing he did after he saw me was hug me.

Shit, I must have worried my friends. Wolf's hug was strong, and we didn't fucking hug a lot. I mean, we weren't opposed to it in my friend group, but we really didn't go around having a whole lot of reasons to do so.

"Hey," I said, the guy pulling back. I slapped his shoulder, and he did the same to mine before pushing his hair out of his face. He normally wore it up, but it wasn't today, all those big-ass curls wavy in his face.

"We thought you skipped town, bro," he said, his jaw clamped up and tight. He braced his arms. "We thought you did after you heard about the murder, thought you were trying to play it safe after what we all did to her."

That made sense, a lot of sense.

He pushed a hand over his hair. "What was worse was we couldn't even tell our parents in good faith you had nothing to do with what ultimately went down."

I twitched. "What?"

"We couldn't until the press confirmed someone else had done it," he said. "I mean, you had stayed behind. Behind with her?"

I had…

And I'd definitely given all my friends strong reasons to think the worst.

I had considering my history with my grandfather. I had tried to off him.

Tried and failed.

Wolf sat down on my bed, and I did with him, silent.

"How are the guys?" My parents had taken my phone away. I'd literally watched my dad shut it off and throw it in a box. Who knew when I'd get it back. "Parents took my phone."

Wolf nodded. "Wells seems cool. You know how laid-back he is, but you pissed Thatch the hell off. The fucker got all up in his feelings, and you know how he doesn't like to get into that shit."

He was worse than all of us, closed off. He had a lot of emotional shit, stuff in his house and with his family specifically, so he never tried to be the burden for anyone else.

It all came out in rage when he was upset like he'd done today with me in the hall. Wells could be that way too, but not nearly as bad.

"You freaked everyone the hell out, D," he said, shaking his head. He leaned in. "Why didn't you call me? I called you. I… I have something to tell you."

He stopped to take a breath, and though Wolf never dealt

with feelings well either, he was generally better than this. Between the two of us, he was actually better at talking shit out.

He seemed ill-equipped today, his hands to his mouth. He ended up bracing his arms, and since I knew I had something I needed to share too, I had no idea where my buddy and I would be by the end of this conversation. I had opened a door I couldn't easily close when I decided to pull my grandfather into this Mayberry shit last summer.

"I got something to tell you too." I forced out a breath. "It's bad, man. So bad."

"What?"

I couldn't even find the fucking words. I wet my lips. "My grandfather's alive."

His eyes expanded, like legit bulged out in front of me. "What are you fucking talking about?"

"Just as I said, man." Even I couldn't believe the words I was saying, but they were true. My throat tightened. "I don't know how. We didn't get that far—"

"What do you mean *we*?" He sat back, eyes in horror. "What are you talking about?"

And so I told him *everything.* It all came out, all the fucked-up details. I left no stone unturned, and the chilling truth brought the shakes back to my own fucking knees. My grandfather not only was here in this town, but he'd survived an attempt against his life. An attempt *I* had unsuccessfully made. My buddies all knew I'd gone upstate to take care of him. I'd kept it a secret at first, but I'd ended up telling them in the end. Wolf had taken the news the hardest. He hadn't agreed with me initially going to see him.

But that didn't mean he disagreed with how I'd chosen to handle it.

Once he found out, he'd put it to bed. *All* my friends had. We weren't going to think about it again.

I guess my grandfather wasn't giving us a choice.

"But how?" Wolf looked entirely haunted, slammed clearly in the same way the news hit me. This was impossible, my grandfather being alive. I'd *poisoned* him. He faced me. "You said you took care of it."

I thought I had. I shook my head, and he got up.

He grabbed his legs. "D, what the fuck?"

"I know." I got up too, my shoulders popping up. "I don't know what happened or how he's alive. Someone must have found him or something." I raised a hand. "I didn't stick around after I watched him go down."

"So you didn't check for a pulse?" My friend was angry now and understandably so. He combed his fingers through his hair. "I don't know shit about this, but you always check for a goddamn pulse."

And he would have had he been there. I'd been dumb.

I should have trusted him.

I should have trusted all of them, Wells and Thatcher too. They never would have agreed with what I'd done, but knowing the mindset I'd been in, I would have done it anyway. I would have, and I know my friends would have been there with me. They would've supported me.

I guess I wasn't good at dealing with heavy shit either.

Like Thatch, I kept my shit to myself. I did that to protect others. I wanted to carry the burden, always, and that left stuff off my buddies' back.

Wolf twitched my way. "But what about Sloane?"

I twitched myself after what he'd said, the last thought I'd ever thought would come out of his fucking mouth. "What—"

He came forward. "You said your grandfather went by Montgomery, right? As in the *Callum Montgomery* who took in Sloane and her brother?"

"Yeah."

"So what's that mean for *them*? What…" His mouth

opened and closed, my buddy's eyes flashing. "What is he doing to them? Sloane and her brother? What is he doing?"

Bruno Sloane had been in our friend group for a brief time, and Wolf had felt guilt after setting him up with that haze.

I also knew Wolf didn't hate the kid. He'd wanted to in the beginning, like all of us. His sister had gotten in the way of things with Charlie.

Fuck… his sister.

They'd both played us, all of us. My jaw moved. "I'm sorry, man. But Bruno's in on shit."

"What are you talking about?"

"I'm talking about his sister, bro." I hated that my throat was fucking thick while talking about her. I forced that shit away, blinking. "Sloane is in deep with my grandfather. She helped him today. All of this was her and him."

I didn't know how much. I didn't know the details, but a lot of fucking things were coincidental when it came to the two of them and my arrest this morning.

My buddy let go of me, and I realized he had his hands on me, my shoulders. "I don't understand."

"I'm saying four people knew where I was today. *Four*, bro, and none of you guys called my fucking grandfather." Grandfather had been smart, I'd give him that. He definitely looked like the hero today. I raised my hands. "Next thing I know, I'm arrested, and my grandfather comes to get me out. He comes there *with her*, the only other person who knew where the fuck I was outside you guys."

Wolf said nothing, his eyes blindly scanning the room. His irises darted left and right as if he were trying to solve the most intricate math problem.

And he appeared pale.

He visibly paled in front of me, sitting down slowly. I could imagine all this shocked him, and maybe, he wasn't surprised. He hated Sloane.

Maybe he'd always known.

I joined him, my hands together. "Between the two of them, they made my grandfather basically look like a hero," I cut, jaw tight. "Fucker comes in on his white horse to save my ass. You should have seen him. He was so fucking smug."

He looked like he pulled one over on me, and he had. I'd been shocked to fucking hell when he showed up.

"Did he say that?"

"What?"

Wolf captured my attention. His swallow worked his throat. "Did he say that's what he was trying to do? That Sloane and her brother were…"

"Working with him?"

Wolf nodded slow.

"He didn't have to," I admitted, all the facts there. "It was pretty goddamn obvious. I told you no one else knew where I was."

It took all I had to say the words, and how I was so easily played. She'd wiggled her way in so *easily*.

Wolf stayed silent for quite a while beside me, his long fingers folding over his arms. "Maybe it's not that simple."

"What?"

His breath eased out. "Maybe they are working for him, but they don't have a choice?" I was surprised he was saying this, his nod firm. "Maybe he has something over on them."

I sat with that, my buddy tapping my arm.

"Right?" Wolf nearly had hope in his eyes, like he really cared about Sloane or her brother. He'd been the first to at least want Bru's sister out of town. "What if they're in trouble?"

He wanted to hope. My buddy was good at his core. I mean, we all were really. We were the good guys. Wolf didn't want to see anyone hurt, regardless of how he felt about them, and maybe this was easier for him.

He hadn't been as wrapped up as me.

I forced the breaths through my nose, my hands together. I said nothing, and Wolf got up. I frowned. "Where are you going?"

"I'm going to tell your parents," he said, and I shot up off the bed. I cut him off right away, and he raised his hands. "What? Dude, they could be in trouble. Hell, you too. You went after the son of a bitch."

"I can't tell my parents my grandfather is back."

"Why?"

"Besides the obvious?" How much my grandfather's return would unsettle my mother? *Enrage* my father? I shot a hand toward the window. "There's about a half a dozen news vans down my fucking street that tell me I've already put my parents through enough shit for a goddamn century. They don't need anything else. Not right now."

"So you're just going to keep this from them?" He got in my face, like actually chest to chest. Fire laced his dark eyes, his finger in my face. "Put yourself and innocent people in danger. I told you, bro. Sloane and her brother could be *trapped*. Your parents need to know your grandpa is back. Fuck, all our parents, so they can help."

I didn't believe I was in immediate danger. My grandfather did let me go today. As far as Sloane and her brother, he didn't see her today, see *the act*. She'd lied so easily, and there was no guilt there.

She didn't look like a victim. Nah, it was so easy for her today. *Too easy* for her to play me. She could be getting just as much out of whatever she had going with my grandfather. Money and only God knew what else.

The possibility enraged me, how I had really been played. "You don't know Sloane and her brother are innocent. You didn't see her today. She lied to my fucking face and didn't think twice about it. Grandpa Prinze could be making this deal awfully sweet for her. She and her brother could be getting just as much out of it."

"What deal?"

"I don't know, but they could have one. I don't know what she's getting out of it, but I told you how smug my grandpa had been. He *wanted* to look like the fucking hero today. Had to have. And I don't think he's coming after me. At least, not right away. He made it seem like he was leaving town soon." I folded my arms. "He might have stopped back here to just throw me off. He let me go and everything."

"Or he's just fucking playing with you." He raised and dropped his hands. "You did try to kill him. He could definitely be back here to settle the goddamn score."

It wouldn't matter if he was. I wouldn't be here. "My parents and I are leaving town in the morning. You heard LJ."

"Yeah, but you're going to come back, D." His eyes narrowed. "And you don't know Sloane and her brother *aren't* innocent."

"Since when do you stand up for Noa Sloane anyway? Her brother?"

His Adam's apple flicked. "I don't, but if she and her brother have nothing to do with this or are trapped, I don't want them hurt. I have a fucking soul." His dark eyebrows descended like storm clouds. "Where's yours?"

I already told Sloane that it'd died, and it had the day I thought I killed my grandpa.

Her deceit only made sure it wasn't resurrected.

I wasn't going to be the victim. I wasn't going to let someone play me or my family. We'd all been through enough here, and there'd be *no more*.

"My family comes first," I said, in my buddy's face. "And I won't put my mom and dad through any more hell. Especially if my grandfather is just rolling through town and trying to make a *fucking* statement. He had an opportunity to take a shot at me. He chose not to." I'd place strong bets he wanted to shake me, and he'd definitely done that. "If he is just playing around and trying to scare me, there's no sense in bringing that shit in for my parents to think about. I'm not letting him win there."

"Letting you go could have just been another game. Something to throw you off before he *actually* strikes," Wolf said, and I supposed he was right. Again, I wasn't going to take that chance. My grandfather being around would fuck with my family like nobody's business, and I wasn't just talking about my mother.

My grandfather really was the one person who could break my dad, and I wasn't going to do that to him. Not if my grandfather really was just playing games.

"I'm just asking for time," I asked my friend. "Time to look into what he may or may not be doing while my family is out of town."

I could have Thatcher peel apart his new identity. We hadn't looked into it long enough when Sloane first came into town.

We hadn't had a reason.

"And what about when you come back?"

"We'll know by then," I stated. "At least, have an idea of what he's up to. I'll do what I can from where I'm at, but I bet Thatch can uncover some shit. We didn't look into my grandpa's pseudonym enough. He made it sound like I should know it." He said a lot of things that could have been bullshit, but I definitely wasn't overlooking anything this time. "My grandpa also made it sound like he'd only be in town for a few days. Said he was just checking on the Sloane kids. I could have Thatch look into that too. See what the link there is. Gramps said Sloane's dad used to work for him."

Wolf panned in my direction. "In what way?"

"No idea." I leaned back against the door. "I just need *time*, Ares. Time to see what may or may not be true. It might not result in anything, but that time is so valuable. My family is already ripping apart, man. I can't upheave their world again. Not so soon."

All this fucking shit was killing me and *ripping me* apart. So much of the drama was stuff I'd unleashed.

I just needed time before more happened.

I thought my buddy would argue with me more. I mean, he'd been going up and down with me, but he stayed silent for a bit.

This was a good thing.

That meant he was thinking about things, his hands sliding in his pockets. His head lifted. "How much time?"

That I didn't know. "Let's just start with my folks and me being out of town. We'll talk more when we come back."

This didn't seem to settle well on my friend's face. He obviously thought I was in danger, and for whatever reason, he wanted to go to bat for Sloane and her brother too. He didn't know all the facts, though. He didn't *see* the evidence with his very eyes like I had. I'd watched Sloane go along with my grandfather's ruse, and it'd been too good.

She'd been perfect.

Not an ounce of a lie could be read on her face, so fluid with my grandpa's script. The girl was incredibly dangerous, and besides the visual evidence of her making out like a bandit in regards to my grandpa being her and her brother's "guardian," she no doubt had lots more she was pocketing. This was going beyond a nice house, a fancy school, and her brother's and her sweet ride.

The shit about her dad dying in a fire could have been bullshit too.

It was the unknown that scared me the most because, if someone could lie that well, they didn't have a soul. They were just as much of a monster as me and the shit I'd gotten wrapped up in recently.

Maybe even worse.

I needed my buddy on this. I needed his and my other friends' help.

"Please, Ares," I pleaded. "Just give me time."

He remained silent, his hand cuffing his arm. He seemed really at war about this decision.

"We'll need an eye on your grandfather," he said, making me blink. "We'll watch him while you're gone. See where he goes, stalk the hell out of him. Hopefully he leaves town in a few days like you said. That'll at least save us from worrying about him here. You could be right he's just trying to scare you. That'd be the best-case scenario for obvious reasons."

He was going to help. I acknowledged what he said, nodding too. "Sloane and her brother will need a detail too."

"I'll take care of it," he said, sitting on the bed again. I joined him. He huffed. "And don't worry about looking into all this mess while you're gone. I mean, you can, but your priority should be taking care of your mom and dad. I'll have Thatch look into your grandpa. We *all* will, and we'll leave no stone unturned." He put his hand on my shoulder. "We'll get to the bottom of this. Just watch out for your parents. Just worry about that, yeah?"

I wasn't sure how much help I could be anyway. I mean my parents took my phone, and I didn't know if and when they'd give it back. I might not have any technology where I'm going.

And I could hug my friend for not letting me worry about anything else but my family, my buddy, ride or die. He obviously didn't agree with all this, but he was going to help me move the pieces.

I thought about the fact that I didn't have any biological brothers or sisters. Hell, my father hadn't either, but he'd found close bonds with his friends. They were stronger than blood ties, unable to be broken, and anyone from the outside might not understand that. You had to live it.

I was happy to say I had that with my friends. These boys were truly my brothers. Bow was in our circle too, but we'd have to keep our knowledge of at least my grandpa away from her. We couldn't risk her wanting to alert the parents, and that'd been the only reason we kept the Mayberry stuff from her.

Rainbow Reed was ride or die as well, but if she thought anyone, i.e., any of us, were in danger of anything, whether physically or mentally, she went for the greater good. She could often be jaded by that, but I didn't consider that a flaw. It just meant she cared and kept her pure. She should never lose that.

It wasn't so easy to get back.

"You're going to have to let Bow know to stay away from Sloane," I growled. "She can't be trusted. Tell her that and everything with the arrest, but don't let her know my grandpa is back in town or his place in it. She'll just worry."

"Yeah, she will," he said, but his voice sounded hollow. It was in that moment I remembered he'd wanted to tell me something too before I unleashed all this shit.

"What did you want to tell me before?" I nudged his leg. "You said you had something."

The way he blinked, it seemed like he'd forgotten. "It was nothing really." He opened his hand, smirking. "I was just being a little bitch. Was going to tell you how worried I was about you."

"Worried about me?"

He eyed the room, probably easier than looking at me. He shrugged. "You going off the grid, I guess, freaked me out."

He said that with his hug before.

Wolf got up, his smile soft but tense. He was definitely putting it on. I didn't know if it was for me or what, but I didn't say anything about it when he pounded my fist. His next move was to give me a hug again before he left the way he came. Nah, my buddies and I weren't good with emotions.

Our actions, *our bonds*, always spoke far louder.

CHAPTER
FIVE

Sloane

My text messages to Dorian had gone unanswered last night, my calls straight to voicemail. I wasn't sure if he had his phone off or was simply shutting me out.

Yesterday hadn't made sense.

He'd accused me of leaking his location yesterday. Initially, he'd demanded if I snitched to the cops myself, but I hadn't. I mean, I'd called for reinforcements to get him out. Of course, I hadn't wanted him arrested.

I supposed he could believe that considering I'd made calls for him, but he also could believe I may have simply slipped something to someone, Bru or someone else, and *that* had gotten around. This was a town where people seemed to like to get in each other's business, but I hadn't done that either. I'd never do that to him, betray his confidence…

He clearly didn't believe me, and unfortunately, I couldn't justify blowing up his phone outside of the few messages and calls I had made to plead my case.

His family was going through some epic shit right now.

The news had his family and the Prinze name all over it. My brother Bru and I had spent most of last night watching everything go down. Dorian's family was being harassed, and it was only by the grace of God Principal Mayberry's kidnapping had all but disappeared in all this. The media was talking about the viral video, yes, but not much surrounding who'd done it. They didn't seem to be concerned with that.

I mean, the woman was dead.

All this was fucking crazy, the added layer that Dorian believed I'd *betrayed him* on top of that. I hadn't. I had no idea how the cops had found him to even arrest yesterday.

I tried him one more time when I got up that morning, but when I got voicemail instantly again, I couldn't help my frustrations. This was probably completely selfish of me feeling frustrated, and there was a strong possibility that his life was chaos right now and he simply didn't want to deal with his thoughts about me on top of it.

I'll talk to him at school.

That was if he *was* at school. I hadn't received any messages that classes had been canceled again, but that didn't necessarily mean he would be there. In fact, I wouldn't blame him for taking the day off if those thirsty pricks known as the media were still cluttering his neighborhood. My brother, Callum, and I watched them literally broadcast outside of the gates of Dorian and his family's cul-de-sac.

Callum really had been a godsend in all this. After I got back home, I'd found him there with Bru in front of the television, but the older man hadn't been watching TV. He'd been on the phone looking into the situation with Dorian, but not for the same reasons as the media.

"Just want to make sure the boy and his family are faring well since he's your friend," he'd said to me. *"I figured you'd want some actual news and not this chaotic drivel."* His expression had gone serious. *"That is one thing I don't miss about living here.*

This town is small enough where everyone wants to know everything."

I was starting to see that, all of this a mess.

I'd been shocked to see Callum making calls on his own and on my behalf. I hadn't asked him to do that, but I couldn't be more grateful. His news updates had actually kept me sane last night since Dorian hadn't texted or called me back. He was able to confirm the media was only talking about Mayberry's murder, and with the updates he and the news did give me, I was able to see that Dorian and the guys would not be implicated for her viral confession. That had been my biggest worry.

When things started getting late, I figured Callum would stay at the house with Bru and me last night. I mean, the place had enough bedrooms, and he technically owned the space. He'd given us literally the roof over our heads, but he'd been adamant about checking into a hotel downtown when he finally wrapped up his calls.

"This is your space," he'd said, his driver behind him and waiting to take him. *"But I will see you children again before I leave. I want to check on everything with the house and make sure it's running smoothly. And of course check in with you too and hear your updates."*

We all hadn't gotten to talk about my brother's and my updates. We'd all been too busy watching Dorian's with the rest of the town, but obviously for different reasons.

Our guardian had left after that, and again, he hadn't asked for anything from Bru or me. My brother and I had never been ones to have a lot of luck. In fact, we could definitely be considered unlucky. We both barely remembered our mother since she'd died when we were so young, and our father had had a slew of mental health issues. My brother and I had constantly moved because of that, and we'd never had much.

Since Callum had come into our lives, we seemed to

suddenly have someone looking out for us, someone we could rely on. My brother and I basically had a fairy godfather, and I was so happy to not have to do all this by myself. I was only eighteen and had nothing to my name besides my father's Chevelle.

It was just my brother and me, and I forced myself to believe everything with Dorian would be okay. There were a lot of emotions that had gone on yesterday, and I just had to stress to him that I had his back the next time I did see him. He and his may not be my family, but I was certainly invested in his well-being. In fact, certainly more than I wanted to admit. It had been my brother and me basically taking care of each other for a while, so trying to wrap my head around being anything to anyone else was hard for me.

So damn hard.

Things would be okay, and I just had to believe it. If Dorian wasn't at school today, at least Bow may be. I'd tried texting her too last night, but Dorian's family was basically hers as well. I wasn't surprised to not hear anything back from her either and tried to be patient with the situation. They were all probably really freaking out right now with everything surrounding Mayberry and Charlie, Dorian's uncle. I needed to respect that.

Things are going to be okay. Things are going to be okay.

This was my mantra as I showered, then got my uniform on. I hadn't heard Bru all morning in the house, so I decided to bug him before getting breakfast.

"Bru?" I knocked on his door, a mumble on the other side. My brow shot up. "Are you still sleeping?"

I normally ran into him at least once in the halls during our morning routines, but I noticed I hadn't today. I'd been so focused on the Dorian stuff I hadn't thought about it.

He didn't answer after my second knock, and I turned the doorknob.

"Cover whatever you don't want seen," I announced, but

pushed open the door when I found him still in bed. He had a sheet over his head, and I sighed. "What are you doing? Get up." We had to be at school in less than an hour. I let go of the door. "Come on."

"Nah, man. I don't feel good."

He moaned under his sheet, and I rolled my eyes. He'd tried similar tactics when we were kids. I frowned. "You're not getting out of school just because you fucked up."

Him and that stupid fucking haze I definitely hadn't forgotten about. He'd tried to get in with Dorian and his clique.

Maybe he thought he might have to answer to that today. From Legacy's Court minions maybe. Either way, he was going to school.

My brother's response was to moan again, and I came over to his bed. I ripped the sheet off and found him down to his boxers, his arms hugging his big body. He was basically in the fetal position, and my brow shot up. "What the fuck?"

I sat on the bed, touching his brow. He was clammy, and his forehead heated my palm the hell up.

Fuck, he is sick.

"I told you I wasn't lying. Fuck." He pulled the sheets back up, covering himself. "I'm not going to school."

"Okay." Christ. He hadn't been sick since we were like kids. I'd gotten sick more than him over the years. I touched his brow again. He was burning up. "Let me go take your temperature."

"Don't bother. Already did. It's ridiculous." The bedding shook when he closed his eyes. Shit, did he have chills too? "I have a fever. I'm staying the fuck home."

He burrowed into his bedding, and I agreed. I sat back. "Well, do you need anything? Should I stay home?"

He laughed a little, shaking his head. He still had his eyes closed, but he smiled. "I'm seventeen, Noa. I'll be fine. Go to school."

"You sure?"

He nudged me back, and I smiled, my worry dying down a little. He was obviously sick, but still acting like himself considering. "Okay, well, I'll make sure to get your school work for everything."

"Goody," he said, laughing again. But he sounded so tired. I started to get up, but his hand came out and touched mine.

"Did you ever hear back from Dorian?" he asked, concerned when he opened his eyes. I hadn't told him about the fallout between Dorian and me, his accusations. For starters, that was between him and me, and after a conversation, I figured I'd get the dark prince to come around.

That issue was personal, and honestly, I hadn't wanted to think about the alternative. That I might not get him to believe me.

He'd been so angry.

"Not yet, but I'm going to try to talk to him today if he's at school," I said. As far as my brother was concerned, Dorian was simply busy with his family and hadn't been returning my calls and texts.

Bru pulled his bedding up, and I snuggled him in. I hadn't done that for him since we were kids. My brother was this big tough football player now. He rested his arms on the bed. "Well, when you see him, tell him I feel for him. The other guys too if you see them. I still haven't heard back from them, but I'm not surprised."

I wasn't either. They were all hella close, family.

I guess my brother knew that too.

I patted his hand. "Sleep and don't play too many video games, please."

I got nothing but a chuckle from that, his eyes closed. "I make no promises. And hey, can you talk to Coach for me? I'm obviously not going to be at practice today."

After promising him I'd do that, I got up. Before I headed downstairs, I told him I'd get him stuff out of the first aid kit for his fever, Tylenol. I headed downstairs to do that and jumped when I came across Callum. The older man had been making coffee, a cup in his hand. He wore a suit, and seeing me, he raised a hand.

"Sorry. Did I scare you?" His head tilted. "I hope you don't mind, but I let myself in. I have a man coming through the house today to check the filters and make sure everything with the house is running smoothly."

He had mentioned he was going to be doing that, and of course, I hadn't minded. He owned the house. "No, you're fine. I'm just jumpy."

A lot had fucking happened in the last few hours, another added layer with my brother being sick.

I came into the room and noticed Callum had two coffee cups going. He gestured to one for me, and I appreciated that. Did I mention I had a fairy godfather? I mean, this man left no stone unturned. I noticed he had a laptop up on the kitchen island like he'd been working, and he sat in front it while I got my breakfast together. I chose cereal.

"How was your evening, Sloane?" he asked me from behind it. I turned, and his frown greeted me when I swiveled in his direction. "Did you ever hear back from your friend?"

Yeah, I'd texted Dorian. Yeah, I'd *called* Dorian. I shook my head, and Callum's frown deepened.

"I can imagine all this is hard on the family," he said, sighing. "I brushed up on the controversy. A terrible sequence of events."

He'd put that lightly. What Dorian and his family... his friends and his family, were going through was something out of a nightmare.

"I'm going to try to see him today at school," I said, my and my brother's guardian also unaware about Dorian's heated issue with me. Again, that was personal. I appreciated Callum and everything he did, but he was still a stranger.

"And I never really got to thank you for making those calls on his behalf."

The man had stepped in like a knight, no questions asked, and that meant so much to me.

He raised a hand, his smile lifting. "It wasn't a problem. In any sense, it sounds as if things were going to work themselves out anyway." I eyed him, and he nodded. "The actual murderer coming forward? It seems your friend really does have some luck on his side."

He did, and thank God for that.

"You met the boy at school, then?" he asked casually. "I don't believe you ever said."

"Yeah, school." And it was crazy how far we were away from that initial place we'd met. There'd been so much tension there and misunderstandings even back then. Dorian had never been easy.

"He's just a friend, then?" he asked, bringing me out of my thoughts. His smile was small. "Sorry. I don't mean to be intrusive. I suppose I was just curious after seeing you both together yesterday. You seem close."

I wondered if that had been obvious, us looking like we were together.

I mean, the way he'd hugged me...

If was as if I'd given him life when he saw me at the police station, but that had changed so quickly. I didn't know why, and we needed to talk.

"He's just a friend," I said, and I didn't find the question invasion. I mean, the man had been willing to open his pocketbook for Dorian. That warranted the question, and I was being honest with him. I didn't know what Dorian and I were. We'd been enemies, *heated* ones, and somewhere along the way that had changed into something else. That something else was just as heated, *passionate*, and where we were at now I didn't now. I hoped friends at least.

I couldn't reach my thoughts higher at the moment, never good at emotional things. Because I wasn't, I forced a smile, putting on that strength I didn't feel I always had. It'd always been needed, though, for my brother and me. We were survivors.

I noticed Callum's attention while in my thoughts, and I was grateful he didn't push the issue. I couldn't talk about it anymore anyway.

"I'm glad you've been able to find friendship in your short time here," he said, his eyes warm. "And I hope you don't mind, but I'm going to work here for a few hours this morning. I plan to step out when maintenance gets here, but I want to at least wait for the doctor."

"Doctor?"

His gaze lifted from his laptop. "For your brother? I ran into him this morning, and he said he was sick. I figured I'd call the doctor for him just in case. There's an excellent physician I know not far from here. He's coming down to see Bru and make a house call."

I mean, I couldn't even think after he said that. That he'd been willing to *do* that. I swallowed. "Do you think it's serious? Bru?"

"Probably not, but it's better to be safe than sorry." His smile widened. "I've also called someone about your car. Your brother mentioned it was giving you issues. They'll be through to tow it to a local shop. Since Bru won't be at school today, you can use his, or if you'd like to have your own, I can work that out too."

I blinked, truly awed here. He'd done all this?

I must have been silent for too long because he made eye contact with me then. He frowned. "I can have whatever you want delivered. Maybe you want Bru to have something here to drive just in case? I can…"

"No, no. It's fine." I waved him off, floored. "And I guess, just thank you."

I didn't feel that warranted any further explaining. I was thanking him for everything.

His eyes warmed. "Not a problem. You have a good day at school, and if you need anything, I'll be around. As you know, I have a room at the Bellaire downtown. I'll either be there, here, or in meetings. I'm looking into some business endeavors based in Maywood Heights. Would give me more of an opportunity to see you children."

Bru and I would be going off to college soon, but I'd be lying if I said I wouldn't mind him around. Coming downstairs, it was like those times back when Dad had had his good days. When he was there in the kitchen and things were just normal.

I couldn't thank Callum enough for giving me that feeling. Even if it was only temporary. In fact, he said he was leaving in a few days. He ran businesses all over, and the fact he'd put my brother and me, of all people, in his schedule to simply check on us?

I simply didn't have words.

"I appreciate everything you're doing for us," I said. "I'm sure Dad appreciates it too."

God, he'd love all this, the security and comfort Callum gave us was something he'd always reached for. He'd wanted to do that for us himself, but his own internal limitations had always kept him guarded. He hadn't been able to keep a job, so we were always struggling.

"Again, it's not a problem," he said. "I'm happy to help."

He went back to work after that, and smiling, I finished up, then headed to school. I drove that morning with finally a little bit of peace when the last few days had been anything but. I was so hopeful when finally showing up to Windsor Prep. Especially when I did spot Legacy.

The boys were by their cars, Bow with them. The little rabbit was digging in her school bag when I drove right past them, and I hurried into a spot.

I hadn't seen Dorian.

Thatcher and Wells were there, Ares too, but no Dorian. The large boys stood in conversation by their cars, Ares's Hummer in the center. He'd chosen not to park in his Student of the Month space today, and I was surprised to see Bow with them. I figured she drove herself.

Maybe she hadn't today considering everything. Quickly, I got out of my brother's car, wanting to catch them. I got my bag, but by the time I made it around the car, the group had already moved on toward the school. They were moving with a group of kids, people I recognized as Legacy groupies around them. I waved my arm. "Bow!"

She started to turn in my direction, like she heard her name, but Thatcher put an arm over her shoulder. He kept her moving forward, and when the others fell in close behind, I lost sight of her all together. All their fan boys and girls seemed to crowd around them as they headed toward the school.

Huffing, I banked on being able to catch them later, Bow later. I tried not to let the anxiety hit me that maybe they wouldn't want to talk to me. I mean, Dorian definitely could have talked to them.

I bet they just didn't hear you.

That was what I made myself believe. At the present, I had no other choice.

CHAPTER
SIX

Sloane

The first half of the day left me anxiety-ridden. I didn't have an opportunity to speak to Bow since she'd dropped the math class we'd had together. I had to wait until lunch, but she wasn't at the table we normally sat together at. I studied the whole lunch room for her and even went out to the courtyard to see if she and the other boys were out there. The Legacy boys often took lunch there, and though their Court groupies were there, none of them were.

I texted Bow after I noticed, asking if maybe she and the boys went out to lunch. They did that sometimes off campus.

She never got back to me.

In fact, the whole school day passed with nothing, and it was a long one because of it. I left the day with no contact and my brother's make-up work. I got everything he needed so he could get caught up, and he was in the same place I'd left him that morning. Actually, he was sleeping, but he left me a text around fourth period that the doctor had checked him out. The guy, I guess, said what my brother had was most likely a temporary bug, but he wrote him a note off from school for the next few days just in case. I didn't want to bother my brother, so I left his work on his desk, then tried Bow again that night.

She hadn't answered.

Me: We really need to talk. We didn't leave things well, and I know you're busy, but I didn't tell anyone anything about you. I wouldn't do that.

That I sent to Dorian, also mentioning I hoped he was okay. He'd gone completely ghost, and if he believed what he had about me, that was probably why.

I wish he'd just talk to me.

We could figure this whole fucking thing out if he did, and I could only hope Bow not getting back to me had nothing to do with this.

The next morning, my brother didn't look any better. He didn't look any worse either, but he was lethargic. This did worry me, so I called his doctor, Dr. Richardson. The man informed me if my brother did have a temporary bug, then he simply needed rest. He offered to come by again if it made me feel more comfortable, but when I proposed that to Bru, his eyes rolled back in his head. He said I was worrying for nothing, and we both just needed to do what the doctor said. I called Callum about everything, and he advised the same.

"I'm sure he'll be fine," our guardian had assured me. *"But do call me if you need anything. I can even stay in town longer if you need me to."*

I definitely wasn't going to do that, and odds were, I might be channeling more worry about my brother's situation because of everything going on with Dorian. The news had still been talking about his family this morning, and the Mayberry situation. They seemed not to want to let it up, and who knew when they finally would.

I told Callum him staying longer wasn't necessary, but he did give me the line of his personal assistant just in case.

Something came up with one of his businesses, I guess, and he had to fly out this evening.

That made me anxious that I wouldn't have his aid, but I forced myself to nut the fuck up. My brother and I were good, and I needed to just stay positive about everything else.

"Chocolate pudding, please."

Her little voice triggered me in the a la carte line at lunch later that day.

Bow.

I angled around, spotting Rainbow Reed about four people behind me. I'd missed her earlier today, and actually, her brother and his friends too. Their cars had been there, but no boys.

Well, everyone but Dorian's car.

He still wasn't here today. At least, if the Windsor Preparatory's parking lot told me anything. I was surprised to see Bow now, actually. She hadn't been at lunch yesterday.

Taking this opportunity, I allowed a few people to pass.

She jumped just about a foot when her head lifted from the pudding cups.

"Sloane," she gasped, her dark lashes blinking. They whipped like fans, easily seen since she sported a messy bun today. "You scared me."

Clearly. I nudged my tray in. "Sorry."

"No, it's fine." Taking her pudding from the lunch lady, she slid it on her tray. "How are you?"

She asked the question, but she wasn't really looking at me, analyzing the salad options. This rich-ass school had enough of them. I watched her. "Good."

This was something she'd know if she'd bothered to return my texts, calls.

Be patient.

I wasn't selfish enough not to know she and hers were going through shit. I was well aware of it.

She said nothing in response to what I said, as if she

hadn't heard me. Next thing I knew, she was grabbing her tray off the line, but I got her arm.

"Not so fast, little rabbit. Uh," I started, not really knowing where to go from there. I mean, she hadn't answered me when I attempted to reach out. "How are things? I haven't heard from you. I texted. Called?" I put her on the spot. I knew. "I'm not sure if you've talked to Dorian, but I think there was a misunderstanding between us the other day. He seems to think I leaked where he was, and that's how he got arrested."

Bow's lashes flashed in my direction. She started to say something, but then her lips pinched tight.

"Has he talked to you?" I asked. "Said *anything*? I know he's not here today. I know he's going through epic shit, but if that's what he's thinking about me, I need to talk to him. He's not returning my calls or texts."

Basically, he was doing the same thing she was doing to me now. Actually, the exact same thing.

A strong feeling told me she knew exactly what I was talking about, but for whatever reason, she wasn't talking to me about it.

She was too busy looking outside.

Something about the Legacy boys was they always stood out. Especially Thatcher Reed, her brother. He was the largest out of the Legacy boys, and I'd seen him pummel through guys like a boulder on the football field. He sat between Ares Mallick and Wells Ambrose, the two of them talking to him about something, but he wasn't a part of the conversation.

He was too busy looking at Bow and me through the window.

Catching wind their buddy no longer had their attention, both Ares and Wells slid their gazes in our direction too. Wells's jaw locked immediately, and I noticed Ares sit back. He started to swing his head in the direction of Thatcher, as if to say something to him, but the large football player was already up and moving. He headed in the direction of the cafeteria doors, throwing them open.

"I need to go," Bow's little voice said beside me. She ducked her head, avoiding my eye contact, and I could do nothing but watch her go to her brother. He took her by the shoulder when she got to him, looking at her.

As if I might have done something to her.

He scanned her like he was looking for any sign she'd been messed with. I guess passing the test, he let her go, and when he started to move in my direction, she grabbed his arm.

Now, I couldn't hear what she said to him, but her little hand was certainly tight on her brother's arm.

He wrapped an arm around her after she finished, guiding her away and back into the courtyard. The two of them sat together at the table, joining the other guys, and it didn't take a genius to see what was going on here. Bow had definitely talked to Dorian. They *all* had.

And that was more than obvious.

CHAPTER
SEVEN

Sloane

I did something I thought I'd never do after school the next day.

I went to Dorian's.

This was a fucking terrible time to do this, confront him, but at the present, I didn't feel I had a choice. He had all of Legacy thinking that I'd snitched on him, but I wished *to God* that'd been the reason I decided to head toward his neighborhood like a crazy ass.

I was more concerned about *him*, hard not to be. He'd looked so betrayed that last day, and that hurt my goddamn heart. I cared about him.

I might more than care.

In any sense, that had to be secondary. I just wanted him to know I was in his corner, and what he did with it after that was his business. I just didn't want to add to the stress.

I couldn't even get anywhere near his cul-de-sac's gate.

News vans literally filled the street, and honest to fuck, I'd completely forgotten that the rest of town was trying to get in his business. This was an oversight on my part. Especially because I did know where to go *because* I'd seen his house on the news.

What were you thinking?

I hadn't been obviously. I ended up hanging back down the street, just watching the news vans and people. None of them were outside the vans, but the vehicles themselves were stacked on top of each other. They were all waiting like invasive assholes, and when any cars passing through did get anywhere near the gate, the reporters were sliding open their van doors for a peek. If someone looked interesting enough (i.e., one of Dorian's neighbors), the newscasters got out and did an interview. That was pretty rare, though. Dorian's neighbors weren't trying to sell him and his family out for a news story for the most part.

I watched on, feeling more than stupid. My car was in the shop, and I'd be lying if I said my brother's Audi hadn't gotten any attention. Eventually, the news assholes had all noticed it was just me in the car and headed back to stalking the gate. I waited for about an hour before the vehicles divided into half. Odds were some of them had to get back for the evening news, but a lot of them stayed.

Why are you staying?

I didn't know. It wasn't like I could actually get past the gate to talk to Dorian. Maybe I hoped I'd get lucky and see him coming in or out.

I'd been stupid.

So stupid in fact, I shook my head when I turned on my brother's car.

Something slammed against my door.

I jumped about a fucking foot only to find Ares Mallick's face staring right back at me. He still had the black eye from when my brother had punched him, the other side of his face socked from the work Dorian had done. They'd gotten in a fight when Dorian found out Ares sent Bruno in on that haze.

Had that only just happened?

It felt like so long ago now, Ares, with his long arms, hanging over my brother's ride. His thick but sculpted eyebrows knitted in tightly, his fist against my window. He had his shaggy hair hoisted up in a man-bun, AirPods in his ears and long running shorts on. His cutoff tee matched the shorts, and he was arrogant enough to wear a shirt that basically gave him male side boob. The thing was a scrap of fabric *at best*, and when his fist rammed into the door again, I realized that'd been what he'd initially done to gain my attention.

"The fuck you doing here, little?" his deep voice growled at me. It was muted through my brother's window, and he gestured for me to put it down.

I did, and he lowered his long body into view.

His dark eyebrows inched in tighter. "You here for an exclusive too?" He gazed around. "Or are you here to *give* one?"

The words stung, my eyes twitching. I mean, I pretty much figured out what was going on here with Legacy.

But still to hear the words…

He'd obviously confirmed my beliefs, beliefs about Dorian and what he *thought* he knew. This was a misunderstanding.

And Ares didn't seem to want to stay to debate anything else.

He pushed off my door, going in the opposite direction, and though I couldn't run for shit, I was out of my car and after him.

Now, when I'd woken up this morning, the last thing I thought I'd ever fucking do would be running. I didn't run *for shit*, let alone run after who could easily be considered my arch nemesis. Ares had given me more than a hard time since I'd gotten to Maywood Heights.

"Eh, Mallick!"

His Nikes skidded to a stop in the street. He whipped around, me fucking huffing behind him. I was still in my school uniform, but even if I'd had the appropriate running gear (i.e., *not* knee-highs and flats), I still wouldn't be able to run for shit. I panted like a psychopath, and he'd only gone a few long strides.

"Keep your fucking ass *down*," he gritted. Next thing I knew, he was grabbing me and taking me with him. I wanted to check his ass for pretty much snatch-grabbing me off the street, but he wasn't running in the opposite direction of me and actually talking. Since that was the point, to talk to him, I went along with his sprint. I was half-running, half-dragged until we came to a stop behind some trees.

Now, if I was a more dainty bitch, I might have tried to pretend I could breathe once we stopped. I wasn't, though, and pretty much choked on any incoming air.

This had Mallick arch one of his bushy eyebrows, and he definitely hadn't tried to hold back his smirk. He folded his arms. "Cardio, much? Jesus, little. You act like you've never run a day in your goddamn life."

He forgot he had a good amount of height over me. I was tall, five-ten, but still. He was a dude and tall as fuck. I coughed. I started to say something, but instead flipped him off.

He chuckled, a little dry but only like half. He seemed to find this whole situation funny, and normally, that'd piss me off. I mean, it still pissed me off, but he and his lot were super mad at me right now.

I found his humor dulled my anxiety a little, irony in that. I hated this guy, but I had an ulterior motive here. He could talk to Dorian for me.

"Anyway, the press doesn't need to know I'm here," he said, and I wanted to face-palm myself for not thinking about that. Of course, they'd want to talk to him too. The Mallicks and the rest of the Legacy families were very buzzworthy in this town. They'd be stalking him just as much as Dorian.

Especially since their families were so close. "I'm house-sitting for the Prinzes while they're gone."

My head shot in his direction. "Gone?"

He flinched, like actually legit flinched as if someone had struck him. He cursed. "Yeah."

Perhaps, he hadn't wanted to admit that detail.

I wondered why he had?

But he did, though, his feet more fascinating now than looking at me. He propped his hands on his hips. "So I suppose you want to go spill that out now? Tell the press or… your guardian?"

I didn't know what Callum had to do with anything. Sure, I'd told him the situation with Dorian, but that'd been after the fact. *To help him.* "Look. I know Dorian thinks I told on him—"

His smirk returning stopped me. He laughed. "You know it really doesn't matter what you say right now," he said, his smile fading. "Because anything that comes out of your lips will always be questionable as fuck as far as I'm concerned." His eyes darkened. "You're right. That is what Dorian thinks, and because he does, *we* stand by him." His throat tightened. "It doesn't matter what you say, little. You're questionable. It's my buddy's word against yours, which means you have no say."

His honesty struck me silent.

And he was right.

It really didn't matter what I said. I was going against *Legacy*, foundations and families. I didn't have a voice here.

I need to talk to Dorian.

"Well, can you have him talk to me, then?" I asked. Ares's head was shaking at this point. I angled in front of him. "At least have him return a fucking text."

"He doesn't have his phone." He braced his big arms. "His parents took him off the grid, and they took the phone too." His eyes lifted to the sky. "I don't even know why I'm fucking telling you this."

I was glad he was.

And he was leaving now.

Actually, he left me standing right there, and I was well aware if this guy went in a full sprint, there was no catching up to him. He could lose me with little effort.

So I stayed.

This really seemed hopeless, *beyond* hopeless. If Dorian didn't want to talk to me, listen to reason, what voice did I truly have here? His friends were loyal to him, his brothers, and Bow was his sister. Those bonds had formed well before me and were generational. Even their fathers were tight.

These people were the epitome of family, and there was no listening to reason here.

Ares stopped a few feet away. "Go home, little. Because there's certainly more for you there than will ever be here."

I blinked, the tall boy sprinting away. He left me there, and eventually, I headed back too. I was going to go to my house, but he was wrong when he called it a home. My brother and I didn't have one of those. We had a *house*, and even that was temporary. It was on loan from our guardian until we grew up and moved on. We didn't have what I could imagine Ares and the rest of Legacy had.

Maybe someone like my brother and me never would.

CHAPTER EIGHT

Sloane - age 6

I bounced the ball hard down the hallway. Mommy put down my brother, Bruno, to take a nap, so I got real bored. I didn't like being bored. I liked to play. I tried to make noise real loud on purpose, but Bruno was a heavy sleeper.

Why can't he just wake up!

I listened outside his door, but I didn't hear anything. Shrugging, I decided to take the ball upstairs. I might play Barbies or something until he wakes up. I started to bounce the ball again, but sat down. I rolled the ball across the hall for a few moments. I'd get my Barbies soon, but this was fun. The ball kept hitting my bedroom door and would roll back. That last time I rolled it, the thing wouldn't roll back, though.

I got on my knees to get it when I heard Mommy's and Daddy's voices. They said my name.

"I can't do this anymore," Mommy said, and I crawled on my knees until I got to their door. I pressed it open with my palm, but could only see Daddy's back. Daddy was a big man.

He sighed. "You have to. You *have to* and you know that. For her sake."

I let go of the door, sitting down. I tried to see around Daddy, but couldn't really. I could only see Mommy's feet between his big legs. She sat on their bed.

"You know what people tell me when I take her out?" Mommy gasped. "They tell me how beautiful she is. How I need to put her in *pageants* because she's so stunning. She is stunning…"

Mommy's voice sounded funny. It sounded sad like when her and Daddy fought. They'd been fighting a lot lately. Especially when I started school last year.

I played with my bracelet, a dangling charm on it. I didn't remember when I'd gotten it. Mommy and Daddy had given it to me when I'd been real little.

"It's not fair," Mommy stated. It sounded like she was crying now. "What kind of people are we to do this to her?"

"We don't have a choice." Daddy's voice was quiet. "And, Marilyn, you have to keep it together."

"She's going to know. As she gets older, she…"

The floor creaked under me, and Daddy whipped around. Daddy and Bruno looked a lot alike. They both had dark brown hair like Mommy. I didn't have dark brown hair. Mine was almost black. Mommy said I looked more like my grandmother. She was an immigrant from Mexico. I didn't know what *immigrant* meant, but I liked that I looked like her. I told people that whenever they asked. I looked like my grandma. I wished I'd gotten to meet her. She died before I was born.

Daddy pulled his hair out of his eyes, blinking down and looking at me. Hurriedly, he closed the door behind him, and I saw Mommy with her face in her hands.

She had been crying. She had her mouth in her hands before Daddy closed the door.

He squatted down to me.

"What are you doing, little punk?" he asked, tugging on

my braid. He grinned, and I giggled. He tugged the other braid. "Playing spy on me and Mommy?"

He started to tickle me, and I couldn't stop laughing. Daddy was always so funny. He tickled until I had tears in my eyes and was on the floor.

"Daddy, Daddy!" I laughed, squealing. "I wasn't spying!"

"You sure?" He laughed too before tickling me again. "You know only spies get ice cream?"

"Ice cream?" I shot up, out of breath. "I'm a spy, then!"

Daddy chuckled, rubbing my head. He helped me up, then took my hand. "Come on. Let's go see if your brother is up from his nap. I'm sure he'd like to come too."

"Bru's lame," I mused, skipping down the hallway with him. "He always has to nap."

"That's because he's younger than you. That doesn't make him lame. It just means he'll always need a little help from you since you're his big sister."

Picking me up, he gave me a piggyback ride. I held on real tight, but spun around when the door opened.

Mommy peeked outside the room, looking really sad. She leaned against the door, raising her hand at me. She waved, so small, and I did back.

"Can Mommy be a spy?" I asked Daddy when he took me downstairs.

Daddy gazed up at me. "Why, honey?"

He placed me down, and I shrugged. "She looks sad, and if spies get ice cream, I want her to be a spy too. Ice cream will make her happy."

Ice cream always made me happy. Made sense.

Daddy started to say something, but then he put his hand over his mouth. He rubbed a second before taking my hand again.

"Let's just go get Bru, huh?" He nodded. "Your mommy will be okay."

I hoped she would. No one should be sad.

And Mommy was sad a lot.

CHAPTER NINE

Sloane - present

I washed my face long and hard that next morning after running into Ares, scrubbing it. I still couldn't believe what had fucking happened.

This was hopeless.

This situation was hopeless, and once again, I found myself at the center of hate. Legacy hate.

Dorian's hate.

The first time, I hadn't been aware of the reasons. Once I was, I hadn't liked it, but I'd gotten it. In the end, it'd all been a big misunderstanding. Actually, quite like this, but this I couldn't get or accept. I wasn't a liar. I *hadn't* betrayed him.

That didn't matter.

He'd made up his mind, and that had made up everyone else's mind.

I braided my hair with wandering thoughts, trying not to feel anything, but that was hard. He'd once again shut me out, but this time was different. *This time* I was invested. I cared about the asshole and fuck us both.

Fuck me.

I wished I hated him. I wished I didn't care for him, Bow, or anyone else. That would make all this easier. I could be alone. I *got* being alone. My brother and I were our own island, and I thrived on how well we always adjusted.

It was different when you actually had something, though. At least the start of something. I didn't know what that was for Dorian and me, but it'd been *something*.

You need to get your shit together.

With a stiff breath, I moved on that morning. I still had a ship to fucking run, and my brother was sick. He hadn't been any different last night before he'd gone to bed. Though he had gotten some homework done. It hadn't been much since he complained about drowsiness, but he'd gotten a little bit done, and I'd worked with him.

Of course, his smart ass hadn't needed me. He was the whiz, but he'd entertained me being there and working alongside him on my own work. In all honestly, I would have preferred working on a series I'd started in my art studio downstairs. I hadn't gotten terribly far with it, but with all the downtime I'd had since coming here, that was where my mind had been at since Bru had been busy himself with football after school.

He obviously wasn't doing that now, and I knocked on his door this morning. "Bru?"

His door was kind of open, so I pushed it the rest of the way. My brother turned over, and I thought he might be still sleeping, but I spotted him texting on his cell phone.

He eyed over his shoulder, some actual color in his face. "Sup?"

Well, that seemed good. He hadn't been talking so much since he'd been tired and achy.

Lounging against the door, I eyed the room before smirking. "Really milking this thing for all it's worth, aren't you?"

His room was filled with video games and takeout

cartons. Clearly, my brother's weird bug hadn't dulled his appetite.

And he seemed to be better now, sitting up. It took him a second to get himself stable, and clearly, some weakness continued to bother him. The fact that he'd been able to rise in itself was good, though. He had the energy enough to do it.

"Whatev," he said, messing with his phone a sec before resting his head back on the wall. He closed his eyes. "Anyway, give me a fucking break. I'm like dying or some shit."

He wasn't dying, my eyes rolling back into my head. I picked up a pizza box, stacking it on another. "Dying people don't eat pizza."

"Says who?" He chuckled, but he must have done it too hard because he stopped. "Don't make me laugh. It hurts."

"What does?"

"How about everything?" His eyes still closed, he folded his arms. "This fucking sucks. Why couldn't you get it?"

"Nice," I said, and after cleaning up some of his stuff, I sat on his bed. "And you obviously aren't contagious; otherwise, I would have gotten it."

Dr. Richardson didn't think this was something my brother could pass to anyone. Just a bug, like he said. Leaning forward, I felt my brother's forehead, and though he was still warm, he wasn't burning up like that first day.

"You seem to be coming around, though. Sitting up? I'm assuming you've been taking your medicine." The doctor had left some stuff for him.

My brother shrugged. "When I remember. I think I missed the last dose or two. I get all foggy, and since I've been sleeping, I just forget."

Well, he couldn't be doing that. Not if he did want to get better.

I'd scold him, but since I didn't know what he was going through, I decided to be helpful by getting his meds together. The doctor hadn't left a ton, but they had different directions on the bottles. I decided to get them ready on his nightstand, and while I did, he looked at his phone again.

"Any word from the guys?" he asked me, thumbing the screen. "I've been texting the hell out of them, asking them if everything is all right and stuff. I haven't heard anything since before the video went viral. Ares isn't good about texting, but Thatcher and Wells always do. I didn't want to bother Dorian. I figured all that stuff with his family had him busy."

I stopped messing with his pills, my eyes up. I shook my head, and my brother sighed.

"I'm not trying to get in their business. I just want to make sure everything is okay, you know?" He put his phone down. "You think they're still mad about the haze? That I didn't do it?"

I fingered a pill, about ninety percent sure the reason my brother was being ignored had something to do with me. If Legacy hated me again, they'd hate him by proxy. They only hadn't the first time because Dorian had been trying to mess with me.

I guess he wasn't bothering with that now, or having the others do that either. I rubbed my arm. "Ares said Dorian is out of town."

"You spoke to Wolf?" Bru leaned forward.

"Barely. I just know Dorian's not here. His parents took his phone too."

"Shit."

I nodded.

Bru's head lifted. "Does that mean he did the video? Him and the other guys? Why would his parents take his phone? Do they think he did it?"

I had nothing to lose by telling my brother the truth, but I didn't want him to think about anything else with him being sick. He didn't need the stress.

"I can imagine all this shit with the press is hard for his

family," I said, still covering for Dorian for some reason. I swallowed. "I don't blame them for leaving. As far as the phone, I mean, I'm not his parents, so…"

He was probably right in what he said. Again, I just didn't want to stress him out. None of this did have anything to do with us and my brother was sick. He shouldn't be thinking about this. His only priority should be getting better.

"Do you know where he went?" Bru continued. "Like I said, I'm not trying to get in his business."

My brother was just worried. He was because he was a good friend.

He was being screwed just as much as I was in this situation.

"I think you should just worry about getting better," I said, then gestured to his table. "I divided up your meds. The right side is the morning. Left, night. Actually, take the first set now while I'm sitting here so I know you have."

Smirking, he picked up a small bottle of water he had on his bedside table. He took a swig before popping the meds, taking them down together.

He even showed me his tongue after.

"Don't be an ass," I said, making him chuckle again.

"And *you* stop worrying," he said.

I'd do that once he got better.

I nudged his leg. I started to get his books so he could do some homework since he was up, but he waved that off.

"Finished it this morning," he said before picking up his video game controller. He had a huge TV in here like he did downstairs. He shrugged. "Was feeling a little better, so I did it."

Well, that was good. I grinned. "Perfect. I'll get you some more today."

He groaned, but I chuckled. I gathered some more of his trash before getting up.

"Did you hear anything from Callum?" he asked, fighting

something on the TV screen. "He said he had to leave early. Some business thing."

He'd said the same to me, but I hadn't heard anything since then.

Taking out my phone, I decided to text him now to see how he was faring. I supposed I didn't need to, but I just wanted to make sure everything was good.

"What are you doing?" My brother wasn't even looking at me, shooting something that had purple guts.

I cringed. "Just texting him. I'll let you know if I hear anything."

"Thank him for me when you can," Bru said. "For that doctor? Really, Callum has been a godsend. He told me he even called Coach just to make sure I didn't lose my spot or anything. The team's real competitive, and I was concerned about that."

I knew he'd called the school since Bru had been out. He was technically Bru's guardian since he was still a minor.

My brother would never know how truly helpful Callum had been surrounding the Dorian thing. I hadn't gone into detail with my brother involving anything with that.

I'd been still trying to support the dark prince.

I had his back from the jump. Even if it didn't matter now, I had.

You still do.

I'd dodged my own brother's questions about him today, and before I could think about why, I got up.

"Let me know if you hear anything from the guys," he said to me. His arms dropped over his legs. "And I'm sure you'll hear from Dorian soon. He and his family are probably just busy like you said. Maybe his parents just need time for all this to blow over."

Normally, I'd pass that off, tell my brother Dorian and I weren't a thing and he needed to mind his own business.

I just nodded today, only one concern on my mind. My

brother was the most important thing, his well-being and our survival. I didn't have time for anything else. The pair of us were alive. We were good, and there wasn't time to think about anything else. Anything else would be foolish.

Anything else *was* foolish.

CHAPTER
TEN

Sloane

I basically ignored Legacy over the next few days.

They made it easy.

When I wasn't ignoring them, they were ignoring me. The only place we really collided was lunch, and since they sat in the courtyard with their groupies, I didn't see them anyway. I was once again on my lonely island, and as the days passed, I preferred it that way. I'd been nothing but anxiety-ridden since I'd gotten to this fucking school, and with my brother being out, one more thing to *not* have to worry about was a good thing. Bruno's fever had broken, but whatever bug that "bit" him still lingered. He still had the aches and chills, and I'd been paranoid enough to call the doctor again. Dr. Richardson happily came out and changed his meds to ease his symptoms more. The meds, in general, made my brother super sleepy, though, so he was basically asleep whenever I saw him now.

It'd been over a week of this, a week of stress and strain. Since Bru wasn't getting any worse, there was that, but something in my mind couldn't help but focus on how he'd gotten this. My brother didn't get sick, and I could only conclude him and that dumb haze had been the cause. Who knew what was in that water that night he'd dove in.

Dorian may have saved my brother only for him to get sick and die anyway. I was probably being dramatic, but the thoughts chilled me.

Don't think about Dorian. Don't.

I did enough—when I wasn't stressing about my brother —while I was working in my studio. I did that just to give my mind something to do. My new series was the second priority in my life. In fact, I worked so much on the project I almost always missed Callum's calls to check in on my brother and me. He had gotten back to me before. He was on business and traveling as per usual. With as freaked out as my brother's situation was making me, I nearly asked him to come back, but I wasn't about to disrupt his life. Not when he'd been so good to us. Our guardian was giving us just what I'd asked for when our father passed away, space.

Even if I felt mad within it.

I actually started working on my series at school too just to get out of my head. I had several advanced art classes at Windsor Prep, but also found myself with a free period. It used to be filled as a student assistant for Principal Mayberry.

That obviously wasn't the case now, and Mr. Keene, our assistant principal, gave me the option to use the time how I wanted. He was taking over for Mayberry at the present, I assumed until the position was filled, and I took full advantage of the situation when I asked him if I could work on my art in one of the academy's art rooms. They had like a dozen in this rich-ass school that weren't being used every period.

I chose one of the biggest rooms with the best gear, my earbuds in when I pushed into the room that day. I hadn't expected the room to be occupied.

Nor to hold a Legacy boy.

Ares Mallick had his legs propped up on a chair, ankles crossed, and a sketchpad in his hands. I should have been able to tell who he was by the sheer size of the guy alone, but it took me a moment to realize he was the large football player. He had a black hoodie on over his academy uniform, his hood up and his curls falling out of the front. I supposed the curls alone would have given him away. Not many had the crazy volume his did when he let them go.

His head lifted when I opened the door and his feet dropped to the floor when I came inside.

He sat up. "What are you doing in here?"

I could ask him the same question. I shrugged. "I chill in here sometimes." I took my bag off. "It's my free period. Not much to do."

No one would know that more than him. He was well aware I'd had my free period with Mayberry this hour. He and his friends had planned to kidnap her and make that video during the time.

They'd obviously ended up doing something else, and Ares watched me under a more than observant gaze when I crossed the room. The way he eyed me, one would think he thought I'd shoot him.

"Right," he said, finger tapping his sketchpad. The thing was huge, and he had a piece of charcoal in his hands. I recalled him saying he liked to do art, but this boy wasn't in any art classes. I took like all of them, so I'd know.

"What are you doing in here?" I asked.

He gave me a look like it was obvious. I supposed we were in an art room, and he did have a sketchpad.

He eased into his hoodie after I said it, and I wondered if he was using it to hide his face. Good tactic really, as hoodies were allowed as long as they had the school's insignia. His read *Windsor Prep Football* and happened to have the king on it, the large gorilla that was the school's mascot.

Catching a glance of his face, I noticed it wasn't as bad as the last time I'd seen him, the bruising more yellow today.

"Was trying to get some work done," he snipped, and I rolled my eyes. This guy just couldn't help but be an aggressive ass. Always had been. He ran the charcoal over the sketchpad. "I usually swipe shit from here, charcoal and pencils. It helps it's quiet too." His brown eyes lifted. "Usually."

I laughed, mostly because he was just such a dick. I folded my arms. "Well, don't let me bother you."

"I won't." Even still, he eyed every move I made. I dropped my bag on a chair, then headed over to the easels. My series was paintings, and I'd brought one in to work on at school. I got my paints together.

Ares studied me for a while before he found me arranging my stuff and putting on my smock boring enough to get back to what he'd been doing. He smirked after a beat. "Calc one?" he questioned, and I noticed he eyed the books falling out of my bag. He tipped his chin. "That's a junior class, little. You that far behind?"

My eyes lifted to the art room's rafters.

"It's actually for Bru," I said, tying my apron. "And I thought you liked it quiet."

He made a noise with his mouth, like he was over me and over it all. This was typical of him. I mean, he was writing me off right now with the whole Dorian situation. His presence was definitely a reminder of the dark prince, which made me more than annoyed. I came in here *not* to think about him.

"Why you got the kid's books?" he asked, though he barely looked up from his work. His fingers on his pad had slowed, so he was actually interested.

I swallowed at that situation, wetting my lips. "He's sick. Something I guess you would've noticed if you actually cared about him?" I eyed him. "I thought you guys were friends. Or did you not notice he hasn't been around at school?"

"I noticed." He swung a glance in my direction. "And sick?"

"Yeah." Though I definitely didn't want to talk about that.

He nodded. "I'm sure he'll be fine, though." He put one of his shined leather shoes up on the chair he'd used for his legs. "You and your brother have that sweet setup. I'm sure your guardian's been taking real good care of you. Probably called out a doctor and everything for the kid."

How did he know? I supposed he could assume. Especially if that's how his own parents handled illness. Rich kids didn't go to hospitals. Hospitals came to them.

But my brother and I weren't rich kids. We *weren't* like them. We might have currently had some of the perks, but that wouldn't be forever. This situation with Callum was nice, but it definitely had a clock on it.

Ares moved his lips. "So is he?"

"What?"

His chin jutted at me. "Your guardian. He's taking care of you. Bru?" He dropped an arm over his leg. "What is it that Montgomery does again?"

My eyes narrowed. "Why?"

"Just curious." Ares passed that off with a shoulder shrug. "Smaller town. Just call us some nosy fucks."

I shook my head. "He's in business."

"What kind?"

"He's an entrepreneur, and is there a reason I'm being interviewed right now?"

"Nah, little. You good." Though I noticed his stare didn't let up. "Just trying to clear up some blanks about you. You came into this town all mysterious and shit. You, your brother, and your guardian."

And with my supposed dishonesty, he was trying to gain some intel on me, something he couldn't find with just an internet search.

If anything, that pissed me off even more. I hadn't lied to him and the others... Dorian.

"Well, you're right about the size of this town and having some nosy fucks," I gritted. "Anyway, if you want to know something about me, why don't you *get to know me* instead of just assuming shit."

"No reason to get heated." He tucked his hands under his arms. "Just trying to figure you out is all. Anyway, I noticed I never see your guardian around. He never came to Bru's games. I'm naturally curious about all you guys."

I frowned. "Callum doesn't come because he's busy. *He has a life*, and I don't ask him to disrupt it just to take care of Bru and me."

"So just take what you need, then?"

I seriously couldn't *with* him. Ignoring him, I got behind my easel.

"That's your stuff over there?"

Considering he wanted quiet when I came in here, he wasn't giving me that now.

I stayed quiet, and eventually, he got up, coming over. I wouldn't break my concentration for him, so I did what I could to forget he hovered.

I was working on the fifth piece of my series, and he watched me pull up a stool and get back into it. I liked to paint space, galaxies in particular.

"You're pretty good." He all but grumbled it. "Actually, very good."

I'd say thanks, but I ended up shaking my head. "Any reason I've never seen you in any of the art classes?"

He studied my hand stroke across the canvas. "Yes."

Elusive much? "And that reason would be...?"

It was as if I hadn't spoken, and the way he watched me paint, intense like he was trying to dissect the work itself, I wondered for a second if he had. He braced his arm. "I find them stifling. I don't want to do shit because people tell me to do shit." He shrugged. "I feel it's a waste of time."

"How do you learn, then?"

"I make my way." Smirking, he looked at me. "I've studied art for what feels like my whole life. Just not from these basic-ass art teachers."

I laughed at what he said, and probably the only reason I didn't find the teachers here sniffling was because I hadn't had such resources before. Half the schools I'd been to didn't even have art programs.

This was all a new world for me, but obviously not for this guy. Rich, he'd probably studied with the best. Especially if he'd been doing it his whole life.

"I've learned the most from my dad," he said, glancing my way again. "He's quite prolific. He owns half the art galleries in town."

More nuggets of surprising information from who was truly the worst out of all the Legacy boys. Over the weeks I'd been here, I'd been able to find some common ground with Thatcher and Wells. Of course, Dorian had been a more difficult case, but Ares had been completely hopeless. The way Ares and I had met set the foundation for nothing but pure, unadulterated hatred on both our parts.

"That's cool."

"Yeah?"

I nodded. "He as much of a delight as you are?"

This quirked a small but genuine smile to his lips, and I nearly fell off my chair. Ares Mallick smiled at me. Chuckling, he tugged his hood down more over his curls.

"Everyone loves my father," he said. "He's a good man. A kind man." His head tilted. "I'm sure even you'd love him."

"Why even me?"

His grin widened. "After all, you're as much of a delight as I am."

That had me laughing, and go figure, *laughing* with this guy.

He continued to watch, and I noticed his sketchpad at his side. I stopped painting. "Can I see what you do?"

Eyeing me, he took a beat, but eventually, he raised it for me to see. I might have hit a nerve there. Artists could be touchy about showing their work, and this guy was nothing but a loose cannon anyway.

And had absolutely no reason to be.

Cars. He liked to sketch cars, boats. He even had a few motorcycles.

"I do some designing," he said. He shifted on his shoes. "Actually, yeah. Designing. It's my thing."

Puffing up, he was kind of looking uncomfortable talking about it or at least showing me. Again, he was an artist, so I got that.

"These are good," I said, no lie there. They were fabulous and so realistic. He had people in his sketchpad too, portraits. I turned the page, hoping to see more of them. Mallick surprisingly had an eye for realism I'd never seen before.

"Okay, little," he stated, stopping me. He took his pad back, and apparently, didn't want to show me more.

I did get that being an artist. I had work myself that would never see the light of day in my own sketchpads.

"You're very talented." I wasn't trying to stroke his ego, facts.

Ares closed the pad. "Thanks. I do a lot of geometric work too. I try to put it into my designs when I can."

"What are you trying to do with it?" I asked. "Your art."

"Design school is first." He dropped an arm on the shelf that housed all the watercolor paints. "Actually, that's what my senior project is. I'm going to use it for my applications."

That was cool. I figured I'd just do an essay for mine. We just needed it to graduate, and since I hadn't thought about going to college, doing anything more than that hadn't crossed my mind.

"I could use some help with it," he said, stealing my attention. His eyes narrowed. "This piece has gotten a little bit away from me, and it'd be nice to have the assistance. I'm still in the design phase, but I can tell it's going to be too much for one person to meet my deadline."

"Wait." Was he asking *me* to help? "Are you asking me to help you out?"

His stare didn't let up. "I guess I am. Like I said, it's too much for one person, and what you're doing with these galaxies flows with what I'm trying to do."

I wondered what that was, but I wondered even more why he was asking me of all people. He didn't trust me. Hell, he couldn't stand me. "Why are you asking me? I thought I couldn't be trusted."

"Lucky for you, what does or doesn't come out of your mouth has nothing to do with how well you can paint." His jaw ticked. "Which is decent. Even if I don't want to admit it."

Shit, he was honest. Like a fucking slap-in-the-face honest.

His hand slid in his pocket. "Anyway, if you decide to commit, you'll get credit for your own senior project." He shrugged. "You can even use the piece on your applications of wherever you decide to go for college."

That sounded really good and was another thing I wouldn't have to think about. I had enough on my mind these days. I shifted on my stool. "What about Dorian?"

He messed with his curls. "What about him?"

I twitched. "Won't he be pissed you asked me to help?"

His thick eyebrows knitted. "Well, I guess it's good things between *my friends* and I have nothing to do with you. You and I are working together. And as far as you're concerned, that's all you need to worry about."

Fuck, this guy was a literal nightmare and definitely didn't give a shit about me.

And his words stung more than I wanted to admit.

In fact, so much so that I was considering working with the asshole. Why should I care about what Dorian thinks about what I do? He didn't care about me. At least, not enough to listen to me. He'd just *left*.

My mouth moved. "When would we start?"

He blinked, as if shocked I'd agree so quickly.

"It'd be right away." He angled his phone out of his pocket. "I'll text you everything. You'd need to sign a contract and an NDA."

"Wait. What?"

His eyes lifted from his device. "The contract is so you don't pussy out if the work starts to get to be too much for you. I don't need you leaving me hanging. The contract locks you in. No getting out once we start." His gaze was sharp. "The NDA is to avoid any potential problematic shit, i.e., loose fucking lips. The art you see stays between us. No photographs. No *talk*. I don't need my shit showing up everywhere."

I didn't miss how he called me problematic again. He really didn't trust me, but apparently that didn't matter since I could hold a brush well enough.

I really didn't want to work with this guy, but I couldn't deny having the school credit wouldn't hurt. I also didn't want to care either about what Dorian would say.

I'd look over his little contract, and if things seemed on the up-and-up, I'd say yes. I wouldn't care about Dorian Prinze, or his opinions about it. He didn't own me.

At least, he wouldn't anymore.

CHAPTER
ELEVEN

Sloane

I ended up signing Ares's little contract, and I told myself it had nothing to do with sticking it to Dorian. I told myself it had nothing to do at all with Dorian, and I was going to look out for myself for once. I could definitely use the help in regards to graduating, and what I did or didn't do had nothing to do with him.

I told myself these things.

Honestly, Ares's project was an inconvenience. My brother was still sick, but at least, it'd get me out the house and not worrying about him. Bru all but pushed me out the door when I told him about it.

Anyway, after I did sign it, Ares's text told me to meet at his house that evening, and I nearly regretted committing to him. The last time I'd been at this house, things had been fucked up as hell with his little lingerie prank, but then, I remembered he'd made my ass sign a contract and NDA.

He'd been serious about it.

Apparently, this guy was Van Gogh and believed his art

held true value. As an artist myself, I believed this for everyone. Anyone who made art should have a sense of protection of it.

But it was Ares's arrogance that truly got me. The guy was a tool and a half, and because he was, I couldn't help but be more than curious about a few things. One was what kind of project was so massive he, of all people, felt the need to ask for help.

The other surrounded him asking me in the first place.

He didn't believe me about the Dorian thing, just like the rest of Legacy, and he'd truly have to need help with something to ask an enemy. We'd been enemies even before.

He really must need help, and I could only sum it up to that. I also wondered if he'd told Dorian, but like he'd said, his relationship with his friends had nothing to do with me.

I cringed thinking about that, but forced myself to put that away. I needed to stay focused and just get this shit done with Ares.

I'd really forgotten about the size of this place.

The football player's home was simply huge, surrounded by fencing, and the white columns on the home matched. His place reminded me of those old Southern estates down in Louisiana or North Carolina. It was quaint and lovely and the exact opposite of the bad boy I'd crossed one too many times for my liking.

Ares did have gates like the Reeds, but they were open, and I let myself inside. I followed the driveway up to the front of the house.

The driveway itself was wraparound, and I started to park before he came outside in a pair of paint-splattered coveralls and a tank. The tank was basically another scrap of a shirt, and I was honest to God surprised he didn't come out here shirtless. This guy was constantly feeling himself.

He waved a hand.

"We're going to the garage," he said, and that made sense.

If we were painting and getting messy, we probably shouldn't be doing that in his nice house. I'd been in there, and it was immaculate.

He walked beside my car as I rolled toward a garage that held five or so cars. He had it open and told me to park in one of the empty spots. I noticed his Hummer there with the silver wolf scrolled on the front of the hood. The work obviously reflected his namesake.

I got out of my car, wearing my own set of work clothes. Funny enough, I wore a pair of paint-splattered bibs too, but my T-shirt beneath definitely left me more clothed than the Wolf himself.

Ares noticed my attire as I got out of my ride. His eyes narrowed with a shake of his head.

"What? No booty shorts today," he quipped, and I rolled my eyes. He always claimed I liked to get attention, so I wasn't surprised about the jab. The fucker had even called me a bimbo when I'd first met him. He clearly believed there wasn't anything up there in my head and made snap judgments about me.

"Let's get one thing straight." I strode right up to him. He turned and was right in my face, and though he was tall, I was too. I only had to stare up at him a little to make eye contact. I cut a hand across my neck. "No insults. No bullshit. I'm here to help you. Not to have you call me names." I shouldered him out of the way. "Now come on, bitch. Where's the canvas?"

I expected an instant retort from my arch enemy, so imagine my surprise when it didn't come. In fact, he was only smirking when I turned around.

He cuffed his arms. "Bitch, huh?" He approached. "So the no-insult thing apparently doesn't go both ways?"

"The contract didn't state otherwise." I smirked now. "Believe me, I read it."

That thing had me doing everything just short of signing

over my unborn child. I couldn't talk about Fight Club, and my life would *become* Fight Club. He had me basically living and breathing this project until it was concluded.

But that didn't mean we wouldn't be establishing some boundaries from the jump.

Ares's eyes darkened as he loomed largely over me. "Well, it does go both ways. You're working with me, so I'll get some goddamn respect from you…"

"Same goes for me." I got in his face. "Got it, Mallick?"

The smirk returned.

"Sure," he said, but I noticed that wasn't a yes. That was probably as close as I'd get from him. "And before we do this, I got some additional rules."

"Depends. Were those in the contract?"

I swear to God, I got a little bit of a growl from him at that, and his eye twitched a little. But surprising *again*, he didn't check me on this. He wanted to and I saw that, but he didn't.

Instead, he took a slow breath, the grimace etched on his face like a dark tattoo.

"This is my project," he established. "Therefore, I call the terms." He put a finger in my face. "Rule number one is I'm in charge. You do what I say, and you take my direction. This won't work if you're going rogue and acting up."

He saw me as a child obviously, but what his bougie ass didn't know was I was just as much of a serious artist as he clearly *felt* he was.

"Well, that's a given." I shrugged. "What else?"

"You don't go in my house." His expression was serious. "Our project's out here. You stay out here."

"Bathroom?"

He directed a finger toward a door in the garage. "Leads to the guesthouse. There's a bathroom in here. Cooler for water. I even got fucking snacks. Basically, you have zero reasons to go inside my house."

For someone who had raging parties during which people stayed over, he was pretty territorial about his space.

Maybe that'd been different before. Different with me. I hadn't betrayed his friend then.

Ares was clearly hung up on this, and I was completely over trying to prove my innocence to him. He was a fucking asshole, and I was only here because he needed me.

His jaw clenched. "Understood?"

"Yeah."

He nodded. "Good." He waved a hand. "Now, follow me. I'll show you what we're doing."

That'd be a breath of fresh air. I wouldn't have to talk to him anymore. Once we got going, I could do my part while he did his. I could blast my music in my earbuds, and we could stay on our own sides of whatever this project was.

We headed over to the cars, one away from the rest on the far side of the garage. He had it under a tarp and pulled the thing off, unveiling an old muscle car. Painted white, the thing reminded me of my dad's Chevelle, except it was brand new.

Ares balled up the tarp. "We're starting here."

"Um, what?"

He jutted a chin toward the pretty ride. The thing was a pearl white, immaculate. He tapped a hand on the front. "We're going to paint the car. *This* is the canvas."

My mouth parted as he walked behind it, pulling another tarp. This one had been over a plain canvas that was about the size of the actual wall. Actually, the canvas itself traveled the entire length of the car.

"And this too," he said, my eyes flashing. He laughed. "Intimidated yet?"

Getting there.

I guess now I know why he needed the help.

"We're going to paint the car," he continued. He put a hand out. "Then blend it into the canvas behind it. It'll create an interesting perspective and be perfect for my design school applications. It'll show I'm multifaceted."

I'll say.

"What are we painting on them?" This actually sounded fun, real fun.

Ares dropped the tarp, then I followed him over to a sketchpad he had on the back of the car's trunk. The ride was completely sweet and easily a hundred-thousand-dollar car.

The fact that we were going to be *painting* on it was something else, and opening his sketchpad, Ares showed me what we were going to do.

I couldn't have been more shocked. He'd told me he did geometric work.

But he'd never said he did constellations.

The pages were filled with them, gorgeous and reminded me so much of my galaxy work it gave me chills. It was like the opposite of what I did. He was all hard lines and tough edges, and I was exploded chaos.

But it worked together. It definitely did.

Ares studied me. "What do you think?"

"Did you just do these?"

"I'd been working on it, but after seeing what you do, I realized your work fit into mine. I've always done constellations."

Crazy that he'd always been into that, the stars. I obviously focused on that.

His eyebrows narrowed. "Anyway, I was able to finish it up this morning." He pointed to the paper. "I figured your stuff would go behind it. You do a little of you, and I do a little of me. It'll be a learning process, and you'll have to keep up…"

I rolled my eyes.

He laughed. "We'll both learn, and I'm not going to bullshit. This is going to be time-consuming. I'm going to need your one hundred percent."

I admit, I wasn't dreading this now. It really could be fun.

He waited patiently beside me, but he fidgeted. His hands slid into his pockets. "So this is your chance. The contract says you can leave after our initial session after seeing the game plan."

It did, and that was the only part of it that I thought was fair. I could bow out if I thought things would be too much.

"This actually sounds like fun," I said, and his eyes twitched. I chuckled. "I don't back down from a challenge, Mallick. And like you said, what we both do will work well together."

"You'll have to sketch your part." He frowned. "I'll have to approve it."

It was like he was trying to convince me out of this, and maybe he was. It couldn't have been easy asking for my help. Especially since he didn't trust me.

That only made me want to say yes more.

"Well, then, maybe we should get started," I said, his eyes only growing in width. "After all, you do have a deadline."

"I do." He put the sketchpad on the car. "I mean it, Sloane. I'm not going to drag your ass."

I knew he did. I nodded, but then leaned forward. "I'm not going to drag *your* ass. So let's get this going."

He stayed in the middle of the garage when I walked around him. I got my bag out of my car, my own sketchpad and pencils in there. I was completely serious about this.

I guess he saw that when I came back with them, and nodding, he gathered his pad.

"We can sketch in the guesthouse," he said, then led the way. This would be an interesting pairing. But considering everything with my brother and, well, everything else, it might be just what I needed. I wanted a distraction.

And all this work would definitely be it.

CHAPTER
TWELVE

Sloane

Mommy jerked me forward, my hand in hers. She tugged me so hard.

It hurt.

I cried, telling her my arm stung, but she didn't stop.

She just kept tugging, the room a blur.

Everything but the animal.

It had big teeth, a large mouth like it'd eat me whole. It would eat me.

Mommy dragged me toward it.

"Mommy, I'm scared," I cried, but Mommy didn't stop tugging me. A door was beside the animal, a big door. Would the animal eat me in there?

"You have to," Mommy said, but I didn't want to. I wanted to go home. Why couldn't we just go home?

I shook my head, the tears falling down my cheeks. I could taste them in my mouth like salty crackers.

"Mommy, please," I called, but she grabbed me by my shoulder.

She was taking me to the animal, the door. She wanted to take me to it.

I didn't want to go.

CHAPTER
THIRTEEN

Sloane

I had a weird dream about my mother last night, weird because I didn't dream about my mother.

I barely remembered her.

She'd died when I was six and Bru was five, and nothing really particularly stood out about her. I mean, I loved my mother.

I just didn't remember her.

I remembered her funeral a little, mostly because Dad hadn't let Bru or me out of his sight the whole time. He'd made us stay with him, our hands in his. After she'd died, we hadn't even had babysitters anymore. He'd become pretty much a recluse after that, outside of his job. It was like he'd been scared he'd lose us too, always scared.

The moving around had started shortly after that, going from school to school and town to town. We'd never stayed anywhere for longer than a year, and Dad had constantly had new jobs in the midst of it. He hadn't been able to hold on to one for longer than a year.

Hence the moves.

I'd resented my father for a long time while in the rough of that. I mean, I was basically socially inept because of it. We'd never been anywhere long enough for me to make friends, and I couldn't deny the fact that wherever I'd gone, trouble had seemed to find my brother and me.

That went triple for Maywood Heights.

I thought about my mother pretty much all morning the next day at school, finding it weird I was suddenly thinking about her. The dream hadn't made sense, and it more so felt like a nightmare than anything else.

I'd actually woken up in a sweat.

My mother had never been heavy-handed or physical with me. Neither of my parents were, so whatever that was last night had been so weird. I was so in my head that morning I hadn't been paying attention. In fact, I slammed right into someone, and had he not been a football player, all my shit would have exploded in the hallway.

"Watch it, little," Ares Mallick growled. His lips pressed together. "Watch it, Sloane."

My brow jumped, him actually making good on not insulting me for once.

"My bad." I had run into him, on me.

And people were staring at us.

More than one set of eyes lingered over Ares, then me. He naturally got attention. I mean, he was Legacy, but I'd all but disappeared since Dorian and the rest of Legacy weren't putting any attention on me. When I'd hung out with Wells and Thatcher for a time, the school had started to get me off their radar a bit in a negative way. Still, being with them definitely got a girl more attention than she wanted. Positive or negative.

I had no idea if the rest of the school knew about Legacy pretty much casting me out. Maybe they just found it weird because Ares was being seen with the likes of me. The two of us had spent pretty much all night working on the sketches for the project, and that was the first thing he showed me when he lounged against my locker.

"Figured we'd start getting things down on canvas tonight," he said. "What do you think of the final design?"

The final was my work and his put together. What I'd worked on last night had just been mine, but what I was seeing now was the two combined.

I didn't know if he'd worked this all out at school, after I left, or what, but he'd done a lot of work in not many hours.

And he was also asking my opinion for some reason.

"What? You fucking hate it?" He pushed a hand over his hair. "Obviously, it's not going to look just like what you did. I had to replicate your style, but I think I got pretty close."

Pretty close was an understatement. Hell, it was like I'd done the galaxies beneath the constellations.

"Pretty good." I gave the pad back to him. I couldn't help but be annoyed he could imitate a style I'd been working on for, well, my whole goddamn life.

He smirked upon looking at it, then me. "Something tells me it's more than pretty good, but all right." He laughed. "So tonight, then? Same time?"

I was about to tell him yeah before our audience suddenly expanded beyond the casual onlookers.

Rainbow Reed had stopped in the middle of the hallway, people passing around her. Her lips parted, she passed a glance between Ares and me.

Ares pushed off the lockers, following the line of my sight in that direction. He faced me. "Tonight?"

I nodded, but he barely waited for that before heading over to Bow. He dropped a long arm around her, walking away with her, and I didn't know what to think about that before closing my locker. I supposed it wasn't my business to think about it.

CHAPTER
FOURTEEN

Sloane

"So, I take it Bow's unaware we're working on a project together?"

Ares's head lifted after what I said, a pencil in his teeth. He'd been working out our objective tonight, i.e., where to start on getting something down on our huge canvases. We had a lot of work ahead of us, and we both needed to be smart about it.

His pencil fell from his teeth with his frown, and I shrugged.

"Bow?" I questioned, hiking back against the white muscle car. "She didn't look like you'd told her we'd be doing this."

Not that I cared really. Like he'd said, all that wasn't my business, but the girl had definitely looked like a deer in headlights today.

Ares pushed the pencil behind his ear, his paint-splattered bibs secured at his hips. I'd purposely worn jeans and a T-shirt to differentiate. We may be working together, but I wasn't *working for him*. Last time I'd shown up in bibs like him, I'd ended up looking like his employee, and I wasn't having that shit.

It seemed he'd noticed our similar choice in dress the other day, or at least, was mixing things up. In any sense, we'd both managed to avoid wearing the same fucking thing.

Ares hooked thumbs in his pockets. "How about you just focus on the *work*," he said, then directed me on the other side of the car. "You start there. Take what I sketched out and replicate it."

I saluted him, which made him scoff. I swear, by the end of this, we'd probably both kill each other. I didn't know what had compelled him to ask me to do this shit with him, or what had compelled me to say yes.

I think I knew when I pulled out my phone, a distraction from everything going on back home.

I checked my phone for texts. I'd told Bru before I left again today I'd be around for him. I had my phone on in case he needed me. He probably wouldn't. He never did, and his response this morning had been the same as when I'd told him about the project.

He'd verbally pushed me out the door, then promptly told me to not make any noise on my way out. He spent most of his days sleeping, and though I often asked if he was feeling any worse, he stressed he was fine.

He was almost stubborn about it.

The thing about my brother was, he had a lot of pride. He did just like me. The pair of us were so used to just looking out for ourselves and each other, when we actually needed help, we refused to seek it.

For all I knew, my brother really could be dying, but he'd never tell me. This made me even more vigilant about checking in despite his doctor telling me (telling the both of us) Bru just had to sweat this shit out. We were informed to tell Dr. Richardson if Bru got any worse, and since he hadn't, we didn't call.

Despite my brother's ailments, he was still acting like himself, so that was good. Definitely didn't stop me from checking my phone every few minutes, and the first person to call attention to that was Ares. He was quick to tap the rubber end of his pencil on the car, getting my attention.

"That going to be a problem?" He directed a finger toward me, my phone. "Because if it is, you should probably leave it somewhere it's not."

So, yeah. Me and this phone? Wasn't negotiable. Not with my brother being sick. I palmed it. "The phone's not a problem."

"Good."

"As long as it's not a problem for you that I'm on it." And might as well let him know that right now. "I told you my brother is sick. He needs me around."

"Your seventeen-year-old brother who can take care of himself," he volleyed. He placed his hands on the trunk. "Anyway, isn't your guardian supposed to do that shit? He is taking care of you, right?"

I really didn't know what his problem was or why he just couldn't help but be, well, himself. I realized he didn't have any siblings. At least, not any that I'd heard about.

I also knew he hated me, but he could stand to have a little sympathy. I shook my head. "No. Because my brother and I take care of ourselves."

"Right." He smirked. "You guys are all about taking care of yourselves in that big-ass house you live in. Your brother's fancy ride and that sweet tuition you both got."

I blanched. "Yeah, well. I'm sorry that my dad *dying* and someone helping us after the fact bothers you." Because that was exactly what had happened. My brother and I were *orphans*, and he knew that because Dorian knew that. The dark prince had admitted himself he'd looked into us, into me. And whatever Dorian knew, his friends definitely did.

I watched the words play on Ares's face, the tall boy saying nothing.

I smirked now. "Well, I don't expect sympathy from you. Someone who obviously has it all and always has." I waved a hand to his garage. The thing alone was as big as some of the places I'd grown up in over the years. "My brother and I have always been number one and number two. And though we had my dad, *he had problems,* so it was always basically just number one and two. My brother and I had to work just so we could fucking eat."

At one point, I'd had like three fucking jobs, taking on the burden for Bru as well. He was the smart one, and I wanted him to do something with himself. I'd never let him work more than what we needed.

Even then, it'd been too much.

Ares's gaze followed me, my movements. I was restlessly checking my phone, which was pointless. My brother was probably asleep because of his meds. I huffed. "So, yeah. We have Callum. But no, I don't *make him* take care of me. Care of us. He may have stepped in when our dad died, but we never asked him for anything. Let alone the house, the car, and your stupid fucking school."

And why was I telling him all this? Mentioning all the dark shit?

Mentioning my dad.

That was *private*, but for whatever the reason, I was talking about it with this asshole.

The asshole had eyes on me, his head cocked. He wet his lips. "How'd he step in?"

"What?"

His shoulders lifted. "Your guardian. You said he stepped in. How?"

Not that any of that was his fucking business. I cuffed my

arms. "It was all my dad. Apparently, he left a will?" Ares's eyebrow arched slowly, and I nodded. "Anyway, my brother and I didn't know about it. It named Callum as our guardian."

Ares cuffed his arms now, his head still angled. "Callum." His lips pinched tight. "You're saying your dad left you with him? Had the foresight to do such a thing when he had all these problems like you said?"

One of his problems had been paranoia, so I guessed that hadn't really surprised me when I thought it.

Ares leaned forward. "He left a will when it didn't sound like y'all had a whole lot."

Surprisingly enough, it didn't sound like he was making fun of me for once. I shrugged. "Our dad was really paranoid. Suffered from anxiety and mental illness."

I studied that pass over Ares's face. Again, I had no idea why I was telling him this stuff. It was just pouring out, all this a lot. Maybe it'd been a long time coming since I'd been stressed.

I scrubbed my face. "Look. I committed to you, and I'm going to be here." He had me locked in on that in case he'd forgotten. "But I need my phone. It won't get in the way, and this may sound stupid to you, but I need to look out for my little brother. I know he's seventeen. I know that, but he's sick, and he's all I have."

There was so much truth in that, and though that may look different from the outside, that was true. Callum had given us stuff, but it was temporary.

His lips pursing, Ares kept silent, and it was obviously pointless to try to reach the human part of him. I sat on a stool, phone in hand, and he came around the car.

"It's not dumb," he said, and my eyes flashed. He frowned. "I have brothers too. They're not blood, but I do. And I have Bow." He paused, his jaw shifting. "She's my sister. The guys my brothers. So no, it's not dumb."

I knew he had them, and though I didn't have that kind of bond, I didn't know if it'd feel the same. Thatcher and Bow probably had a connection that he'd never had with her. There's nothing wrong with that, but they weren't blood.

Blood was different, I think.

Of course, I didn't know the alternative, so I couldn't say, and in his silence this time, Ares tapped the car.

"We can't start like this," he grunted, grabbing a hoodie off the car. He slid it on over his head. "Let's go on a field trip. The energy is all fucked in here, and we can't start that way."

I agreed about the energy being fucked, but what kind of field trip?

What that apparently was had him heading to his car. He opened the door. "Come on. I got a place where we can get out of these negative vibes. I don't work well in my head."

Had what I said managed to affect him in some way and, I don't know, actually give me some fucking sympathy?

Maybe not, but he was right about one thing. I didn't work well in my head either.

I got up. "Where we going?"

Of course, he didn't say, looming by his big-ass ride. Smirking, I got my own hoodie. I zipped it over my clothes, and even though it was against my better judgment, I did get in his Hummer. The thing was honestly built for combat, not a teenage boy.

It did fit him, though, both obnoxious and large. Ares definitely liked to have a big presence.

"Get ready to put some work in," he said, revving the thing up. Sometime between getting in the car and turning it on, he'd lit a joint. The thing currently smoked from the side of his lips. He grinned around it. "But by the end of it, we'll actually be able to get some stuff done here."

———

Ares's field trip was only a partial ride. The rest was a *fucking trek* through the sewage systems of Maywood Heights, and he had us huffing it the whole way. My only saving grace was there was no actual sewage going through the pipes, and Ares did stress the city used these for rainwater to prevent flooding.

Still, I was ankle deep in shit and muck. He'd driven us to the outskirts of town, and only the arrogance of the abundant and privileged would allow someone to leave their expensive-ass Hummer out and about for anyone to take. We literally left it behind to take the pipes, and Ares not only did it, but acted like he'd done it many times before. His next move was to throw me a bag from the back of his trunk, and it was heavier than shit. He strapped one about twice the size on his own back and had the nerve to sprint after that. He left me behind for a good solid length before realizing. He stopped every few feet for me to catch up and didn't hesitate to flash that smug fucking grin of his.

"We really got to get your cardio up, little," he said, jogging *backward*. We'd made it out of the pipes at this point, walking a concrete channel that water from the pipes spilled off into. He smirked. "It's a good thing you're not running for your life."

Yeah, good thing, and fuck me for taking a hit of his joint when he'd offered it. I hadn't smoked in a while, and the buzz definitely wasn't helping my situation.

It only seemed to push more power into Ares's football legs, but I had enough energy to realize that I'd been insulted again.

"We said no insults," I said, trying not to gasp for breath, but then gave the hell up. I didn't run *at all*. I grimaced. "I'm not little."

The frown was only partial on Ares's lips. Stopping his jog, he sprinted up to me. He leveled a hand high above me. "You're little to me."

Okay, so we both knew that wasn't what he meant by the word. "You're calling me little as in beneath you," I growled, which made him chuckle.

"Or maybe it just means you're *little*," he chortled. He raised a hand. "Give me a break. Everyone is smaller to me."

And I was sure that was exactly what he felt about most people, him and his friends.

He laughed. "I'm sorry, but it's a hard habit to break. I literally associate you with the word. I don't think of you any other way."

Nice.

His head cocked. "I'm just saying that's your name. *That* is what I associate with you." He'd tugged his hair down in the car, his hand scrubbing into his curls. "Just give me that one, and if you want, you can call me something else too."

I opened my lips.

He frowned. "And no. It ain't going to be *bitch*."

Well, that certainly limited things. I chuckled, which only made his frown deepen.

He waved a hand. "Come on. You think about it as we walk."

He let me walk this time, which was good, and for once, he held back the length of his strides. I knew because he kept pace with me more often than not. I almost made a joke about him being an actual decent person for once, but he took us into another pipe. This one was bigger than the rest, and neither of us had to duck.

On the other side was a hill, scenic, which jarred me for a second. We'd been surrounded by concrete only a breath ago.

"Watch your step," Ares called, ahead on the hill. "One false step, you're rolling down this thing."

Yeah, I got that.

But the view was definitely something.

The hills rolled ahead of us, a sea of green that led into the city. Smokestacks from local factories puffed into the setting sun, but there weren't a ton, which made them less of an eyesore.

"You good?" Ares had turned back at this point, his hand on the hill. Even he needed it to keep from sliding.

I was good, so I followed, but his bag on my back wasn't helping. Ares navigated the trek like Spider-Man. We were angled, but you wouldn't have known it with the way he navigated the hill. His bag clearly wasn't bothering him.

"It's just up here," he said, and when I saw it, well, I saw it. A fresh wall of concrete from the channel was on the other side.

And it was tagged.

Graffiti completely painted the wall, the colors rich and buttery. Ares stood beneath the wide work, and when I got to him, I did too.

It was all seriously sweet, some of it abstract and some of it not. There were portraits too, childlike faces. Someone had done a lot of work here. Well, some people. It seemed like a lot for just one person.

Taking off his bag, Ares revealed the contents. Aerosol cans lined the interior. He took one out and proceeded to head to the wall.

I cut in front of him. "What the fuck are you doing?" I knew he was a rich kid, but I refused to think he was *this* dense. "You can't just fucking tag a wall."

His brow hiked. "Uh, yeah. I can."

"Nah." He may be stupid, but I wasn't going to let him get killed for his stupidity. "You can't just tag walls." I raised a hand. "Someone's already been here." And depending on who that was could get his ass shot. He didn't grow up where I grew up. There were territories, *gangs*. "You could piss someone off."

He chuckled. "Well, I don't think my dad *or me* will mind." He lowered his arm. "This is our wall. We did this."

He stood back, letting me see.

"You did this?" I directed a finger. "You and your *dad* tagged a wall."

Ares's eyes lifted, and he proceeded to head to the wall again. He shook up his can, then blended into the art.

The transition was seamless.

He knew this wall obviously, and he was showing me.

"When Dad first took me here, I thought he'd lost his fucking mind." He directed a look at me. "You saw that fucking trek."

I did, huffing it the whole way.

I approached him, watching behind. I'd never seen him work right in front of me, and the kid was talented. Like epically. I was good, but he was great.

I really didn't know how I felt about that. The competitor in me was annoyed, which was silly. I was sure he'd worked with the greats.

"I was in middle school then. Things were kind of rough." He spoke casually while he sprayed, his back to me. "Dad took me out here to deal with my attitude."

I recalled him saying his dad was a kind man. If he was, something told me his childhood couldn't have been that bad. I supposed I didn't know his mom, though. I mean if she was still around.

I propped hands on my hips. "You got issues with your mom or something."

"Nah." He shook his head, turning. He laughed. "I was just a little shit."

I rolled my eyes.

He tossed me his can. "Come on. It helps. Dad called it illegal art therapy."

Shaking the can, I took him up on his dare. I got that color going before Ares directed me to take off my bag. He had more cans in there, and I used them.

I painted one of my galaxies, and funny enough, I'd never

tagged a wall before. I guessed I hadn't wanted to deal with the territory shit.

Ares stood behind me for a while, nodding at my work before joining in himself with another spray can. He let loose on the wall, the pair of us doing our thing.

We didn't talk while we worked, nothing but the sound of our spray paint in the air, and he was right. It was definitely therapeutic.

"What does your mom think about all of this, then?" I asked him, wondering about her. If she wasn't terrible, why was he such a little shit? I mean, his life seemed pretty fucking good, privileged.

He smiled. "Dad said it was our little secret. My mom would hate this shit. She's in politics."

"Is she cool?"

His painting slowed a little but didn't stop. He was adding to something he'd already started, geometric work. This didn't surprise me since he said he was into that too.

"She's the best woman I know. Strong." He looked at me. "I wish I deserved her. I guess she and my dad got stuck with my attitude. Stuck with me."

A muscle flexed in his jaw, his eyes narrowed. Shaking his can, he proceeded in his therapy, and maybe it did work.

He was telling me things about him too, things about his family and his respect for them. He seemed not to have a lot of that for anyone outside of his friends.

Family, bonds, obviously meant a lot to him, and that reminded me so much of someone.

"Where are your parents now?" I asked, painting too. I needed another distraction. I swallowed. "Just wondering. I mean, you have parties and stuff. Didn't know if they were workaholics or something."

That would explain a lot of his aggression, *his attitude*. I also hadn't seen his parents at the house, but I hadn't gone inside recently.

"They work, but they're not workaholics. They're actually out of town now."

"Where?"

He didn't answer for a second, and honestly, I just kind of asked the question off the cuff. We'd been talking, vibing. I faced him, and he'd stopped painting.

"They're visiting D and his family," he said, my eyes flashing. He sprayed a line. "And I got another rule."

He didn't give me a chance to ask, lowering his can.

Tension narrowed his eyes. "Personal shit isn't needed with what we're doing. In fact, it's completely unnecessary to do what we have to do." He fingered his hair. "So let's not get into it. And that goes double for anything that has to do with D."

I heard the words, the rule, but a request lingered there in his tone and the way he looked at me. It was like he was asking me for this new rule, and it was one that didn't bother me. I didn't want to tell him about my own shit.

I just had.

I told him more things than I ever thought I would about my brother and my worries about him and who we were before Maywood Heights. He hadn't even pulled my arm.

"I can be about that, Wolf," I said, putting out a hand. "I can call you Wolf, right?"

That was something that only his football friends called him, and something that should trigger him.

But I had given him an inch. I couldn't stand the name *little*.

His grin started slow.

"It's on loan," he said, putting his hand in mine. "While we're working together."

He shook once, then let go. He proceeded in his art therapy, and I did with mine. It must have worked in the end.

I didn't check my phone once.

CHAPTER
FIFTEEN

Sloane

My time spent with Ares "Wolf" Mallick required long days and even longer hours when we finally got started on our piece. The transition to the canvas had been seamless, and we hammered out a ton of work over the next few days. Actually, we worked so hard I found myself dreaming about galaxies instead of my usual stress and strain. It was a nice release.

And go figure working with him.

The two of us surprisingly worked pretty well together. He didn't like to talk, and I didn't either. I definitely *knew* who I was working with. Whenever I seemed to move, I felt his eyes in my direction, which was a stiff reminder of what we actually were. We weren't friends.

But we weren't feeling like enemies as much.

We'd been able to find some common ground, and that common ground kept me sane and working. He never gave me crap about checking my phone, and even less when I had no messages from my brother. He just kept working beside me, his earbuds in. I did the same while I brushed strokes along the car and canvas, and even though we were two planets working in our own little worlds, it felt as if we were on the same planet. It was probably one only another artist could get.

We had plans to work tonight too, but he sent me a text telling me he had to bow out. I was surprised until he mentioned it was football. His coach was having some of the varsity run drills. I wondered how long something like that could last since we did work long hours, but then he said he had a student council meeting after that.

Student of the Month indeed.

Something told me there was more to the boy with the attitude than met the eye. I told him fine and would probably just work on my series. I hadn't gotten to work on it at all this week. It'd also be nice to be close to Bru even though he'd probably be sleeping, and Dr. Richardson was supposed to come by tomorrow to check on him. It was hard to tell how my brother was doing since he did sleep so much, and it'd be nice to talk to the doctor myself.

Since I did have my evening free, I decided to get some paints after school. I was coming out of the art supply store when I noticed a girl in a Windsor Prep uniform rushing into the street. She'd come from the direction of the grocery store next door, and the bottom of her bag exploded, oranges spilling into the street.

"Crap," she squeaked, running after them. Hiking out to assist, I grabbed the closest orange, and it took me getting that close to realize who she was. She'd had her head down as she scrambled, her dark hair covering her face.

Of course, Rainbow Reed would be chasing oranges in the middle of a mini mall. I just felt like that was literally something she would do. She gathered a bunch before she followed my knee-highs up to me.

Her eyes expanded in width, but before she could say anything, a blond woman raced up behind us.

"Rainbow, honestly," she said, laughing with the words. The woman was gorgeous, Bow's height and with blond hair nearly the color of Wells Ambrose's. Hers was natural blond, though, and the woman's bib overalls gave her a more youthful appearance. She sported them with cute heels. "Darling, you had twenty feet to the car."

"Sorry, Mom. You know I'm a klutz."

"Something I've apparently cursed you with." The woman grinned. "Catch your father looking at us, he'd be laughing at us both."

The woman nearly dropped her own bag when she said it, making her laugh. Her laughter was so high-pitched it reminded me of her daughter's voice. If anyone questioned this woman was Bow's mother, they wouldn't. I definitely saw it.

Her mother was scattered grabbing the oranges, but Bow was still looking at me. It took her a moment to start helping her mom and her mom a moment to realize I was helping. I'd gathered a couple before she saw me.

"Oh, thank you," the woman said, standing. She took me in. "Oh, are you from the school?" She faced Bow. "Bow, is this your friend?"

Bow's lips parted. *Friend* was definitely a strong word. I hadn't been her and the rest of Legacy's favorite person as of late, though, I didn't know exactly how Bow herself felt about the situation. The boys were her brothers, and she obviously followed along with them.

But then, she looked at me, really stared. A harshness met a normally soft gaze, and when she pushed away her hair, she barely gave me her eyes.

"Mom, this is Sloane," she said, the tone of her soft voice matching how she looked at me. It was rare I saw Bow Reed angry. Actually, she was entirely too sweet, but today, my appearance was met with aggression. Bow lifted a hand in my direction. "She is from school. Yeah."

I'd say ouch, but I knew what this was. She still believed I'd crossed her brother, no blood tie or not, and the only reason Ares was being decent to me was because he needed something *from me*.

And don't forget that.

I couldn't forget my place amongst them, and this bond Ares himself had mentioned. They were family, and this was their world.

Mrs. Reed didn't know about all this drama, though, and I put my hand out when she gave me hers. "Hi, Mrs. Reed."

"Sloane?" She tested my name before facing her daughter. "Is this the same Noa Sloane who came to our house? Janet mentioned her."

I knew Janet to be the Reeds' housekeeper.

"Yeah." Again, Bow was looking at anything but me. "But she's probably busy, so..."

"Of course." And realizing I still had the oranges, Mrs. Reed had me put them in her grocery bag. Mrs. Reed managed to lift a hand below the bag. "One second, Sloane, before you go."

I didn't know what this was about, but she had her daughter assist her to the car. Bow still had her broken bag and the oranges she'd gathered.

Using her foot, Mrs. Reed motioned the sensor for her automatic trunk to open. She placed the bag in the back. Bow followed her with her items, but only Mrs. Reed came back.

"What are you doing for dinner this evening?" she asked, and at this point Bow was coming back.

Bow shook her head. "Mom..."

"Oh, stop it. You never have friends over." She braced her daughter. "Please join us. Bow and I were just out gathering a few things. It's our night to make dinner, right, sweetie?"

Bow appeared at odds with what to say. I mean, she didn't want me to come over, clearly. I was a traitor to her.

"I probably shouldn't," I started, making her mother

frown. "My brother's at home, and he's been feeling under the weather."

Bow's lips parted after I said that. Had she not known? I didn't think they were friends or anything, but she was acquainted with my brother. She wet her lips. "Sorry to hear that."

She did sound sorry. She probably was. Bow had a heart. She wasn't like these boys, and though she was obviously as loyal, she wasn't so hard-edged.

Mrs. Reed frowned. "Oh. I'm sorry. Hope it's nothing serious."

I did too, and I waved her off, trying not to make a big thing of it. I had no reason to according to Dr. Richardson. "We're thinking it's just something he has to sweat out."

"Oh?"

I nodded. "Though he's not making it easy." I shrugged. "He's seventeen, so he thinks he's invincible."

"Well, I definitely know something about that with this one's brother." Mrs. Reed shook Bow, which made her smirk.

"Yeah, Thatcher's stubborn," Bow said. "Real stubborn."

She said it to me, and I noticed the initial aggression had faded. She might be going along with her brothers, supported them, but she may not actually feel the same way. At this point, Legacy, Dorian, and everything was just one more thing I didn't want to think about. If Dorian had made up his mind about me, then he had and I...

"You know what?" I stated, getting Mrs. Reed's attention. "Bru, my brother, he's fine. In fact, he's been pushing me to stay out longer." I lifted my bag of paints. "I was at the art store so I could do something else other than be in his face tonight."

This made Mrs. Reed smile. "Does that mean you'll come over? Have dinner?" Mrs. Reed pumped her fist, and that too reminded me of her daughter. She nudged her. "Bow, isn't that great?"

Bow's enthusiasm definitely didn't match her mother's, but she didn't appear as annoyed either. Maybe I'd been right that she might not be on the Sloane-hating train as the others. We had been friends.

We might be able to be again if I could just talk to her, and Ares's text did say varsity was running drills tonight. Odds were, her brother wouldn't even be there, and I wouldn't have to deal with his mess.

Bow nodded at her mother, and Mrs. Reed tapped her chin. I didn't know what that was about, but I did know Bow didn't seem like she had a whole lot of friends. Bow herself had been very enthusiastic to have me over the last time, and that definitely could have something to do with the guys in her life. I mean, they had chased me away.

He chased you away.

I swallowed. "I'd love to come over."

"Perfect. Dinner's at seven, but if you come over early, we can chat while we prepare," Mrs. Reed said, and I forced myself not to backpedal. I forced myself to believe I was going over there to talk to Bow and maybe just be cool with her again. It wouldn't be about anything else.

It couldn't be about anything else.

CHAPTER
SIXTEEN

Sloane

"Do I know your parents, Sloane? Your mom? Your dad?"
Mrs. Reed asked while she mashed a bowl of potatoes. She,
Bow, and I were in the Reeds' kitchen, and though I'd been
there before, I still couldn't get over how completely ritzy the
whole place was. Their kitchen was just a stunning top-off to
the exquisite picture that was the entire Reed manor. I mean,
these people had *gardens* and people to tend them.

Coming over tonight, I was surprised Mrs. Reed and her
daughter were cooking. I knew they had household staff, but
I hadn't seen any today. Well, no one but Janet. She'd let me in
when I got here, but it appeared they'd given her and the rest
of their staff the night off.

I thought it was nice the pair of them were making dinner
tonight. I even offered to help, but Mrs. Reed waved a hand at
me. The woman certainly didn't mind getting her hands dirty.
She had flour on her nose from the homemade rolls she'd put
in the oven earlier. Mrs. Reed grinned. "I feel like I know you,
or have seen you before? I must know your parents."

Bow studied the pair of us from the kitchen island. She was preparing a salad, and she was definitely aware I was here. Her eyes hadn't left me. I hadn't gotten a chance to talk to her tonight yet. Her mom was busy chatting with me most of the evening so far.

I shook my head at Mrs. Reed. "I don't think so. My brother, Bru, and I just moved here."

"Really? Where from?"

"Chicago. Well, most recently. We've been all over before coming here."

Bow's eyes lifted in our direction again, and between the two of them, there was enough food here to feed an army.

Though judging by the size of the guys in their household...

Mr. Reed hadn't shown up yet, but he was just as large as Thatcher. Mrs. Reed said he was still at work, but would be around for dinner. As far as Thatcher, I was sure a hefty part of this meal would be for him once he did get back from practice. The guy was a fucking building.

"Interesting," Mrs. Reed said, looking at me, and I wondered why. In any sense, she smiled before waving Bow over.

"Can you finish mashing these, sweetie? I'm going to take a plate of what we got to your grandma."

Bow nodded at her mother, and after the woman left, Bow sighed.

"My gram's too sick to come down," Bow said, mashing. Her jaw moved. "It's best she eats upstairs so..."

Last time I was here, she mentioned a sick grandma. "Is she okay?"

That felt like a dumb question, and I instantly regretted it.

Bow's attention stayed on the potatoes. She shrugged. "Every day is different. Some days it feels like yeah. Others, no. She's my dad's mom."

She moved the potatoes over to the kitchen island, putting them next to the salad.

"I'm sorry to hear that."

Bow acknowledged what I said, her head bobbing once. "You said Bru's sick?"

I eased over to her. I grabbed my arm. "We honestly don't know what's up. It's kept him out of school."

"I know," she said, and my eyes flashed. Her head tilted. "We haven't seen him around, and Ares mentioned something."

Which meant my brother's friends, i.e., *all* the guys, knew my brother was sick but were still ignoring him. They were doing that because of me and a lie, which was fucked up.

"He also mentioned you guys were doing some kind of project together…"

"I didn't say anything, Bow."

Her eyes flashed this time, big, wide. She blinked. "I want to believe you."

Then why *wouldn't* she? Why would she let them get to her?

Her head lowered, hands on the counter. "I even told them that I didn't believe you would, and if you did, it was probably an accident." She lifted a hand. "You said something to someone, and it got to the wrong people…"

So she stood up for me. At least, tried.

Her jaw shifted. "I want to be on your side."

"Then *be* on it. Don't group with them."

She bunched fingers into her hair. "I want to. I do, but there are things I don't get."

"What things?"

Her expression fell. "They said I can't trust you, and if I can't, I don't know if I can trust what you say."

I started to say something, and she hugged her arms.

"It's hard, Sloane, because I trust them," she said. "I trust them with everything. They're my family, and you've…" She started, sighing. "You've *lied* to me before."

I had lied to her.

And apparently, that had damned me.

The room was silent when her mom bounced into it.

"I found the wine on the way back." Mrs. Reed waved two bottles. She set them down on the counter. "Though obviously not for you kiddos."

The woman booty-bumped her daughter, but it didn't elicit much of a reaction out of her. Mrs. Reed placed an arm around her. "Everything okay?"

Bow, of course, nodded and even stapled on her cuter-than-heck grin. She was terribly good at that, but I always knew when she was putting it on. When she didn't mean it, her smile didn't reach her eyes.

Coming over was a bad idea, huge, but I was already here.

If Mrs. Reed knew her daughter was off, she didn't make a thing of it. She let go of her daughter, then proceeded to get some wineglasses. She'd just placed them down when a large man sauntered into the room and surprised her from the back. Crazy big, he pulled her clear off her feet, and I'd never heard a grown woman squeal so loud.

"Knight Reed," she gritted, shocked but laughing at the same time. She slapped at his hands. "One day, you're going to catch me with something hot in my hands."

"I know the feeling, baby," the man crooned, and Bow palmed her face when her dad literally planted a kiss on her mother in the middle of the kitchen.

Bow rolled her eyes. "Dad, please. We have guests."

He seemed not to be bothered by this, definitely bending his wife over *in the kitchen*, but Mrs. Reed wasn't having that. She kicked at him until he let go of her, her face flushed. She physically had to force a man the size of a good portion of this kitchen away from her.

"Honestly, Knight," Mrs. Reed said, but did smile. She

eyed me. "And Bow does have guests. Her friend is here to join us tonight for dinner."

"A friend, eh?" Mr. Reed worked around, his hands sliding into his pockets. He was dressed more casual than the last time I'd seen him. He wore a dark sweater with lightly colored pants. He put a finger out. "Noa Sloane? The friend who is not a boy."

I laughed at that, and surprisingly, Bow did a little too. When I'd first met her dad, he had believed I was a boy because of my name. I waved. "Still not a boy, Mr. Reed."

"Very good," Mr. Reed grunted, but he smiled. He placed an arm around Mrs. Reed. "And a friend of Bow. Always nice to see that."

He eyed back to Bow, and her eyes lifted again. She really didn't have a lot of people over, and after talking to her, some pieces were definitely getting put together.

Legacy held a solid place in this girl's life, which only pissed me off more. Dorian had left bodies in his wake. He'd not only left me, but left me to burn. He didn't care *about me* and definitely didn't care how his friends treated me.

I really wanted to leave. I felt *sick*, but worse, I felt sick *because* I felt sick. I didn't want to feel anything. I wanted to feel *nothing*.

"The hell are you doing here?"

The bark came from across the room, the laughter from Mr. and Mrs. Reed fading. The pair of them swiveled around to find their son in the middle of the kitchen. His hair was wet and his teeth bared. He had a gym bag on his shoulder, a Windsor Prep Football T-shirt across his bulky chest, and he hadn't come alone.

Wells Ambrose backed him up, his bottle-blond locks also wet with shine. He cleared them from rage-filled eyes. "Why are you here?"

"And why are you both speaking to her like that?" Laughter completely gone, Mrs. Reed clacked her heels in that direction. She folded her arms. "And, Thatcher, what are you and Wells doing? I thought your practice was running long. Why are you here?"

"Coach let some of us out early. Invited Wells over after showers to get food." He growled it out, that same rage in Wells's eyes lacing his own. He shot a finger at me. "You're not supposed to be here."

"And apparently, *you've* forgotten who you are in this kitchen, *son*, and who you are to me. Your mother?" A similar blaze hit Mr. Reed's eyes. Actually, the man was snarling to the point where I checked *myself*, and he hadn't even been talking to me. His dark eyebrows narrowed. "What's with the disrespect, and why are you speaking to Bow's friend like this?"

Thatcher laser-focused on Bow. The sophomore had her hands on the bar, but she didn't look away.

Some kind of exchange passed between them then, but not long before Mr. Reed cut Thatcher's focus off. He cut his hand in the air. "You got a half a second to speak, son. Don't make me repeat myself."

"She's trouble," he said, point-blank. He obviously wasn't wasting those seconds, and I noticed he didn't look away from his father again. "Dad—"

"To your room."

"But, Dad—"

Just a *look* made Thatcher shut up. He wet his lips, his earrings reflecting the light off the kitchen's chandelier.

Saying he snorted like an actual bull before leaving that kitchen was an understatement. With his own glare (in my direction), Wells started to follow him.

Mr. Reed raised a hand. "My son needs to cool off," he said, then nodded. "And you need to explain why you both came in here so hot. Hot toward her?"

Mr. Reed directed the room's attention on me, and I was solid in place. I never should have come over here.

Wells's gaze landed on me, his shrug subtle before he pocketed his hands.

"You have nothing to say, then?" Mrs. Reed said this time. She frowned. "You sure had a lot before."

"It was a rough practice," Wells ground out. His eyes blazed at me. "We just weren't trying to deal with folks from school." He jutted his chin toward me. "Girls like her like to gossip. *Talk.*"

There was so much laced there in what he said, so much while saying so little. This was their turf, and I wasn't welcome.

"Sounds like another field trip might be warranted to the ballet," Mr. Reed growled, and though I didn't understand the reference, it certainly got Wells's attention. The tall blond shot ramrod straight.

"No, sir. That's not necessary," he said, and something I noticed was their dynamic. He spoke to Mr. Reed with respect, and Mr. Reed spoke to him like his kid.

They really were brothers.

There was some deep shit here, shit I clearly didn't understand.

Mr. Reed bunched his hair. "Go get seated for dinner. After, you head home."

Wells nodded, placing a glance my way one more time.

The parents watched him on his way out. Bow watched him.

I grabbed my purse off the counter.

It was Bow to notice that first, then Mr. and Mrs. Reed. Mrs. Reed came around the island. "Sloane—"

"I need to go," I said, shaking my head. "I shouldn't have come. I have my brother anyway. I mentioned he's sick so… I, uh, I should head home."

It took all I had not to physically *cry*, and I didn't cry. I wasn't that girl. But I was embarrassed. Angry.

Frustrated.

I visibly shook in the Reeds' kitchen, and it took everything not to be rude and run from the room.

Mr. Reed frowned. "I don't know what's going on with
you kids, but the boys have a habit of being chronically inept
when it comes to treating others with respect as of late."

"They do," Mrs. Reed agreed. "Please don't let them scare
you off. You're our guest. Bow's guest."

I didn't feel like Bow's guest either. I mean, she didn't
want me here.

She'd told me that herself.

Even now, she was finding it hard to look at me.

I nodded at that. "I need to go but thank you. So much…"

"Sloane. Dear…"

I couldn't stay to hear what Mrs. Reed said, and I guessed
I was the trash that Legacy treated me like when they first
met me. I just couldn't stay.

I was done.

CHAPTER
SEVENTEEN

Dorian

My father slid my phone across the counter, something I hadn't seen since we'd all left town. I turned off the water from the kitchen sink, then wiped my hands on a dish towel. I'd finished rinsing the dishes from dinner anyway.

Dad nodded at the phone, more casual today and in both demeanor and dress. All his buddies and friends were out here with us, visiting us for the next couple days. It was the first time we'd all been a group since, well, things had happened.

My god dads and their wives had even brought my friends too, all of us really together.

Dad folded his arms. "I figured since your friends are here anyway," he said, shrugging. "Might as well give that back to you."

My friends were all cleaning up from dinner, something all us guys had opted to do. We figured it was the least we could all do and that freed up Bow, the moms, and Billie (LJ's wife) to head out and go shopping. It'd also get them out of the house.

We needed to talk.

The guys and I waited, cleaning. I'd offered to do the dishes after the group dinner with the families while my friends cleared the dining room and handed me stuff. The dads and LJ liked to talk, though, so it'd taken them a while to leave the dining room. They'd cooked barbecue for the whole group this evening, all of us at another one of my parents' cabins. This one was out of state. It took a drive to get here, but it was quiet.

It'd been nice as fuck actually, and the first time I hadn't been worried about bullshit. Of course, that worry could never really leave.

My grandfather was still out there.

I needed news today, limited here out in the boonies. Outside of my laptop (which I could only use for school), I had nothing to link me to the outside world. As far as my parents were concerned, that'd been a good thing. I'd fucked up, majorly. I got internet access for school, then my dad effectively cut it off. He and Mom used their own devices and a hotspot for working remotely.

Needless to say, they didn't give me the password.

I'd take all the hits in the world, a small price to pay. They were here, and *they were safe*, and I'd play solitaire all damn day for that.

My father's logic sound, I took my phone back and happily. "Thanks."

"Don't make me regret it," he said, but I noticed he didn't leave my side. He hitched a hip against the counter. "The guys and I are going to go meet the girls at the shops. We're going to catch an evening movie if you boys want to join."

Normally, I might. Especially to get out of the cabin, but I couldn't right now. I'd literally heard nothing from the outside world since we'd gotten here. I needed news about back home and my friends were going to give me that.

Everyone being out at a movie was the perfect opportunity for us guys to sit down and go over stuff. "Probably will just stick around here."

"Figured. Your friends being here and all that." He pushed off the counter. "If you reconsider, you can join us."

My parents had been doing well since I got here. Especially my mother. She and my dad took the boat out on the lake all the time, and Mom was sailing better than him these days.

She really had been doing much better since she'd gotten here, which was another reason I stayed quiet and didn't complain about being restricted. I wanted her to feel good, get better. It was these days she was waking *me* up. She and my dad went for runs in the morning before their remote workdays, and when I did get my ass up, I joined them. It kept me in shape for football, the team ready and waiting for me when I got back. Dad had talked to Coach about my spot and informed me the team would manage until my return. Dad even practiced with me to keep up with my game when he had time, and he hated football.

Being up here had been our family's own little oasis and so easy to forget the shit back home, shit I'd created. There were true horrors outside these walls, shit that kept me up at night and dreading the day my dad decided to come back to the town of Maywood Heights.

Dad lingered for a second, outlining his mouth. He only did that when he wanted to talk. He lifted a hand. "You know, we never really talked about everything after it all happened. What you did and why regarding your uncle."

We hadn't, and I was well aware of that. I was *happy* for that. Both my parents had been tiptoeing around the issue, and fuck if I'd bring it up. There was already enough bullshit.

There was already enough pain.

"Charlie's truth needed to come out," I said, and I didn't regret what I'd done. I may have regretted the fallout, and the way I'd gone about it, but I didn't regret it. "I'm sorry, but…"

"I'm not talking about that, Dorian."

My eyebrow arched, and he folded his hand over his face.

"I'm talking about the fact that my son is in pain," he said, my heart jolting. "He is, and he won't talk to me. He won't talk to his mother. He'd rather do stuff like this, *stuff with his friends* instead of trusting me or his mother."

I said nothing, my throat constricting. "I'm sorry."

"*I'm* sorry," he stated, my eyes twitching. He nodded. "Because you're so much like me. So, *so* much, son."

But that wasn't a bad thing. That was a *great* thing. I admired my father so much. "I didn't want to hurt you and Mom. Especially if I was wrong about more going on that night. That night with Charlie?"

I'd only had a feeling, and why cause unnecessary pain if I didn't *know*? It was the same reason I was keeping shit from them now. For all I knew, this shit with my grandfather… it could be nothing. He could just be trying to scare me.

I hoped he was only trying to scare me.

"And we don't want you hurting." Dad's hand folded on my shoulder. "So just talk to us next time. Vent to us." His lips tightened. "That stuff with the video shouldn't have happened. You should have trusted me and your mother if you believed something more was going on." He sighed. "You should have trusted me."

I did trust him, and he was right.

I was so much like him. I was, and because I was, I couldn't do what he said. I *had* to protect him too, him and Mom.

I have to know the truth.

I nodded because I had to in that moment, hating lying to my dad. He'd go to the ends of the earth for me.

"If you boys leave, don't go far," he said. He left, but I

only stood in the kitchen for a few moments. After feeding Chestnut (we'd brought her with us), I looked around the cabin for my friends.

I ended up finding Wells and Thatcher in the dining room still. They had the rags they'd used to wipe down the table folded. Sitting in two of the dining room chairs, they had their thumbs dashing across their phones.

They stopped when I came in, my thoughts still turning from the conversation with my dad. Wells frowned. "You okay?"

"Yeah," I lied, outlining my mouth. I would talk to my dad. I would, but only if and when I thought it was necessary. I wasn't quite sure yet as I approached my friends. I gazed around. "Where's Wolf?"

"Smoking." This came from Thatcher. He sat up. "Said he needed to think. Went outside after we finished in here."

I wished I was out there with him, a strong blunt needed to calm me down right now.

Wells said he texted him to come inside, and while we waited, Thatcher got his laptop out. He booted it up. "Where's your dad?"

"He, the dads, and LJ all went to the shops. They're meeting up with our moms, Billie, and Bow for a movie."

Thatcher tapped some keys. "That gives us some solid hours, then."

My gaze directed to my buddy at the door, Wolf sauntering in. He had a beanie on over his hair, one he pulled off when he came into the room.

I gave him my hand. "Hey."

"Hey." He pulled me in, real quiet at dinner. We'd *all* been, and I was surprised none of our parents had called us out. We'd definitely exchanged looks between us. We had shit to talk about, but no opportunity.

At least until now, the cabin quiet. I tapped Wolf's fist. "You were smoking?"

"Yeah, just needed to get out of my head." He angled his gaze around. "Where are the dads?"

We told him, and after we did, he closed the door. We all convened at a corner of the large oak table, long enough to literally seat everyone, our parents and Bow included. When my parents had bought this place, my dad had intended for the cabin to be a home away from home, one all the families could go to and had over the years. My buddies and I had spent countless summers here, so many good times had.

"Where's my grandfather?" I asked, getting right into things. "He still in town?"

"Nah." Wolf put his hands together. "Had Thatcher track him."

"He made it easy." Thatcher shrugged. "I didn't have to do much, and actually, I thought it'd be harder. You never told Wolf where you thought he went after he dropped you off, but fucker popped up at the first hotel I called. I started with those, the nicest ones I could think of downtown, thinking maybe he was staying at one."

"Good idea," I said. "That's where he was staying?"

"Yeah, and using that fake-ass name he's been going under." He swiveled his computer around, his screen filled with pinpoints on a Maywood Heights's town map. "There wasn't much movement after that. Though I don't know where he was before I identified him. I was able to get his whereabouts the next day in the evening." Thatcher clicked around. "He was at that hotel and didn't really move after that. He went to the store a couple times, *late*. But other than that, nothing. We had some stoner asshole track his movements for a hundred bucks while we were all at school or with our parents."

"I took up the shifts after that, watching him?" Wells lifted a hand. "He didn't really do anything, D. Nothing weird anyway."

"And he only stayed a few days." Wolf nodded. "He left just like he told you he would."

That didn't mean much to me. "Where is he now?"

Thatcher clicked a button on his computer. "Last we could track him was the airport. Stoner guy told us he booked a flight to India."

"India?"

Thatcher put his hands together. "He's got businesses there. Just built an airport actually and has a nice little paper trail for that fake-ass name. If he was trying to hide something from someone, he's doing a shitty-ass job. Callum Montgomery has lots of businesses in India, and they *appear* legitimate. In fact, all his businesses do. He's a land developer. Been out there for years, I guess."

"What about the name Montgomery?"

"Couldn't find any ties back to you or your family." Thatcher sat back. "It's a pretty common name, and the only thing I could find was another Callum Montgomery, but that was way before Callum *Prinze's* time, your grandfather?" Thatcher shook his head. "Anyway, that family was a bunch of bootleggers."

"Basically nothing of note." Wolf captured my attention, frowning. "I don't know what your grandfather is doing, but we couldn't find anything out of the ordinary. He and his new name seem to be on the up-and-up."

Squeaky clean, which was in itself very telling.

"What about Sloane and her brother?" I asked, surprised by my initial reaction. I managed to contain everything inside me, my anger, *my rage* wrapped all up in a tight little box. Noa Sloane had crossed my thoughts more than once.

Enough where my runs hadn't just been in the mornings with my parents.

I'd sweated that shit out, *nightly* for what felt like a solid week, and even then, rogue thoughts lingered. Her poison had embedded deep, but I managed to keep my shit together.

I managed to not do something stupid.

I kept it all on lock, good at that, and coming out of my head, I noticed my buddies. They'd gotten real quiet, and Thatcher and Wells diverted their attention to Wolf. He had offered to look into the Sloane situation for me.

"Wolf?" I questioned. "What did you find out?"

Again, I surprised myself. My voice was level, even.

Bracing his arms, my buddy leaned forward and a silver chain hung from around his neck. I hadn't seen the thing in years, something he'd gotten as a kid. He said his parents had given it to him.

The bottom of the emblem grazed the table, Wolf wetting his lips. "Didn't find anything off about her either. Her brother?" He placed a hand on the table. "I kept an eye on them both. Even set up a camera outside their house."

"And?"

"Normal shit. They do normal shit. Sloane goes to school. Her brother at home." He raised a hand. "He even seems to be sick. They had some doctor come over for him the other day. Had Thatch run the guy's plates."

Thatcher pulled thick fingers through his hair. "Yeah. Guy works in pediatrics. Some doctor who runs a private practice upstate."

"What about her parents?" My jaw tightened. "Her connection to my grandfather?"

"Thatch looked into that." Wells patted Thatch's arm. "Her dad's name is Godfrey Sloane. He was on your grandfather's payroll before your gramps went to prison. Worked for one of his factories."

"He's deceased," Thatcher confirmed. "Found his death certificate. Marilyn Sloane, Sloane and Bru's mom, too. She died in—"

"A home break-in."

Thatcher looked at me. The room did. Thatcher nodded. "Yeah." He frowned. "How did you know?"

I knew what she'd told me. I knew the facts, but what I didn't know were the lies.

I had a feeling they stacked.

Her backstory only supported that, a girl with nothing, her and her brother…

Trash.

That had been Wolf's word for her once upon a time, but then, I'd had no reason to have thoughts about it. I'd been neutral in that regard. Noa had only been the girl in the way back then.

Not a device my grandfather was using.

Her place in this town didn't make sense, a rogue piece, and I didn't like rogue fucking variables.

"She came over to my house."

The room's attention shifted back to Thatcher after what he said. He grunted. "The little bitch weaseled her way into my house. Got close to *my* family."

"The fuck?" I sat up. "Why? *How?*"

"Bow made it sound like Mom invited her for dinner. The two of them ran into her at the store, I guess, but it doesn't sound much like my sister fought her on the decision." Sighing, Thatcher pulled a hand down his face. "We might just want to bring my sister in. She doesn't understand why Noa's a threat. The girl got in my house, bro. *Again*, after already manipulating my little sister once, and that does not sit well with me. I don't know what the fuck she was up to this time, but she came over while Wells and I were at practice."

"It was a good thing we got out early." Wells shrugged. "She left after we got there, and that girl's a good fucking actress. Thatcher and I saw her crying in her car on her way off the property, really hamming shit up after Thatcher and I got to her."

"Or maybe we should consider that she wasn't."

Wolf had, again, been quiet up to this point. He'd been

present for this part of the conversation, but he'd been quiet nonetheless.

He had his fingers laced together, his thumb flicking that emblem at his neck, and I turned completely in his direction. I shook my head. "What are you talking about?"

He'd said some shit like this before, questioning my thoughts on the matter. He did this even when no other conclusions made sense, and that only heightened the situation.

This shit was already enough for me, *enduring* this shit and the deceit Noa Sloane clearly had no issue taking part in. I didn't know what my grandfather was doing either, but she was right in the center of it.

Wolf opened his hands, looking at me. "I talked to her."

My brow jumped. "What?"

He put a finger on the table. "You told me to look into this situation. You told me to get the truth." He huffed. "Now, I'm not saying I have that, but we might want to consider a scenario in which she and her brother have nothing to do with your grandfather."

"They have nothing to do with him." I smirked, but nothing was fucking funny here. "They're living *in his* house, bro. Playing around with his money. Going to *my* school, a school where his grandson happens to go."

Wolf rubbed his mouth. "According to Sloane, her dad had a will. A will in which *he* named your grandpa as guardian."

"So?"

"So the man was the guy's boss." Wolf put out a hand. "He *worked* for your grandfather like Thatcher confirmed, and according to Sloane, their dad didn't even have much to fucking fill a will *with*. Their family couldn't even rub two cents together, so what kind of poor fuck has a will in the first place—"

"Someone who's lying." I swallowed. "Someone who's a

liar, and by talking to his daughter, you've probably put all this shit on my grandfather's radar. That we're looking into him and this? Sloane probably walked that information right up to my grandpa."

"I was careful." Wolf nodded. "I'd always be careful." He lifted a hand. "I got her thinking we're working on a project together."

"A project?"

He acknowledged that, his hands tucking under his arms. "Yeah. She's into art. I got her talking. It was a casual conversation while we worked. I made sure of that."

Thatcher and Wells remained silent at this point in the conversation. They exchanged a glance before Wolf sighed.

"Of course, I'd be careful, D," he started, but then his phone buzzed. With another sigh, he picked it up. I wondered who was texting him since we were all here. I guess it could have been his parents.

"Fuck," he growled, getting up. "I need to go do something. It can't wait. I..." His teeth lodged into his lip. "Just trust me, okay? I'm doing *everything* I can to figure this out for you. I swear to God."

I knew he was. He was the first one to take the reins with all this, tell me not to worry, and I only did that because I trusted him.

"Wolf—"

He didn't answer me, leaving the room. I put my hands together, and Wells and Thatcher shifted in their seats. They studied the other again, and I opened my hands.

"What?" I asked, and Wells shrugged.

"They've just been spending a lot of time together," he said.

"Who?"

"Wolf. Sloane?" Wells returned. "And he wasn't telling you the whole truth about that project." Wells jutted his chin at Thatcher. "Tell him."

Thatcher closed his laptop. "Bow saw Wolf and Sloane together at school. She thought it was weird because *we* told her to stay the fuck away from the girl. She asked me what was up with that, and since I didn't know, I asked Wolf. That's when Wells and I found out about his little CIA undercover mission." He waved a hand between Wells and himself. "He didn't even tell us about it."

He didn't have to technically. I mean, he probably should have, but he didn't have to. Especially if he was trying to keep it quiet and suspicions low.

"I told him to watch her," I said. "He's just doing what I asked."

"Yeah, well, he's doing a real good job of it." Thatcher leaned back. "He's spending all kinds of time with her, and we know that because I had Wells *watch him* after Bow told us what kind of project it was."

I didn't understand, and Wells huffed.

"It's Ares's senior project, bro," Wells stated, my brow twitching. "Exactly. Why the fuck would he have her work on that with him? That shit means too much to him."

"He's acting weird," Thatcher surmised. "Real weird. You know how protective Wolf is over any of his art. Let alone the thing that's supposed to get him into *fucking* college."

I did know, my buddy's art rarely seen. Outside of us and his family, Wolf's art was his life. He didn't expose that part of himself to people a lot.

And he was sharing that with Sloane?

That didn't make any fucking sense. None of us guys got to see his shit all the time, and we were his best friends.

Something didn't sit right, something weird like what Thatcher said. I picked up the phone, texting Wolf. I was going to give him a second to explain himself.

Because he had a lot to fucking explain.

CHAPTER
EIGHTEEN

Sloane

The animal kept getting closer. Its angry teeth *kept getting closer.*

Its monster eyes...

Mommy kept tugging me toward it, my feet skidding on the floor.

"You have to. You have to go," she said, tears in her eyes. Why was Mommy crying? "I'm so sorry, baby."

"No!" I screamed, jerking at her hand. She let go, and I raced away.

"Noa!"

I kept running. Running so fast. There were so many people around, and I kept pushing through them, stumbling.

I tripped.

I fell.

My sleeve caught on something, and it ripped.

There was so much blood.

I didn't see it long before someone pushed me into a wall. I hit my head.

The world went black.

CHAPTER
NINETEEN

Sloane

I was pacing the hospital when Ares Mallick waltzed into the ER, and I twitched.

What the fuck?

The past few hours had been a complete mess, and I was still trying to figure them out. It'd started when I'd been ripped from my sleep by my brother. I'd been having another weird nightmare about my mother when I heard him vomiting.

He hadn't stopped.

I'd run into his room to find his head in a trash can, body halfway off the bed. Immediately, I raced out of my room. He'd been sick, but he hadn't been vomiting. I started to call 911, but he stopped, and after, somehow convinced me to let him go back to bed. I had for a time, coming back to my room myself, but I'd ended up texting Ares.

Honestly, I didn't know why.

I supposed I'd been panicking, and with everything going

on with Legacy, he should have been the last person I texted. Technically, he'd been the second person I'd attempted to contact, the first being Callum. He hadn't picked up since it'd been so late, and I guess I thought Ares might be a good alternative to help try to convince my brother to go to the hospital with me. Being Bru's friend from the football team, I figured he may have some pull with him where I didn't. My brother was freaking stubborn as hell.

Within moments of the text, Ares had gotten back to me. He'd texted right away I should call 911 after I'd explained what happened, and I felt like an idiot for hesitating in the first place. I'd started to call, but then I'd heard a thud. I'd returned to my brother's bedroom to find him collapsed on the floor, unresponsive and barely breathing.

Yeah, I hadn't fucked around after that.

I'd called an ambulance right away, and though the whole event in question happened hours ago, it seemed like it just happened. It kept replaying in my head. The paramedics rushing in, my brother on the floor. My brother *not* moving.

I felt like I'd died inside, every moment pulling me closer and closer to that point of insanity I'd teetered on since I'd gotten to this town. If I lost Bruno, I didn't know what I'd do.

He was all I had.

They had been able to get my brother stable in the end, get him *responsive*. He'd woken up, but he was barely lucid, and I'd ridden with him and the paramedics over to the hospital. I'd tried calling Callum on the way, but again, hadn't been able to reach him. I'd tried calling Dr. Richardson too, my brother's doctor, but it just must have been too late. He hadn't answered either, and he'd *just* seen my brother this morning. What was crazy was he'd said he was doing better.

This wasn't better. This wasn't better *at all*, and here I was with no answers. When Bru and I had arrived at the hospital, the staff wouldn't let me in the back. Some kind of accident had happened on the highway, I guess, and they weren't allowing a lot of foot traffic back there. Hospital reception told me a doctor would come out, see me and give me an update on my brother, but they never had.

This had left me basically walking a hole through the fucking floor, and though not many things could shock me further tonight, *Ares Mallick* showing up did. For starters, he'd told me he was out of town when I'd initially texted. I hadn't asked him. He'd just told me.

Spotting me now, he sprinted over, actually here in the fucking ER.

"Hey," he said, casual like this was normal. He tugged the hood of his football hoodie down, pushing rain from the front of his curls. The guy was basically soaked, and it had been raining pretty much all night. He gazed around. "Where's Bru?"

I blinked, still shocked he was here. "I... I... I don't know. I..."

You need to breathe. Breathe.

I tried to, but fear from the situation still lassoed me like a wild stallion. I felt on the cusp of breaking from it. In my silence, Ares cut around me like he'd actually spot my brother just casually waiting in the ER, and maybe he thought he could. For all he knew, my brother's condition wasn't as serious as I'd made it sound.

I followed after him, my high-tops squeaking in the puddles his sneakers left. "What are you doing here?"

His big legs swiveled around, his keys in hand. His chest heaved with heavy breath, and the way he breathed, it appeared like he'd sprinted all the way over here. "Well, you texted me, right? To help?"

I had, but I didn't ask him to come. I approached. "Weren't you like somewhere else? Out of town or something..."

"Obviously, not now, little," he snipped. His hand pushed

over his hair. "What's going on with Bru? It sounded serious."

Reality set in again, that we *were here* and I was dealing with this current state of events. Air flow thinned, and next thing I knew, I was bending to catch my breath.

Ares's eyes flashed. "Little, hey."

I gasped, and Ares waved someone over.

"A little help, please," he said, but I shrugged it off. I just needed to calm down. I needed…

Ares held the person coming over from reception off, looking at me. "What do you need? You need to sit?"

It was like he read my mind, or we were strangely in sync or something. I nodded, and he joined me over in the waiting area.

"One second. Just stay here," he said. He sprinted over to the water machine, bought a bottle, then brought it back to me. "This will help."

It actually did and gave me something to focus on.

Ares folded himself into the chair beside me. "Better?"

Like one hundred percent. I capped the water. "Yeah. Thanks."

"No problem." He eyed me. "You need anything else?"

He appeared genuine about the ask and almost worried, which was a new look for him. Ares definitely cared about few people outside himself, and like a million percent not about me. He and his friends were cut from the same cloth.

I rubbed my hands on my shorts, saying nothing. I shook my head, and he sat back.

"Is it that bad?" he asked, *sounding* worried now. "Bru? He all right?"

I wished I could tell him. I shrugged. "I don't know."

"You don't know?"

"No, they won't tell me anything." These people were being assholes, point-blank. I wet my lips. "I rode over in the ambulance with Bru, but when I got here, they took him back and told me I had to wait in the waiting room. He was stable, but they wouldn't let me go with him because some kind of accident just happened in the area."

"An accident?"

"Yeah, something on the highway," I said. "Basically, they aren't letting a lot of people back there. Just doctors and staff." That'd been *hours* ago, hours with no news. "I keep asking for updates, but they aren't telling me anything."

I pushed my hands over my face, still in my fucking bed clothes. I'd barely gotten a chance to put shoes on in the middle of all this.

I literally thought I was going to lose my shit, all this too fucking much.

Ares got up. "I'm going to go talk to someone." He shrugged. "Get some answers."

I pulled my hands over my head, lacing my fingers behind my neck. "I already tried that. These people are being complete bitches."

What I said made him chuckle, his hands diving into his hoodie pockets. He leaned forward. "No offense, little, but you're not me."

He sauntered away after that, casually striding up to the front desk. I watched in fascination as he chatted up who was easily a *college* girl behind the reception desk.

Her cheeks colored the tint of a stop sign, and right away, she got up after talking to him. My lips parted when she waved him to follow her.

He did, of course, but not before passing me a wink. He disappeared behind the hospital doors after her and was gone for about ten minutes before he returned. He came back with a chocolate bar and a smile on his lips.

He tossed the chocolate to me. "Bru's fine. He's sleeping." *What the fuck?* "I didn't see him, but I spoke to his doctor personally. He's resting and stable, and you're welcome for the chocolate, by the way." He leaned forward. "Blair showed me where all the good snacks were."

I noticed *Blair* was missing, and I wondered what other delights might have been exchanged back there. Ares had only had a few minutes, but something told me that probably didn't matter. I sat back. "How did you just do that?"

He might have gotten a college girl to do what he wanted, but getting a doctor to stop and talk to him was different.

Then again, if she'd been a female doctor...

His big shoulders popped. "My family has a lot of influence over this hospital. When I come through, people move their feet."

Aka they most likely donated a crap-ton of money. He didn't say this, but he might as well have. Money was influence. Money talked.

His lips tightened a beat before he continued. He outlined his lips. "Anyway, his doctor says he's fine. Bru's actually not even down here anymore."

I stood. "Where is he?"

"Since he's stable, they've moved him to another wing of the hospital. He needs to stay overnight for observation."

"Why didn't they tell me?"

Ares pushed his hands into his pockets. "I guess they got a hold of y'all's guardian. Spoke to the guy personally, and he agreed with the plan of action." His eyebrows narrowed. "It seems your Montgomery took care of everything."

He did, but he hadn't called me. In fact, I'd been trying to get a hold of him most of the night. At least, I had before my phone died. *That's* how much I'd called him.

I pushed my hair around. "Can I go see him?"

Ares shook his head, and my heart sunk. He put a hand on his chest. "I couldn't even go. It's past visiting hours, and I'm not family."

"Well, I am."

"But it's still past visiting hours, little. And you were right about that accident. The hospital is a clusterfuck right now, and I was lucky to get the few moments I did get with the kid's doctor. The hospital doesn't want a bunch of people wandering around. It's a bad time, and they're not making exceptions for anyone. Not even me."

This was complete bullshit, all of it. I wanted to go back there and punch someone in the face. They couldn't treat people this way.

Ares's head tilted. "But it sounds like the kid's doing okay. The doctor advises you to go home and apologizes for not coming out to speak to you. Once they got a hold of your Montgomery, they didn't do anything more after that. They were busy with that accident, I guess, and got sidetracked."

And I was nobody. I wasn't like Ares. People didn't move because of me. I growled. "So they forgot about me. Nice." My teeth gnashed. "Someone should fucking sue these people. They don't have their shit together."

"Yeah, oversights definitely tend to happen here," he said, looking over my head. His eyes had narrowed when he made eye contact again. "But you should go home. Get some sleep. Parking out in the lobby isn't going to get you anywhere."

He was right, of course, but it made me feel better to be at least in the same place my brother was. At least, until visiting hours. "I should just stay. I don't even have a ride home anyway." I could call a ride share, but I wanted to stay anyway.

Ares studied me. "I could give you a ride." He pocketed his hands. "I'm already here, and I'm not getting on the road to head back out of town tonight. It's too late."

"Where were you coming from?"

"Lake Shelley," he stated, and my jaw fucking dropped. That was like out of state.

I started to mention that, but Ares was waltzing toward the door.

He lifted a hand. "Come on. I'll swing you home."

He didn't give me a chance to negotiate, and apparently, Ares really did move people.

I went begrudgingly, but it was hard to argue knowing someone had driven a state over to help. I didn't know why he did, but I didn't argue with that either.

He'd gotten me answers.

CHAPTER
TWENTY

Sloane

Ares Mallick took me home.

Consider that one a win for the record books.

Another was that we managed to not kill each other on the way. We didn't even argue. It was actually a nice quiet drive. Well, quiet outside of the blaring rock music that Ares blasted throughout his Hummer. Arm hanging out the window, he blasted that shit despite it being the middle of the night, and I didn't complain because that was what I would have played.

It was kind of crazy how we had so much in common. I seemed to discover more and more, as we spent time together. A big commonality was our art, and it may be because we had so much in common, we fought so much. We were like two alphas constantly knocking heads. He was obviously more aggressive, but I didn't stand down from him.

That was probably a big reason *I* pissed *him* off so much. I didn't stand down like the rest of his sheep at school, and call me crazy, but it seemed he didn't hate me as much either.

Besides helping me out tonight, I think he played his music so loud *because* he witnessed me enjoying it. He caught me bobbing my head to the beat from the radio more than once.

"You need anything else before I cut out?" he asked, eyeing my living room. He mentioned some shit about not letting me walk into a dark house, which fucking floored me. He did something nice, normal even. He was surprising me just like someone else I'd rather forget.

Dorian himself had impressed me more than once in the past. He'd been kind before. He was kind until he wasn't, a constant reminder of what Legacy was, and I couldn't soon forget. Ares may have my back now, but I was still aware he needed me for that project. We were far from finishing it.

I kept that thought in the back of my mind as I left Ares to deposit my bag in the hall closest. I returned to find Ares in the kitchen, actually studying the area like he was looking for something or *someone.* I chuckled, and he turned around.

"We have home security," I said. He saw me turn it off. "No one's getting in here. Callum made sure of that."

I'd been able to juice up my phone on the way here since Ares had a charger in his car, and Callum had left me a couple messages. He mentioned basically the same thing Ares had told me at the hospital, so I hadn't bothered calling him back. It was late, so I left him a text I'd call him in the morning.

"Did he now?" Ares's gaze bored over the room. He studied the light fixtures and cabinets before finding my eyes. "Any reason why the dude left you hanging tonight?" He shrugged. "He's supposed to be your guardian, right? Where was he and why did I have to tell you what was going on with your brother?"

I frowned. "He didn't leave me hanging."

"He did." Ares took a step, and I didn't get the attitude change. "And where does he go anyway? He just leaves you guys here? All alone and shit."

"Because he's not our dad," I stated, not that I had to

explain it to him. I braced my arms. "And he didn't leave me hanging. He tried to call me, but my phone died."

"Hmm," Ares grunted, like an actual grunt. He stood tall. "Well, where is he? Is he coming?"

His phone message said he'd try. I didn't know where he was right now, but I assumed on business. He always was when he wasn't here.

But again, I didn't need to tell him that. I wet my lips. "You know what? Thanks for tonight. Thanks for taking me home, but I'm probably good at this point."

That was my nice way of saying he needed to go home, and there went our record for not arguing. He just couldn't help but be himself.

I left him standing in the middle of the kitchen, opening the cabinets for some hard liquor. I needed a shot, and he laughed behind me.

"You're getting tanked this late?"

"Doesn't hurt the situation." Things were already fucked. I pulled out the bourbon.

"Going straight for the hard stuff, I see."

I turned to find him smirking.

He leaned back against the counter. "Wouldn't have taken you for a bourbon drinker, little. Maybe one of those fuzzy pink drinks." His eyebrow arched. "Those ones with the sugar crystals on the top."

I flipped him off, and that got me another smirk. It pissed me off enough that I grabbed two glasses instead of the one. The first I poured my shot, and the second I decided to fill with some milk from the fridge.

I got it nice and high, Ares watching me the whole time. His lips thinned. "What are you doing?"

"Pouring a glass for the big boy," I said, then pushed it to him. "How's that for your fuzzy pink drinks?"

I'd give it to Ares. He took it and actually lifted his glass to me. "Salut."

I said it back, completely aware I didn't know what the word meant. I tossed back my shot the same time he drank his milk.

And the fucker managed to make a competition out of it.

He chugged back his milk with greedy gulps, taking it down just as easily and effortlessly as I did with my small shot. I growled, starting to fill my glass again.

"Okay, little. Slow down." He raised a hand. "This isn't a competition."

I didn't listen, taking another shot. The burn triggered a coughing fit, and Ares pushed off the counter.

"That's enough," he said. He slid the whiskey down the counter. "Why the fuck are you always at me?"

My head shot back. "I think that's the other way around." He'd been attacking me from day one, attacking me *now*. "You come in here jumping down my throat when I'm going through all this shit. My brother could be fucking dying right now, and here I am with you when all I want... All I want..."

His lips parted. "What?"

I didn't know what. I just knew I was *scared*, and I felt so alone. I'd felt it for so long, and the only time I had a *shred* of not feeling that way it'd been taken away. *Trampled* all over.

And by his fucking friend.

I didn't want to admit that now, that what I felt not long ago might have been real. Especially in front of Ares. He wouldn't care. Instead, I swallowed, Ares looking at me from across the kitchen.

He flicked at his curls. "I wasn't trying to jump down your throat."

Then what was he trying to do?

His gaze found the floor. He cursed. "Got an actual shot glass in this bitch?" he asked, my brow jumping. His jaw shifted. "I don't drink shots out of fucking milk glasses."

He pulled the bourbon over, completely serious. I eyed him. "I'm not driving your ass home."

"I'll call a ride share. Just get the fucking glass."

I did, giving him what he asked for. He downed that shit like it was nothing before taking another. He chuckled. "You actually have good taste in bourbon, little."

A compliment, and from this guy. I smiled. "Some stuff I brought down from Chi-Town." I'd gotten it with my fake ID.

Ares nodded. "It's good," he said, but he didn't take another glass. He studied the room. "Got any snacks or are you going to continue being a piss-poor hostess?"

He said this, but he smiled, and for some reason, I didn't immediately throw an insult at him. I chuckled. "What do you like to eat?"

As it turned out, everything, and I ended up defrosting what felt like half the freezer. Bru kept a lot of garbage around the house, frozen cheese sticks and wings. I ended up being pretty hungry too, so I made it all, and Ares didn't protest. I really didn't know why I was entertaining his presence here. When we'd gotten here, I'd wanted him out of my house.

"Pick your poison." I tossed him the remote from the living room. We'd assembled all the garbage food out there with our booze, and seeing Ares in my brother's easy chair was frickin' hilarious. Bru may be a large boy but he wasn't nearly as tall as Ares. With his legs stretched out, my brother's teammate basically had his long legs breaching the opposite side beneath the coffee table.

Ares barked a laugh, a bowl of cheese puffs in his lap. "You're giving me a lot of trust, little."

"Just pick something, *Wolf*," I tossed. I popped a piece of popcorn chicken in my mouth. "And it better be good."

I angled back to see him actually smiling from my brother's chair. He said that name was on loan, but I was only forty percent sure I'd get away with calling him that.

"I got something for you," he said, and when he grinned, it appeared I did get away with what I said. He proceeded to change the channel to *The Office*, and I was surprised. That was like my favorite television show.

"You like *The Office*?" I asked, taking a blanket from behind the couch. I put it over my legs while I ate chicken.

Ares grabbed a wing off our island of junk. We'd arranged it all out on the coffee table for easy access. He lifted a shoulder. "It's cool. Jim fucking kills me."

"And Dwight."

"Yeah." He faced me. "Wanna binge-watch? Now that I'm up, I don't think I'm going to sleep anytime soon."

I probably wouldn't either. Not with everything that just happened.

I could use a laugh or two. "Only if you don't fucking talk. I hate when people talk while I'm watching stuff."

He lifted a hand, then proceeded to turn up the television. This was not how I'd thought the evening would go, and though Ares's laughter boomed over the set almost right away at the show, his distraction didn't annoy me. If anything, his laughter made me laugh too.

We laughed *together* which should be weird, but as we watched, it wasn't. Actually, watching TV with him felt a lot like painting with him. It felt, I don't know, easy.

I really didn't think I'd sleep that night, but my lids definitely started feeling heavy during the show. I fought sleep for as long as I could, but I must have drifted off sometime between episodes. I was totally in and out of sleep because, at one point, I thought I felt a set of hands tugging my blanket up when it slid.

"Night, P," I heard a voice say, but that couldn't have been true. My name didn't begin with a P.

I must have been dreaming.

CHAPTER
TWENTY-ONE

Sloane

A crash jerked me awake, my head rising from a couch pillow.

What time is it?

I looked around for my phone, but then I realized I'd left it in my bag. I pulled my legs off the couch only to hear a thud hit from inside the house. It sounded like something literally hit a wall.

"Dorian, bro, *calm* down."

What the fuck?

Wide awake now, I got feet to the floor. That sounded like Ares's voice.

"This was your plan the whole fucking time?" Another thud, something physical colliding with something else. "Alcohol and shit? You fucking sleep with her?"

"Nah, man. It's not like that."

This time, there was no thud. There was no crash.

This time, it was a *smack* like flesh hit flesh, and I got up, stumbling a little. I was disoriented. I'd fallen asleep on the damn couch, and I'd also had shots last night. I didn't feel hungover or anything, but I definitely had a strong headache.

I padded my way through the house, pausing when I made it to the foyer.

My lips parted where I stood.

Down the hall, Dorian Prinze had Ares against the front door. He had his fist raised, his hair tousled. His shoulders roved under a thin T-shirt, and a crush of red tint crept from the neckline of his shirt all the way up to his chiseled cheekbones. He looked *pissed*, and his fist raised in his friend's direction only made the fact more obvious.

Dorian's nostrils flared. "What the fuck, Ares?"

"Come *on*, D." Ares's voice was even, calm. He was clearly trying to talk down whatever this was. He placed a hand on Dorian's fist. "It's not like that with her. *Believe me*. It's not like that at all."

"What's it like, then, Ares?" Dorian's jaw worked, and between the two boys, they filled the small hallway. Ares had height, but Dorian was huge too. The football player crushed dudes well beyond his height, and I'd seen it on the field.

Really, the two of them barely fit in my entryway, and what the fuck was all this? I started to move in that direction, but Dorian slammed Ares against the wall.

"You let me in here, and all I see is *fucking* shot glasses and her sleeping on the goddamn couch." Dorian leaned in, his Adam's apple flicking. "So tell me what it's like?"

"Not what you're thinking."

"Fuck *you*, Ares," Dorian growled. "The guys told me you were hanging with her, but I passed that shit off until your phone showed me where you were. We can track each other's phones, and you know that."

Ares's blink was slow. "I had to. She needed help and texted me. Her brother—"

Dorian's fist collided with Ares's jaw so sharply I screamed, both boys whipping in my direction.

"What the fuck!" I charged over, stepping over an actual plant. It lay shattered on the floor like something had been tossed into it.

Or someone.

Both boys watched my strides with wide eyes, but it was Dorian to pin me still. His body heaved with charged heat, and I hadn't seen him in so long.

I hadn't been in his presence.

He absolutely filled the entire space he was in, and I was only ninety percent sure that had to do with his actual size. Lips parted, that flush blazed all over his face, his hair silky and curled over his eyes. It appeared longer, blond spools cutting over his dark irises. He was still ridiculously beautiful.

And I hated him for that.

I hated him for what I still felt, and forcing myself to ignore it, I shoved him off of Ares.

Dorian's eyes twitched. Like actually twitched as if I'd slapped him. He watched in what appeared to be shocked fascination as I got between him and his friend. I put a hand out. "What the fuck is your problem, Prinze?"

Another eye twitch, a tic this time in his right eye. He said nothing, his full lips closing, and when I spotted Ares, he stood the same way.

Ares exchanged a glance between both me and his friend, not a word said, but I had enough for both of them.

I shoved a finger in Dorian's direction. "How fucking dare you? What the fuck is this, huh?"

My words ricocheted off the walls like I was in my own amphitheater, and I noticed neither boy was immediately speaking. Dorian stood there, just looking at me, and on my other side, Ares just rubbed his jaw. It seemed that was where his buddy had hit him, and that just pissed me the hell off.

I heard what it *sounded* like I came in on, Dorian in a jealous rage that made no fucking sense at all. He'd left me.

He'd *left* me.

He'd abandoned me here and what was worse about that was it had nothing to do with the obligations to his family. He'd called me a liar, thought I'd betrayed him.

I fought the quiver in my lips, standing tall. "You have no right."

"Sloane..."

He had no right to say my *name*, and I shoved at his meaty chest. He didn't move an inch, but that wasn't the point. "You and I are *nothing*. You left me over bullshit and then you come back in here and pull this shit?"

His jaw locked, and the muscle that feathered in it pulsed his skin. He obviously had something to say, but he was going to fucking wait.

"This fucker was actually there for me, you know?" I stated, directing a finger at Ares. "Last night he showed up, and it didn't matter if he believed in me." I got in Dorian's face. "It didn't matter what he believed you told him. He came through like..." I raised and dropped my hand. "Like an actual friend."

It felt weird saying the words. The term *friend* was nowhere near where Ares and I were.

But recently, it felt that way. It did. Especially when I looked back. He did look past things he believed about me, and when things had been rough, things with my brother, he didn't hound me about them. He took me to do street art. Shared his weed with me and that'd been even before last night and our binge fest. He'd showed up.

He'd acted like a friend.

Dorian hadn't been the only one shocked by the words. Ares stood ramrod straight as if he too didn't know what the fuck I was talking about. I would admit I came in here hot with some madness backing me, but I wasn't going to let Dorian Prinze push anyone around. Especially me.

Ares studied me a second, a long hard second before he faced his friend. He wet his lips. "D..."

Dorian had his hands up, backing away. His attention jumped to me, the dark prince borderline snarling. I'd seen his rage in my direction before, his hate. That I recognized and completely understood, but this now was harder. Before, he'd looked like I had betrayed him.

But now, it was as if I disgusted him.

Dorian's attention cut to his friend. "Then go be fucking friends."

He left in a sharp pivot and threw the door open so hard he broke the glass in my window. He stalked down the stairs with Ares striding after him.

"Dorian!" he called, but I noticed he passed a glance back. He stood in the middle of my entryway, as if conflicted.

In the end, he chose to whirl in the other direction, after his friend, and I might have given the situation another thought had my phone not rung. Since I was in the hallway, I heard it.

I've got my own shit to deal with.

That was what I put in my mind as I went in the closet and pulled my phone out of my bag. Seeing Callum's name, I felt a sense of relief. He seemed to be the only thing I could rely on these days, the constant and always supportive.

I hadn't called him back last night it'd been so late, and I was happy to hear from him. "Callum?"

"Sloane. Good," he said, sounding busy in the background. He was always busy, so this didn't surprise me. "I'm glad I'm getting you. Did you not get my calls last night?"

"I did, but it was late. I got your messages, but I didn't know if I should call you."

"I'm always available to you, Sloane. Especially now, considering the situation."

I swallowed. "Have you heard anything else about my brother?"

"I did. Actually, I just got done talking to Dr. Richardson. He's taken over his care this morning, and he apologizes for not being around for you both last night. He and his family left for a family vacation after he saw Bruno. Didn't even know anything was wrong until I got a hold of him last night."

Oh my God.

"He caught a quick flight this morning. He's with Bru now, and from how it sounds, your brother is doing very well."

I couldn't believe he'd gotten the doctor to come to him. Leave his vacation. My lips parted. "What's wrong with my brother?"

Callum's sigh was heavy into the phone, and even though he said Bru was doing well, my heart raced. "Unfortunately, Dr. Richardson is still unable to diagnose. What appeared to be a temporary virus your brother obviously can't seem to shake. His fever keeps coming and going. Your brother collapsed last night due to lack of fluids. He was severely dehydrated amongst other things."

I was sure the vomiting contributed to that. My throat constricted.

"Good news is Bru's fever has come down this morning," Callum continued. "He did very well through the night, and Dr. Richardson is hopeful."

"Did you speak to him? Bru?"

"I have, and he does sound good. I'm trying to do everything I can to be there. I was on a flight myself last night, which was why I missed your calls. I was working on a deal overseas."

He was always working and had no obligation to us at all.

You should have called him sooner.

My brother had just been sick for too long, his meds making him sleep all the time. He hadn't been well at all, and if I'd been proactive, maybe more could have been done to prevent all this. Obviously, Dr. Richardson was a doctor, but to him, my brother was a patient. He cared for him like a patient, facts only and not instincts. Instincts, a gut feeling, came from those closer to home, and I should have pushed more.

That was all in the past now. Things were what they were, and this was the hand we all had been dealt now.

An engine charged in the air, and my gaze shot outside to see Dorian's Audi.

He peeled off out of my driveway, Ares physically behind him. Ares had his hands up, his head shaking. The next thing I knew, he was getting into his Hummer.

I watched as he cut after him too, chasing after him, and I realized Ares must have fallen asleep too. He couldn't have gotten past the gate if he hadn't.

I realized exactly how this did look to Dorian, but I couldn't bring myself to care. He had no right to come here.

My heart surged as Callum continued to speak.

"I'm doing what I can to get there, but just wanted to give you the update. I assume you're on your way to the hospital this morning? I'm sorry they blocked you last night. Dr. Richardson spoke to Bru's attending, and he told him they wouldn't allow you entry. From what I hear, there was some type of traffic collision?"

"Yeah, there was." I pulled my keys out of my bag but decided to head to my room for a fresh change of clothes first. I was still in my pajamas. "The place was full. They wouldn't let me back."

"Well, I've made a few calls, and that shouldn't be the case now. You should even be able to stay there while your brother is admitted."

"Do you think he'll be there long, or…" I chewed my lip. "Callum, how bad is this?"

I hated how worried I sounded. I hated that I was asking him, a virtual stranger in my life only a year ago again, for aid but I couldn't help it. I couldn't do this on my own. I had nothing. I was *no one.*

"We're going to figure this out," Callum assured. "For now, I don't want you to worry. The doctor sounds hopeful. All Bru's vitals are stable. He was even joking this morning on the phone."

Of course he was, the fool. He was also the same one last night who didn't want to go to the hospital. It hadn't been until he'd passed out and had no way to protest I finally got him into an ambulance.

"Thank you, Callum."

"Of course. I'll keep you updated on my status. As soon as I can, I'll meet you, and don't hesitate to call until then."

He really was the only thing constant in my and my brother's lives. And I also noticed, he was the one person who never asked for anything. He hadn't left me broken. He hadn't left me *hurting,* but most of all, he hadn't abandoned my brother and me. Even with his distance, he hadn't. He was always there, no questions asked, and never, not once had he abandoned us.

He'd never abandoned me.

CHAPTER
TWENTY-TWO

Dorian

Wolf's house was dark when he finally dragged his ass home. It was dark because *his parents* were supporting my family. They were still back at the cabin, and he should have been too.

I kicked back a beer on his front stoop. I'd actually gotten here a couple of hours ago, driving all around town. I needed to fucking think, and I assumed it had taken him so long to come home because he'd been out looking for me. He'd followed me when I'd left Sloane's house today, but I turned off my phone so he couldn't track me.

Sloane…

Her very name charged me up like a goddamn bull, my fingers gripping my beer bottle. When I'd tracked Wolf to her house, I hadn't known what I'd do. I hadn't known what I'd expected to find, but it wasn't him answering her door.

He'd stayed at her house.

The beer soured in my mouth. It twisted in my gut when I forced it down, and that wasn't the only thing I tucked away when I stood. Wolf's Hummer pulled into his parents' circle driveway, and he must have seen me on the stoop. He normally would have rolled around back and parked in the garage. I'd parked back there and came around.

I waited, patient. I respected my buddy enough not to break into his house as I waited for him tonight. I could have. He always left the window open for me.

We both did.

We were *brothers*, blood without the biology. I would *die* for this motherfucker if I needed to.

My insides seared, splitting in two when I watched Wolf pull his ass out of his ride. Hating the feeling, I tossed back another drink. I didn't know how many beers I'd had, but the bottles were in my car. I'd driven over here drunk, completely stupid.

I was getting all up in my head, and for what? A girl who'd fucking betrayed me? She was in cahoots with my grandfather.

So why are you here?

Finishing off my beer, I wiped my lip.

"D?" Coming around his ride, Wolf eyed me. He pocketed his hands. "You drunk, man?"

What the fuck did he care about it?

The only thing keeping me from tossing the bottle at his ass was my god dad and Brielle. I didn't want them to have to deal with the exploded glass.

I jerked my chin toward the back of the house, leaving him and heading there. I heard him sigh behind me, but he did follow.

His cadence heavy, he kept up. I opened the gate that led to the backyard, easy since I knew the combination. Wolf closed it behind me after he came through, and that was when I tossed my bottle to the grass.

I took my varsity jacket off, cold tonight.

Wolf's mouth parted, his eyes narrow. "Dorian, what are you doing?"

My buddy appeared fatigued in the moonlight. He had bags under his eyes like he hadn't slept or anything, and that had to be a joke.

He'd slept with my girl.

Noa Sloane was mine, *mine*, and regardless of what she was up to. In fact, since she had betrayed me, that only made it more so.

I controlled her. I *owned* her. Her fate and what happened to her was mine to decide.

Mine.

The haze hit me after that, fucking blind, and I saw myself unravel from a bird's-eye view. It was like I was out of my body when I tossed my jacket on the lawn.

It was the same when I hit my friend.

I clocked him clear across the jaw, and it was like he'd let me. He stood there, like he was ready to just fucking take it. The second time I reared back, he just blocked, and that only pissed me off.

"Fight back!" I spat at him, and when he blocked me this time, we went down. We tumbled on the lawn, me throwing punches and him just blocking them.

"I'm not going to fight you!" He roared, guarding his face. "D, I won't fight you."

He should. He'd been bold enough. He'd betrayed me today. He'd betrayed all of us.

"I don't want her like that," he called, and hearing the words only unfurled more rage through my veins. I shouldn't care if he wanted her or not. He'd admitted he was playing her for information. Maybe that was this, and I definitely shouldn't care about that. If anything, I should be celebrating it, get off on it even.

My vision red, I threw a fist so hard I questioned if I broke my hand and my buddy's jaw, and at this point, Wolf grabbed my shirt. "Stop it. It's not like that with her."

He said that, but he was lying, *lying*. I'd seen him with her with my own two eyes. The two had had a fucking pajama party. Noa's shorts had barely covered her ass, and Wolf's hair was all over the fucking place like when he screwed bitches in the computer lab. They liked to put their hands all through it.

She'd put her hands through it.

In my distraction, Wolf got me off him, taking his own corner and holding up his hand. His face was already changing color on the right side. "Dorian…"

"You betrayed us," I snarled. "You betrayed *me*, your boy, knowing she's with my grandfather."

"You don't know that."

"And you do?"

His gaze fell to the ground, his hands in the grass. "I don't, but…"

"No."

His head shot up.

My mouth dried. "You don't, but it definitely didn't stop you from going after her, you fucking asshole—"

"You're one to talk about betrayal." His nostrils flared. Eyes wild, they *cut* in my direction. He put a finger out. "You're one to talk about people going behind people's backs."

"The fuck you talking about—"

"You brought this bullshit into our lives, Dorian." He raised and dropped his hand. "You brought your grandfather in when you fucking knew better. *You knew*."

I bared teeth. "I didn't have a choice."

"You didn't give any of us one." His expression sobered. "And now, we all have to worry about it. You, me, and the guys. Your mom and dad?" Wolf shook his head. "And

Sloane. Sloane and her brother could be victims in all this, but you're too fucking blind to see it."

He'd said something like this before, *standing up* for her. My throat tightened. "Well, if you don't want her so bad, why do you keep coming to bat for her, then?"

He forced fingers into his hair. "I just don't want her hurt. She *can't* get hurt. She…" He stopped on his own accord.

But I think me stepping back definitely had something to do with it.

Angling my head, I held up a hand.

Wolf frowned, getting up. "D…"

"I'm done, Ares. Done with this," I huffed. "Done with you."

He cringed. "It's not what you think."

But he couldn't offer me anything else. Even now, he just let those words sit between us.

They filled the fucking air.

I lifted my hands. "I said I'm done."

He did call after me. He did a couple times, but I noticed he didn't follow. In fact, I didn't see him again until I closed the gate. Who I'd called a friend and a brother was down to his knees on the lawn.

He had his head in his hands.

CHAPTER
TWENTY-THREE

Sloane

My brother tossed a Funyun at me.

He was obviously feeling better.

Dr. Richardson had said something similar about an hour ago. He'd checked in on Bruno several times throughout the day. After the final check, the doctor said he had felt good about leaving him for the evening but advised the hospital (or Bru and me) to call him if anything changed. My brother was up and wiry, joking with me, and though he couldn't possibly eat any Funyuns, that didn't stop him from tossing mine at me.

"You worry too much," he said, like I hadn't seen his ass *collapse* last night. Dr. Richardson had confirmed what Callum had told me when I'd arrived. My brother had collapsed due to dehydration and lack of fluids. His throwing up had only made it worse. This had ultimately caused him to pass out, and though his fever had broken, he was still weak. A Funyun was about the only thing he could pick up.

I'd taken Dr. Richardson aside at multiple points in the

day. I wanted the hard facts about what was going on, but Bru's ailments seemed to be a mystery to him. My brother gave symptoms as if he had the flu, his fever coming and going.

"We're going to get to the bottom of this," he said before he left for the evening. I'd come back into Bru's room after that, and Bru definitely knew what had been talked about.

Hence him tossing Funyuns at me now.

"I just don't know why they can't figure this out," I said, tossing a Funyun back. "I mean, they're supposed to be doctors."

I'd been informed by Dr. Richardson that he'd consulted with a couple of doctors here at the hospital before I'd arrived. He'd wanted a second opinion, I guess. He'd had the doctors here do bloodwork, and even after analyzing it, he and the other doctors still couldn't discover a diagnosis for my brother's symptoms.

Bru shrugged. Sitting up, he was in a hospital gown, and it was hard not to notice the dark circles under his eyes. He'd also lost a ton of weight.

Mere weeks ago, he'd been a teenage boy tossing footballs across the field. Now, it was touch and go whether he could pick one up depending on the day. His head tilted. "They may be doctors, but they're practicing medicine."

"Well, they need to practice better."

"And you should know because of your degree. Right, Dr. Sloane?" He smirked. "I'm feeling a lot better."

"Who knows for how long." Whatever was going on with him seemed to be tremendously better or worse depending on what breath he took. I cuffed my arms. "I just want you to be okay."

He said nothing, but I noticed him shift in my direction. My brother and I had never been the touchy-feely types, but we did care about each other. We both loved and *worried* about each other.

We were all we had.

Bru took my hand over the sheet, and I let him because I was vulnerable. Hell, I should have been the one taking his hand.

"I'm going to be okay."

"You don't know that."

He smiled a little. "I am because I have you." His head cocked. "You won't let me die. *I know* you."

He said that with a laugh, but it was a little dry, and I wondered if he was just as scared as I was. If he was worried about dying.

I squeezed his hand. "You're right. I won't let you die." I frowned. "I still have to kick your ass for trying to get into the Court in the first place."

Whatever was happening with him now seemed to have come right after he'd jumped into that lake. Who knew what the fuck he'd caught? He could have been stung or bitten. Who knew?

Bru pressed his lips together, huffing. "I don't think any of that matters anyway." He studied me. "You were right about those guys. Not one of them has come to see me while I've been gone." His back touched his elevated bed. "I can't even get any of them to text me back. Friends don't do that."

If it meant anything, I didn't want to be right.

Honestly, I *believed* Legacy had been pushing Bru away because of me, but I just hadn't wanted to stress Bruno out.

I still didn't, squeezing his hand.

"Knock, knock. Anyone home?"

I let go of my brother's hand when Ares Mallick entered the doorframe. Basically, I was surprised as fuck.

I wasn't the only one.

Bruno's jaw dropped, mine even lower.

Ares had brought... flowers.

He had like a huge fucking display of them, in a pot and everything. He balanced that on one hand, his hood up and all his curly hair pushing out. He laughed. "You seeing visitors, bro?"

Pure shock stiffened me as I watched my brother brighten up, then *sit up*. Bru attempted, but he struggled, so I elevated his bed more.

"I got it," he growled, still trying to be strong. Bru waved Ares over. "Of course, man. Come on in, and good to see you."

"Good to see you, kid," Ares returned. He came into the room with his plant, and my expression dropped.

The side of his face was a completely different color.

Like *legit*, his face had transformed. Red and purple marred his usually golden skin, and he'd healed pretty well since his run-in with my brother, and Dorian after that. Dorian had actually hit him over that haze at the lake.

And again this morning.

Dorian had hit him earlier today, but I didn't recall Ares's face looking *like that*. I definitely would have noticed.

Ares had obviously tried to hide it as he gave my brother the pot he brought. He had his hood up and his hair around his face, but there was no hiding that bruise. Ares lifted the pot. "Sorry I wasn't around sooner. I, um…"

"Nah, you're fine." Bru visibly brightened. Ares looked like he didn't know what to do with the pot, and Bru advised to place it on the table near the door. Ares had to double back to do this, and when he did, I got up.

I told Bru I'd be back, then asked Ares if we could talk out of the room for a second. He was hesitant, but he followed me out. We made it into the hallway, and I propped my hands on my hips. "I want to see it."

"What?"

I eyed him like it was obvious, *his face*. His gaze caught the ceiling, and I took it upon myself to tug his hood down.

I covered my mouth. He looked like someone had

assaulted him, over and over someone had kicked his ass, and growling, he tugged the hood back up.

"Who did that to you?"

His attention reached the lights again. "What's it to you?"

It wasn't, but this was fucked up. I shifted on my high-tops. "Was it Dorian?" They'd fought before.

Had they fought again?

The way that Ares avoided my eye contact told me this appeared to be the case, and I was floored by this. *This* didn't make sense. Dorian getting all territorial and shit. He hadn't cared about me at all.

"What's *his problem*?" I gritted, trying to keep my voice down because my brother was basically behind us. We'd gone into the hall, but I hadn't closed the door. "Why is he acting like he fucking cares?"

"Probably because he does."

I blinked, ramrod straight in that fucking hallway. "He doesn't. He thinks I lied to him."

"But that obviously hasn't stopped him from acting the way he's acting." He was being so candid with me, real. He braced his arms. "Why did you call me a friend, little? You did, and that fucking set him off." He leaned in. "We're not friends."

I didn't know why, but my chest tightened a little when he said that. Stupid, I knew. We weren't friends. My jaw shifted. "Then why have you been acting like one?"

The question of the hour, right? He was and continued to roll through my life like someone who actually cared too.

"Maybe I have my reasons."

I smirked. "Meaning you need me for that project." He was using me, and it was obvious. I laughed. "Okay, now that we got that settled."

His hand cut across the way. This kept me from leaving. He eased his hands into his pockets. "Maybe I want to believe you." His shoulders rose. "About the not ratting out D and shit. Maybe I want to believe that, and it's fucking with my head."

Again, he was being so candid, but it was the first time anyone had given me an indicator of that. Bow had said the same thing, but I had messed with her before. I'd given her no reason to trust me now.

This obviously wasn't the same case with Ares, and when he chuckled, my lips parted.

"You know, it was a lot easier to hate you when I had no fucking reason." His head shook. "When the only reason was because you were coming between me and my boy."

"Wait. What?"

"I was jealous, little." The very admission had him rolling his eyes. Probably at himself. He wet his lips. "You put this mind-fucking voodoo on him. Thatch? Wells? And let's not even talk about Bow."

I raised a hand. "You were jealous of me?"

His sight grappled the ceiling tiles once more. "Maybe a little bit of you getting close to my friend. You were getting up in my clique. Pissed me off." He shrugged. "People like you. You get *attention*, and attention on you takes attention away from me."

Oh, what a complete and arrogant fucker this guy was.

But he was smiling.

He actually *smiled* at me, and this whole conversation was crazy. I hugged my arms. "So what does all this mean?"

"It means the jury is still out on you." His lips pinched together. "I stand by Dorian and will always stand by Dorian."

"But?"

His jaw shifted. "But I personally feel like things are complicated with you. I do, and I'm acknowledging that."

I didn't know what to feel about that. And all of this was so screwed up. His boy was a complete idiot.

"Why is he like this?" I asked, an idiot myself for saying it. "I didn't lie to him."

Of course, there was no point in saying this. Ares knew my position. I could preach it from the rafters.

"Guys, everything okay?"

My brother's voice came from the other room, and giving up, I headed that way.

Ares raised his hand again, stopping me. "You're not the only one who's complicated," he said, then pointed to his face. "This happened for a reason, little. We don't fight over shit like this. We don't *fight*. We're brothers, but this is the second time my buddy came at me since you came around."

My mouth dried, and Ares's chin lifted.

He adjusted his hood. "I guess I'm not the only one who feels you're complicated."

He lowered his arm after that and went into my brother's room, and I stood there for a second. I stood there for *too long*.

Don't.

I refused to let my mind go anywhere with what he said, and if Ares wasn't trying to be a friend, he was doing a sucky job at it. He was definitely acing like one.

It seemed the complications didn't lie with just Dorian and me.

CHAPTER
TWENTY-FOUR

Sloane

I stopped by the house to get some clothes the next morning and a few things for Bruno too. He wanted his handheld video game and something to cover himself with, something that wasn't a backless hospital gown.

I planned to reject the latter request but did tell him I'd bring him his video game. We didn't know how long he'd be in the hospital, but we might as well prepare for however long it took.

As far as school, I didn't know about that either. Hell, I didn't know about it for me. We were off on a holiday today, but I went ahead and had Callum call me in for the rest of the week. I didn't plan to leave the hospital.

I thought Ares might give me a harder time about that. We obviously hadn't worked on the project since before the weekend, but he hadn't mentioned it once yesterday when he came by. He'd been cool, and in any sense, school and his project were the last things on my mind anyway. I was still stressing out about my brother.

Amongst other things.

I kept that all out of my mind as I pulled up toward the house. Upon rolling up the hill, I was mulling over the list of items I wanted to grab, but it all fell out of my head when I realized a car was parked outside of the gate.

I recognized it.

Dorian Prinze had his arm out of the window, his head angled in my direction when I came up. He had sunglasses on, the morning light flickering across his sun-spun locks.

Wetting his lips, he pulled them off his eyes, squinting like the sun bothered him. His mouth pulled into a tight line, and I thought he was about to get out of his car.

Which had been why I pulled on.

I had *no* idea why he was here, but I didn't fucking care. My window was still broken from him and his crazier-than-fuck rage.

I cruised on and believed he'd get the hint.

He didn't.

Right away, the growl of his Audi hit the air, the sports car following behind me. I let him get as far as my garage before I hopped out of the car.

He did too, the thing snapping shut when he came around. He'd returned his glasses to his face, but he tugged them off when I stalked toward him.

He looked like a wreck, and completely different than when I'd seen him yesterday. For starters, he had bags under his eyes, his hair messed about on one side. He worked his shoulder as he strode toward me, and I wondered how long he'd been in his car.

I wondered how long he'd been outside *my house.*

This begged the question why, and his split knuckles definitely gave me pause when I saw them. They hadn't been like that yesterday either.

But then again, *Ares's face* hadn't looked that way until I'd seen him the second time. Dorian's hand was obviously the source of this.

"We need to talk." He didn't acknowledge his hand, and his eyes were red too. In fact, they were bloodshot. His throat worked. "We're going to talk."

He stated this to me as if it were a command.

The audacity.

He wanted to talk. *Now*, he wanted to talk, and I was apparently supposed to listen. I cocked my head. "What makes you think I want to talk to you?"

His growl sounded low, deep and predatory. He pinched the bridge of his nose.

"I'm not playing a game with you, Noa," he said, the only one who ever called me Noa. Like ever. He forced a breath through his lips. "So as much as you love your fucking *sass*, I don't need it right now."

Why would I care about what he needed? I shook my head. "Go to hell."

I whipped around, but he was fast.

He cut me off before I even hit the garage and had hands on me even quicker.

"Stop," I gritted, his hands too hot through my shirt, his gaze too pointed on me. Dark and ignited, his smoky irises pinned me in place. "Let me go, Dorian."

He ignored the warning in my voice, the plea to *stop this*. Every moment with him tore at my insides.

I felt cut to ribbons.

I swallowed it all back as my breath hiked and he homed in.

"Tell me the truth." Harsh breaths heated my face, his nostrils flaring. "I'll know if you're lying. I'll know if you're *fucking* lying, so don't lie to me, Noa."

His words were anything but steady.

His hold on me matched.

He was visibly shaking above me, on me. His jaw shifted. "Did something happen between you and Ares?"

"What?"

His eyes closed in that moment. Like it was taking everything inside him not to level the world as it stood. He gripped my arms. "Did something happen between you and him?"

Out of all the things he could ask me...

I didn't think it'd be that.

I thought he'd come at me about anything else. I was the liar to him. The traitor, but that wasn't what he asked about.

I shoved him off me, and I think he only let go due to pure shock. He hadn't been anticipating it. "There is no me and Ares, you *stupid* fucker."

His eyes flashed, mine too actually. The words exploded out of me, and I felt like I too would level the world in this second.

I gasped. "I was *worried* about you." I blinked, my eyes fucking cloudy for some reason. "Before you left, I was freaking out about you and your family. What you all had to be going through after that video came out..."

His mouth parted, his eyes narrowing. It was like he couldn't compute, and I couldn't either.

My jaw moved. "And what's worse is, I still did that." I nodded. "You still crossed my mind, even though you called me a liar." I lifted and dropped my hands. "I can't see past you, and I hate myself for it."

He was wrapped in my head, a fucking tether I couldn't even use a machete to hack through.

Dorian distanced slightly, his chest rising with breath. He probably saw me as pathetic, another groupie Court bitch who was falling all over herself for him. I mean, what other girl still thought about someone when they did that to them?

I cringed. "There's no me and anyone else. There's no Ares and me because even after you left, left *me*, you're still in my fucking head."

He'd once called me the head-fuck, but he had played the worst game of all. He'd etched himself into my brain, and I couldn't escape him.

I cared about him.

Shunning away from it, I raised my hands. "You stay away from me, Dorian Prinze." My throat jumped. "You *get away* from me."

He twitched, the words he'd said repeated back to him. I'd done it on purpose. I wanted to cut him. I wanted to hurt him as bad as he'd hurt me, and it might have worked had I actually believed what I said. I would have been able to make him believe. I would have been able to *lie*.

But I was such a bad liar.

His hand braced behind my neck, and when he swiveled me around, he collided our mouths. I gasped.

"Stop," I cried, my words saying one thing but my mouth another. He deepened our kiss, and I kissed right back. "I can't."

I couldn't do this anymore, the head trip.

"Don't fight me," he gritted, my lip pinched between his teeth. He bit down. "Don't. I need this. *Please...* I need this."

He released my lip, his mouth closing down on mine. He drank me in, and I did cry.

Our faces were wet between us.

Where the emotion flowed from, *my tears*, I didn't know. Maybe because I knew I'd regret it the minute I let him kiss me. I *knew* this was wrong, and that I'd both hate myself and him even more after it was over.

But that didn't stop me from letting him into my house.

It didn't stop me from letting him in my bed. We shed clothes along the way, toeing off shoes, socks. I jumped, and he caught me, falling down on the bed with me.

The springs labored under his weight, Dorian down to his jeans. He kissed me hard into the sheets, his bulky arms crowding around me.

"Tell me you're not fucking with me," he rasped, shaking above me. He pulled my lips apart. "Tell me I'm not an idiot."

He was an idiot, and I was too. We were both so toxic to each other. We were this mass of chaos, sex, and anger...

But if he thought I was lying, lying about his arrest and anything else, that wasn't true.

"I'm not fucking with you." And God did I wish I was. I wanted to play him. I wanted to be the bad guy after what he'd done to me. That would have made all this easier.

It would have made these feelings go away.

I would have deserved everything that happened, but I didn't.

A noise rumbled from Dorian's chest, his mouth chasing a line to my navel. He had me down to my bra and panties, his teeth nipping small bites to my inner thighs.

"Open your legs for me," he gritted, his hair tangled in my fingers. "I need your fucking taste."

I called out as his tongue lapped through my underwear. He got a handful of my ass before he shoved two fingers past my panties.

I bucked on his digits, grinding against his face. I touched my breast, and he blew heat over my panty-covered sex.

"Be my dirty girl, Noa," he stated, pulling his fingers out of me. He outlined my lips before pushing past them. I sucked them hard, and his eyes flared. "Fuck. Why are you so fucking good at this?"

As if he needed a taste, he kissed me after, his tongue hot and greedy. He got a handful of my underwear before tugging them off me so hard they ripped.

"These are mine," he growled, shoving them in his pocket. I didn't know what he'd do with them, but he was obviously taking them. He gripped my face. "No one else gets to taste you."

I let him think that, almost believing it when he disappeared between my legs. He wrapped my legs behind his neck, then proceeded to suck my lower lips into his mouth.

"Dorian," I ground out, my sex *aching*. He had the nerve to chuckle over me.

"No one else makes you feel this way, Noa," he said, his tongue shoving into my heat. "No one else can do this for you."

It was as if he was telling himself that as much as me, and how I wanted him to be wrong. I *needed* him to be wrong. Dorian Prinze wasn't good for me. I didn't want him.

But the way my body sang for him.

I didn't need to say a word, my body responding to every lick and flick of his tongue. His laughter, deep and gravelly, only egged it on. He knew exactly what he was doing both to me and for me. He had full control over my body.

But that didn't mean he owned it.

It didn't mean he owned *me*, his fingers pulling through blond strands when he came up. He unstrapped my bra, freeing my breasts. He bit me with a wet mouth, sucking my nipples and coating them with my own juices. His tongue swirled, and I nearly came on his leg.

He forced my sex away.

"Taste me," he commanded, his tongue flicking my nipple. "I want to feel your mouth on me."

It wasn't a request, his fingers curling in my hair. Dorian never asked for anything. He took, and I hated that I wanted to give him exactly what he wanted. I couldn't stand that I wanted to taste him, that *I missed him*. I wet my lips, and he grinned.

"Let me feel your throat," he coached, his fly open and his jeans sagging low on his hips. He shoved them down, his dick tenting his boxers. "Noa…"

I rubbed him, his growl heavy, feral. He probed into my hand, steel in my palm. I pulled him out, and he angled toward my face.

A tight, "Fuck," fell from his lips as he pushed past my lips. I hadn't sucked him off in a while. "Fuck, yes, Noa."

His taste affected me more than I liked, my head bobbing. I moaned, and the moment he stiffened, I thought he'd come down my throat.

He didn't, angling off me. He kissed me again, pinching my nipples, and I cursed.

"Oh my God," I panted, his hand pushing between my legs. He gripped my sex, and I grabbed his biceps. "Dorian."

"Don't talk. Just scream." He bit my mouth, *hard* and my eyes rolled back so far I thought I'd see the inside of my skull.

My hips bucked against his hand, his other one forming around my neck.

He leaned me back while he took the seconds required to sheath himself. He kicked his jeans off, then didn't ask permission before he angled himself inside.

He cursed with every thrust, stabbing me, and I bit his shoulder, my attempt not to scream and do once again what he said. He had me under his command so well.

It didn't work in the end, his name falling from my lips. In fact, I screamed so loud when I came I had ringing in my ears.

"You didn't wait for me," he said, smiling before taking my lips. He squeezed my neck, fucking me harder and harder until he too was shaking.

Until we both collapsed.

He slowed as he milked my sex and didn't stop kissing me even after his hips stopped. He just kept saying one word again and again.

"Mine," he said, biting, tonguing my mouth. "Mine."

He was disillusioned enough to think it. All of his words obviously that. Dorian Prinze was reminding me of his claim on my body.

And I let him because, in that moment, I was disillusioned enough to believe it too.

CHAPTER
TWENTY-FIVE

Dorian

What am I doing?

Sloane fell asleep. We were both good about that shit when we were together. We did stupid shit *together*.

I peeled myself away from her, sitting on the edge of the bed. I scrubbed my face before gazing back at her.

Who are you?

Most importantly, was she lying to me? Wolf sure didn't seem to think so.

Wolf.

I didn't know if something happened between them. I didn't know a lot of things, but I had been drunk last night, and things with Wolf had gotten out of hand. I'd been sick about it. Sick enough to come over here and ask her about *that* of all things.

Why did you?

My stomach tightened, clenched to fucking hell. This girl was playing me, and I was letting her.

Fucking obsessed.

Sloane had a leg out of the sheets, golden, luscious. Her ass was outlined by the silk, and I wanted to rip it off her and shove my cock inside her. I was *hard* for her, even now, and that made her so dangerous. I didn't know a damn thing about her.

But I wanted her.

Being inside her... being close to her only reminded me of how it'd been before I'd left. She maddened me, drove me crazy, and her sassy-ass mouth only made me want her more.

She's playing you.

Shaking, I got up. This, what had happened here in her bed, should have been some kind of fucked-up triumph. It should have been me showing what I could do to her.

"You're still in my fucking head," she'd said, and what I'd so obviously done this morning showed her place in mine. She was tearing my whole world apart. Helen of Troy caused less bullshit.

I scrubbed my face, getting up. I put my clothes on, then made my way downstairs. Her front door was still broken, something I'd done.

Get the fuck out of here.

I could. I should, but I was here. I was in the Sloane household, and maybe something here might tell me something. It'd tell me who Sloane was, she and her brother. It'd let me know something about my grandfather. He'd paid for this house, all this his stuff.

I told myself that was what I was doing, searching through mail and other things to find out dirt about my grandfather. I needed to dig into the devil's lair, and anything I found out about Sloane herself was just a byproduct. I told myself this. She was secondary.

But that didn't feel like the case as I searched, my hands flying through mail and shoving shit around. A desperation backed me, opening and closing cabinets and drawers. I just kept hearing words in my head, her words playing back. She said she'd been worried about me, me and my family.

Swallowing, I ended up in the kitchen, forcing shit open. I wasn't being careful at all, messing shit around and making too much noise.

"Do you normally go through people's private things, grandson?"

I stiffened, my back ramrod straight. I whipped around, and my gaze clashed with an old man.

Grandpa Prinze was in a suit, his fingers laced and sitting at the Sloane kids' kitchen island. He had a curious look about him as he stared at me, and I instinctually cut my gaze across the room. There was a set of kitchen knives readily available, a meat tenderizer.

I studied them both, but Grandfather's smirk stole my attention.

"So ready to try again, my boy?" He placed a hand in the direction of the knives. "Please. Since you're so obviously ready to kill me."

I was ready to kill him. I was ready to do what I had to do.

I'd done it once, hadn't I? At least, I thought I had.

My grandfather found my lack of action amusing. Chuckling, he tilted his head. "I thought so."

"Well, don't think shit," I growled, my voice low for some reason. I didn't know why I cared if Sloane knew this conversation was happening. Especially if she was in on whatever this shit was with my grandfather. I stood tall. "And how are you alive?"

I placed the poison in his tea myself, watched him drink it. The poison should have took and *quickly*. Especially with his age.

He smiled, almost coy about it. "You mean, how did your last attempt on my life fail so poorly?" His hands opened. "You always check the body, son. What's the point in starting the job unless you're going to finish it?"

He said it like a seasoned pro, like this wasn't his first rodeo with death, murder.

I wouldn't put it past him.

His hand touched the island. "Someone got to me in time. I have call buttons all over the house for emergencies." His head lowered. "Managed to get to one before it was too late."

And escape death, my grandfather immortal. He seemed to be able to escape all kinds of fates. He definitely should have served life for that shit with my aunt Paige.

Grandfather folded his hands. "I'd like to say I didn't know you had it in you. But then again, you are my grandson."

"Take out a few bodies yourself, then?" I smirked. "You've definitely covered up a murder." I didn't mask the growl in my voice.

Grandfather's chin lifted. "I was protecting my son then, your father." He pointed at me. "Though he obviously doesn't feel the same way."

"Well, considering that's his wife's sister," I said, my throat tight and constricted. I shook my head. "You're a monster."

"Some may think that." He nodded. "But whenever I act, it's necessary. Just like you, I can imagine, with me and your failed attempted."

"I'm nothing like you."

"But aren't you?" he asked, my eyes blinking. He waved a hand. "You saw an obstacle and what you felt was a threat to your family, and you *attempted* to take care of it." The smile graced his lips again. "And how is my son and his wife? I can imagine Royal is going stir-crazy at that cabin, seeing as how he's a workaholic just like his old man."

My mouth dried.

He grinned. "Of course, I know where they are, Dorian." He sat back. "I even know you've had people tailing me. Well, you and your friends can rest knowing that my stay here will once again be short. I don't have a place here in Maywood Heights anymore, as I'm sure you know."

The way he continued to trivialize what had happened to my aunt had me snarling.

Grandfather's head cocked. "Fortunately, I've been able to create a new life for myself. A handsome one with privacy and no ridicule from this town."

"Hence your new name." My eyes narrowed. "Montgomery?"

His chuckle was light. "Yes, an old family name actually," he said, his lips pulling in. "Something you'd know if my son ever bothered to tell his own son about his family history. The Montgomery name is tied to my mother's side. I merely took it up again. It allowed me to start over with no retribution. The name wasn't classy, you see. Left behind, but never forgotten."

Thatcher had said it came from some bootleggers—*not classy* as my grandfather said.

"And so a Prinze becomes a Montgomery." My laughter dry, I braced my arms. "And right. You really had to start over with all your money, your power?" My eyes narrowed. "I'm sure that was so hard for you."

He studied me, and the lack of emotion in his eyes shouldn't surprise me, but it did. This man was a vault, showed even less emotion than my father. Dad had obviously gotten it from this man.

"You roll through here like a fucking freight train," I said. "Destroying lives, and boo-hoo, you have to start over."

He let me go off on my rant, entertaining it. He appeared to find me and this whole conversation amusing.

"I told you. I do what needs to be done for my family. *To protect* my family, even if they don't agree with how I go about it." His brow lifted slightly. "Who knew what that Mayberry woman would have done after you and your friends kidnapped her. You're eighteen, son, and though you may feel you're above the law, it's best not to test it."

He said this so casually, and I stiffened.

He nodded. "Yes, I took care of that too. Didn't take much. I told you the woman had enemies. I just had to direct them where to go."

My stomach soured, suspecting this. "You did that," I said, gut turning. "And the police coming to get me?"

"That was a warning." Grandpa's eyes narrowed. "I forgive you for that situation at my home. You believed your family was threatened, and I understand that, but going forward, nothing like that is ever to occur again. *Ever*, grandson."

"But…" I started, blinking. "I tried to kill you."

He appeared casual about this, his hand lifting from the table. "Like I said, I understand. You were trying to protect your family and no one gets that more than me." His lips tightened. "And I'd never hurt your father, Dorian. I'd never hurt my son nor you."

"Only my mother." I hated how my voice shook, that this asswipe affected me.

His head shook. "I act when I need to. I don't go by emotions. Something you yourself can learn from."

I swallowed.

"Anything I ever do is to protect you. And anything I'll ever do will." He sighed. "I don't wish to be at war with my only grandson. I merely wanted to get to know him. You may not believe it, but those last few months I had with you I enjoyed immensely. I'm getting along in years, boy. These moments are all I have, and I have no interest in harming your mother." His head tilted. "Truly. I just wanted to get to know you."

He made himself sound like an aging man with innocent desires, not the cruel bastard who not only threatened my mom, but used to *beat* my father. Where had his protection been then?

Where was it now when it came to me?

"And is using Sloane to do your dirty work part of that plan?" I asked. "She helped you with my arrest, right? Told you where I was?"

Again, my grandfather's poker face was a great one. His cane rested against the island, and he braced it. "Why would you think that?"

This fucker was playing with me too much. I sneered. "You admitted to getting me arrested."

"But I never said Sloane had anything to do with it," he said, my eyes blinking. He gazed around. "Where is Sloane anyway? I've just come from seeing her brother. He said she'd be here…"

I had no words at the moment, completely fucking confused.

He faced me. "And why are you here, grandson? It's very early and not exactly a decent hour. She expressed to me you're just friends, but if my grandson is anything like his father and his father before that—" He almost laughed, arrogant about it. "Is something going on between you and Sloane? If so, this is a surprise. My grandson and my ward. Very interesting."

None of this made sense. He had to be fucking with me, *lying*.

"You said I couldn't trust her," I forced out. "You said that at the fucking police station—"

"What I asked is how well you *knew* her. I asked how close you were, and that's a question you should always be asking outside of family."

My pulsed pounded, the blood charging through my veins.

Grandpa Prinze frowned. "I feared my son had spread more of his weakness in you, which is why I said what I had.

He's always been too trusting with his friends." He waved that off, pulling out his phone. "Only a Prinze can truly be trusted. *Family*. It was merely a lesson I was trying to say, and no, Sloane wasn't aware of your arrest. In fact, I was quite surprised when she plead to me about you the way she had. She really does seem to care about you, son."

My throat tightened, my mind dizzy.

"Who is she to you?" I breathed out. "Sloane and her brother. Who are they to you?"

He'd been studying his phone, like this conversation was just another of many for him.

And I felt sick, so fucking sick before he gazed up.

"Sloane and Bru's father used to work for me." Graying eyebrows pulled in. "I mentioned that in the car."

"And what? You're just, out of the kindness of your heart, looking after them?"

His nod about that was casual, and my brow jumped. His head cocked. "He was a trusted associate. A good man." He pocketed his phone. "What's with this line of questioning?"

My questioning was that my grandfather didn't have a kind fucking bone in his body. He was a monster. Point-blank. "You yourself said you don't do anything unless you need to. Why would you care for a bunch of strangers to you? Orphans..."

Sloane.

My hands shook, and I steadied myself on the counter. If my grandfather noticed, he said nothing. He wet his lips. "Like I said, grandson. I knew their father and well. I was honored to watch over them. Bring them here for a new life? They've both had it pretty rough, and I was happy to give them an opportunity to start over."

I said nothing, my mouth dry.

"I thought Maywood Heights would grant that opportunity for them. It's a smaller town, and they could blend in." His head lifted. "Unfortunately, in order to do that, I had to conceal who I really was to them. They couldn't know. They'd be ridiculed. I'm not a favorite in this town, as you know, and I didn't want that for them. They'd both had enough with the loss of their father."

I couldn't breathe.

"Though I'm sure you've noticed Sloane isn't aware of who I am to this town. To you?" His eyes narrowed. "But what I don't understand is why you haven't told her." He pointed a finger. "Why you lied? I figured I'd have to deal with that after you left the car that day."

He should have had to deal with it. It should have come out.

"In any sense, I can't see why her peace should be upheaved now." He leveled me with his gaze. "She and her brother live a very nice life. A quiet life, and I'd like to continue to provide that for them. No need for the noise, and if you and your friends are worried about me, you don't have to be." He moved his cane. "Sloane and I have an agreement. She and her brother take care of themselves, and that works for me anyway. I'd like to continue living my quiet life and do plan to return home after my visit. I'm only here now because her brother is sick, and I came to see about his care."

Wolf had mentioned that Bru was sick. Said *Sloane* had said that.

I just hadn't put much stake in it.

I gripped that counter now, the world tilting on its axis.

"Might be too late for the truth now anyway."

I focused on my grandfather after what he said, his fingers folded.

He nodded. "I mean, you lied to her. Lied to her about me and who I am to you." He opened his hands. "I can't imagine that will sit well with her. She should be able to trust you. *Her friend*, should she not?"

And how the tables had turned. He'd made me the liar.

And I'd let him.

He'd created a world in which he now looked like the hero, and I was the bastard who'd fallen into the trap. I was the *liar* who looked for secrets in all the wrong places. My grandfather had been up to something, and with my help, he'd gotten it. He now had a place in Sloane and her brother's life.

I'd given it to him.

"Callum?"

Sloane entered the kitchen, my grandfather between us. She'd gotten dressed, her hair up and out of her face. She flashed her tight little waist with one of her bare midriff tops, a hoodie she'd cut off well above her hips. Her head tilted. "What are you doing here?"

She asked the question, but there was only a mild curiosity there. This wasn't unusual to find my grandfather here.

My stomach twisted, her attention focusing on me next. A heat hit her eyes, and in a manner of seconds, she placed distance between me...

And moved closer to *him*.

"What's going on?" she asked, and my grandpa stood from his chair.

He smiled at her. "Just talking to Dorian here," he said and so coolly. "We ran into each other. Didn't we, son?"

My grandfather obviously wanted to continue his ruse.

His smile stretched. "I was just telling him how I've come from seeing Bruno at the hospital. He's doing well this morning, which is good."

The... hospital.

I really hadn't been listening. About so many things, I hadn't been listening.

"What's wrong with him?" I asked, but out of the two, only my grandfather shifted in my direction.

He frowned. "The boy's been sick, but he seems to be coming around," he said, and Sloane's response to that made my stomach crawl. She flushed all over, cradling her arms. She stayed near my grandfather, clearly comfortable with him.

I was well aware of her distance and her body language, and her reaction to me when she came in versus my grandfather was definitely telling. She trusted him. She was *comfortable* with him.

And definitely not with me.

"Bru said you were at the house, Sloane, which was why I stopped by. I hoped to catch you," my grandfather continued. "The school informed me your tuition bill was sent here, and I wanted to pick it up and take care of it." My grandfather's sight fell on me. "Dorian, did you say you saw it? The mail?"

I twitched.

How long had he been watching me?

Obviously, for a long enough time to watch me circulating the house. My jaw locked. "By the front door. The hallway on the table."

Grandpa smiled a little at me, a knowing smile. This was a test.

I guess I passed.

I didn't give a fuck about my grandfather's secrets. I didn't care about his lies, but I did care about Sloane.

Even if I had been too fucked in the head to realize it.

My buddy, not long ago, had said I'd been blind. He'd said I couldn't see, but it wasn't because I didn't.

It was because I hadn't wanted to.

The reality was this now. My grandfather had moved his way in, and now, I was the idiot.

I was the one she didn't trust.

Calling my grandfather out on the carpet now would just make things worse. He had her too invested, and her reaction to me today stripped me of all my power when it came to her. I had no *validation* when it came to her.

I came forward. "Sloane—"

"Dorian was just leaving," she said, effectively cutting me off when she hugged her arms. "He wanted to talk, and we did that." She wet her lips. "Did you get what you wanted out of it all?"

A dagger could have dug less. She obviously felt I'd used her, gotten her to fuck me, and why shouldn't she think that? That was basically exactly how it looked. We had talked. We had fucked, and when she woke up, I hadn't been there. I'd been going through her house, sneaking around.

I was the liar.

I started to say her name, but her head whipped in my grandfather's direction.

"Are you going back to the hospital?" she asked, dismissing me and my presence here.

My grandfather nodded. "Eventually. Just want to take care of that bill so you both don't have to think about it." Bracing his cane, he studied me. "Good to see you again, Dorian. Maybe we'll run into each other in the future."

He didn't want to say such things to me, my knuckles digging into my palm.

Sloane faced me. "Goodbye, Dorian," she said, and my grandfather's manservant/driver chose that opportunity to enter the kitchen.

Lucas (the guy was still a gorilla) had his billed hat on. He took it off. "Is everything all right, sir? You told me to leave the car running, so I thought I'd check."

I didn't miss Lucas's glance in my direction. My grandfather's manservant was his safety net obviously.

He'd probably been watching me too.

I had three sets of eyes on me in the moment, but out of all of them, my attention stayed on Sloane. I didn't want her anywhere near my grandfather.

Lucas's hand on his jacket let me know that may not be my choice today. I wet my lips. "I'll see you at school."

My grandfather was joking if he thought I actually

believed what he said about his presence in Sloane's life. My grandfather had an agenda, and win today or not, he wasn't going to do that another time. He wouldn't *have her*, and I wasn't going anywhere.

Sloane appeared confused about what I said, but I meant the words. I wouldn't be returning to my parents' cabin. I wouldn't be leaving Maywood Heights.

I shouldn't have left the first time.

My phone was in my hand the moment I hit my car. Thatcher and Wells were still at the lake with the families, but they'd come back today once they heard from me. We all needed to be here, but I didn't even think about contacting them until I heard from Wolf. I needed to talk to him the most and for obvious reasons. I'd fucked up when it came to my brother, and I could only hope he hadn't given up on me, that he had more trust *for me…*

Than I clearly had for him.

CHAPTER
TWENTY-SIX

Sloane

Ares was in my brother's room when I arrived back at the hospital, and I was surprised to see him. He'd stayed until visiting hours wrapped last night, and yet, here he was there again today.

He and my brother sat on his bed when I came in, playing a loud-as-fuck video game that bled into the hallway.

"Watch my back, kid," Ares barked, laughing. "Next time, we're not going to be on teams, bro, if you can't cover me."

He chuckled after it, but my brother rolled his eyes. They were playing some kind of first-person shooter, blood and guts everywhere. There definitely hadn't been any games in my brother's room when I'd left this morning.

Yet, here it was, along with Ares. It was a newer system too, the thing rigged up to the television the hospital had provided for my brother. The TV was ancient as fuck, so it looked pretty hilarious with that system.

"What's going on?" I asked, sliding my brother's bag off

my arm as a character on the screen exploded. Really, its head had been completely blown off.

"Christ, sis." My brother growled at me, and Ares did too when his guy, I guess, exploded in the same way.

Ares shook his head, and his hood was up again. I wasn't sure what story he'd told my brother about his face, but he was still trying to hide it. The hood did pretty well for the most part, but his face was still another color. Ares tossed his controller. "Yeah, little. What the fuck?"

I raised my hands, rolling *my* eyes. I tossed the bag by the door. "I thought I was bringing your game." I mean, it wasn't this thing, but I'd brought it.

My brother exposed teeth with his grin. "Wolf brought this over. Pretty pro, right?"

I'd say, thing was sleek as fuck.

Ares stood as he slapped my brother's hand. "No problem," he said, bumping his fist after. "Kid looked bored as hell."

"I brought him something." I gestured toward the bag. "And what are you doing here?"

"Came to visit the kid like he said," Ares returned, and I nearly fell on my ass. I'd heard what my brother had mentioned, but still, Ares was here *again*. Like stated, he stayed pretty late last night. Ares joined me by the door. "And what took you so long? The kid said you left hours ago."

I really didn't want to rehash my last few hours with Dorian. I scrubbed into my hair. "Had some interference."

Ares's thick dark eyebrows drew inward. At this point, my brother was playing his video game again.

Ares studied him before finding me.

"What kind of interference?" he asked, and though casual about it, I noticed an edge to his voice. He angled outside the room a bit. I joined him but didn't really feel like talking about this. Especially because he was right about us not being friends.

I wagered he was only here now *because* of my brother. They at least played on the football team together and had hung out.

I opened my mouth but didn't have the opportunity to say anything at the approaching steps of another. Callum came down the hallway, his driver, Lucas, behind him, and I was surprised to see them both. Callum had said he was staying behind to pay that bill.

He was apparently right behind me, his suit jacket over his arm, and I'd never get over the ritzy life he held. I mean, the man had a *driver*, the guy hanging back when Callum strode down the hall. Callum lifted a hand. "Sloane."

"Hey, Callum," I said, immediately turning toward Ares. I had to angle a bit.

Ares had distanced. Like legit, he was behind me, and I had to make a full rotation.

The football player was basically on my back, and I had to distance just to get some breathing room.

He glanced down at my few steps, his head shooting up when Callum joined us.

The older man grinned. "Hello, again. Finished up, so I thought I'd head on over here." Callum's attention directed to Ares. "A friend of yours?"

It was funny how that word kept coming up. Ares Mallick had definitely expressed he was no friend of mine, but for the sake of conversation, I nodded. "This is Ares. A friend from school."

"I see. Nice to meet you, young man. My name is Callum Montgomery." Callum put out a hand. "For all intents and purposes, I'm this one's guardian. Her and her brother's."

I'd never seen Callum joke, but the smile in his voice gave that as an indicator. It was nice to see him being casual, like he really was starting to become a close friend, and I liked that. I didn't have a lot of those. None actually.

Callum's hand lingered in the presence of *my friend*, Ares

merely studying him. I didn't know what was up with that, but he made no move to shake.

"Ares," the tall boy said, finally taking Callum's hand. "Nice to meet you. Heard a lot about you."

Once Ares had Callum's hand, he didn't let go, a nice long shake. Callum continued to shake Ares's hand too, his head tilted.

"Ares," Callum stated, a question in his voice. "A last name go with that, son?"

"Yeah. Mallick." A noticeable snip hit Ares's voice, and Callum let go of his hand.

The man returned it to his pocket. "I see."

"Mmm," Ares returned, being weirder than he already was. Really, he was being borderline rude. He took a step, but paused when Lucas approached.

Ares's gaze flicked over to Callum's driver, but his attention refocused when Callum regarded Lucas.

"You can wait in the car, Lucas," he said to him before facing Ares. He smiled. "Good to meet you."

Ares might have said something, but Callum had already entered Bru's room. I heard his voice inside shortly after, greeting my brother.

Lucas tipped his hat at Ares and me, the large man nodding. He didn't stay long before he was rerouting back down the hallway, and with his exit, Ares glanced into my brother's room.

I did too. My brother and Callum were chatting in there, but more of my attention settled on Ares. "You okay?"

"Yeah. You?" The snip had returned, and my brow jumped. Ares looked at me. "You okay?"

I shook my head, confused as fuck. I wasn't really okay. Not by a long shot, but that had nothing to do with the weird way he was acting now.

I didn't say anything, and Ares angled in. "Little..."

"It's Dorian." I hugged my arms, and though I hadn't

wanted to say anything, for some reason, I was flapping my lips. I kept doing that with him, and I didn't get it. I sighed. "He was at the house when I got there."

"What?" Ares got close. I started to say something more, but his eyes flashed. "Wait. Was he there when—"

Ares didn't get to say because in the next moment, Callum returned to the hallway. He was putting his suit jacket back on, and I frowned. "Are you leaving?"

"I am." He straightened his jacket. "But I'll be back. Wanted to stop by and see Bru again before I checked into my hotel. I drove straight here from the airport, so I'm going to go take care of that now. Especially since you kids are entertaining." He leaned in. "Don't want to cramp your style."

He wouldn't be, but it was nice he was thinking about that.

Ares's lips pulled tight. "Staying in town long, Callum?"

Callum's sight fell on Ares. His head lifted. "I'm in town for Bru, so as long as he needs me." He faced me. "But the way your brother was laughing and joking with me just now, I can't imagine that will be for long."

I hoped he was right about that.

"I'll be back after a while," Callum stated, then pointed at Ares. "Again. Good meeting you. It's nice to see the kids have made some friends at school."

Hands in his pockets, Ares didn't get a chance to respond. Callum strode away, and Ares followed him with his gaze.

"What's your deal, Mallick?"

"What happened at your house?" Ares swiveled in my direction. "You said Dorian was there. That you had interference. What happened while he was there?"

So, yeah. None of that was his business, and I definitely didn't want to talk about that.

I was already embarrassed.

I gave in *so* easily to him, and I didn't want to think about it.

"Sloane."

My sight clashed with Ares's, his eyes narrowed.

His jaw shifted. "Did something happen while D was there? Did Montgomery show up?"

I didn't know what that had to do with anything. "Dorian wanted to talk, and yeah, Callum came by. I think they were actually talking for a second."

Which I hadn't liked, Dorian in my life and acting like he had a place in it. I didn't know what they had been talking about when I'd come in, but I prayed Dorian hadn't been rude to the one person outside of my brother who I had.

Dorian had been so out of line, and Ares's cursing stole my attention.

He had his phone in his hand, his head shaking.

"It's D," he said, but his phone silenced in his hand. He messed around on it, his thumbs moving at rapid fire. His eyes bugged out. "Shit, he's called me like five times. Texted too."

The guy's thumbs dashed on his phone screen like his friend hadn't turned his face a completely different color yesterday. I could imagine Callum hadn't mentioned it because he hadn't wanted to be rude, but the evidence of what Dorian had done was there.

"I must not have heard him since Bru and I were gaming." Ares pushed his hand over his hood. "He wants to meet."

He had to be joking.

"Yeah, and he also did that to your face." I was actually really angry at this point, angry that Dorian could think people would just bend and move for him. He'd done that to me.

I didn't know why I cared he was doing that to Ares too or at least, cared enough to say something.

"It's not so simple." Ares's focus didn't leave from his phone. "He's my brother, little. I'd take a bullet for that kid. Even when he's being stupid, I would."

I blanched. The guy was completely serious about what he said. "Why?"

"Because he'd do the same for me when *I'm* being stupid." His gaze dragged up. "We're there for each other. Same with Wells and Thatch. Those guys aren't just my friends."

They were family, something he'd said before, and Dorian too. This obviously all extended to Bow Reed too. Hell, I'd seen it firsthand.

"You think he's being stupid?" I asked, for some reason that coming out of my mouth. "Stupid about me and everything?"

Last time we talked, the jury had still been out on me.

Ares's head lifted, his eyes narrowed. "I need to go see about him. He says it's important. I'm sorry."

He breezed past my side, but stopped in the middle of the hallway.

He turned. "I was thinking, with your brother being sick, it might be a good thing to bring the project over to your house." He waved a hand. "That way you can work on it and not be too far from him. You know, when he gets home?"

The project? I hadn't even been thinking about that. My mouth parted. "You'd be willing to do that?"

"Not much of an adjustment," he said. "That okay? I can bring it by. Today even."

"I'm not sure when I'll be able to work on it. Bru and I could be here for a little while." My brother's condition was temperamental at best.

He nodded. "That's okay. I'll work on it in the meantime, and you can join whenever."

He was being so lax, and Ares had never given me an inch on his deadline. He'd been really serious about it.

"I'll text you the garage code. It's the same one to get past our gate," I said, shrugging. "That'd be nice to work on it from home and thank you."

"No problem. Tell the kid to feel better. He can text me if

he needs anything." His mouth moved. "You can too. I'll be around."

His phone rang again, and he gazed down at it.

His hand lifted before I could answer, and shifting around, he strode down the hall. His phone pressed to his ear, his low words quiet and muted. He disappeared from my sight when he turned the corner, and I headed back into my brother's room. I let Bru know what his friend had told me to relay to him.

Even if the conversation had, once again, left me confused.

CHAPTER
TWENTY-SEVEN

Dorian

Wolf sat completely still while I spoke, and when I finished, he moved even less. I honest to fuck was surprised he'd even come over after I'd called him. I'd screwed up, and he'd been right.

He'd been right about everything.

I had been blind. I'd been foolish, and I'd pushed in all the wrong places. I'd pushed at him and…

"Ares?"

My buddy looked up after I spoke, and I fought myself from cringing. I'd done that to his face, the side completely bruised. I swallowed. "I need your help." And it was the hardest ask I could have probably ever made. I didn't deserve his help, and I definitely didn't deserve Sloane. I'd betrayed her as much as I had him. I put my hands together. "You have to help me. She trusts him, and I don't know what to do."

My grandfather had her, and I was at a complete loss.

Wolf rubbed his hands after what I said, eyeing the floor.

He got up and placed an arm on one of my bookshelves. I had them lining my bedroom, reading something I liked to do outside of football, though I never preached that shit. He tapped the shelf. "He's not the only one she trusts," he said, frowning. "And if your grandfather is bullshitting as much as you think, we might need that."

I got up, coming over to him.

"We need to call Wells and Thatcher," he said, nodding. "And once they get here, I think we may be able to figure out how to use that trust." He lifted a hand. "She trusts me, D. Sloane does."

I blinked. "How?"

He looked away, picking at the shelf. He dropped his arm. "It all has to do with that project I told you about." His expression turned serious. "I never lied, Dorian. I've always had your back."

I could see that now, more and more I was seeing things. I swallowed. "I'm so sorry, man."

I didn't have the words, and he shouldn't want to help me. Like I said, I didn't deserve it, but that might not matter.

We were brothers.

The guy would probably do much more than this for me, and I knew even if he had betrayed me, I would have come running had he needed me. Our bond was deeper than even a falling out. It was deeper than *betrayal*. It was so much tougher than blood, and my grandfather would never understand that. My father had the same with his friends.

"We need Wells and Thatcher here," Wolf returned, and though he hadn't acknowledged what I said, I didn't think he had to. That was just us. No malice when there were more important things. "We all need to be here, and once they are, I can explain things better. Things with Sloane and what's been going on while you've been gone."

It seemed like a lot, but one thing I wasn't doing this time was closing my ears. I was listening. My grandfather wouldn't fuck with me again.

And he *wasn't* going to get her.

CHAPTER
TWENTY-EIGHT

Sloane

"Are you sure you don't need anything, Bru?" Callum asked, folding his jacket over his arm. "If not, I was going to go ahead and hit the road."

When Callum and Dr. Richardson had informed me my brother would be home in a few short days, I hadn't believed him. I mean, Bru had been a mess when he came in.

But he wasn't now, my brother taking a seat on our couch. One better, he took one *without assistance*. He even walked into the house by himself too, up the stairs.

That didn't mean he did it all without taking a few staggered breaths, and when I raised a hand for assistance, he growled at me.

"If you haven't noticed, sis, I'm alive," he said, chuckling. He smiled at Callum. "And I'm good, Callum. Thank you."

He did seem good, relaxing into his seat. He hadn't had a fever since he'd arrived at the hospital and his systems had seemed to all but clear, despite his weakness and general malaise.

This was all something Dr. Richardson said should clear too once my brother got his strength up. Bru was told to keep moving, ambulate and *eat*. The doctor had even taken him off his meds, and I was astounded by what several days in the hospital could do. It was like Bru was getting back to himself.

I couldn't be more relieved. Whatever bug this was, a hospital stay seemed to have been just the trick.

Callum grinned. "Are you sure?" He eyed him. "I can stay a few extra days and even call the school to hold off on you going back."

The doctor had pretty much cleared Bru to go back as long as he felt up to it. Since Bru was behind in school, he said he'd start this week, and I'd been surprised by that.

I assumed my brother was trying to prove to the rest of the world he was good, my brother being stubborn as per usual.

I believed him for the most part since he wasn't currently keeled over. Bru rubbed his legs. "Nah, I'm good. I'm going to go back. I need to. Get things back to normal again." His head lifted. "Did you talk to Coach for me?"

"I did, and though he'd love to have you on the field right away, he believes it might be good for you to sit out the rest of the season. You're still a full-fledged member of the team and he said you're welcome to sit in on practices."

This didn't seem to sit well with my brother, and I sat next to him. I jerked my chin at him. "Let's focus on you getting through the rest of the term academically. There's always next year, and Coach still says you're on the team."

"Yeah, I guess." He rubbed his hands. "I'm the one who messed up by getting sick, I guess. I was stupid."

It had come up that Bru had taken a dip in Murphy's lake on my end. I'd never said why or anything about that haze, but I'd been worried about something in the lake affecting him.

The doctor had assured us that couldn't be the case, but Bruno was obviously holding on to that.

Callum tilted his head. "You did nothing wrong. Getting sick can happen to anyone."

Bru nodded, but again, he was holding on to that.

Callum asked him once more if he was okay, but Bru was adamant he'd be fine. Callum must have believed him enough because eventually, our guardian did head out. He asked to speak to me before he did, so I followed him to the door.

"As always, my phone is on for you both," he said. "I'm not going to be leaving the country this time, so I'll be close."

After the not-being-able-to-reach-him fiasco, Callum put me in contact with one of his personal assistants. He said that'd be the quickest way to get to him if needed.

Our guardian had taken these past few days to be there for us, and though I wasn't certain where he was traveling for business this time, I, at least, had a way to reach him quickly.

It was crazy that, these days, I enjoyed the security. He'd come through so much for us.

"And before I go, I wanted to mention something I've been working on," he said. "I suppose I wanted your opinion on it before I relayed anything to your brother. I don't want to step on any toes."

"Okay." I leaned back against the wall.

"As you both know, I travel a lot for work, but I was thinking about doing more work closer to you both. What happened with Bruno was quite alarming and put things into perspective for me. I've been looking into purchasing a home here in Maywood Heights."

I blinked.

He raised a hand. "But only if that's all right with you both. I'm having people look into it now, and I think we've found something appropriate and not far from here." His head lowered. "What do you think about that?"

I was kind of at a loss really. He wanted to be here.

He wanted to be here for us.

My lips parted. "Bru would really like that. I know he would." Callum was like his favorite person ever.

Callum's head tilted. "And what about you? Like I said, I don't want to step on any toes." He put his jacket on. "I know you're both going to be in college soon, and me relocating here wouldn't just be for the sake of proximity. I've got quite a few business ties out of Maywood Heights, and it'd be nice to be nearer and grow them."

I really didn't know what to say. "I think that'd be cool. Actually, really cool."

The older man smiled. "Excellent. I'll let my people know to continue with the planning."

"Thank you, Callum. Just…" I felt myself smiling fully for the first time in days. "Thank you for everything. Everything with my brother and just everything."

I felt like I was thanking this man every five seconds.

He lifted a hand. "No need. I'll have my people let you know the status."

The house was quiet after he left, but I didn't get to sit long before I was up and answering the door. Someone knocked, and I thought it was Callum. I figured he was trying to be polite or something since my brother and I were home.

It wasn't Callum, and in fact, I angled to look up at Ares Mallick.

"Little," he said, a paint cloth on his shoulder. He had his paint bibs on and his signature man-bun tugged tight. He eyed me. "You and the kid home, then? He was supposed to come back today, right? He texted me this morning."

I panned to see his Hummer parked outside my garage. The garage doors were open. "You just get here?"

Ares had been scarce since that day at the hospital when he'd left abruptly. Actually, he only came by a time or two, and when he did, he'd spent more time playing video games with my brother than talking.

I hadn't minded it. I was happy Bru had a friend, but I had wondered about that day he'd left.

This was obvious considering the reason *why* he left.

"Uh, yeah." He angled around. "Came by to paint. Guess I got good timing running into you."

I'd say excellent time. We'd just gotten here.

"Saw your guardian leave." His stance widened. He clasped his long arms. "He mind if I work out here? I can get pretty loud. I've been coming here every night to work on the piece and play my music since y'all don't have neighbors."

Every night? Really?

I supposed I had given him the code, but he hadn't mentioned the project since that day.

I braced the door. "Yeah, it's cool." I widened the door. "And he doesn't live here. Doesn't care what we do. When you passed him, he was leaving town anyway. He's got to go back to work. I told you he travels."

"Mmm," he said, his hand on the doorframe. He shoved a thumb back. "I'm going to get started. I'll say hi to the kid on my way out. Since he just settled in, I don't want to bother him."

That was very considerate of him, and knowing my brother, he'd want to entertain all night.

Ares waltzed back down the steps, but swiveled around when I came up on his heels.

I passed him. "I want to see what you've been doing." I walked backwards. "Got to make sure you didn't fuck up anything."

He chuckled, picking up his pace. "Yeah. Definitely don't need to worry about that."

He let me go the rest of the way by myself to the garage, and if I saw anything but perfection, I would have handled him good.

His work on the piece didn't give me the chance.

Midnight blues and dark tones swirled on what used to be a mostly blank canvas, pops of purples and pinks both on the backdrop and the car itself. He'd done a lot of work on them both. So much, in fact, I wasn't sure how much longer completion would take. This must have taken him hours.

Days.

"I feel like silence is good."

Ares came up on me, his smirk high, and I shook my head.

"It's all right," I said, more than all right. He'd even managed to mimic my style so well. I had no idea what he'd painted versus what I'd painted.

"Thank you."

I faced him after what he said, and his expression transformed into a full smile. His head lowered. "You said you loved it."

I hadn't even heard myself say it.

But it was definitely true.

"It's great, Ares. Amazing." I eyed the muscle car blending into the background. The transition was so seamless it stole my breath. "We'll finish this thing in no time."

"That's what I was thinking." His hands propped on his hips. "Wanted to do as much as I could so I could free you up. You know, for the kid."

Again, really considerate, and he was being modest. This would have taken him countless hours. I started to say that, but his phone buzzed.

He pulled it out, texting someone.

"That Dorian?" The words had vomited out of my mouth.

I couldn't take them back.

They lingered in the air, and Ares dragged his head up slow.

He frowned. "Yeah," he rushed, then quickly dashed his thumbs on his phone.

"So he's officially back, then?" I asked. He had mentioned

he'd see me at school. "He's back, and you guys are a bro couple again."

Ares's fingers slowed. I didn't know if he'd finished his text, but he pocketed his phone.

"We worked it out," he said, his big shoulders lifting. "He made a mistake. He did, and he acknowledged it."

Yet not one word to me.

As it turned out, the dark prince ended up being my biggest mistake.

"He told me what happened, little," he said, my head shooting up. His nod was firm. "How he came over and stuff."

I was sure it was a nice little bro talk for him. I smirked. "He bragged about his conquest, then?"

"It wasn't like that."

"Okay."

"It wasn't, and he didn't go into specifics. At least, not about that." He lounged back against his Hummer. "I assumed that bit. You looked like hell when I saw you at the hospital, and he didn't look much better."

"Then guilt, then?" I gritted, and Ares sighed.

"Nah, little. He looked fucked up." His eyes narrowed. "Like *you* fucked him up. I've never seen him look that way and definitely not over a girl."

"Well, he can get over it." I swallowed. "He fucked and dashed, and that was *after* accusing me of messing around with you. Oh, the sprinkles on top were that he never acknowledged if he believed me or not."

"He does," he said, and I shrugged. So what if he believed me now?

It was too late.

I'd waited long enough, and I shouldn't have had to…

I hadn't done anything wrong.

My throat tightened. "Well, he's too late, and even if he

wasn't, your friend could use a crash course in vulnerability. To be *human* and admit his faults."

Ares's head rose, and I threw my hands up.

"I want to paint," I grumbled. "But if I do, no talking. I don't want to fucking talk."

I just wanted to do what I did best—*calm down*—and a paintbrush only did that for me. Now was a good time anyway since Bru was inside relaxing. I'd just let him know I'd be out here if he needed me.

Ares pushed off his ride. "I'll get everything set up." He lifted a palm. "And I promise no talking."

I'd done that for him once.

I was happy he was doing that for me.

CHAPTER
TWENTY-NINE

Sloane

"Is this really necessary?"

My brother groaned as we passed under Windsor Preparatory's familiar crest. I'd driven him to school on his first day back.

And yes, it was necessary.

He may be cleared for school, cleared for driving, but I wanted to drive him. I also didn't mind it, and he'd get the fuck over it.

"You'll be fine." I patted his leg, and he shoved it over. I chuckled. "Anyway, we're bonding. Let us bond."

"You mean you're hovering." He cut his eyes in my direction, but he did grin at me. He shook his head. "Whatever, but I'm driving my own ass the rest of the week. What the fuck would I look like?"

He'd look like a kid who'd been sick out of school for a while. A *long* while. Me driving him, at least for today, was me making sure he didn't have any trouble with anything.

I obviously couldn't be with him in his classes, but during our video call with Callum at breakfast this morning, Callum had said he'd spoken to the school. The academy said they'd make any accommodations my brother would need. Bru could also opt for shorter days as needed if he was feeling too weak or anything.

As of today, Bru was pretty much good as far as his strength, but since none of us knew what bug he'd had, it was better safe than sorry.

I pulled into a parking space. "Just humor me for like a solid minute," I growled. "I basically watched you die for like ever."

"I wasn't dying." He said this, but he really couldn't say that. He hadn't been on the other end. He hadn't had to *watch* him be sick. In my silence, Bru faced me. "I'll be fine. If I wasn't, I sure as fuck wouldn't be going back to school. Please, just stop worrying for once."

I made no promises and jumped when someone tapped Bru's window.

Ares lowered his head of curly hair directly in front of Bru's side. He grinned. "He lives!"

"Hell, yeah." Bru chuckled, and I rolled my eyes, getting out. Bru did too, and I grabbed our bags out of the back while he greeted Ares.

"Back at school and in the fucking flesh." Ares shook Bru's hand, giving him one of those handshake-hug things that guys did. Ares snapped his fingers. "I see your sister didn't make you come in a wheelchair today."

"Not for lack of trying," Bru joshed, and I snarled at him.

"Yeah, screw you," I shot, then jutted a chin at Ares. "And screw you even more."

Ares mock-pouted. "I'm hurt, little. And here I was trying to bid you both good morning."

That would be a first, but apparently, one of many when it came to him.

In addition to visiting my brother in the hospital, we'd worked on our project every night this week. He was also often the first person I saw in the mornings recently too. The pair of us had to do double duty with that mural since my brother had gotten sick.

I'd been seeing Ares Mallick's face way more than I thought I would, and interestingly enough, not in a bad away. We really did work well together, and I'd be lying if I said the project hadn't been therapy since Bru had returned home. I got to do that instead of hovering over my brother.

Ares dropped an arm across Bru's shoulders. "In all seriousness, it's good to see you back."

"It's good to be back," Bru said, the pair of them jostling each other like they did on the field. I missed that, seeing my brother with friends. Things had been so different before he'd gotten sick, and well, other things.

Those other things loomed in the air when I noticed we had an audience. The three of us may have been by ourselves, but there were definitely three onlookers nearby.

Dorian, Wells, and Thatcher hung out by their Audis, the three of them passing a joint around. In fact, they appeared so much like that first day I'd seen them I got chills. That hadn't been a good day and had basically set the tone for a lot of crap that came after.

I supposed a lot of that had been my fault, and though I was over Legacy and how hot and cold they were being, I couldn't help how it felt to see Dorian again. I'd been at school since Bru had come home. I had to. If anything, to make sure Bru and I graduated on time. I had to get his coursework and stay up on mine, but in all that time, I'd never seen Dorian. I'd seen Thatcher, Wells, and even Wolf in the courtyard at lunch, but Dorian had always been absent.

I never knew the reason why. Didn't care why, so seeing him now definitely jarred me.

His gaze roved in my direction, a military boot on his car

while a cloud of smoke puffed around him. Thatcher and Wells were sharing a blunt, but when they passed it to Dorian, he lifted a hand.

He had eyes on me, and his academy jacket was off, his shoulders all big and bulky in his dress shirt. Gripping the back of his ride, he pushed off it, but stopped when movement occurred beside me.

Ares still had his arm around my brother. Bruno still chatted with him, but Ares's attention appeared only partially in that direction.

The rest he had on his friends and Dorian in particular. Mallick shook his head, the movement just slight, but I definitely noticed it.

My brow twitched when Dorian shifted on his boots. He snatched his jacket off the trunk of his car with a growl before barking at Wells and Thatcher to follow.

Wells and Thatcher were definitely aware of the exchange, Thatcher's fingers cutting through his dark hair while Wells strode along beside him. The platinum blond glanced in our direction before picking up his pace and joining Dorian and Thatcher.

My brother was also privy to all this at this point, frowning. He faced me, but I was too busy looking at Ares.

"What was that about?" I asked, and Ares waved it off.

He dropped his arm from my brother. "Told him to hang back. Dorian?" Ares's big shoulders popped up. "The other day you didn't seem like you wanted the drama. Thought it best he kind of keep his distance."

I hadn't asked him to do that.

But I'd be lying if I said I wasn't glad.

I followed Dorian's back as he ventured toward the school. He shoved his thick arms in his jacket along the way, and something I didn't miss was how my breath released. I was relieved Ares had talked to him.

But again, I hadn't asked.

Ares joined us inside the school, apparently opting out from walking with his friends today. I noticed I hadn't seen Bow with the guys' clique, but then again, I generally never saw her with them in the mornings anyway. I assumed she drove herself.

While we walked with Ares, my brother had nothing but questions in his eyes. These, I assumed, were about what he'd witnessed outside, but he kept them to himself. He did until Ares caught a couple of friends in the hallway.

Mallick tapped the guys' fists, but my brother, on the other hand, moseyed over to me outside my locker.

"So what the fuck happened while I was gone?" He leaned in. "What was that back there? You and Dorian are over?"

I'd told my brother absolutely nothing about the situation with Dorian. Made sense he was confused. He didn't even know Dorian thought I lied to him. I rooted in my locker. "We were never on, Bruno."

"Well, if that's not on, I don't have fucking eyes." He frowned. "You guys were definitely a thing before he left town—"

"We're not now," I gritted, causing my brother to blink.

He shook his head. "It's like I'm in the fucking Twilight Zone. You and Dorian are apparently not a thing, and then Wells and Thatcher out there." He lifted a hand. "They didn't say shit to me just now. Not to mention they never did get back to me after all those texts I sent them."

Again, that was probably about me. Especially if Ares told Dorian to hold off. They obviously walked away with him.

Bru bunched his fingers in his hair. "Ironically enough, the only one who's come the fuck around was Wolf... who I punched. Then there's you two working on that project when I thought he had beef with you or you had beef with him or whatever." His back hit the lockers. "Like I said, we're in the goddamn Twilight Zone."

He may have been right about the whole Wolf thing. I mean, that was weird, but as far as his friends ignoring him initially, I could clear that up.

"Wells and Thatcher staying away from you isn't your fault." I closed my locker. "At least, not initially."

My brother's eyebrow arched slow, and I proceeded to tell him about the fallout. Well, what I felt comfortable. This whole thing started because Dorian had zero faith in me at all to have his back.

For whatever reason, I didn't want to prove him right and didn't tell Bru too many specifics. I wasn't sure why I cared, but I did tell my brother there'd been a misunderstand. One in which Dorian believed I said something that had gotten him in trouble. I left out what that was, but it had happened right before he'd left and so I hadn't gotten a chance to clear things up.

That had left me at war with Legacy again and Bru by association.

My semi-vague explanation left my brother slack-jawed during the whole conversation. He gripped his bag. "Shit, Sloane. Why didn't you tell me?"

"You were sick." I lifted a hand. "And I didn't want to make you deal with that."

"So you dealt with it all alone?" he asked. "I may have been sick, but my ears weren't. You should have told me. Taking care of each other is a two-way street, you know."

I didn't want it to be. I wanted to be strong. "I'm sorry."

His sigh was heavy. "Well, did the misunderstanding at least get cleared up?" His brow lifted. "Because if not, I'm going to go talk to—"

I raised my hand, cutting that shit off. "I don't need you getting into my shit and punching folks again." I eyed him. "Especially not the most popular boy in school…"

"Most popular?" Ares slid into the conversation. He grinned. "Was I called?"

He would think I'd been talking about him, the arrogant fuck.

Ares had left his fan party, his fist tapping a few passersby. He dropped his arm around Bru. "Y'all talking about me?"

"We were talking about how it's the Twilight Zone around here," Bru huffed and might have explained, but the intercom sounded.

"Good morning, students and faculty. I'm sure some of you have heard, but the academy is currently in search of a new headmaster following the recent tragedy our community has experienced with Principal Mayberry's passing."

"Tragedy," Ares gritted. He shook his head. "Always trying to keep the peace. I suppose she can't help it."

"Who?"

He didn't say, the voice continuing.

"In the meantime, I will be returning as headmaster for the time being. Many of you also know that I've served in this position before, and I'm happy to do so while the board recruits a new headmaster. For those of you who don't know, my name is Dr. Brielle Mallick," the woman said, causing me to blink. "And I invite you all at any time to stop by the headmaster's office and say hello. And for those who need it, counseling services will continue to be available regarding anything you need to discuss. Myself and the rest of the academy staff urge you not to keep your feelings to yourself. There are resources available, and my door is open to all of you if you should ever need it. I bid you a good rest of your day, and here's to a brighter outlook for the rest of the year."

The announcement ended, activity in the hallway continuing. I exchanged a glance with my brother, and when we looked at Ares, he had his fist tight in his curls.

"That's my mother," he said, shocking the fuck out of me. He sighed. "I tried to talk her out of it. She's too fucking busy to come back here, but there was no way she wasn't with all of us going to school here. She thinks she's helping."

Ares tugged his hair back so hard I questioned him pulling it out, and now that I thought about it, that was definitely the woman who'd been speaking that day we'd all gotten the video about Mayberry.

I wondered if his mom had come back to help with the situation then, and I thought to ask Ares about it, but the warning bell rang for first classes.

Ares shoved his hands in his pockets. He jerked his chin at Bru. "You okay with getting around to your classes today?"

"If I'm not, I'm sure she'll do something about it." Bru rolled his eyes at me. "I'm good. Headed to the north building."

"I'm headed in that direction. I'll go with you."

Bru started to walk, but Ares hung back.

"Did you decide what you were doing about your free period?" he asked, and I nodded. He suggested I look into an independent study during our last few sessions in the garage. I still had that free period open with Mayberry being gone. Mr. Keene, the assistant principal, allowed me to do with it what I wished, but I still had to check in with him before I went to the art room every day to make sure he didn't need anything. I wouldn't have to do that anymore if I did an independent study, and I would get course credit for it too.

I forgot how this topic came up during my sessions with Ares, but when he suggested it, I jumped at the chance. Especially since I could do art and get credit.

"The school approved an art class for me," I said. I'd looked right into it after he said something. The class was even college level, and I got to work with an online instructor. I'd get college credit too which was cool. "Thanks for the suggestion."

"No problem. See you around."

"See ya."

He hooked an arm around my brother, and as I watched the pair of them leave, I understood what my brother had said. Him walking with my brother and me. Him talking to *Dorian* for me…

Things definitely felt like the Twilight Zone.

CHAPTER
THIRTY

Dorian

It was the guys' idea to stay away. Well, Wolf's idea.

He was the one calling the shots these days.

My buddy had graciously heard me out the night I needed him, and after, he'd had me listen to him.

Wolf had been working this shit for weeks.

He'd gotten in with my grandfather's wards. He had relationships with them, good ones, and now that he had them, he could cash them in. He was keeping watch over Sloane and her brother.

Because he'd trusted them the whole time.

It'd been me who'd had his head in his ass. My grandfather had taken me down a rabbit hole of lies and deceit, and I'd allowed him because it'd been easy. It had been *easy* to want to believe the lies and go off the grid with my family. I did that, and I could avoid other mental shit going on in my head. It'd been that shit that had me calling Sloane to that cabin in the first place.

I wanted her.

I wanted her so fucking bad I couldn't even think straight, and I didn't do that shit. I didn't *feel* shit, not like that.

As it turned out, my feelings for Sloane had ended up being the very thing to jade me. I'd been in deep with her, and maybe I'd put that out there the day my grandfather had gotten me arrested. He'd read something on me that day, manipulated me.

I wasn't going to be manipulated anymore.

Wolf and I had had to wait until Wells and Thatcher returned to talk more, discuss details and make plans, and it had taken all I had not to act up and play my cards. Not for a second did I believe Grandpa Prinze wasn't up to something when it came to Sloane and her brother, but acting too swiftly could cause problems. He couldn't know I was onto him. He couldn't know my friends and *I* were onto him.

Which we were.

Grandfather had told me himself he didn't act unless he needed to. He'd told me that point-blank in Sloane's kitchen. He'd set up this whole operation, *labored to hell* to make all this shit happen. He had Sloane and her brother living in this town, going to our school, and living off his money. All these things took effort.

Especially since they weren't family.

That was another thing that set off red flags. My grandfather valued family, blood, and he'd told me that himself. Taking care of virtual strangers would be unusual to his character, and even though my friends and I had discovered he'd later left town (after another brief visit), he wouldn't be gone for long.

We found the fucker's house.

He'd purchased one, but this time, it was under his own name. Thatcher had found this, more pieces, more moves...

My grandfather was making plans to return to Maywood

Heights, and he wasn't hiding this time. A second house wouldn't be for Sloane and her brother.

This was another reason Wolf told me to stay away from Sloane and only partially because he found out she was pissed at me. I needed to look impartial to his ward, like she was just another fuck buddy that meant nothing to me. If he thought he'd played me, he wouldn't be looking *at me* while we looked into him.

But ignoring Sloane wasn't easy, and hundred percent not that day when her brother came back. The initial days even before that, I'd made sure to smoke quick with my friends before leaving in the morning. I'd gone on to class and hadn't even sat with them at lunch. That too had been Wolf's idea. He knew personally what I was capable of when it came to Sloane.

I'd punched him in the goddamn face over it.

I lost all sense when it came to her. Fucked in the head. Knowing my grandfather was close to her... could be around her at any moment only made me crazier. My friends had had to talk me down more than once to keep from going over to her house and putting my foot through her door. It didn't sit well my grandfather could just come and go out of her life, *out of her house*, as he pleased. I didn't care if he was out of town or not. He still could.

The only thing keeping me from going truly crazy was that Wolf had been able to get a camera actually in her house recently. Like he'd stated, that project of his was another one of his proactive measures. He and Sloane were working on his senior project, but he'd been using it to gain more intel and get closer to her. He really did have my back the whole time.

I trusted my friend. I trusted all my friends, but ignoring Sloane was easier said than done.

It felt like she was everywhere at school, which made her easy to stalk. I knew her schedule like the back of my hand. I had since that day Thatcher had gotten a hold of it when Sloane had first arrived. It'd been burned in my memory since I'd basically been stalking her then. She'd crossed me, and it'd been necessary.

I knew where Noa Sloane was supposed to be every hour on the hour, and because I did, I should have known better than to hit up the vending machines right outside the room she held her independent study in. This happened to be an art room, and her independent study had also been Wolf's idea. With his mom being the new headmaster now, he wanted to keep Brielle away from anything Sloane kids-related. Getting Sloane to opt for an independent study got her out of the headmaster's office, and if that gave Wolf a little security in regard to his mother, well, I got that. I'd probably do the same thing. This was my grandfather we were dealing with here.

I saw Sloane's ponytail that day by the vending machines. It glided in a sea of dark strands across her back, the girl waltzing right past me.

She hadn't seen me.

She pushed inside the bathroom, her thighs thick and her calves shapely. Her skirts never fit her right, too short since she was so tall.

And too fucking tempting.

I called myself on my madness in the next moment. I didn't follow her in the bathroom, but I might as well have. The girls' restroom was right next door to the tech room, and since I had keys, I opened it up and hid out inside. I *waited*, telling myself all kinds of things. I was just going to watch her when she left the bathroom. I'd get a look at her and wouldn't do anything else. If anything, the glance would just check my obsessive thoughts about her for a second so I could go about my day.

It didn't.

She was coming back, adjusting her ponytail. I watched

those silky strands move and sway through the glass on the door, and I wasn't thinking when I opened the door.

I just took her hand.

I took *her*, yanking her inside the room with me. She shrieked, of course, fought me. I mean, it was dark in here, and she probably thought a crazy person grabbed her.

I was crazy.

I was crazy enough to pin her to the wall. I was crazy enough to *kiss her*, her fists punching at my chest and her teeth and mouth fighting me. She tried to bite my fucking face off at first.

But then, she recognized me.

It was slow, her mouth in delayed recognition. Her eyes opened, studying me and the situation. I got her to kiss back for all of a second before she pushed me off her.

"What the fuck," she growled, shaking, but I didn't stop. I grabbed her by the back of the neck and fused our mouths together.

Euphoria. Goddamn heaven in a single taste.

"Sloane." Her name fell from my mouth in desperation, my tongue flicking hers. "Little fighter."

I'd missed her. I missed her in my head, my dreams. She'd been in there enough.

She curbed the nightmares.

They'd been nonstop since what had happened to Charlie, fear, *loss* a staple in my life.

I didn't want to lose another thing.

"Please stop," she whimpered, our kiss salty. She was crying. "It hurts."

It did hurt. The pain was deep and violent. I crowded her. "Don't fight."

She always fought me. She always fucking fought me. She didn't like fighting.

I was tired of it myself.

I was tired of pain. I was tired of *suffering*. I just wanted this. I wanted fucking something that didn't hurt, and she was the one thing that never had. She was my peace always.

She was my refuge.

"I want you," I admitted, making her gasp. "Please, Sloane. I'm sorry. I'm so fucking sorry…"

Her breath stolen, her fingers clenched tight on my shirt. They relaxed as I braced her face.

"I should have believed you," I ground out, my tongue diving into her mouth. "I want you so bad. I should have—"

She shoved me off her, and so quickly, it took me a second to realize what had happened.

Especially when she slapped me.

The hit burned hot, searing hard into my flesh, but I'd been hit harder. Sloane was a chick. She wasn't hitting as hard as one of my boys when things got rough.

"You're so fucked up." Her chest hiked, trembling up and down. "You are, and you're trying to drag me down in that shit with you."

I didn't understand, and she only laughed.

She lifted a finger. "You're a headcase, Dorian Prinze. You're *fucked* and you're…" She swallowed. "You're too late."

Too late.

Her laughter continued, so fucking dry. I'd pulled some of her hair out of her ponytail, and she pushed a veil of it out of her face. "You don't want me. It's your ego. It's…" She raised and dropped her hands. "I don't know what the fuck it is, but people who want people don't treat them the way you have me. They don't *abandon* them and call them liars."

I'd made a mistake, shaking my head. My throat jumped. "I know I've fucked up."

"You don't know the half." She pulled her ponytail down. "I told you to stay the hell away from me, and I meant it. You don't know what you want, and even if you did, *I* want nothing to do with it. You treat people like shit, and you've especially treated me like shit."

I wished I could just tell her, *tell her everything*. She needed to know my grandfather was playing her and her brother. She needed to know he was my grandfather.

But there was too much risk.

My buddies and I didn't know the answers. In fact, we knew little to nothing, and Grandfather was right. It might be too late for the truth now with her, and her going rogue and doing something random once we told her our theories could cause more harm than good. My grandfather was a determined man, a violent man.

And if she got hurt…

She couldn't know, not yet, and I said nothing after what she said.

Her smile was haunted, as sad as it was gorgeous. Noa Sloane could bring a man to his fucking knees with her beauty.

She had me.

Maybe she wanted me to fight, fight her and what she said. Maybe she wanted me to *fight for her*.

I should have.

Shaking her head, she left me, and before I thought better of it, I went after her. She ran right into someone the moment the door opened, my buddy grabbing her.

Wolf glanced up, probably roaming the halls. We'd all been taking details. Just keeping our eyes open in case my grandfather attempted to try something at school.

This must have been Wolf's shift.

"Sloane?" he questioned, but then she shoved him away. She speed-walked down the hall, and he started to go after, but then spotted me.

He blinked then, his eyes flashing. "What did you do?"

I blinked myself, not expecting that reaction.

Especially when his eyes narrowed.

They cut *hard* in my direction, his dark eyebrows descending like storm clouds. Before I had a chance to get a word in edgewise, my buddy was striding down the hallway. He headed in the same direction as Sloane, and I fell back against the door, knowing I'd fucked up. I'd told my buddies I'd stay away. I'd told them I'd keep my distance.

But today, what just happened told me I obviously couldn't.

CHAPTER
THIRTY-ONE

Sloane

Ares was really quiet that night when we worked in my garage. He was always quiet, but this time it was different. He didn't have his earbuds in, which, for some reason, made me super aware of him. Or maybe it was that I knew he was aware *of me*, and that made all the awkward shit that had happened with his friend this afternoon that much worse. Ares had come after me following that, but I'd told him to fuck off and hadn't seen him again until we met tonight.

It was a long goddamn night. It was one full of Ares Mallick's glances. It was like he was checking to make sure I was okay or some shit, and eventually, I threw my paintbrush at him. He was working at the trunk of the car, and the brush caught him right in the face.

"The fuck?" He popped up, snarling. We'd almost finished the side he was on and probably only had a few more days on this thing before the piece came together. He tipped his chin at me. "What was up with that?"

I rolled my eyes, shaking my head and turning back toward the mural. "That's because you won't stop fucking looking at me. You've been doing that shit since we started the night."

And he'd been more than obvious about it. If he had something to say, he might as well say it.

A sigh occurred behind me, loud enough where I heard it. Eventually, I heard him make his way over, and he watched me paint for a while.

"It's looking good," he chose to say. I supposed it was easier than actually talking about anything else. When we did talk, it was about art. He'd said never to bring personal shit in here, so we didn't.

Ares started to walk away, but then he braced his arms.

"You good?" he asked, but when I didn't say anything, he pushed himself into view. His brow arched. "Sloane."

"Ares?" I continued to paint, barely looking at him. He sighed again, and I didn't miss when he sat back down on his stool. He didn't stare at me this time, but he also didn't put his earbuds in.

"I talked to him."

I turned after what he said, and unlike most of the night, he had his head down, his full concentration on the paint.

He swirled a long stroke. "He told me what happened, and I told him that wasn't cool. Especially after I told him to back off."

"Why even bother?"

His shrug was subtle. "You seemed upset."

Again, why would he *care*?

"You better be careful, Mallick," I said, pausing. "You're kind of looking like a friend. Actually, you look like a friend a lot."

He stopped painting. He gazed up. "Or maybe I'm not an asshole." His lips tightened. "Maybe in all your judgment, I'm not as much of a dick as you want me to be."

"And maybe I'm not a bitch." I tilted my head. "And I never did get an apology for that. That first day?"

Not to mention he'd called me a cunt, and God only knew what else. He'd been a tool. He knew it, and that was outside of him not believing me either at first.

His nod was slow. "I did snap-judge you. I did *judge* you, but I was wrong, little."

He was wrong…

"I'm sorry." He opened his hands. "I was in the wrong, and about more than a few things since then. I'm sorry for all of it."

I honestly didn't know what to say to that. I never thought I'd *hear* that.

"Anyway, are you okay? I mean…" He pulled the paint towel off his shoulder, twisting it. "I'd like not to be enemies. I know I've called a truce in the past, but I actually mean it this time."

I definitely hadn't forgotten about the whole lingerie-party thing.

Nor the fact that he just asked me if I was okay.

"Dude, this is looking sweet."

We both angled around, Bru waltzing into the garage. Bru stepped over a few paint cans, and with his arrival, he'd cracked the weird fucking vibe in here.

My brother lifted a hand to Ares, and though his teammate didn't seem like the type to appreciate people poking in to stare at his work, Ares was cool about it.

"Thanks, man," Ares said. "It's really coming together."

"I'll say." Bru angled in to look, and it was crazy that he'd just been sick. He had so much of his strength back, seeming really well. He propped his hands on his hips. "Anything I can do?"

"No."

Bru whirled around. Ares and I both had said that at the same time. In fact, at the exact same time.

I laughed, Ares too, and my brother rolled his eyes.

I patted the air. "It's just, we put a lot of work into this." Dozens of man hours, in fact, and the last thing we needed was a rogue stroke mucking it up. Not to mention Ares would probably annihilate my brother if he did. I pointed to the garage doors. "But you can make yourself nice and cozy on that chair and watch."

The chair currently housed a couple cans of paint, and helping me out, Ares cleared it. Ares dusted if off with his rag. "Perfect place for you, brother."

I couldn't help it. I busted out laughing, and Ares did too. It was nice since things had been weird before.

My brother lifted his hands.

"I can tell when I'm not wanted." He eyed us, but then laughed too. "And you two have been spending far too much time together. You're even starting to laugh like each other."

That had me rolling my eyes, and I hopped over a paint can to my brother. I mock-kicked him out of the garage. "Go to bed. It's late."

It was well after midnight, and we both had school tomorrow.

Walking away, my brother waved a hand behind his head. I shook my head. "Pardon him. He's aware we need to finish this, but he just doesn't care."

He'd probably be in here all night if I let him.

Ares didn't say anything, and when I pivoted, he had his hands on a part of the trunk we hadn't painted. He was staring off into the garage, and I waved my hand. "Earth to Mallick."

He blinked, his gaze colliding with mine. He pushed off the car. "Actually, it is getting kind of late." He tapped the air. "Probably should wrap it up for the night."

He'd never cared about it being late before, but since I was tired too, I didn't disagree.

Ares immediately bent down to start cleaning up, and when he did, I noticed a chain slip out of his tank top.

"What's that?"

Ares angled his head down, his hand clamping the necklace. I came over and nodded at it, and he opened his hand.

"I used to have something like that," I said, recognizing the emblem. "But mine wasn't a necklace."

It'd been a bracelet actually, a charm like that on it.

I studied his, smiling. "I lost it a long time ago, but yeah. It looked just like it."

In fact, it was uncanny, same shape and everything.

Ares's finger moved across his. "How did you get it?"

"My parents." I shrugged. "I don't remember when. I kind of just always had it."

Ares's head tilted. "You said you lost it?"

"Yeah." I leaned back. I realized then I'd gotten closer to see it. Like real close. "Probably something a bunch of parents give out or something. Is that how you got yours?"

"Yeah." He let it go. "Do you remember where you lost it? When?"

Laughing, I cuffed my arms. "If I did, I'd probably still have it, right?"

"Right." He laughed, but not quite like me. It was short as he studied the garage. He grabbed his hoodie. "I'll see you tomorrow. We'll work first thing."

I told him that was cool, thinking about the bracelet as he got into his Hummer. I wished I could remember where I'd lost it. I recalled loving that thing and had always worn it.

I'd probably loved it more because my mom specifically had given it to me. I didn't have a lot of things from her and even fewer memories. They seemed to wipe away each year I got older, my memories of her fading.

I drew her that night in my studio before bed, her face. I tried to remember the slants and curves and just about fell asleep with a paintbrush in my hand. I never could get the face right, though. She looked oblong, blank. My memory was grasping at things I didn't have.

Maybe, in the morning, I'd try again.

CHAPTER
THIRTY-TWO

Sloane

I'd woken up Friday morning to find the Legacy boys outside my house.

They'd brought a flatbed truck.

It was just after 5 AM, and I'd only gotten up to pee. I had swift plans to go back to bed after that, but after spying them all through the window, I raced downstairs. I had a hoodie hanging up on the door, and after tugging that on (mostly to account for the fact I didn't have a *bra on*), I slipped on a pair of high-tops. I was rushing so damn quick, I was lucky I didn't put my brother's shoes on.

I bristled in the garage. All of them were in there. Wells and Thatcher were waving and directing the car Ares and I'd been painting.

The dark prince was inside it.

Dorian had his arm hooked behind the headrest, backing the car up with the guidance of his two friends. The flatbed was apparently for the car because they were having Dorian drive the thing in line with the truck. The only one *not* messing with the car was Ares, who was currently tethering the other part of our project to the top of his Hummer.

He'd covered it and everything, and with all the activity behind him, he hadn't noticed me until I was all up on him.

None of them had.

All the activity stopped the moment I was in front of Ares. Wells and Thatcher were literally mid-wave, and without the guidance, Dorian himself stopped the car. He faced forward, gazing through the windshield.

He stopped on me, his big fist clenching and unclenching the wheel. He had his school uniform on, though the tie was undone and his shirt was open. Apparently, he had plans to go to class after whatever they were doing here.

I hated that I studied him as long as I did before noticing the others. Wells and Thatcher had their uniforms on too, both guys rocking on their patent leather shoes. They were obviously at a standstill on what to do like Dorian.

"Fuck, we were trying to get this done before you got up."

This came from Ares, his hands lowering from the tethers. He too had his uniform on. Though his was minus the jacket. Upon further observation, I noticed he had it in the front seat of his ride.

The tall boy came around his Hummer, tugging his shirt down. "Shit, we woke you. Didn't we?" he asked, and after waving off his friends, he came over to me.

I noticed right away Wells and Thatcher continued what they'd been doing. Wells proceeded in waving Dorian while Thatcher got everything going with the truck. The only person who *hadn't* moved was Dorian himself.

He was at a standstill behind the wheel, his wrist resting on it. Ares caught me watching and turned toward his friend.

The two made eye contact for several seconds until the dark prince decided to let it go.

Hooking an arm around the back of the headrest again, he

continued to back up the car, and the next thing *I knew*, Ares Mallick was waving me to come with him.

"What is this?" I asked, staring behind him. Business as usual proceeded to continue on without the distraction of me.

Ares shoved his hands in his pockets. "Well, you know we're finished. I asked the guys to help me move everything. We're taking the piece to the school."

Well, it would have been nice to know *that* was happening. And we had finished last night, I supposed. Technically, a couple days ago. We'd wanted to make sure everything looked okay after the paint dried, and last night had just been more of a touch-up session.

I'd ended up going to bed about three hours ago, but before that, there hadn't been any talk about moving everything right away.

Let alone who he was going to recruit for help.

This made sense since these guys were his friends, but Ares also knew how strongly I felt about one of them specifically. I growled. "You could have asked me. I could have driven the car over to the school."

His eyes narrowed. "No offense, little. But no one is driving that thing. Not after all that fucking work we did on it."

I got that but still.

"And if you haven't noticed, this thing also weighs a ton." He jerked his thumb back toward the mural. "I wasn't going to ask you or Bru to help me with it. I think you know why. Your brother and I probably could have handled it, but I wasn't about to risk you raging on my ass for even asking him."

My smile started slow. We really had been spending too much time together. He was really starting to get me and how I worked. I *would* have raged on his ass.

He smiled too. "Anyway, we'll be out of your hair soon. Go back to bed. We don't need anything from you."

Well, now that I was up, trying to go back to sleep would be hilarious.

Especially knowing Dorian was here.

He was currently out of the car, helping the guys to finish loading up, and I didn't miss him pass a glance in our direction.

Ares hadn't either. He'd returned back to the other part of our piece, but still had eyes on the situation. Currently, he messed with tethers while his friends completed the other job. Thatcher and Wells eventually got inside the flatbed once their group finished, but Dorian hadn't joined them.

He came over to help Ares, and I twitched when I was forced to share more space than was comfortable with him. I mean, my garage wasn't a small garage, but he was in there with me.

I shifted in my high-tops, hands clenching in my hoodie. I tried to put off disinterest, that I didn't care one way or the other that Dorian was in my space, but who was I kidding? I did care.

I still did.

But this didn't mean anything to me. I told him things were too late. His apology was too late, and I meant that.

I kicked back a foot against my Chevelle, making sure both boys knew I was there. This was still my space, and they were both inside it.

"D, you still got those extra bungie cords in your car?"

"Yeah, in the trunk." The dark prince tossed him his keys. "Should be some in the roadside emergency kit."

Now Dorian's car wasn't far away. But it *looked* like miles.

Especially when Ares left us.

The tall boy sprinted away to his friend's Audi—also parked outside my house. Ares opened the trunk, and Dorian kept his distance while he waited. I averted my eyes, and his head lowered, a sea of perfect blond breezing in the wind.

"Hey."

I panned in his direction, clashing suddenly with dark eyes. I was surprised he'd actually spoke to me.

I'd been more than clear before.

But here he was, hands in his pockets. His dress pants fitted tight to his muscular legs, his stance wide and his signature combat boots gracing his feet. He never did give a fuck about the school's dress code. His sleeves were shoved up above his thick forearms. His shoulders lifted. "How you been?"

How have I *been?*

I wondered if I should tell him before or *after* he'd once again made a fool out of me. Who knew how far things would have gone in the computer lab had I not stopped it.

In fact, I knew exactly what would have happened. He would have made me his whore once again. How easy he got me to bend for him.

I looked away again, and by then, Ares had come back. He was well aware his friend had been talking to me, waving him back to help. For whatever reason, Ares "Wolf" Mallick continued to look out for me, and how weird their dynamic had changed. When I'd first met them, Ares had clearly answered to him.

Today, as it seemed, something different was happening, because not only did Dorian leave, but he also assisted Ares with no hesitation. Ares directed, and Dorian did what he asked, shocking the fuck out of me. Dorian was so crazy, *his control* crazy. He'd made me bend *to that* more than a few times too.

I watched, nearly fascinated by the dynamic. Ares tossed a tether, and Dorian secured it, doing it exactly how Ares wanted it. After the boys were done, Ares mentioned he was going to tell Wells and Thatcher to go ahead and take off, and at this point, I'd been standing idle. I mean, there was nothing for me to do.

Well, nothing but watch Dorian Prinze come back over to me.

Which he did, his advance strong and with clear intentions. I just wished I knew what those intentions were.

"Can I talk to you?" He clasped fingers behind his neck, rubbing. It was almost an *awkward* gesture, and the dark prince wasn't awkward. His lips pulled tight. "I understand if you don't want to. In fact, I fucking get that completely."

I blinked, not expecting that. For one thing, he was asking and not being an asshole about it. I hugged my arms. "You actually want to talk?" I popped a shoulder. "Well, that's new."

This boy didn't talk. He *took*.

His hands cuffed his biceps, his nod slow. "I deserve that."

He deserved more than that.

And I was done with this conversation.

I started to walk away, but he called my name.

And why did I always stop?

I closed my eyes, pivoting. He hadn't gotten any closer, but that didn't matter. I still felt his reach, didn't matter the proximity.

I could even smell him, taste him. His clear cool scent wafted in the air like a drug, and it was a habit I couldn't seem to kick.

"I just wanted to say I'm sorry," he said, frowning. "I'm sorry I didn't believe you. I'm sorry for how I left you and how I left things."

"You already said that." He'd forced himself on me yet again, taken from me because that was what he did. He knew how fucked up we *both* were, and how I always responded to it. I lifted my chin. "In the computer lab, remember?"

I definitely hadn't forgotten.

"Well, I'm saying it again." He started to come closer, but his fists clenched, and he stopped. "And I shouldn't have done that. And definitely not in there." He cringed. "We take girls in there."

Even better. I nodded. "Nice."

"But that's…" He cut around, finding my eyes. "That's not what I wanted to do that day."

"What had you wanted to do?"

"I don't know." The words were low. "I guess I just wanted to be close to you."

Why did he keep *saying* things like this?

He was making this so much worse.

I didn't want to push him away. *He'd made me.* "You're an asshole."

"I know, and I'm not trying to be. Fuck, it's driving me crazy. *You* drive me crazy." He shook his head. "I hate what I've done to you and how I made you feel. I hate that I didn't believe you—"

"Why didn't you?" I'd never given him a reason to think he couldn't trust me. "I never said a word about where you were that day. I'd never do that to you. I…"

I stopped myself before I said something stupid, and what did I really know about feelings and bullshit anyway?

Let alone anything deeper.

The one time I tried he'd done what he had to me.

His jaw moved. "I know. *I know.* I just…" He stared away. "I'm not good at this."

"Good at what?"

He put a hand out. "*This.* This shit. Us."

"This shit?" A perfect sum-up of what we were or were not. I squeezed my arms. "I don't want you."

"Well, I want you." He closed the distance, disappeared *space*, and I thought he'd do what he always did. He'd take.

He waited.

He stood there *waiting*, and the side of his neck flushed in so much color. His nostrils flared. "Sloane…"

"I told you it's too late." My throat tight, I tried so hard not to fucking blink, *cry*. If I blinked, I knew the tears would come down. "I can't do this anymore, Dorian. We're so bad for each other."

It used to be a joke, our madness. We were hate-fucks and anger.

We were aggression and heaven.

Combined, it just made for a recipe of chaos and disaster, and my heart couldn't physically take anymore.

"We aren't, and it doesn't have to be how it's been." He wet his lips. "I know I screwed up with you. I know I'm *fucked up*, and everything you said was right. It's always been right, but I want to try to not be so fucked up." His throat worked. "I want to take you out. On a date. A real fucking date and not me being an asshole for once."

I twitched.

He smiled. "I want to show you I'm serious. Serious about this, and that I'm not afraid to admit when I'm wrong. That I have faults, and I'm human."

Blinking, I noticed Ares over Dorian's shoulder. At this point, he'd gotten in his car, but he was still looking at us. He'd obviously gone into detail with Dorian about conversations Ares himself and I'd had.

I mean, those were my words coming out of Dorian's mouth.

For some reason, Ares was going to bat for us. He was *rooting* for us.

As my thoughts mulled over that, Dorian managed to advance closer. I could make out every various shade of brown in his eyes now.

"Please give me a chance to show that," he continued, and he was really pleading here in front of me. He grinned. "I'm not a complete asshole. I swear, I'm not."

There were these moments, a time or two. Sometimes that dark filter would slip, and he let a part of himself out. A part that wasn't so cold and thorny.

A part that wasn't so distant.

He let me get close, but so quickly he'd pull it right away.

"It's..." I started to say. "It's not that easy. *You're* not that easy."

His head lifted, his nod firm. Ares's window pulled down, and Dorian and I both angled around.

"You coming, D?" Ares tipped his chin. "Probably should get this thing to school. Wells and Thatch will wonder what's up."

They'd apparently left while Dorian and I were talking. The flatbed truck was gone, and it was only the three of us now.

"Two seconds," Dorian said, facing me. "What do you say? It doesn't have to be what you think. You and me?"

But it very well could, and he hadn't given me reason enough to go that way and take the risk.

At least, not yet.

"You should probably get that stuff to school," I said. "You go do that, and I might think about it after that."

His eyebrow rose slow. "You might?"

I couldn't help but smile, shaking my head. Why did this boy get me like this? In my head and *girly*. "I might."

His grin was wiry, and completely knowing. My poker face completely sucked, and he knew it.

He laughed, rolling his shoulders back. "You're not going to make this easy, are you?"

Probably as easy as he'd made it for me since I got wrapped up with him. He'd put me through hell.

Maybe it was time he went through a little of his own.

CHAPTER
THIRTY-THREE

Sloane

Reason #1 why I'm fucked up: *I tend to not trust my instincts. If I had, I wouldn't have lost you.*

What I'm going to do about it: *This note is a start.*

- Dorian

———

That was the first note I'd gotten from Dorian Prinze. It fell out of my locker that morning I'd seen him and the others at my house.

They didn't stop.

The next few days we had at school, they arrived in the most random places. I found them in my bookbag, as well as in my *gym locker* of all places. He was obviously recruiting his Court minions to help him out, and each note started the same way. They consisted of a reason as to why he was fucked up, his own words, and then a solution as to how he was going to fix it. Reason number two was that he had trouble admitting his own faults. These were obviously my words, and his solution then had been simple. He was going to give me notes until he proved to me that wasn't the case. That solution sounded a lot like his first, but with the rest, he started to get more creative...

As well as even more personal.

Reason #6: I don't like anything that threatens me. That goes for anything from people to my performance on the field. I actually went vegan so I could play better, but hated it so much those first few months I thought I was going to bitch out. I've since learned to appreciate it, and now, I'm vegan because I actually like it—mostly. Don't tell the boys and especially don't tell my father. He'd look at my ass like I was crazy. My mother is a vegan, and he never understood it.

What I'm going to do about it: I'm going to try new things like I handled veganism. I hope you'll see that soon. You're the ultimate threat, Noa Sloane.

- Dorian

Reason #12: Personal shit gives me hives, whether it's learning about others or giving them things about myself. This is mostly because I hate fucking small talk. Every minute means something. Every hour. Every second. I don't like wasting anything for the sake of goddamn normalcy and societal expectations. Fuck society.

What I'm going to do about it: Refer to reason #6. I literally thought telling you about actually liking veganism would kill me. It didn't. Reason #12 is officially corrected.

- D

Reason #15: *I find myself thinking about what your reasons are, i.e., the things about yourself you might not like, but I could never see myself asking you about them. For some reason these notes are easier.*

What I'm going to do about it: *One day I will ask you, but one better—I won't expect anything back. This will lead into my next reason why I'm fucked up. Just wait for it. It's coming soon.*

- *dark prince (yeah, I remember your nickname for me)*

Reason #16: *I have issues with anger and control. I could blame everything on what happened with Charlie, and though that contributed, that isn't the reason. I believe, at the heart, it's ingrained in me if that's at all possible. You wouldn't think shit could be passed down, but if you knew some of the fucked-up things in my family history, you'd think different. It actually scares me sometimes (Reason #12 corrected again, hah), which is a huge reason I respect the hell out of my father. He has these same issues, but you'd never know it unless you know him. He's learned to embrace his darkness and has somehow conquered it. He's the best person I know outside of my mother.*

What I'm going to do about it: *Listen to the announcements today.*

- *whatever you want me to be*

———

That last note, his reason number sixteen, I read at my locker that day. It'd fallen out like many of the others before, but this one felt different.

It was also the first one that made me want to see him.

His reasons were diving deeper, like he was exposing himself on lined paper right in front of me. Obviously, he hadn't said these things to me, but he'd written them.

I didn't know how to feel about that, and even though I'd been shamelessly looking forward to every one of his reasons, I hadn't been so willing to let him back into my life. He was fucked up, and him *professing his affection now* could have just been a ploy. This boy got what he wanted *from everyone*, so why should I be any different than a toy he suddenly couldn't have? I was probably the first person who'd said no to him.

"You got one minute, Dorian."

The voice came from the intercom, female and who I knew to be Ares's mom, Mrs. Mallick. I'd yet to see her, but I had heard her voice over the intercom every morning when she did the announcements.

"That's all I need," came a deep voice, *Dorian's* voice. He chuckled, and judging by the female laughter that followed, something told me he'd gotten Ares's mom in on this. I was well aware all of the Legacy families were close. Some shuffling occurred through the speakers. "Listen up. This message is for one person, so the rest of you fuckers can go about your business."

"*Dorian*," Mrs. Mallick gritted, but the smile in her voice couldn't be denied. She was disciplining him *clearly* because she felt she had to in that moment. "That's your one warning. I mean it."

"Sorry," he said, though he didn't sound sorry. He sounded playful, and my tummy tossed. It was rare I saw him this way. In fact, only one time.

It was the day we'd destroyed that house together, Principal Mayberry's house. Ironically enough, I'd goaded him to do it, and surprisingly, it'd been one of the best times of my life. It'd been freeing for me too.

"Like I said, this is for one person," Dorian stated again,

and my stomach clenched. I didn't necessarily know if I wanted to hear what he had to say. Honestly, it was easier just being mad at him. It was easier pushing him away and not having to feel the brevity of my own reasons. I may have called him fucked up, but I definitely had my own issues. He cleared his throat. "So if you're not Noa Sloane, you can continue on with your previously scheduled broadcast."

People stopped talking in the hallway.

Some even gasped.

For all they knew, Dorian was about to ruin my life again. The last time he'd placed me before the entire student body, he'd been removing my name.

"I messed up with this girl," he continued on, my heart racing. "And I told her in a letter, many letters, how I was going to not mess up anymore. I promised her I'm going to be human, and this is me being that."

I stared around the hallway. All eyes were on me.

"My reason number sixteen talked about anger, *control*. So this is me putting it all out there and handing it completely over to you, Noa."

More gasps sounded, and I hugged my books.

"I've asked you out recently, and you both swiftly and reasonably shut my ass down. Sorry, Brielle. I mean, Principal Mallick."

Muted laughter occurred over the speaker. I was assuming from our temporary headmaster.

"Ten seconds, Dorian," she said.

"Noted," he returned, chuckling, and I listened with bated breath for what he was about to say. I was actually anticipating it like an idiot. I really needed to stop getting my hopes up for this boy.

"So here is my official declaration, in which the public humiliation following said declaration will only be for the benefit of this girl. She's trying to teach me a lesson, and I deserve to be taught one."

He sounded serious, no humor at all in his voice.

"So once again, I'm asking you to go out with me, Noa," he said. "I want you to get to know me and see that I'm for real about all I've said to you. I also want to get to know you, but I'm a stubborn SOB, so here's some incentive so I don't have to wait too long for your answer. I, Dorian Riley Prinze, will play in a dress every home football game until I hear back from you. I've never worn a dress, but I have a feeling it will be just as humiliating as it sounds. The ball's in your court now. Have fun with it."

He handed the mic over after that, saying as much to Ares's mom, and I stood in the hallway slack-jawed.

"Proceed with your classes, everyone," Mrs. Mallick said, and both snickers and gasps in the hallway commenced. Almost instantly, I got a text from my brother. He wanted to know if I heard the announcement just now.

I definitely had.

Shaking my head, I told my brother as much, and I laughed too. Dorian couldn't be serious.

"I see he stopped being an idiot."

I looked up to spot a familiar face, but I'd be honest. It was one I was starting to forget as of late.

Bow Reed had still been keeping her distance from me, but I noticed she hadn't been sitting with the rest of Legacy at lunch when I saw them. I didn't know if she was opting to eat somewhere else or what, but she hadn't been sitting with them.

She had a gray sweater on with the Windsor Prep crest, her signature ruby brooch right in the center of her dress shirt. The bright ruby matched the ones in her ears. Her hair was up in two space buns. This girl couldn't manage to *not* look cute for the life of her. Her head tilted. "And I'm pretty sure he's actually going to do it. He's never gone to such lengths before. Hell, I don't even know if I've ever seen him date."

Boys like him probably didn't. Not when they could get anything they wanted.

"I'm glad he is." She pushed a tendril of hair behind her ear. "And though I didn't need to be told, I knew he was wrong about you."

So she'd been told the truth, had she? Of course, she had. Dorian and all the guys were her family. My back hit the lockers. "I never lied to you, Bow. And I'm sorry I gave you a reason to think any different."

Her blink was slow. She pressed a hand to her chest. "You're apologizing to me?" she asked, those lashes rapid-firing now. "But I've been an ass. Like a big ole ass."

I smiled. Bow Reed cursing was like the most adorable fucking thing. She was so dang chipper and couldn't even do it right.

"I'm sorry, Sloane. I messed up. We all did." Her head shook. "It'd been my brother to tell me the truth, and he looked sick while he did."

"He did?" My brow hiked.

She nodded. "He feels terrible. I heard him talking about it on his computer with the others one night." She adjusted her bag. "I guess Ares told him and the guys to give you space, which was why I'm surprised Dorian just did what he did. Ares mentioned you were pissed at him, and I'm sure none of them were in your good graces after they didn't believe you."

Well, that explained the parking lot, and the Wells-and-Thatcher-keeping-their-distance thing. My brother had been there, but I had as well. Them staying back had been about me.

As it turned out, Ares Mallick struck again.

"I would have come forward sooner, but I didn't want to make things worse," she continued. "I hadn't believed you either."

Again, I'd given her reason not to. I shrugged. "You're

right about what you said. I'd been dishonest with you before."

"Even still I should have been better." She frowned. "I'm really sorry, Sloane. I wanted to be there for the guys, for Dorian. It was such a bad time. His parents had to leave town, and the press has *just* left them all alone…"

"I get it," I said, because I did. It was just a complicated time, and I understood.

But it was still hard, Dorian and our situation so hard for me.

"I hope you'll consider forgiving me," she said, and I grinned.

"What would I look like not forgiving you," I told her being honest. "You forgave me that one time, but if I do, I have a condition."

She appeared legit hopeful, on the toes of her Mary Janes. "What's that?"

"You come with me to this football game." I was actually considering it, more than considering it. "If I'm going to watch Dorian Prinze be an idiot, I'm not doing it alone."

Her brow jumped. "You're really going to go?"

I shouldn't. In fact, I should flat-out refuse. I should let go and let him be an idiot.

But like most things with us, it wasn't that simple. Dorian had gotten in deep.

Enough for me to tell Bow Reed yes.

CHAPTER
THIRTY-FOUR

Sloane

Bru came with me to Friday's game, and I was surprised. Though he was technically still on the Windsor Prep football team, he wasn't allowed to play. He'd spoken to the head coach about possibly reversing his thoughts on the rest of the season, but his coach held firm on the decision. There was too much risk that the players' workouts would be too strenuous for him, and Bru was too far behind in his academics anyway to play at all. At least for this year's season.

This bummed my brother enough where he hadn't wanted to talk about football at all, but perhaps, he came to simply see if Dorian Prinze would make good on his promise tonight to play all home games in a dress.

He like the rest of the stadium.

Windsor Prep football fans always turned out, but this was even unusual for them. There was barely any bench space and even the opposing side had jam-packed bleachers. My brother and I came in right before the national anthem, and I wished we had arrived early. Gratefully, I ended up spotting the little rabbit at the top of the stands. She waved her arms, guiding us to come to her.

Bow had her spirit paint on and held a sign with the academy's giant-ass mascot on it. Known as simply *the king*, the ape growled with a furious bite, and that was partly why I made Bow out so quickly. Her sign was huge, the gorilla large.

"Sloane!" Bow called, a flush in her cheeks. I wasn't surprised since I was shivering myself down to my jeans. Maywood Heights's weather was about to take a turn for the worst toward the end of the fall season. My jacket was barely enough for today. Bow moved her hoodie off the bleachers when we got there. "Saved us some seats."

She seemed like the type to plan ahead, and I grinned, my brother and I taking them. Bow had a blanket too, and I took full advantage of it next to her. I offered it to my brother, but of course, *like a dude*, he said no.

I gave it to him anyway, putting it over his legs. "We don't need another reason for you to get sick."

His eyes lifted to the sky, and Bow frowned.

"Heard about that. You okay now?" she asked him.

"Doing fine. Though you'd never know judging by my sister." He elbowed at my hands. I was still arranging his part of the blanket. He growled. "If you're going to make me wear it, at least let me fucking do it."

"Then do *it*," I growled now, shaking my head and noticed right away we had an audience. Half the people in our section of the stands were looking at *me*, not us. I waved a hand. "You all want to take a picture? No? Then move along. The show will be over there."

I wasn't stupid. I knew everyone knew that I was at the center of what had happened at school, but I wasn't happy about it. Dorian was trying to prove a point here today, and I really didn't want to show up, but I'd already told Bow.

"Sloane," Bow *and my brother* said together. Bow chuckled. "Why are you so combative?"

"Right. People are just curious. Curious about you?" My brother cocked his head. "You going to take him back if he actually does this?"

I scoffed then, pulled out my cell phone. "I'm just here to capture him doing this crazy shit," I said, actually telling myself that. It was the only reason I could justify being here tonight.

"Sure." Bru exchanged a glance with Bow, and my eyes nearly rolled to the back of my head. They could think what they wanted. I was here to see Dorian Prinze make an ass of himself, point-blank. I was pretty sure this whole thing was just a ploy to get me out here anyway and more of his mind games.

Odds were, he wouldn't even put on the dress, and he better hope for his sake he did. I was already pissed off at him enough.

"Hey. It's about to start." Bow stood up. Everyone else did as well as when the announcer got everything going for tonight's game. They started with the anthem and everything, the school's pep band playing. After that, they announced the opposing team, but it wasn't until the king came out that everyone started freaking out.

The academy's mascot flipped down the field. I was sure that was a nice little feat since he was a big-ass gorilla.

"Here they come." Bow waved her sign, chanting, and though I looked around, I couldn't see anything.

Mostly because the stands exploded.

Everyone was hooting, hollering, and pumping their fists. Bru was pumping his too, but since he was taller than me, he got a better vantage point. People were even standing on the bleachers, and it wasn't until Bow and I joined them that I could see our team dancing down the field.

Our football team was a bunch of arrogant fuckers, the lot

of them shaking their hips and dancing. They liked to intimidate the other team this way, but I had to say, I couldn't find Dorian and the Legacy boys in the bunch.

"There. There. Look." Bow pointed, and I should have known they'd all be last. Dorian and his crew always made up the rear.

They were the stars of the show.

Ares came roaring out. He actually roared at full volume, his namesake "Wolf" on the back of his jersey. I didn't know how he'd gotten away with that, but Thatcher and Wells weren't far behind.

Thatcher threw his hands up, saying, "Let's go!" while Wells threw himself on top of him, chanting the same. The academy's quarterback came out last, and I think it was to everyone's surprise to find Dorian dressed the same way as his teammates. His huge thighs were housed in his regular uniform pants, the gear underneath his jersey making him big and bulky. He appeared the same as he normally would except he held his helmet instead of wore it.

Tucked under his arm, Dorian waved to the crowd with a gloved hand. He scanned the area, our bleachers.

The air horn sound came out of nowhere.

I literally almost fell off the back of the bleachers when Bow tooted a loud-ass horn. It was just like the one my dad kept in the back of the Chevelle and freaked everyone else the fuck out. They all covered their ears, and the sound definitely had the entire arena looking in this direction.

It had *Dorian* looking in this direction.

His hand lowered when he so obviously heard it. Smirking, he pointed in *our* direction, and that's when I realized what Bow was holding. She'd flipped that dang sign over, and on the other side wasn't the school's mascot.

She's here! the sign said in glittery orange paint. She even outlined it with navy to emphasize it. I grabbed her arm. "What the fuck, Bow?"

She shrugged. As if she wasn't completely guilty for whatever the fuck this was. The crowd started laughing, and that was when I shot my gaze forward. Dorian was no longer staring at the bleachers.

He was in the middle of field, stripping. He'd tossed his helmet off to the side, jerking off his uniform top.

"Holy fuck. He's actually wearing it," Bru chanted, punching at the air. Dorian had discarded all his gear, his broad chest covered in dark silk. It sparkled and shined.

He wore a dress, an *A line*. He pulled the skirt out of his pants, and when it hung all wrinkled and fucked up around his hips, I roared in laughter.

"No fucking way." I was losing my shit, *epically*. One of the biggest boys and thickest boys I'd ever seen was wearing a sleeveless dress in the middle of the football field. It even had a plunging neckline.

And he wore the shit out of it.

Dorian danced in the field, completely making an ass out of himself, and when I tell you, this boy had *hype* men. Wells, Thatcher, and Ares backed him up, and even though they weren't wearing dresses, they supported him. The clique gathered around him in a semicircle, shouting and amping him up. All the while, Dorian flexed his biceps in his little black dress, and I thought I was going to throw up I was laughing so hard.

I honestly thought their coaches might have something to say about all this, but they stood off to the side. Their arms crossed, they simply shook their heads at the antics before waving the boys in.

They did come, *eventually*. They slapped hands before sprinting back to the team. Dorian brought up the rear, and though he put his uniform back on, he left the skirt out. He got to the sidelines, and after he put his helmet on, he whirled around and pointed in the stands.

The fact that it was at me was obvious, and of course, I

was mortified. Shaking my head, I covered my face, and Bru nudged me.

"Well, it seems he was serious," he said, grinning.

Yeah, I guess he was.

I returned to my seat with everyone else, and once the crowd calmed down, the game started. I got to witness who was easily the most popular boy in school wear a black dress the entire game.

And I recorded every minute of it.

———

Windsor Prep won against the Valley Creek Panthers in a clean sweep. This wasn't surprising. Our team won all their games, but the talk of the evening was definitely the quarterback. He played in a skirt that whole time, and it hadn't phased him once. He wore the dress like he played in it every game.

He even wore it after.

I hadn't waited for Dorian on purpose. Really, waiting outside the locker room with the rest of the team's groupies had only been for Bow's benefit. The last time I'd seen her left to her own devices at a game, she'd nearly gotten assaulted. The pair of us waited while my brother pulled the car around for me.

The dark prince had nice legs.

They were thick and chiseled just like the rest of him. His gym bag strapped across his front, Dorian strode out from the locker room with that black dress hugging his muscled frame, and he even sported his combat boots with it.

This guy was something else.

He hadn't even noticed me at first, nor the other guys. The four came out to their legions of fans, and I was the last person they'd take notice of since I was hiding. Bow and I had decided to take our real estate far away from their thirsty groupies, and it was her to nudge me that the guys came out.

Dorian broke away from his friends when she did, and though he got more than a few catcalls (from both guys and girls) on the way over to Bow and me, he ignored them all. The dark prince sauntered my way with nothing but confidence in his step, that black number bursting at the seams with his bulky frame.

Bow nudged me. "I'll see you at school on Monday."

A snicker in her voice, she skipped off in the direction of her brother. Basically, she ditched me, the traitor.

And here I thought I was being nice by waiting with her.

She sprinted past Dorian, a knowing look between them both. I could have strangled that little rabbit for her sign tonight. The two had obviously planned that.

It felt like all of Legacy had a place in Dorian's spectacle because, despite their legion of fans, Wells, Thatcher, and Ares had their attention on Dorian's strides toward me. Ares in particular stood out because he had two girls under his arms.

He watched on and was more than obvious about it. This thing with Dorian he kept pushing, and if I knew anything about them all, I knew why. If Ares would take a bullet for the dark prince, getting Dorian back in a girl's good graces would be nothing for him.

"I'm sure you witnessed tonight's festivities." He smelled strongly of heat, *boy*. Angling in, Dorian presented himself. His hair was wet and so obviously freshly showered. He grinned. "But in case you didn't, I wanted to make sure you saw up close and personal."

I definitely saw him, but didn't put off like that meant anything. My butt touched the wall. "Hard to miss."

He had better legs than I did, chuckling when he pressed an arm against the wall. This brought him way too close, and the only thing keeping my head right was the fact the most popular boy in school had me against the wall while he spit game... in a dress.

But damn if a familiar heat didn't ghost my cheeks. I was rocked where I stood, but I wasn't going to let him see that. I tipped my chin. "I didn't ask you to do that. Or for your notes."

"And yet, you got them." He managed to get closer, but kept his hands to himself. He crowded me. "And now that I got your attention, what day and time can I pick you up?"

I never said I'd actually go out with him after he made a fool of himself. I smirked. "See, your first mistake was thinking I'd go out with you after you did that. I said I *might* think about going out with you. *Might*."

His smile was slow. "Okay."

I angled from underneath him, his laughter gravelly. I left him standing there.

"Noa..."

"Still thinking," I called, and ready to do more. He said he'd play every home game like this, and honestly, I wanted to see how long he'd hold out. I wanted to see if he thought it was worth it.

I didn't know why, but I ignored any thoughts that he wouldn't.

"I'm not giving up," he said behind me. He laughed again. "I mean it, Sloane. You made this the best challenge for me."

I didn't want to be his challenge or conquest. I didn't want to be his anything. Truth be told, I wanted *nothing* to do with him, but each moment of every passing day showed my defeat more and more. I mean, I came to the game tonight wanting him to wear that dress. I wanted to see him try. I wanted him to want me, but that wasn't the scariest thing. What was truly scary was what I wanted in addition, and that was way harder than getting me to go out with him. I wanted all his gestures to mean something.

I wasn't a fool enough to wonder about what that something was, walking away.

My brother had pulled up our dad's Chevelle outside the stadium when I spotted him. Standing next to it, he was chatting with a couple guys, and when I realized who they were, my brow twitched.

When Wells Ambrose and Thatcher Reed had left their pack, I didn't know, but I'd spoken with Dorian long enough for them to leave. They had Bow with them, and the guys tipped their chin at my brother before striding away. It wasn't until I got closer that Bru noticed me, and he got in the car like nothing had happened.

"Uh, what was that?" I strapped myself in.

"What?"

I rolled my eyes, waving toward the outside. "Wells and Thatcher? You were talking to them."

I was aware of Wells and Thatcher's position after everything with Dorian. I mean, Bow had told me about them giving me space, and though that shouldn't have anything to do with my brother, they were obviously keeping their distance.

My brother's shrug was subtle. "We were just talking about the game. They were walking to the parking lot, and I was standing here. They mentioned Coach wanted to see me back out on the field."

"And…"

"And what?"

"You guys cool or…"

"I was standing here, and we talked." His eyes lifted. He started the car. "You want to talk to me about if you're going out with Dorian?" He chuckled. "According to the guys, Coach nearly had a coronary. Dorian didn't tell him, or the assistant coaches he was going to do that."

He'd obviously gotten away with it, though, and I noticed my brother evaded what I'd asked.

I started to ask him again, but I didn't want to be asked about Dorian.

I couldn't give him answers I didn't have.

CHAPTER
THIRTY-FIVE

Sloane

Dorian played every home game in that dress after that. Well, not *that* dress. He mixed it up on occasion.

At least, from what I heard.

With Bru not playing anymore, I didn't make it to every game, but I certainly heard about his antics. Especially when I also heard his coaches still weren't too keen on what he was doing out there on the field. Word around the academy was, there was talk of trying to bench Dorian for the rest of the season until he stopped with his impromptu fashion shows, and I'd gotten more than enough flack for that around the halls. Dorian Prinze was this school's golden boy out on the field.

He continued to wear the dresses, though, and he never asked me out again, but that didn't stop his letters. He left them strictly in my locker now.

I'd even caught him putting one in.

I'd assumed he always had his flunkies doing it, and maybe in the beginning, he had.

The one he left today, though, he slid right into my locker and stayed there when he spotted me.

"Number twenty," he said, absolutely relentless. His grin high, he nodded toward the locker. "Aren't you curious?"

I was, but I played that off. Instead of opening my locker, I stared at him. "Why should I be? They're all the same."

They were all him, each and every one. Some days they weren't as deep as number sixteen or number twelve, but they were still him. Like he was trying to peel open his heart and let me in for a little peek. Honestly, I was starting to hate them as much as anticipate them. I was starting to feel a lot of pressure with each one I found and not to give in for a date.

I thought, one day, he may want me to reciprocate. He'd want me to open myself up, and I wasn't ready for that. Things were difficult after he left, the scars.

Dorian's grin slipped a little in my direction, and he averted his eyes as I opened my locker. The note fell out like it always did, and I opened it up.

It was blank.

I even turned it around to see if I'd missed something.

"You know, you're acting like you don't care, little fighter…" He edged closer, his heat close. His lips parted. "But it sure looks like you do."

I hated that I did.

It didn't matter.

It couldn't matter.

Why does he keep doing this?

I felt ripped open right in front of him, peeled apart as he rested an arm against the locker.

Blond eyebrows narrowed hard. "You want more, you're gonna have to give me something." His brow lifted slow. "I'm serious about all the things I said. I am, and I'm willing to work for them, but…"

Our gazes clashed, his frown hard.

"I need something from you." He scanned my eyes. "Just… *something*."

He was so close now, and he didn't have to explain. He needed something from me.

He needed something *back*.

He needed to know all this wasn't pointless, and I was well aware I wasn't giving him anything.

I didn't want to.

Pride was something else. *Hurt* was something else. This boy had hurt me, multiple times, and I couldn't easily forget.

I wished I could.

With no response from me, Dorian's head lowered, that silky blond brushing his brow. I wanted to touch it so bad.

I wanted to touch him.

I resisted the devil in all his dark temptation. Dorian may be willing to change, but that part of him would always be there. He'd always have the capability of massive destruction, even if he had changed.

He could always destroy me whether he wanted to or not.

Reaching up, he played with my hair, and I let him for a second because I was stupid.

The hair slipped from his fingers.

"Let me know when you have that," he said, avoiding my gaze, and it took everything in me to let him walk away.

But in the end, I did.

———

Later that night, my brother surprised me when he asked if we could go see a movie. Typically, he played video games or brushed up on homework, and since I'd finished my project with Ares, I stayed in my studio most nights. It kept my thoughts about everything else surrounding Dorian Prinze away.

Needless to say, I said yes. Getting out of the house would

definitely help. My brother decided to drive us in his Audi, and I noticed his gaze more than once in my direction while we drove. More specifically, his gaze lingered on my Windsor Prep hoodie and leggings. He frowned. "I wished you would have put something else on, or at least *tried* not to look like you just got off the couch."

I had just gotten off the couch. I'd been eating dinner when he asked to go to the movie.

I flipped him off. He'd said something similar before we left. Actually, he'd made a big deal about it, saying I looked lazy, but he didn't appear much different. He wore jeans and a polo.

"I'm not trying to impress anyone," I said, hugging my arms, and he chuckled.

"Clearly," he returned, and it took all I had not to knock his head forward. I did get him in the side, though, and it was nice that we were getting back to normal. I liked my brother not being sick anymore.

Gratefully, Bruno laid off while we continued to drive *for the most part.* I still got his eye, but when we traveled in the opposite direction of the movie theater, I sat up. Maywood Heights only had a couple movie theaters, and they weren't this way. My brow lifted. "Where are we going?"

"The movies."

"Newsflash. We're nowhere near where we need to be going for the movies." I angled around. Actually, we seemed to be heading in the direction of the academy.

Which was why I wasn't surprised when that was exactly where we turned up.

We passed under the academy's crest, then next thing I knew, my brother was pulling into the football stadium's parking lot. My lips parted. "Bruno Sloane, why are we here?"

He didn't answer me.

The first thing I noticed was the lights were on at the

stadium. So bright they flooded the parking lot, which didn't make sense. The school never had them on unless there was a game going. The second thing that stole my attention was that, yes, this was our destination. Bru parked his car, getting out. He came around, opening my door, and I stayed in my seat.

"Why are we here?" I asked, but only got my brother's grin. I started to ask him about that, but he didn't give me a chance.

My brother shot off running, like legit *running.* Unstrapping, I got out. His car chirped after I closed the door, my brother running backward.

"Come on, sis. You shouldn't be slower than the sick kid!" he called, reminding me of Ares with the statement.

I really did need to work on my cardio and was huffing by the time I did catch up to him. My brother had disappeared in the direction of the players' locker rooms, but I caught him when I got around the corner.

He wasn't alone. In fact, I counted one, two, three boys, my brother the shortest.

But everyone was shorter than a Legacy boy. Thatcher Reed and Wells Ambrose surrounded my brother. They were chatting with him, laughing, but when the group spotted me, they eased around.

Both Thatcher's and Wells's eyebrows hiked high, but it was Thatcher to cover his face.

He pushed his hand into his dark hair, his dangly earrings twinkling. "Bro, why the fuck does she look like trash?"

I twitched, and Wells groaned. He laced his fingers atop his head. "Right?" He jutted his chin at my brother. "That's the best you could do?"

"I mean, it's not like I had a choice." Bru shook his head. "She's stubborn as hell."

"Where the fuck did you tell her she was going?" Thatcher asked this question, and at this point, I was beyond confused.

Bru lifted a shoulder. "The movies."

"No fucking wonder." Thatcher's sigh was heavy. "I mean, give her a fucking reason to put something decent on. Girls I take to the movies don't dress up for shit."

"Well, I'm not sure that's saying much considering the girls who want his dumb ass." Wells chided, nudging my brother. Bru put a fist to his mouth, trying not to laugh, but Wells was doing enough laughter for them both.

The platinum blond was roaring at this point, which shot Thatcher's snarl in his direction.

I stalked over. "What the fuck is going on?"

All the boys' gazes dashed in my direction. I stated the question as a blanketed one, but it was mostly directed toward my brother. I pointed toward Legacy. "What are you doing with these jerks?"

They had been jerks to me, and though Bow had given me some insight into why they were still hanging back, that didn't deny what they'd done. Nor how they'd treated my brother. I mean, they hadn't even gone to see him in the hospital.

Wells's lips pinched together as if to say "ouch" after what I said, but he shouldn't be surprised by this response. Facts were facts.

Bru cuffed his arms. "They asked me for help."

"With what?"

"Setting you up," Thatcher said from behind him. He shoved his hands in his pockets. "This is a setup."

I eyed my brother, needing further explanation here, and at this point, Bru guided me away. We didn't go far but enough for us to have some semblance of a private conversation.

"What's going on?" I gritted. The other boys lingered over by the locker rooms. "What are they talking about?"

"Just what they said." Bru gestured to the stadium around

us. "This is a setup, and the only way to get you to come around."

"Come around?"

Bru said nothing, Thatcher and Wells rocking on their high-tops behind us. I didn't see Ares or Dorian around, but Thatcher and Wells didn't do anything unless one of them asked them to do so.

They didn't do anything unless *Dorian* asked them.

The dark prince was their leader, point-blank, and just today, he'd been pretty open about needing something from me.

I guess he got tired of waiting.

"Dorian," I growled, and Bru raised his hands.

"Now, before you freak—"

"Oh, I'm already freaking out." I shoved my hands in my hoodie. "This is a setup, and *Dorian* put you guys up to this."

Bru popped a shoulder, and I started laughing at this point but found nothing funny. This was so *him*, and completely the opposite of what he was trying to prove to me. He said he was going to let go of control.

I had my hands laced on my head, but Bru tugged them down.

"Look. Anyone can see that you want to say yes to him," Bru stated, his eyes serious. "That you do, but you're so damn stubborn."

I didn't want him to be right. I gazed away. "He's an asshole, Bruno. He's *been* an asshole, and once again, you're out here having his back and not mine."

"I do have your back, sis." He frowned. "That's why I'm doing this."

I couldn't even look at him, but he angled in front of me.

"You do want to say yes." He nodded. "I know you do because I know you."

I wished he didn't, and like hell, I wanted to protest, but I couldn't.

I wanted him to be wrong. I wanted to say I didn't think about Dorian, or I didn't care. I wanted to say that I threw out every letter he gave me.

But I hadn't.

I had each and every one, and I probably wouldn't ever throw them away.

Bru's smile was slow. "I'm also saving you from yourself. Fuck, I'm saving you from the *school*," he said, chuckling. "If the coaches keep him from playing because of that dress shit, the pitchforks will definitely come out for your stubborn ass."

He rocked my shoulders, and I shoved at him, trying to not smile, but I couldn't help it.

His head tilted. "I'm not happy about how you said he treated you, and you were totally right for being as unmovable as you were on the issue."

He was right about that.

"But I also know how you feel about him." He rubbed my arm. "I know what I've seen, and as far as I'm concerned, that trumps any way I feel about the situation. If I had it my way, I'd deck his ass, which would probably not be a good idea because dude's like twice my size."

That hadn't stopped him from hitting Ares and standing up for me.

He probably only hadn't done anything *because* he knew how I felt about him fighting.

"You and your happiness come first, Sloane," he said, then faced back toward Wells and Thatcher. "It does, and regardless of how I feel about it."

But going along with Thatcher and Wells on this, really? I waved my hand toward them. "But *those guys* weren't here for you. They didn't even come to see you when you were at the hospital."

"And that's on us."

Thatcher came over after he spoke, Wells behind him. I had a feeling they'd been listening the whole time, and I hadn't been trying to keep quiet about anything. Thatcher stopped in front of me. "We talked to Bru at the game. Told him we were idiots. We shouldn't have given you the cold shoulder like that."

"We came at you fucked up." Wells dropped an arm over Thatcher's shoulder. Wells's lips pulled tight. "We should have given you the benefit of the doubt. Wolf did that, and we should have had enough brain cells to do it too."

"We were assholes." Thatcher opened his hands. "Point-blank. We went about shit with a mob mentality, and that wasn't cool." He gestured toward Bru. "Not to mention ghosting you, bro, over that shit. Was so messed up. *We* messed up."

Bru acknowledged that, nodding. "I get standing up for people you care about. If it was my sis, I would have done the same thing, which is why I've forgiven them," he said, facing me. "I did mostly for you. This thing with you and Dorian anyone can see. I wanted to help. Like I said, I want you to be happy."

I studied my kid brother, really looked at him. These boys had more than treated him like shit too, but here he was teaming up with them. He'd done that for me.

My brother definitely hadn't been in my corner in the past. More than once, he favored his interests over mine but that wasn't the case now.

"And we owe you an apology too." Thatcher waved a hand between him and Wells. "Wolf tried to talk some common sense into us, but we didn't listen."

"Yeah, which is why we did after we finally stopped being assholes." Wells frowned. "Ares said you were pissed at D, and that we should all give you breathing room. Especially after what we did and shutting you out. He said talking to you should be on your terms."

I'd been told this, him of all people looking out for me. "Where is he? Ares?"

Thatcher grinned. "He's actually at the school presenting the project you both worked on. I guess some big-time art school reps wanted to see it in person after getting his applications." Thatcher nodded. "Seems you guys worked really well together."

Well, congrats to beast boy. He really did deserve it. He worked hard. We both did.

How crazy how things had changed. I really did wish him well and even more after what Thatcher said. I had a feeling he'd been fighting for me, and though I still didn't know why, I wasn't going to slap that in the face. I supposed kindness can be found in the most unusual places.

Even enemies.

The dark prince and I had been that too, but for some reason, I found it easier to look over things like what Ares had done. I didn't know why.

Yeah, you do.

I stood with those thoughts as Thatcher eased forward.

"So *are* you ready to talk to us?" Thatcher stated, almost sounding hopeful. He studied Wells. "We were hard on you. Too hard, and that goes double for me."

He was obviously referring to that nightmare dinner I hadn't even gotten to have.

And why did my chest squeeze after what he said?

It was like he cared and truly did feel remorse. Hell, it was like *I* cared to even get the remorse in the first place.

Because you do.

I recalled Thatcher's gifts after what I'd done for his sister at that football game. How he and Wells had come to sit with me nearly every day after that. I remembered their jokes and liking being around them even if I didn't want to put that off. I liked being in their airspace, as if they were little brothers like my own. I liked *them*.

Wells smiled a little. "What do you say, Pretty Pretty Princess?" he asked, and why did my heart dance at that stupid fucking nickname. His smile stretched. "At least forgive me if you're not going to forgive this big asshole."

"Fuck you and your weak ass." Thatcher brought Wells under his arm, mussing up the boy's platinum-blond hair. This had both Bru *and me* roaring, and I'd missed that too. The two boys had often done that at lunch.

"She's laughing, bro," Wells said under Thatcher's arm. He shoved him off him. "I think she's forgiven us."

"Have you? I mean, uh..." Thatcher passed that off. He rubbed the back of his neck. "Have you? And make it quick. D's going to annihilate our asses for taking so long with you anyway."

I wondered what "D" had in store. I cuffed my arms, sighing. "I mean, I might consider it if..." The two boys let go of each other, and I grinned. "I get Jax's Burgers every day until holiday break."

"Oh, easy fucking mode." Wells pounded Thatcher's fist. Wells put a hand on his chest. "Jax is my dad, and I will personally make sure you get them."

The two Legacy boys locked hands, snapping after. I pointed at them. "But if you two fuck with me again, I'm going to annihilate your asses."

"Oh, wouldn't dream of it, princess. Wouldn't dream of it." Thatcher raised his hands before rubbing them. "So you ready for this, then? We've been told to get you set."

His thumb shot back toward the field, and though I had no idea what that meant, I shrugged. "Might as well."

Whatever was going on obviously would be occurring on the field. I started to eye that way, but the boys cut me off.

"No peeking." Thatcher shot a finger at me, and almost seemed giddy of all things. Wells rubbed his shoulders before Thatcher took his big fist to the door leading to the locker rooms.

"She's ready," he said, and I had no idea who he was

talking to, but then, the door opened and a little rabbit came out. Well, not an actual rabbit but his sister.

"Took you guys long enough," she said, wearing another one of her bright brooches. She had it pinned to her dress top and was all grins.

That was until she saw me.

Her expression legit flatlined, and next thing I knew, she approached me.

"Oh, Sloane," she tsked, shaking her head. She made eye contact with Bru. "Where did you tell her she was going?"

"Yeah, we definitely got on her bro for this shit already." Thatcher slapped my brother's chest. "Girl looks like she rolled out of a dumpster." I shot a look in his direction, and he immediately raised his hand. His tongue slid out with his grin. "I mean, a pretty dumpster."

"Fuck you," I gritted, but at this point, Bow was taking me away. I shot a finger at him. "I'm coming for you."

His grin stretched. "That a promise, princess?"

Wells dropped an elbow on his shoulder. "Dorian would kill your ass."

Thatcher appraised me. "Shit, it'd be fucking worth it."

Wells gave him an expression as if he'd be right for the statement. The fucker even nodded in agreement.

The two were a pair of horny fucks, and I noticed my brother shoved them as the door closed. I heard him say, "Really, man?" after the door cut me off from them, but I could only shake my head. I was currently being led to the visitor's locker room.

Bow hooked her arm in mine. "Good thing for you I was prepared," she said, patting my arm. We rounded a corner, and she'd changed the locker room into a fashion studio.

That was really the only way I could describe it. Bow had several outfits hanging, the dresses hooked on the locker doors, and she even had a makeup station on the benches.

Tubes upon tubes of lipstick lined the bench, and her

makeup bag was open with more of the same. She had a ton of heels too, and I eyed her.

"Bru helped us with the sizing," she said, completely giddy. She pumped her fists. "Dorian thought you might need some help, so I'm helping."

I didn't know if I should be appalled or flattered. I mean, it was kind of thoughtful he'd gotten all this set up for me, but clearly, he thought I was hopeless. I unhooked a dress. "He bought all this stuff?"

Leaning against the lockers, she passed that off with a shrug. "I mean, I bought everything, but yeah. You like anything?"

I liked it all.

Why is he doing this?

Because he was a control freak, but for some reason, I didn't mind it. One of the things that had initially stood out about him was his power, his control.

He exuded it.

When the dark prince wanted something, he took it, and part of me hated to admit that turned me on. I hooked the dress. "You pick."

It was all gorgeous, and I couldn't.

With free rein, Bow dove right in. She immediately picked a black number with poofy stuff beneath and a plunging neckline. I looked like I was going to prom, but not in a bad way. Honestly, I probably would have picked something similar for myself.

The heels were to die for.

She picked a stiletto that buckled at my ankles. This basically made me look more like a giraffe than I already did, but I didn't care. They were super cute, and I sat down while Bow applied the final touches. She'd already put my makeup on, but had waited for the lipstick since we hadn't picked the dress yet.

She decided on a red, and I let her apply it. My phone buzzed while she did.

Ares: Don't hate D too much for doing this shit. I tried to talk him out of it.

So he had heard about tonight's... whatever the fuck this was. I smirked.

Me: As you like to say, the jury is still out. I'm currently getting dolled the fuck up by Bow.

I snapped a picture to show him, flipping off the camera when I did. This had Bow eyeing me, but as sweet as she was, she didn't ask.

Ares: LOL. Right back at you, and good for you. You managed not to look completely hopeless.

I swear to *God* I didn't let people get away with talking to me like that, but time and time again, he did. Maybe it was because I was around him enough to know that was just his personality, as weirdly fucked as it was.

Me: Nice, you asshole. Anyway, don't fuck up your art thing. The guys told me about it.

If he could dish it, he better take it.

Ares: I'm not going to fuck it up. Hard not to. Our shit is awesome.

It was awesome.

Ares: Anyway, good luck tonight. Hope it's nice and don't hurt my boy. I feel like since he's met you, there's no coming back for him.

I started to text something back but stopped when I noticed Bow just staring at me. She lowered her tube of lipstick, a small smile on her lips. I faced the mirror, and my lips parted.

I'd never seen myself so dressed up, and dare I say, I pulled this shit off. I looked pretty, real pretty. Bow had my hair bumped underneath with a curling iron she had, my eyelids a smoky black and lips a matte red. I'd say I appeared very femme fatale, which I fucking loved.

"Wow," Bow stated, her head tilted. "Gorgeous, Sloane, and something about it is just…" She shook her head. "So familiar. You remind me of someone."

"Who?" I pushed some hair behind my ear.

She hugged her arms. "I don't know. This is all just familiar."

Well, whoever the person was must have been a knockout, and I told her as such, making her laugh. She rushed me out of the locker room after that, telling me to go out the doors and follow the hallway down to the far exits. She said I'd know what to do from there.

I did.

I just kind of stood there for a moment actually. I supposed I didn't really know what to do first.

This boy had had *planes* delivered on the field. Like actual planes. He had biplanes and a couple of helicopters. Each one had Prinze Aviation stamped on the side, and I crossed my arms.

He's something else.

I had a feeling I wasn't alone in that moment, a light prickle on the back of my neck. The heavy cadence that followed confirmed it. My lips lifted. "You get off just creeping around watching people?"

Dorian arrived beside me too quick, and I hadn't been expecting it. My skin buzzing, I turned.

He hadn't just rolled off the couch, his navy blazer hugging his thick arms. He had the nerve to appear some-what dashing tonight, the collar of his dress shirt open and his twill pants tight around his muscular thighs. He caught me looking and fingered his dirty-blond hair.

"I see nothing's changed." He caged me in between two firm biceps, grabbing the bar that separated the high bleachers from the lower ones. His dress shirt laboring at the seams, he grinned. "You still never pass up a chance to eye-fuck me."

"And what were you doing just now?" I countered, ignoring his proximity.

As well as my fucking heart racing.

I swallowed. "How long were you watching me?"

"I never said I wasn't." His dark eyes roamed, stopping at my breasts. He found my eyes. "Still am."

"Well, don't." I put a hand on his chest, my fingers burning from the heat. I meant to push him off, but something had me hesitating.

He noticed, the smile falling from his lips. He didn't give me breathing room, but he didn't advance either.

I wet my lips. "What is this, Dorian?" He had said he'd wait, and whatever this was *wasn't* waiting. He'd also said I had to give him something.

He scanned my eyes. "Maybe I don't care."

"Don't care?"

He nodded. "Maybe I'm going to try something out." He pushed off the bar. "Maybe I'm going to take a chance."

I didn't understand.

He angled around. "This is my legacy," he said, waving toward the planes on the field. He smiled. "Well, part of it. My dad is a pilot, amongst other things. These are his planes." He eyed me. "He taught me everything I know."

"As in you fly these?" I asked, and when he acknowledged that, his head bobbing once, my brow twitched. "Does your dad know you have his planes?"

"I'd like to think so since he signed off the paperwork." He eased his hands into his pockets. "They're on loan for the night."

"On loan?"

Dorian's head cocked. "I want to show you my life, Noa Sloane. I'm going to do that, and maybe I don't care how you feel about it. Maybe I'm going to put myself out there regardless of what you're giving me back."

"Maybe I'm going to take a chance."

His previous words in my head, my lips parted. "Your dad's just cool with you taking his planes?"

He rolled his shoulders. "He wanted to know what for, and when I told him, he was cool." His smile started slow. "I told him I wanted to impress a girl."

I didn't know what to say to that, watching as he put out his hand.

"Outside of football, flying is my life," he said, his expression serious. "It's something my dad shared with me, and I value that."

His *reasons* came to mind when he said that, his notes. He was opening himself up. I eyed his hand. "This looks a lot like a date."

"It's whatever you want to call it." He didn't lower his hand. "And my notes said control was something I was *working* on."

His wink that followed had me laughing. I took his hand, and as it turned out, that was a good thing in these stilettos. He helped me down to the sidelines, and with all that grass, I really wasn't trying to sink into the ground with these heels.

I stepped down daintily, and he must have noticed my difficulty because he gave me his back. He like literally hunkered down, and when he physically put me on his back, I squealed like a motherfucker.

"Dorian!"

"Probably not the ride you thought you were getting tonight, huh?" he stated, chuckling, then proceeded to be an asshole and race across the field.

"Dorian, stop!"

He merely picked up pace, and I screamed for my damn life. The dickwad showboated too when he spun me around, and I grabbed on to him so tight he'd probably see the marks for days. He didn't slow until we arrived at one of his dad's helicopters.

He placed me down then, only appearing slightly out of

breath, unlike me. I hadn't run but my adrenaline was through the roof. I pointed at him. "I'm going to kill you. This is not how you impress a girl."

"Like you'd have it any other way." He crowded me again, his hands on the plane. "You say we don't work, but this is how we *work*, Noa. We fuck around. We fuck with each other."

He was right, of course. We were burning flames, wild and insane.

But those flames worked in the wrong way most often. We charred everything in sight most of the time. Especially each other.

Dorian's smile fell away, and when he curled a finger over my cheek, I swallowed.

"Stop using this." He touched my temple. His smile returning, he gave me space. "Just have fun with me. We're going to have fun. I swear."

I didn't trust him, and I definitely didn't trust me. I didn't trust what I'd *do* with him, but I allowed him to hop into his plane and take me with him.

Dorian took the pilot's seat right away, helping me into mine. He happened to have a couple of headsets, and after he assisted me with mine, he put his own on.

"Now, I know this may disappoint you, but I've been strictly told we can't leave the ground today," he said, smirking. "Dad mentioned something about insurance or liability or some shit."

I laughed, and he grinned.

"But this will give you the idea." He sat back. "Imagine we're in the sky. Limitless in the night, and there's nothing but the lights of the city below us."

It sounded amazing, yeah. "You fly with your dad?"

"When I can." Threading his fingers, he propped them behind his head. "It's been a while. Actually, not since Charlie died. My uncle didn't fly, but he liked to come with us."

He said this casually, but I knew how his uncle's death had affected him. The lengths he'd gone to tell Charlie's story showed me that. "Can you tell me about him? Charlie?"

A slight wince touched his eyes, his nostrils flaring. "Why do you want to hear about him?"

I didn't know why, but probably because his uncle was a part of him. It might help me understand him.

I supposed this was a selfish request, callous enough.

His look was dismissive. "I mean, what can I say? Charlie was my brother." His head turned on the seat, his eyes hard. "The kid was my hero. We were Batman and Robin." He smirked as if at the memory. "He was Batman, and I was his shitty-ass Robin."

He took off his headset, tucking it under his arm, and I wished I hadn't asked. I took mine off too. "You still blame yourself."

"Hard not to, Sloane." He lifted a hand. "We've talked about this. If I had nutted the fuck up, *opened my goddamn mouth* about him and Mayberry, he'd be here right now."

"You don't know that."

"And neither do you." He scanned my eyes. "That's my reality." He shook his head. "You probably wouldn't understand."

I think I did, a little. I shrugged. "Bru getting sick I think is my fault."

"How so?"

I lay back. "We can't prove it, but I think he might have gotten sick because he went into that lake."

He frowned. "That's what the doctor said?"

"No, but they can't prove it."

He studied the floor, his head shaking. "Well, I guess that's my fault too, then." His head tilted. "I got involved with your brother. He wouldn't have even done that haze and tried to get into my crew had I not been fucking with you and him."

"No more your fault than mine." I nodded when he shook his head. "You and I…"

"Yeah?"

I shouldn't have looked at him in that moment, my mouth dry. "We're what you said. We fuck around. We fuck with each other, and people get affected by that."

We really were chaos, madness.

"Maybe." His shoulders lifted. "But it doesn't always have to be that way. We can be whatever we want."

"How?" We'd only been one way; he'd only been one way. "Why did you leave me?"

I hadn't meant to ask that.

But the words were said.

I put them out there, and they hung between us. My throat tightened. "Where did you go, Dorian?"

I asked him this, but I didn't want a physical place. I knew he'd been with his family, but I needed to know the *why*. He'd left me both physically and mentally.

That was what I asked.

I wasn't sure if he got that, and when soft music played from somewhere in the stands, he faced me.

"Dance with me," he said, putting out his hand. "Make this a real date."

The plea in his tone matched his eyes. I didn't want to dance with him. I wanted to run away and take back what I'd asked.

Instead, I took his hand.

Dorian helped me back on the field, and when he placed me in his arms, I hated how familiar that felt. I hated how it felt like *home*. I wanted it to feel as dark and foreign as how he'd initially been in my life. I didn't want to feel comfort in our madness.

But I did. I felt warm…

I even felt safe.

He felt as soothing around me as he always had, and I hated that.

"Number twenty."

I gazed up, my gaze clashing with his. "What?"

"Where I went was number twenty." His throat jumped. "Where I went… *Why I left* was reason number twenty why I'm fucked up. It's not blank like my last note."

He stopped our sway, gentle music playing around us. I gauged now it was playing from the stadium's speakers.

"And it's not the last reason I am." His throat jumped. "It's not, but it's a big one. Maybe even the biggest."

His breath was shallow, weighted as he took my hands.

"When things get real, I don't handle it. It's easier not to trust my instincts. It's easier to question shit even when shit is good. Even when…" He blinked. "I question *everything*. I don't trust myself to do the right thing. I always fuck up like with that shit with Charlie."

"Dorian…"

He squeezed my hands. "Now, ask me what I'm going to do about it. Tell me to *tell you* what I'm going to do to fix it."

I didn't know if I wanted to know, my hands shaking in his. I didn't know if I was ready to know.

"What are you going to do about it?" I didn't know how he heard me. My voice was so quiet.

"I'm going to take a chance." His hand covered the back of my neck. He wet his lips. "Because I'm so fucking into this girl. I'm into her, and even though she thinks we're fucked up, I think we're perfect."

I gasped, my chest trembling. "You do?"

He nodded, a flush across his neck. "We make sense, and I'm going to take a chance against my own odds."

Because he didn't trust himself and still didn't. This probably didn't look right to him.

But it felt right.

It did for me too, and my gaze averted, tears in my eyes. It felt right, but he'd hurt me.

He caged my face, bringing me back. "Let me show you how much we make sense." His eyes narrowed. "Let me kiss you."

Dorian never asked for permission. He didn't bother.

But he did today.

"Is it going to hurt?" Giving in to him had hurt before. It had hurt so bad.

His fingers curled against my jaw. "If it does, I'll make it fucking better." He covered my face. "And never stop fighting until it is."

His thumb grazed my chin, and I gasped. "You promise?"

"I fucking promise." He touched our foreheads together, hugging me close. "I promise."

The words whispered in a breath, and when I lifted my head, I nodded. "I want you to kiss me."

"Yeah?" His eyes crinkled, his grin slow. He tipped my chin. "Fuck, yeah."

He covered my mouth, and when I gripped his lapels, he pretty much hugged me off my feet. He fused us together, his tongue easing into my mouth, and I smiled when he spun us around.

It was like we were still dancing, or up in that sky like he'd mentioned. It was night, and there was nothing but lights.

We were the stars.

Dorian returned me to my feet in a sway, but even still, he didn't stop kissing me. He hugged me to him, pressing me close, and it took me a second to hear we had an audience.

"Hell, yeah, bitches!" shot from the stands and caused both Dorian and me to fall apart in laughter. Wells, Thatcher, Bow, and my brother chanted at the top of their lungs, and though I couldn't determine who'd initially called out to us, Wells was the one standing on the bleachers. He charged his fist. "Whoop! Whoop! Get that ass, D. Get that, get that ass, D!"

"Whoop! Get that ass, D! Get that, get that ass, D!" Thatcher shouted, backing Wells up. He tried to get up on the bleachers himself, but he fell off like a goddamn fucking idiot.

Bru and Bow both shook their heads at his ass, and Wells was roaring.

Despite his fall, Thatcher continued to chant for Dorian to "get that ass," and Dorian flipped him off before kissing me again. He dipped me down and everything, and I let him because I was swept up in the moment too. The dark prince just made another declaration to me, but this was deeper than his notes. He'd promised me something, and a lot came with that. Being with him may always hurt.

Even if he did promise he'd make it better.

CHAPTER
THIRTY-SIX

Sloane

Dorian took me on a few dates after that, and they were ones I actually agreed to. These, as it seemed, appeared to be legitimate gestures by him, so I was game. He took me to the museum and even to the park for a picnic on the swings.

He even packed the lunch.

My favorite date, by far, was the art gallery, and Maywood Heights had several. I recalled Ares saying his dad owned a few of them, and Dorian confirmed the one we went to was established by Mallick Enterprises. We didn't run into Ares's dad or anything, but Dorian said the gallery was his. It was huge, and I loved it. I also liked that I got to show Dorian a part of myself and my interests. He asked about them a lot, and though I told him things, I found myself guarded.

It was still hard for me after everything that had happened, and I wasn't so sure I was ready for all this. I cared about Dorian, sure.

I mean, I really fucking cared.

I found him in my thoughts during my very first breaths

in the morning, and hell, he appeared at the last breaths too. He circulated my thoughts constantly, and if that wasn't more than *care*, I didn't know what was. It wasn't a question of whether I had feelings for him or not. It was if I was ready to have them. He'd screwed with my heart something crazy, and the last time I'd been vulnerable with him had kicked me in the ass. I was still sore from our last fall together.

Fear was something else, wasn't it?

If Dorian had picked up on my reservations, he never mentioned them. He simply took me on dates, and not once did things get physical. I mean, he touched me. He held my hand, and we kissed (a lot) in his car both before and after school.

Sometimes even during.

Yes, there was a lot of kissing, but no fucking. He surprisingly hadn't pushed for that, and I found myself wondering every day if he really had changed. I wondered if he was truly putting himself out there and not rushing things. Maybe he actually was serious about this, about us.

Maybe he won't hurt me again.

This thought was also a constant in my mind and something I thought about before meeting him at his locker that day. Sometimes he met me at mine, but today, he'd said he wanted to take me on another date after school.

I found myself rushing just to get to him after last period, and I knew right away *how that* sounded. Again, I pushed myself past the thoughts. I had to in order to remain sane.

He wasn't by himself at his locker, his back to me. Ares had a shoulder lounged against the lockers with him, and I barely saw the two at all in the crowded hallway. People were rushing around to get out of school.

"It's time, don't you think?" I heard Ares say as I strode up, and I hadn't been seeing a lot of him these days. At least, not as much as we had been. Since our project had wrapped up, I typically only saw him and the rest of Legacy at lunch.

I'd recently started eating there with them and Bow, and my brother joined us too when he wasn't trying to catch up on school work in the library. Ares sighed. "We need to rope her in. It's time."

Dorian braced his big arms, his head shaking. He still had his back to me when I stopped behind him. I frowned. "Rope who in?"

Dorian swung around, an easy smile gracing his lips. He'd started doing that, *smiling* whenever he saw me. It was as if the lazy grin was instinctual, and its presence gave me more butterflies than I'd readily admit.

"Snooping on me, little fighter?" Framing my face, he angled my mouth in his direction. "Why you always so bad?"

He growled before sealing our lips and *biting* mine. His teeth embedded in my flesh tingled down to my toes and had Ares rolling his eyes by the time the dark prince let go of me.

"She's always good for that," Ares announced. He hooked one of his long arms over his open locker. I recalled he had caught me snooping before, so I let him get away with that. He tipped his chin. "Sup, little?"

As well as *that*. I shook my head. "Nothing, *Wolf*," I countered. This made him chuckle, so I obviously got away with that. I smiled. "And what are you guys talking about? Bring who in?"

The pair exchanged a glance before Ares closed his locker.

Ares bunched his jacket sleeves up. "Imma see you two around, then," he said, but then pointed at Dorian. "I'm assuming you're still ditching practice today."

Dorian's brawny arm hooked around my waist, which apparently gave Wolf his answer. I didn't know he was ditching practice for whatever we were going to do today.

Wolf nodded. "Have fun, then."

His statement accompanied a look in Dorian's direction. Ares started to pass us, but stopped. He frowned. "Your hair always like that?"

It took me a second to realize he was talking to me and another to figure out what the fuck he was talking about.

I supposed I had worn my hair differently today, curly. Thick and frizzy curls hadn't held up today, and I shrugged. "I'm naturally curly. I just usually straighten it."

I'd been running late this morning, which was the only reason I hadn't. I guessed the only reason he hadn't seen it in all its frizzy glory was because I'd worn a messy bun at lunch. I'd tugged my hair free toward the end of the day.

Ares opened his mouth, as if to say something, but in the end, he didn't. He simply told Dorian he'd catch him later, and after I texted Bru he could go on home without me, I joined Dorian in his car. My brother and I had been driving to school together since he didn't have his football obligation anymore.

"So, uh, you going to keep pretending like I didn't ask you guys a question?"

We were driving by the time I asked, and the question caused the dark prince to cock his head at me.

"You're relentless as fuck, you know that?" he stated, his fingers tapping on my knee. His meaty hand had found a permanent place on my thigh, and I let him since I fucking liked it. Long fingers massaged through my jeans. "Wolf and I were just talking."

"Talking about what?" I cocked *my head*, and he smiled.

"Wolf wants to bring you into our crew." He adjusted in his seat, his eyes on the road. He glanced my way. "Be one of us, I guess."

One of us.

I folded my arms. "You mean your little Court?" I laughed. "You guys must be on crack."

I wasn't interested in being in anything that had to do with that, whether they did hazes still or not.

Dorian grinned. "The Court isn't a bad thing. Hasn't been for a long time."

"How do you explain what happened to Bru?"

"A mistake." His expression was serious, his nod firm. "And something Wolf has owned up to. He knows he messed up." He shrugged. "He thought he was looking out for me. The way he went about it was fucked, but he did. He was being a brother and supporting me, but stuff like that doesn't usually happen. Not anymore."

I recalled my own conversations with Ares. He had believed I was a threat.

He'd even said he was jealous.

We really had come a long way, our ease together in the hallway definitely saying that and not to mention all the stuff he'd done before for my brother.

"The Court is about brother and sisterhood." Dorian raised a hand. "We're a community."

"A community?"

"Yeah." He draped his arm around me, that chunky gorilla ring with the ruby eyes below his knuckle. "It's about unity, and it's not bad. Members look out for each other and do a lot of good for the city. We volunteer and stuff."

"You volunteer?"

His grin was wiry. "Some of us more than others."

I played with his fingers over my shoulder. "You want me to be a part of that?" I swung my gaze over. "Your community."

He almost made it sound like another family.

Dorian's stare felt weighted in my direction in that moment. He sat up, and when he did, he outlined his lips.

"I want you with me," he said, glancing over. "I want you with us, yes."

At this point, all I could tell him was that I'd think about it. I still didn't know how I felt. All his talk about community came across really strong.

Especially with that last bit.

I knew he wanted to be with me, but whenever he kept

saying things like that, it scared me. Hard not to with our history.

Maybe he picked up on that because he mentioned nothing more about the topic as we drove. I asked him where we were going a few times, but he kept the information tight-lipped.

I got an indicator when we pulled up to his gated community.

I sat up. "We're going to your house?" I asked him this as we passed through the gate. At this point, the area looked way different. For starters, there were no creepy reporters, and Bow mentioned they were starting to lay off. I faced him. "Am I meeting your family?"

My swallow was hard, but his chuckle was jovial.

"Well, it's a good fucking thing you're not with the way you're looking at me," he stated, taking my head and mashing ticklish kisses and bites into my neck. I swear he was such a dude the way he manhandled me. He bumped a laugh. "And no. We're just hanging out. My parents are still out of town."

"They coming home soon?" His neighborhood was gorgeous, nothing but old-timey castles, and actually kind of reminded me of Bow's neighborhood. Most of those proper-ties in her neighborhood were more modern, though.

Dorian didn't say anything, and I swung my gaze in his direction.

He rubbed the steering wheel, the rubies on his ring flick-ering the sun. "Yeah, soon." He studied me. "So no pressure today, yeah?"

I was glad for that, nodding.

He took my hand again, pointing out some of the history of the homes. Some pretty famous people had settled down here in the past, and that surprised me. According to Dorian, his neighborhood had had a president or two come through it and loads of influential people.

This didn't surprise me since Bow had mentioned stuff like this when I'd first come to the city. Dorian kept us moving, and surprise, *surprise*, he lived in probably the biggest castle in the neighborhood. It was old smoky brick, the spokes high. It had dark shutters too, which made it look like a spell had been placed on it, but kind of in a cool way.

The establishment appeared perfect for a dark prince, and Dorian waved his hand at a couple of women watering the hedges next door. The two were outside another old-timey property, their hands raised high.

"Old family friends," he said, then later explained his dad grew up in the house Dorian lived in today. Anyway, the women next door happened to be the mothers of his dad's best friend, Jax. *Jax* was both Dorian's god dad and Wells's real dad, which made the women next door Wells's grand-mothers.

I found it hard to keep up with all the family Dorian had and all the ways in which the Legacy boys and Bow were connected. It took a second to sink in that we were really at the dark prince's house, but once we were in his garage, reality hit something good.

He was sharing himself with me again, a big something. He came around and opened the door for me, and after he helped me out, he pinched my chin.

"Try not to look completely scared shitless." His eyebrow arched slow. "I told you my parents are out of town, and even if they weren't, they aren't *those parents.* They're cool, and they wouldn't grill you. They're not like that."

The way he spoke of them, with so much admiration and even *adoration*… I'd never thought that about them anyway. My reservations came from internal pressures I'd manifested.

If he was doing all this, what did he want? But one better…

Was I ready to give it?

"I'm not scared." I nudged him away, but he caught up easy.

He threw that heavy arm on me again, and though I nearly fell to the floor every time, I'd be lying if I said I hated the possessive nature of it. He kept me close, and I didn't know what that said about me since I was enjoying the possession.

"I find that hard to believe." He opened the door. "I mean, my mom still remembers that pregnancy test."

I'd forgotten about that. I swallowed. "Is she still upset about that?"

His shrug was passive. "She's over it, but she hasn't forgotten about it." He frowned. "Actually, my ass got handled for it. I don't think you ever came up. They were more pissed at me for doing something to you that made you do it in the first place."

Okay, so I *really* liked his parents. I grinned. "Well, that makes me feel better."

"I'm sure it does."

He said the words as he got assaulted from the front, a large brown Labrador racing into the entryway. The dog was all over him, and he immediately dropped to the floor with it.

"This is Chestnut," he said, the dog leaping at him. "She's my mom's dog, but since I came home early, I brought her back. Didn't I, girl?"

Um, so he was being *super* cute with this dog, and I'd never seen him so, well, normal. He was grinning and laughing with her, and I felt like had I not been standing here, the two would be on the floor rolling around together.

"This is Sloane," he said to her, holding her by the collar. He eyed me. "You okay with dogs?"

It was nice that he asked, and since I was, he let her go. She, of course, attacked me, and though I fell on my back, I laughed too. She was really friendly.

Dorian continued to smile as he watched us, letting us

play for a bit before he patted Chestnut away. He helped me up and asked me if I wanted his butler to make something for us.

"Ronald's an excellent cook," he said, and I had to roll my eyes. Of course, this boy had a butler. I declined the offer since I wasn't hungry at the moment. I actually wanted to see the rest of this balling-ass house, but Dorian said we had to tour the garden first.

"It's my favorite place," he stated, opening the door to something out of a film. It was like another world out there, huge hedges and cobblestone walks. Dorian smiled. "It was my grandmother's before she passed."

This house had obviously been with his family for a little while, and Chestnut came with us as we headed outside. Dorian tossed a ball into the sea of flowers and tall trees, and Chestnut raced after it every time.

"Charlie and I used to play explorers out here," he said at one point, Chestnut coming back to him. He threw the ball again, and the pair of us took a seat on a concrete bench. A large koi pond surrounded it, and I watched the fish weave about it with their long tails. Dorian put his hands together. "Seems like so long ago."

It seemed easier for him to talk about his uncle here, but only in the natural sense. He tossed the ball to Chestnut between sentences as if to distract himself.

"We all played, the guys, Charlie, and me." He drew the ball back, following through with a long toss. "Had a blast back then."

"Sounds like it." I didn't know what to really say.

And he was doing it again.

He was letting me in, and when Chestnut came back this time, he didn't toss the ball.

"I'm really trying, Noa." His fingers ghosted along my leg, his smile slow. "I don't know how to do this, and I don't want to fuck it up."

He didn't elaborate, but I wasn't sure he needed to, and he was wrong. He was good at this, *trying*.

At least way better than me.

"I want to talk to you. I want to..." He touched my fingers. "It's just hard, you know? I wish I was better at this."

Seeing him struggle tightened something in my chest. "We don't have to talk about anything you don't want to talk about."

"But I do want to." His lips pulled tight. "It's important, and Wolf's right. I..."

"Master Prinze, I took the liberty of making you and your guest buffalo wings. Yours are vegan, of course. I made two options."

Dorian angled around, his butler Ronald standing at the hedges leading into the garden. I hadn't met him yet, but I assumed this was him. Dude wore a suit, white gloves, and everything.

The man put his hands together. "Would you like me to lay them out anywhere specific for you? If not, I can leave them in the kitchen."

Dorian smiled. "I'll take care of it, Ronald. Thank you."

This world he lived in was so different from mine. This was old hat for him.

We were so different.

He said we were right, but how could we be? I mean, he was privilege and butlers, and though my brother and I had Callum, we really didn't. Callum was temporary, and I could never be privileged.

Did I ever want to be?

Dorian faced me in that moment, taking my hand, and things felt really crowded despite us being outside.

"Actually, could we get the wings?" I shrugged. "I think I'm hungry now."

This would take some of the pressure off him too.

Dorian didn't get up right away, but eventually, he waved

Chestnut in. She trotted on after us, and Dorian and I ended up taking the food to his room.

He had his own wing.

Apparently, he lived in the west, a real honest-to-goodness prince. He left Chestnut out to play in the house and started a movie on a flat-screen above the fireplace.

Once he got that going, the pair of us lay on a bed made fit for a king. He had draping around it, the bedding silk, and he even had his own mini library. The walls surrounding the fireplace were lined with books, and when I asked him about them, he said he'd read them all. Before this moment, I figured he might just be a dumb jock, but I didn't know why I continued to assume things about him.

We lounged on his bed for nearly half the movie before he touched me, and like all those other times, I felt no pressure for sex. He merely took my hand, and it was me to initiate the kissing. His hand moved to my hip then, but even with it, he didn't take things too far. Could I tell he wanted to? Sure. His kisses grew hot, hungry. His tongue delved into my mouth with delicious intent, but eventually, he growled and pulled back. He was physically restraining himself and so obviously for my benefit.

Reason #16: I have issues with anger and control.

He seemed to have corrected them both. I felt no danger with this boy. At least, not physical danger. I felt like the dangerous one at this point. *I* wanted to lose control, his chest hard, his body heated and solid above me.

"I want you," I said, my lips pinching his. This was so hard for me to admit. I didn't want to admit how much I wanted him.

Dorian's nose brushed mine, his fingers ghosting across my neck. A devilish smirk pressed into his full lips. "You have me, little fighter. Always have."

But I didn't. Not always. I gripped his shirt. "Make love to me."

And he needed to do it before I changed my mind. He *had to* before I pushed him away and got too in my head again.

He scanned my eyes, as if questioning the validity of what I said.

He didn't question long.

On his knees, he caged me beneath him, his tongue probing and hot when it dove into my mouth.

"Tell me what you want." His teeth lodged into my bottom lip, tugging. "Tell me so I know how far I can go."

His kisses slowed, almost hesitant. He hovered above me, and when he touched my face, waiting, I knew he was serious about what he said. He didn't want to push me, and I guessed I couldn't blame him.

He was the first to admit how fucked up he was, but I was too. I was because I almost *wanted* him to be fucked up. If he was the screwed-up one, I wouldn't have to think about myself.

He wasn't the only one who had control issues.

I had a history of fighting and for a reason. I got people before they could get me. If I did that, they couldn't hurt me, and that was how I always operated.

I needed Dorian's dark and beautiful void. I needed it to mask my own issues. We both very much loved power.

Which made his darkness light for me.

We did work well together, almost too well.

"Tell me." His thumb brushed over my lip. "Tell me what I can do. I'll do anything, Noa."

He covered my mouth with a hard kiss, and his dress shirt bunched in my fists.

"Fuck me," I gritted, my back arching, my hips rising. "Get me out of my head."

I wanted him to push me.

I wanted him.

Gripping my jaw, Dorian forced my mouth open, his kiss

aggressive, carnal. His hand captured my neck, and I gasped for breath, the adrenaline charging my veins.

"I want it to hurt," he announced, pinning me beneath him. His weight sunk me into the bed, his eyes wild, his tongue in my mouth untamed. "I want you raw. I want it *painful* until I can't feel anything and you can't think. I want you *mine*, Noa. All mine and no one else's."

My breathing labored, a fluttering inside my chest.

"What else?" I was stupid to ask the question, his lips pinching mine apart.

"I want it to be rough. Sweet." His mouth pressed hard, his hold on my neck tighter. "Because that's how you feel. That's how you feel every fucking day."

I gasped.

"I want to make love to you," he rasped, his cock probing through his pants. "Because that's what you deserve, but reason number whatever the fuck is I hate that I want it. I *hate* that I want your taste, and that I do want it to feel good too. I hate that I need you."

"Why?"

I was trembling now, and he stopped kissing me. His fingers bunched my curls, his thumb trailing down my cheek. It came away wet, and I knew why.

He always was so good at making me cry.

"Because hating you would be easier, smarter." His jaw shifted. "I could let go of this, of you, and not give a fuck."

He was being so honest.

His throat jumped. "Hating you is easier than loving you," he said, his nostrils flaring. "And you loving me back…"

Back?

His thumb brushed my cheek, and the digit came away wet again.

"Is this," he said before his mouth touched the tear's trail on my check. He closed his eyes. "It might always be, but I don't fucking care." His tongue drew down my skin. "I can't fucking care."

He licked away tears before unbuckling his pants.

"I can't care, Noa." Leaving the pants open, he unbuttoned his shirt. "I won't care."

He tugged me to him by the thighs and didn't even take my panties off before shoving my skirt up and burying his face between my legs.

"This is mine," he ground out, the cry falling from my lips. I wriggled against his face, and he growled. "This is mine, and I don't fucking care. I'm going to have it. You're mine."

His.

He nibbled my lower lips through my underwear, my chest hiking with hard pants. I wanted him to stop. This was starting to hurt, but not physically. My stupid goddamn heart was taking the brunt of this.

Especially when he slowed down.

He kissed me down there, light and feathery kisses across my sex. He hooked my panties over and his tongue did a sweep between my lower lips.

"Please," I whimpered. "Please stop."

It hurt, *killed* being this close to him, physically, emotionally. It did, and my chest tightened, his hair bunching in my hands.

"No," he rasped, warm breath so gentle against my sensitive flesh. "No, Sloane. I can't. I won't."

He continued to kiss me, making love to me between my legs. I'd told him to make love to me, but I hadn't thought it was possible. He was too hard, too callous.

Too perfect.

My lids squeezed down more fucking tears, bucking when his kisses picked up. Dorian held me to his mouth, his fingers embedded in my thighs and his tongue fucking me.

"You'll come for me," he commanded, and I did so damn hard I thought I'd pass out, my back arching off his bed.

He funneled me down, lapping at my sex hungrily. He didn't wait for me to finish before he tugged his shirt off and pressed that huge body on top of me. He pumped himself in his pants, grinding against my stomach.

"Taste what you fucking do to me." He kissed me hard, solid. He swept my own juices across my tongue. "Taste it, Sloane."

I did, trembling. I cradled his head, and he opened my blouse.

His kisses were even softer there, one by one *softer*. I didn't think I could fucking take it. It was easier to do this, *be with him*, when he was fucking me and making it hurt. I didn't know how to deal with anything different.

He wet my nipples through my bra, sucking and letting them pop out of his mouth. He didn't stop until I had my legs hooked around his waist, and I was bucking against him again.

Only then did he strip me bare, *only then* did he push his pants down his muscled legs. In boxers and on his knees, he appeared godlike.

And almost sad.

He studied me, his hand sliding up to my neck. His fingers flicked my curls. "You're so beautiful."

I couldn't breathe, my chest *tight*. "Shut up."

His jaw shifted, his head shaking. "You're beautiful."

I swallowed, letting him lean over and claim my mouth.

"Beautiful," he whispered, his eyes closed. "So goddamn beautiful."

It sounded almost as sad as he spoke, his kisses rough and angry. Shoving his boxers down, he put a condom on.

"I love you." He tongued my lips apart, arching hard inside me. "I fucking love you."

The tightening in my chest constricted harder, the burn matching the one between my legs. I wanted to love him...

I wanted to *not* love him.

He consumed me way more than body or mind. We were ingrained together with no beginning or end.

I hugged him to me, gasping when his lips pinched kisses over my arms. We came about the same time, and he held my arms while he milked me into my high.

"Fucking *fuck*." His teeth bit down on my flesh, my eyes rolling back. His hands braced me to him, his hold tight and unyielding. His nose buried into my neck. "Fuck."

I said nothing, unable to say anything. The dark prince had said he loved me.

He'd said it twice.

I had no words, but when Dorian secured his big arms around me, it seemed he had enough for the both of us.

"Tell me a reason," he said, his brow touching mine. "Just give me *one*. I... I need to feel not so fucking crazy."

He hadn't asked me to tell him I loved him back, but for some reason, what he was asking felt harder.

"You." I hid my face in his arms. This was *my* biggest reason for being fucked up. "You are my reason."

The air stayed silent between us, and as he held me, he gratefully didn't make me say I loved him too.

I didn't think he had to.

CHAPTER
THIRTY-SEVEN

Sloane

I was alone in one of the art rooms the following Monday. I held my independent study during this hour, so that hadn't been surprising. I had my head deep in my sketchbook, which was why I basically dropped it when someone opened the door in full conversation.

Dorian never visited during my independent study. He had other classes, so it surprised me to see him come in and with a woman I didn't recognize. They'd been laughing, and when Dorian spotted me, he waved.

My feet on a chair, I got up. I didn't know what was going on here.

Dorian touched my shoulder. "Hey, sorry to bombard you like this."

His hand lingered at my neck, and this was the first time I'd seen him since *that* night.

The one where I'd basically been chickenshit.

I was completely hiding from my own feelings, and I was

aware of that. My weekend had been spent with me pretty much in my own seclusion.

Bru had even gone out.

As far as I knew, he'd been hanging with Wells and Thatcher, but I chose to stay inside and hide from the dark prince.

I frowned at him. "What's going..."

"School's headmaster... well, for the time being, wanted to meet you," he said, guiding me forward. "Brielle—I mean, Principal Mallick. This is Sloane. My girl."

His girl.

We hadn't discussed that at all.

So why are you getting butterflies hearing him say that?

Because I liked it. I did.

Just get out of your head.

That was so hard and definitely in front of the academy's headmaster. I knew this woman to be Ares's mom, but I hadn't met her. I'd only heard her voice during the morning announcements.

Dorian presented me forward to her, and when I say this woman was one of the loveliest women I'd ever seen, I meant it. She had long dark hair, which was bumped under just slightly. She wore the style over one shoulder, her dark blouse and black trousers accompanying it. Since she wore so much black, that made the pop of red on her lips stand out, as well as the little bit of silvery gray hair she had. She had only a little bit on one side, the style similar to Rogue from those X-Men movies.

Standing in front of her, I assumed this woman was older, but it was only because of her hair could I tell. She was so very lovely and had a familiarity about her I didn't quite understand. It was as if I'd seen her before, but that didn't make sense. Perhaps, it was because I knew Ares, and I supposed he did look like her a little.

Blinking, the woman had a hand on her blouse, and I realized in that moment I was just staring at her. The woman put out her hand, and I was glad she had. I was being rude.

"Brielle Mallick," she said, our hands connecting. Her head tilted. "I wanted to meet the girl who's responsible for getting my son into design school."

She faced Dorian in that next second, and when he nodded, grinning, her attention drifted back to me.

"Sloane," I returned, happy to hear that news. I had no idea Ares had already gotten in. I smiled. "And I doubt I'm responsible for Ares getting into school. He's a great artist."

Our hands were still shaking, but Brielle stopped them. I let go, and when Dorian ventured back to me, her gaze followed him.

He hooked an arm around me. "She's being modest." He looked down at me. "Sloane's very talented."

"I've seen it." Brielle glanced between the two of us, back and forth a couple times before her hand closed. She pushed some of her gray hair back. "I've just come from the piece you both worked on. Dorian's been telling me you helped Ares, and it's nothing like what my son has done before." She wet her lips. "I'm sorry. You said your name is Sloane?"

"Noa Sloane," I said. "But yeah, I do go by Sloane."

"I see." She eased closer, her hands coming together. "So you're into art, then? Art like Ares?"

I was and decided to show her some of it. I had my sketch-book still in my hands, so I flipped a few pages for her.

Brielle studied them over my shoulder, glancing between the drawings and me. I was taller than her, like most people, so I angled to give her a good vantage point.

"These are wonderful." She actually sounded awed, and that made me feel good. I wasn't sure what Ares got from her, but if she had passion like he seemed to, that might be it. Her lashes shifted in my direction. "You are very talented. To which schools are you applying?"

I stopped for a beat. "This is going to sound hilarious, but I haven't thought about it."

"Oh. Why not?"

"I moved around a lot growing up." I closed my sketch-book. "My brother and I—"

"You have a brother?" she angled in, and I nodded.

"Bru and I—short for Bruno—moved a bunch," I said. "Us and our dad. At least, we used to."

"Used to?"

I started to say, but Dorian's arm returned to my waist.

"He passed," he said for me, and I was happy he had. I could talk about my dad, but I didn't necessarily like talking about the fact I was an orphan.

"I'm sorry to hear that." Brielle's hands came together. Her lips parted, but then they closed. She smiled. "Well, I would like to hear more about you. Your college plans? I'm always available to offer guidance on that."

She had time for something like that? I didn't know her schedule, but she was the headmaster.

Brielle started to say more, but her phone rang. She had it clipped to her hip, and though she checked it, I noticed she didn't answer it.

She silenced it once before it rang again, and this time, she unclipped it.

"Unfortunately, I find myself trying to balance two gigs at the present," she said, silencing it again. She merely clipped the thing before it was ringing once more, but this time, she didn't even look at it. Her head tilted. "But I would like to speak with you again and help. I have to pull an early day today due to my other job, but let's make an appointment for you to come by the headmaster's office. I'll pull your file, and we'll go over things. Come up with a plan for you?"

That sounded really cool actually. I hugged my sketch-book. "Sure. And thanks."

"Of course. Tomorrow. First period? I'll make sure you have a pass with whoever your teacher is. I'll pull that off your file."

Sounded good to me.

I said that was fine, and when her phone rang between us again, she ignored it and took my hand.

"Good to meet you, Sloane."

"Good to meet you."

"Yes. Tomorrow?"

"Tomorrow."

"Perfect." Her hand easing out of mine, she smiled quickly at Dorian. "See you."

He lifted a hand to her, the woman stepping away. With her phone ringing, she finally answered it, and the door closed on her conversation when she slipped into the hall.

"No idea how she's balancing it all." Dorian pocketed his big hands. "I'm sure the mayor's office needs her more than we do."

"The mayor's office? What does she do there?"

Dorian swung smoky irises in my direction. "What does she do?" he asked, laughing. He directed a thumb toward the door. "Uh, Brielle is the mayor of Maywood Heights."

Um, what?

"Wolf didn't tell you?" His chuckle hit the air. "You both spent all that time painting, and he never, not once, mentioned his mother was the mayor of our city?" His eyebrow arched. "Fucker gloats about that shit. Thinks it makes him king of the world."

Or at least the prince of the city.

These boys really were royalty. I frowned. "We painted more than talked."

"I guess so." He weaved our fingers together. "Anyway, Brielle is here because she's babysitting. After everything with Charlie, she wants to make sure we're all okay, but she doesn't have time *at all* to be here." He shook his head. "But that's how she is. She's stubborn, and though my buddy won't admit it, the apple doesn't fall far."

He didn't need to admit it. He showed that shit. Once Ares put his mind to a thought or belief, that tended to be what stuck.

It had benefited me recently.

Dorian ran his hands down my shoulders. "You really haven't thought about college or anything? What were your plans after you graduate?"

I was kind of focused on his hands on me. They made it hard to think, and I was definitely aware we hadn't spent time in close proximity together since this last weekend. It'd been on purpose, excuses on my part. We had a lot of weight between us right now and…

My knuckles touched his chest. "Like I said, Bru and I moved around a lot. Didn't think college was possible. We were poor. At least before Callum."

Even then, his money wasn't ours.

He checked in with my brother and me a few times a week, and though he was moving closer to us, we couldn't forget our place. The man wasn't our father, and regardless of how he'd been good to us.

Dorian's hands left my shoulders after what I said, and his jaw shifted before he tipped my chin. "Well, I'd start thinking about it. This is your home, Noa Sloane, and you're not going anywhere."

He leaned in, and I thought he'd go for the lips. I hoped he would.

They were easier.

His lips on my mouth wouldn't allow me to think. I could just be with him and not think about other things between us. Things like what I did or did not say the other night.

That wasn't what Dorian did, though, and his mouth

brushing my check did terrible damage. He lingered there, his breath heating my skin. He let me *think* in that position.

You're not going anywhere.

I didn't want to. I wanted to just be, but my rogue thoughts wouldn't let me. I kept remembering what it was like to *not* be with him.

I kept remembering how it was when he'd left.

That wound stayed open, and though I wished to forget, it was so hard.

If Dorian saw that in my eyes, he didn't say. He simply kissed my cheek, then pulled back. He told me I'd see him later. He had to get back to class, and I was happy he once again hadn't pushed me. I wasn't ready to tell him I loved him yet, but it was almost worse he didn't push. It meant he was willing to wait.

I hoped secretly he wouldn't always be.

I preferred lunchtime with the dark prince. Lunch with him, Bow, and the rest of Legacy was filled with general boy debauchery and with little to no time for direct conversation with Dorian himself. He was usually engulfed in conversation, and I just blended in.

My brother actually joined the group for lunch today. He was finally starting to get caught up, and to celebrate, Wells and Thatcher suggested we all go to Jax's Burgers. The two made good on their promise to bring me food. When we ate at school, a bag of greasy goodness was always there for me at our lunch table.

The two jocks were well on their way to getting me to forget about what assholes they'd been, and it was kind of hard to be annoyed by them when they were so fucking goofy. They had me roaring in laughter most of the time. Especially because their antics constantly pissed off the two older boys. Ares and Dorian may only be a year older than them, but their lack of patience when it came to the two definitely showed. Dorian was pretty laid-back about it, but Ares spent more time knocking their heads together than anyone else. He always had a short fuse in general, but since Dorian had left, I hadn't noticed it as much. He seemed more at ease whenever I saw him.

"Wait. The fuck?"

Which was why his voice elevating on the other side of the booth caught me off guard. He had his hand raised, his finger shooting in Dorian's direction. "You took my mother to what?"

Dorian's arm dropped from my shoulders, and at this point, Bow stopped her conversation with my brother and the other guys. We'd had to push two tables together today at Jax's just to accommodate with the boys' grub. Dorian put his hands together. "I took her to meet Sloane."

"Why?"

Dorian's brow lifted slow. "Because she asked." He leaned back. "She wanted to meet the girl who'd helped you with your project. I ran into her in the hallway, and we got to talking about it." He tossed a fry at him. "What's your deal?"

He seemed to have one, Ares's gaze shifting in my direction. He had an audience, and once he realized he did, he sat back and gripped his arms. "My mom's busy, bro. She doesn't have time for that shit."

That… *shit*?

He grunted. "What did she have to say about it? The project? Sloane?" He shook his head. "I wasn't trying to bother her with that shit. She's obviously seen it and everything. I just don't want to bother her with any unnecessary shit while she's trying to work."

Again, I didn't know what he was calling shit, but whether he was talking about our project *or me*, I was insulted either way. I cocked my head. "What is your problem—"

"I was talking to D, little." Once more, he dismissed me, and what the fuck?

I twitched at his response, and he put his hands to his mouth.

"D, you know how busy my mom is."

"I'm aware." His arm returned behind me. "But like I said, she asked me." He eyed him. "And what's with you coming at Sloane like that?"

The question was on my mind too, everyone else watching on.

Ares's jaw shifted. "We just agreed that, even though my mom is at school, she *isn't*." His lips pulled together. "I obviously can't stop her from doing what she wants to do, but when it comes to us." He waved a hand at him and the guys. "We do our thing until she gets this out of her system and leaves."

Was he embarrassed by his mom? He shouldn't be. I mean, she was really cool. I cuffed my arms. "Your mom's really nice." I glanced between him and Dorian. "She even asked if I needed help figuring out college stuff."

His digit touching the table, his gaze flicked my way. "She did?"

I nodded, and Dorian did too. He put a hand out. "She was happy to help Sloane." He nudged me. "Especially when she realized she didn't have anything figured out."

My eyes lifted. "She was cool about it. Wants to meet with me tomorrow." I put my hands on the table. "But if this is going to be a thing, I can cancel."

I wasn't trying to piss beast boy off.

Even if I hadn't done anything wrong.

Ares's lips closed, and the rest of the group stayed real quiet. Wells leaned forward. "Wolf, bro. You okay?"

Ares tossed a fry in his basket. He shrugged. "My mom being there is just stressing me out." He eyed the table. "I'm sure none of y'all would want your parents around either."

The general consensus appeared yes from the way the guys all looked at each other, and it was rather stereotypical they wouldn't want their parents around them. I mean, what were we in? Grade school? I wished I had a parent to be around.

I wished I had parents.

I studied my brother on Bow's other side. He appeared just as confused as I felt. In fact, Bow looked that way too, silent as she nibbled her chicken fries. Maybe she didn't feel the same way they did as well.

"Nah, you can keep your appointment, little," Wolf stated, swallowing. He faced Dorian. "And I'm assuming we're not seeing you tonight? You and her are hanging out, right?"

I wasn't sure when I became a *her* or *shit*, but I really wasn't liking how he was both talking and referring to me.

What's his problem?

It felt like I was dealing with Dr. Jekyll and Mr. Hyde at the moment. True, Ares was always a prick. He was gruff in his delivery and often colder than the rest of the boys, but he had been coming around. At least when it came to me.

It appeared I wasn't the only one looking at Ares funny. He had the whole table's attention, but it was Dorian to tip his chin. The dark prince outlined his lips before he tossed an arm behind the booth. He glanced my way. "Actually, do you want to hang out with us tonight? The guys and I usually have a pizza night once a week at one of our houses. This one's at Wolf's." His attention drifted over to him. "That okay with you?"

Wolf sat up, but before he could speak, Thatcher shook Wolf's arms.

"Yeah, bro. That'd be fucking cool." He slapped my brother's chest. "You come too, man."

Alerted into this conversation, my brother opened his hands. "That'd be fun."

"Right?" Thatcher tipped his chin across the table. "Bow, you can come too since Sloane will be there."

"Well, thanks." The sarcasm absolutely lined her voice.

She glanced my way. "Will you be there? Probably shouldn't go unless you're there." She shrugged. "I don't want to get in the way. They do guy things, you know?"

I noticed her study the other end of the table. The only one there was Wells, and he was barely paying attention to the conversation anymore. In fact, he had his mouth full of burger bits, and Bow's cheeks completely colored.

I wondered if the little rabbit may have a bit of a crush. This wasn't the first time I'd caught her looking at him, but if a crush was the case, I wished her luck. Dude was a complete man ho like her brother, and it was lucky she or I could find table space at lunch whenever her brother and his friend brought their harems over.

They also weren't shy about their make-out sessions at the table, which made lunch hella fun. Between the two bros, I gagged on my milk most days.

"Now, I never said there was any goddamn party at my house." Ares's toned snipped, his eyes fire. "D…"

"It might be good to mix things up." He eyed him, his brow arched, and whatever was going on between these boys had me confused as fuck. Dorian nodded. "We'll all hang out and talk. It'll be good."

Ares said nothing, his gaze averting. He waved a hand, and it seemed all this was settled.

"So tonight?" Dorian's fingers folded behind my neck. "You should come. It'll be nice for us to all hang out, and you can get to know the guys more."

I felt put on the spot when he said that, but I'd be lying if I said I didn't prefer a group gathering. He may not mean to put pressure on me, but I felt it whenever it was just us.

I mean, he'd said he loved me.

That was still obviously there between us, and until I could get over myself and my reservations, it would for the present.

I agreed to meet up and quickly. With that all done, the

conversation flowed back to what it had been, but I noticed Ares wasn't a part of much of it. Actually, he stared more out the window than participated in the conversation with his friends, which bothered me more than I'd ever admit. He'd seemed to be cool with me. Like we really had a truce, but how he'd just been acting now didn't feel like one.

In fact, it felt like the opposite.

CHAPTER
THIRTY-EIGHT

Sloane

"We're not staying very long." I didn't want to come at all really, but Bru convinced me otherwise about the pizza night tonight.

He'd called me a lame-ass, and after nearly punching him out cold, I decided to get up and go. I didn't want to go, God did I not want to, and I told my brother that all the way over to Ares's house. We'd just gotten to his wrought-iron gate, and after pulling in front of the house, my brother turned off his Audi.

He scoffed. "We're going to leave when we're *both* ready." Since that wasn't our deal, I frowned, and his eyes lifted. "What's your problem? I thought you and Mallick were cool."

We had been cool until he'd gotten all weird at lunch. I shook my head. "I'm not staying long."

"Well, then your ass is calling a ride share." Bru got out of his car, and I growled. Our vehicle wasn't the only one in front of Ares's big-ass house. I noticed Dorian's ride and Thatcher's and Wells's too.

Ares's Hummer wasn't there, but I assumed he'd parked in the garage since this was his house. I caught up to my brother on the home's steps. "Bruno, I'm not joking."

"And I'm not joking about your butt finding a ride." He sighed. "Just chill for one goddamn night. Odds are, you and Dorian will be all over each other anyway."

"What's that supposed to mean?"

"What doesn't it mean?" His eyebrows wagged. "Ever since he got you all mushy on the football field, you guys have been inseparable."

He may be right about that, but that'd been before our last night together.

The pressure from that moment was still there, and I hoped we could all just hang out tonight. I wanted to commit to Dorian...

I loved Dorian.

I'd stupidly managed to fall for the dark prince, but my head was telling me another thing. I physically couldn't tell him what he needed to hear like something inside me was tugging me back. I was on a tether, and Dorian Prinze was the goal just out of reach.

I braced my arms. "I'm here for Bow too. She's my friend."

"Oh, I'm sure of it." Bru came down a step. "But dare I say, she might be pretty lonely tonight? I'm sure Dorian will have all your attention."

My lips closed.

Bru arched an eyebrow. "If I didn't know any better, sis, I'd say you were in love with Dorian Prinze."

He mussed my hair like an asshole, and I stayed back. I wondered if he wasn't the only one having these thoughts.

I wondered if it was that obvious. I wondered if I wore it all over me as deep as it was felt.

I hoped I didn't. Because even though Dorian was practicing patience, he might not for long, knowing I really truly did feel the same way. I couldn't ever see him pressure me, but that wasn't what scared me. What if he gave me another ultimatum?

And what if this time he meant it?

"Sup, kid?"

The door was open, Ares Mallick standing at it. My brother must have knocked because currently he tapped the fist of his teammate.

It was always weird seeing the boys out of their academy uniforms, Ares in a T-shirt and jeans. I'd obviously seen him up to his elbows in paint, but casual Ares jarred me. It was like those days we used to work together. We'd had so much fun, but that seemed like so long ago.

This seemed even more the case considering the way he'd treated me at lunch. I took a step, and he appraised my jeans and hoodie. Actually, he focused on me for a good long second, a frown pinching his lips. He hiked an arm against the doorframe. "Last to arrive, little. Any reason for that?"

I wanted to take my high-top and literally shove it down his throat for that. He obviously was still going through his PMS. I started to say something, but my brother got in front of me. "We both took a while getting ready. Sorry."

He lied for me, but since this was my fault, I stayed quiet.

A deep "hmm" passed between Ares's lips. He opened the door, telling my brother it was cool. Warm air touched my cheeks when Ares allowed my brother and me into his space, and immediately the spicy notes of fall and pumpkin spice hit my lungs. The foyer had been decorated with a fall theme, and the place felt homey right away. It was like a family lived here and not an angsty teen who had nothing but raging parties.

"Everyone is in the living room," Ares stated, *eyeing me again*. I didn't know his deal, but I didn't care enough to ask him about it. "We already ordered the pizzas. Got a bunch of options. The delivery guy said about a half hour."

"Cool." My brother had his hands in his pockets. Ares immediately started walking us through his large home, and Bru caught up. "Eh, Wolf. Your parents going to be around? Haven't met them. Just wondering."

I'd met his mom but not his dad, curious too.

Ares angled around. "No. Mom's been working late since she's got her two gigs." For some reason, that warranted another appraisal like that was *my* fault. He faced my brother. "Dad's been hanging there with her at night. Brings her dinner, and they spend time together."

Well, that was ridiculously sweet and nothing this guy would ever do. His parents seemed, well, normal.

With that, Ares brought us into his living room, and the place looked quite different without a bunch of partygoers. Bow, Dorian, and the gang were all in there, but people weren't lining the walls like they'd been. Just Ares's couches.

With the appearance of my brother and me, Bow bounced off the couch. She immediately hugged me in a squeeze. "Saved you a seat."

She'd been sitting near Dorian on the biggest couch, and the dark prince grinned from his seat next to Thatcher.

Dorian looked delicious, of course, his T-shirt tight across his broad chest, and whenever he wore jeans, I paid attention probably more than I should. He slapped Thatcher's chest. "She's eye-fucking me again, bro. What do I do?"

Fucking bastard.

I started to pivot around, but he grabbed me and tugged me onto his lap. He got a hand full of my ass and caused the rest of the room to groan. Especially my brother.

"This going to be a thing all night, you think?" Bru tossed the words at Thatcher, but he smiled.

Still, he was being an asshole. I flipped him off, and he passed that off to slap Thatcher's hand.

Thatcher snapped after. "Well, considering my boy is in love... I'd say that's a given."

My heart stopped, and Dorian sneered in his direction.

Thatcher raised his hands. "Please, bro. You didn't even have to tell us."

"It's so goddamn obvious." Wells stated this from his seat on the only other couch in the room. He lounged on it, his leg over one of the arms. He had his thumbs speed-typing across his phone and hadn't even looked up. "Like ridiculously obvious."

I nearly fell off Dorian's lap when he shot a pillow at Wells so hard the guy fell to his ass on the floor. He like legit rolled off the couch, his phone flying. Dorian had apparently put some oomph into it, and Thatcher exploded in so much laughter *he* almost fell off the couch. Dorian directed a finger at Wells. "You shut the fuck up, or I'll make you shut the fuck up."

"Jesus, bro. I was just messing with you." Wells rubbed his bottle-blond locks, his grin wiry. He got back on the couch. "I mean, this is only love in your direction."

"Yeah." Dorian growled it before his arms cradled me back into him. He glanced my way. "Sorry."

Both his look and tone were apologetic, and I hated that. I hated that he felt sorry. Even if he hadn't been talking to his friends about us.

I said nothing, and at this point, the room had settled enough where no objects were being thrown about. Bow sat at my side, but before Ares took a seat himself, he stood in front of the room. He clasped long fingers on his big arms. "And with that, we got some fucking rules tonight." He directed a look at Thatcher and Wells. "Especially with you two fuckers."

Thatcher and Wells exchanged a glance, and Ares snarled.

"The last time we got together, shit got crazy, and I'm not trying to clean up after you fools." Ares ticked a finger. "So rule number one is you eat off anything, you fucking clean it."

Wells snorted. "Well, that means Thatcher will be in the kitchen all fucking night."

Picking up Dorian's discarded pillow, Thatcher shot it at Wells, but Wells was quicker this time. He caught it, then reached over and slammed it on Thatcher's head. Thatcher firmly lost his shit, and the only thing keeping him from retaliating was Ares's bark at the front of the room.

Ares glared at the two. "Rule number two is no one outside of this room is coming in this house. Which means no calling fuck buddies over."

Thatcher kicked his boot at Wells. "Wells, you better take your ass home, brother. We know he's talking about you."

Wells clicked his tongue. "The fuck ever and don't get jealous because my fuck buddy pool is a ten when yours is like a five—at best."

"Who haven't *both* you two assholes fucked?" Ares's brow lift was slow. "I'm still trying to get the stains out of shit the pair of you left the last time you were here."

"Me too." Dorian lifted a finger. Dorian tipped his chin at Thatcher. "And, Thatch, we all know the rule applies to both of you."

Thatcher frowned. "What we all *know* is we're not the only ones." Thatcher waved a hand between him and Wells.

Wells's smile was coy when he placed it in Dorian's direction. He eyed him. "At least that used to be the case for all of us."

Dorian's smile wiped away. He sat up, but when I shifted, he stayed in place. I glared at Wells. "You, fucker, are a cocky son of a bitch." I glanced at Thatcher. "Same goes for you, and there's nothing wrong with not having to get your dick wet whenever the invitation's open." My eyebrows narrowed. "So why don't you both lay the fuck off Dorian? Off us?"

They had no right, but what I hadn't expected was both Thatcher and Wells to angle back.

Nor gain the rest of the room's attention.

Dorian had his brow up, obviously surprised by me jumping in and defending him.

You defended both of you.

Wells raised his hands. "Sorry, princess," he said before nodding at Dorian. "It seems we've crossed your queen."

"And don't do it again." Dorian's hand settled at my waist. He smiled at me, and something about it felt knowing. Something else about it had butterflies buzzing in my stomach.

They weren't bad.

"So rule number three, then," Ares said, watching us. He nodded. "No wandering the house and getting into shit. I don't need anything fucking broken, and my parents getting on me for it. You respect my stuff and my space." He glanced my way. "And I respect you."

Like a few things tonight, I had no idea where Ares's attention was coming from. Maybe it was because my brother and I were pretty new in *his space*, but Bru or I had never given Ares a reason to think we'd destroy anything.

I recalled him being very territorial the last time I was over here as well. He kept us outside the whole time when we painted.

Ares took a seat next to Wells with a grunt, and Dorian slow-clapped for him.

"Nicely delivered TedTalk, buddy," he joshed, and Ares grumbled.

Ares lifted a hand.

"Just don't want anyone fucking with my shit." He settled back. "We all do that, and we're cool."

The room got rather quiet then, awkward, and that may be why Dorian got the guys to start up a video game. The pizza still wasn't here yet, and he suggested the game while we waited. The boys were just starting to get it geared up when I got up. I needed to go to the bathroom.

"Want me to go with you?" Dorian got up, and even Bow

asked, but I remembered where at least one of the bathrooms was in this house. I'd been here before.

I told both him and Bow no and stepped past Ares. He'd been getting additional controllers set up. He stopped in front of me. "Where are you going?"

"The bathroom, that okay?" I crossed around him. "I remember where it is. Down the hall, right?"

"Yeah, but—"

I started to go, but he crossed in front of me again. I rolled my eyes. "Ares, I know where it's at."

"And this is a big fucking house." His lips pulled tight. "D or I should take you."

"I already told him I had it covered." Again, I crossed in front of him. "Lay off. I won't break anything."

I left him standing there, and it was by the grace of God he actually let me go by myself. The guy was being super anal about his stupid fucking rules.

I felt his eyes on my back the whole way, and when I eventually did come out, I was surprised he wasn't waiting outside the door for me. I started to go back to the others, but stopped when I took a second to admire all the art pieces on the walls. I'd noticed them when I passed them initially, but with Ares's eyes on my back, I couldn't study them.

I did now, truly in awe of them. There was lots of metal-work gracing the walls, bent steel in abstract pieces. I'd never done anything like that myself, and I wondered if Ares had created these.

"There you are."

Wells came sauntering down the hallway, his hands in his pockets. His grin easy, he angled in beside me. "His Majesty asked me to see what the holdup was with you."

My eyes narrowed. "Dorian asked that?"

"Nah, Wolf." Wells scrubbed into his hair, my brow twitching up. "Guy's on hundred today about these fucking rules. Wanted to make sure you didn't get lost on your way back."

Oh, dear God. I growled. "What the fuck is his problem?"

"Don't know, but it's probably us, Thatcher and me," Wells stated, chuckling. "I guess you break a thing or two in your buddy's house, and he gets some kind of way."

Apparently.

Wells glanced at the artwork. "Wolf probably should have assumed this would hold you up, though." He grinned, folding his arms. "He's an artist just like you, and this shit is so sweet."

He was right about that. I studied the angles. "I didn't know he was into this kind of stuff. Well, this kind of art."

"This one looks like his pop's actually." Wells hiked an arm against the wall, staring up. He pointed at a corner of the piece. "His dad's name is on this one. Ramses Mallick."

Leaning in, I did see the R and M bent into the work. "He likes to work with metals?" I recalled Ares saying his dad was an artist.

"Oh, yeah," he said, putting his fingers to his lips. He waved. "Wolf will kill me, but his dad keeps the good stuff in his home studio. Come on. We'll take a quick peek. Wolf won't even notice."

I didn't know how I felt about that. Especially since Ares was acting crazy right now.

The artist in me was intrigued, though, so I did follow the tall football player farther into the house. We didn't go far, just navigating a couple halls. On the way, Wells was smart and texted Ares the toilet was backed up. He wanted to give Ares an excuse so he didn't freak out and come looking for us.

Wells's cover was that he was currently helping me plunge it, and Ares apparently didn't want to fuck with that. He just barked at him to hurry the hell up, and the tone of the text was just as aggressive as hearing him say it.

"He's straight trippin' right now," Wells said when we arrived at the art studio's door. There was a lock on it, I guess, a finger pad above the knob.

I pointed at it. "Why's there a lock?"

Wells waved that off. "Ramses put it on when we were kids. We kept messing around in there."

"Uh, should we be going in there now, then?" It was one thing to take a peek, but if Ares's dad minded...

Again, Wells passed that off, and my brow jumped when he keyed in the code. The lock clicked, and he pushed the door open. He waggled his eyebrows. "It's fine. Wolf would care more than Ramses. His dad's so busy he like never works in here anymore, and Wolf's more protective over everything than he is. I think the lock is still on just because Ramses hasn't gotten around to taking it off. We're obviously not kids anymore."

Still, this felt kind of weird. I hesitated. "Why do you know the code?"

"Thatcher." Wells smirked. "He cracked it for us one day. Wolf wanted to get in there. Says it gives him inspiration or some shit." He stepped inside. "Come in. I know you're curious."

He left me before I could protest, and I groaned because *I was* curious. I strode inside, and let's just say the goods around didn't disappoint.

Especially when Wells clicked on the lights.

Large sculptures covered pretty much all available surface area, all metal and all... gorgeous. Ares's dad had turned a regular office into a museum, the place a treasure trove of both big and small pieces. For the most part, they were all metal, but there were painted canvases as well.

My jaw dropped. "Holy shit."

"Right?" Wells propped his back against a wall. He jutted his chin forward. "Check out the tower."

I pivoted and didn't need to ask what he meant.

Whoa.

A piece the height of the ceiling faced a large window, a step stool by it. It had all these cool sweeping angles, like a tree in a forest of metal, and I got why he called it the tower. The ceiling in here was at least fourteen feet.

"We all used to stare at this thing all the time *and* play on it." Wells came up beside me. I hadn't even realized I'd ventured over to the structure. Wells chuckled. "Hence the lock on the door. It's a shame Ramses doesn't really have time to get in here more. He's so good at what he does."

And this came from a non-artist. Even Wells could see how awesome this thing was, which was true. I hovered a hand over it. "You said his dad is busy…"

"Yeah, he is," he said, but his voice grew quiet. His jaw shifted. "Sometimes life gets in the way, I guess. He's a businessman like the rest of our fathers, so there's that."

He made it sound like that might not be the man's only obligation, or at least, not the only reason.

I guessed that wasn't any of my business.

Wells stepped over to the sole desk in the room. He nodded. "Seems Wolf might be working in here now, though."

Sketchbooks lined the desk where a computer would normally be. A couple were open, and I recognized the geometric work.

"Wolf likes to draw this kind of stuff," he said, picking one up. He glanced around the room. "I guess it's good this room is getting some use. Ramses told us it was soundproof once, so that's good for Wolf's tunes. He can blast them and stuff."

He did like to listen to music while he worked like me.

Wells's phone buzzed, and he handed me the sketchbook. I thought that may be Ares being ridiculous, but considering all the eggplant emojis pouring in from a contact by the name of *Ms. Deep Throat*, I may be wrong in that assumption.

Catching me looking, Wells waggled his eyebrows, then

proceeded to text back so many filthy words I had to avert my attention to avoid, well, *that shit.* I started flipping through Ares's sketchbook haphazardly, but a photo fell out of it.

I picked it up and was kind of confused by what I was seeing.

"Who's this?" I asked, and Wells got off his phone long enough to look. There were four people in the photo, a family. There was a woman I recognized as Ares's mother, Brielle. I mean, I'd just met her, so I recognized her even though she was younger. The man in the photo, I recognized too. Not only did he look like Ares, but I'd seen a younger photo of the guy at Bow's house.

The man was Ares's dad, Ramses. He was older than that photo I'd seen, but this was him. God, he was the spitting image of his son.

My confusion lay with the others in the photo. Ramses and Brielle held two children, babies, and the couple had one in each of their arms. Brielle lay in a hospital bed, the baby in her arms swaddled, and Ramses held the other by her side. He sat on Brielle's bed, the couple smiling into the camera.

I assumed one of these children was Ares, and Brielle clearly had just given birth. She had a tired glow about her face, but looked so happy.

I didn't get why there were two babies, though, and Wells took the photo when I handed it to him.

"Ares's parents." The frown pinched hard into Wells's lips. He pointed at the baby in Ramses's arms. "This is Wolf."

"Who's the other kid?"

"Ares's sister," he said, shocking me. Wells nodded. "Ares has a twin. *Had* a twin." He shook his head. "Though he's obviously only been told about her. He never got to meet her." He glanced my way, his sigh heavy. "They didn't even get to make it out of the hospital with her. Ramses and Brielle?"

Oh my God.

I didn't know what to say. I mean, what could be said to that?

"Wolf would never say, but I think a lot of his shitty attitude comes from that." His shoulders lifted. "I think the guy might have some survivor's guilt or some shit. He used to butt heads real hard with his parents, and Brielle and Ramses couldn't be nicer folks. Brielle is pretty tough, but she's cool. I think Ares just feels bad."

"Feels bad?"

Wells's lips turned down. "I think he feels like they got left with him. He'll say shit like that sometimes. Real fucked-up shit. Dark shit."

"I guess she and my dad got stuck with my attitude. Stuck with me."

Ares had said that when he took me to do the graffiti, but I had no idea he meant it literally.

Wells handed me back the photo when his phone buzzed again. He cursed. "I need to call this girl before she starts losing her shit. I told her we can't hang tonight, so she's freaking. Ares let her over last time, so she's giving me issues. I need to handle it."

I was still thinking about what he'd said about Ares, but pulled out of it.

Wells backed up. "Don't go anywhere. This will just take two seconds. I'll come back for you and walk you back."

I nodded, watching him escape to handle his *business.* I heard his voice hit the hall before I shifted my attention back to the photo.

It was so tragic.

I hated that what Wells stated about Ares made sense, things Ares had said and his attitude.

All this definitely didn't feel like my place to know, and I really didn't know how happy Ares would be that Wells had shared this information with me. Ares was very protective over his life, guarded.

I returned the photo to the sketchbook, then put it back on the desk where I'd found it. It felt really weird being in here now, but I did wait since Wells had told me to.

I glanced around the room, but my gaze caught on another sketchbook. This one was shoved between several boxes that were stacked, and the only reason I noticed it was because it was open.

And well, the image on the first page.

I could only see the top half of the sketch, but it was enough for me to pull the sketchbook out for a closer look.

But once I did…

It was *me*. Like I'd been sketched, and the rendering had been full body. I recognized my painting overalls, my hair up in a bun. The realism was spot on.

What?

I turned the page, seeing more of me. There were tiny sketches, three or so little *mes* in various poses on the page. Nearly all of them had me painting.

Some had me laughing.

I kept turning the pages. There were more and more of myself, and as I continued to flip pages, things somehow managed to get creepier.

There were some of me sleeping. In fact, it was the night I'd fallen asleep when Ares had come over. I was under the blanket I'd put on.

My heart raced, sketches of me eating on the next page. I was at the school and sitting at a lunch table by myself. I was in the hall and at my locker. There were just tons of me living life, but none of this felt flattering.

It felt obsessive.

Toward the end of the sketchbook a folder fell out, and that's when I stepped back. There weren't just sketches of me.

There were pictures.

Actual shots were taken of me. Bru and I were mostly in

these. They had to have been recent because my brother looked thinner. Some were at school, but others…

Were in my house.

There were photos *inside* with my brother and me on the couch. They were all from the same angle, our living room. They had timestamps like they were screenshots off a recording.

I was completely fucking shaking at this point. Especially when I looked up. A spot had been left where the sketchbook had been and tucked in it was a DVD. It was labeled two words: Sloane's House.

Oh my God.

"Why are you in here?"

Ares Mallick stood at the door of his father's office.

But he didn't have his eyes on me.

He was looking at what was in my hands, the folder, sketchbook, and some of the photos. He was blinking *rapidly*, and when our gazes clashed, he stepped forward.

I stepped back. "What is this?"

A swallow flicked his throat.

And he wasn't talking fast enough.

"What the *fuck* is this?" I waved the evidence. "Why do you have all this and a *DVD* of my house, Ares?"

But it wasn't just my house. He had it in my house.

I wondered for how long.

Ares stared at me, his hands coming up and locking over his head. "I can explain."

What could he explain?

How could he possibly?

This looked like he was… obsessed with me. I stepped back. "This is some stalker shit, Ares."

"I know what it looks like—"

"This doesn't just look it." I threw it all in his face, all of it exploding all over the floor. The sketchbook and folder, the photos… My throat tightened. "Are you like *in love* with me or something?"

He blanched. Like it was really so far-fetched that I'd said such a thing. He raised his hands. "No, and if you would just calm down, I'll tell you what all this is."

I couldn't calm down. I was freaked the hell out, so no. I couldn't fucking calm down.

It was all enough for me to make a wide fucking berth around him, and when he grabbed my arm, I shoved him off me.

"You touch me again, I'll fucking scream!" I was already screaming, and Ares looked horrified.

I think me shaking might have had something to do with it.

I was. My hands were actually trembling, and Ares backed up. It was at this point, Wells shot into the room and blinked at the pair of us.

"What's going on?" he asked, his phone midair. A voice drifted out of it, and he must have still been on his call. I had no idea where he'd taken it if he'd missed Ares coming in here. Wells's mouth parted. "What's with the shouting? What's going—"

He backed into the door when I shouldered past him, taking the opportunity. Ares and Wells were quick on my heels, but I didn't slow down.

"Sloane, stop."

It was Ares to speak, but I ignored him. I cut into the living room, my brother and Thatcher sitting on the floor. They had game controllers in their hands, shooting shit on the screen while Bow watched them from the couch. Dorian sat on her other side, his thumb tapping his phone, but when I came in, his head lifted.

He started to smile, but with all that shit trailing behind me, the expression was only the *start* of one. Ares's and Wells's heavy cadences stormed into the room, and when

Ares asked me to slow down again, Dorian lowered his phone. He looked at me, then Ares and Wells. "Um—"

"Ask your friend," was all I could say in explanation before ripping the controller out of my brother's hands.

Bru glared. "What the fuck—"

"We're leaving," I commanded and not fucking joking. To prove the point, I snatched his keys off the floor. I started to go, but Dorian got me this time.

The dark prince got his big hands on my shoulders. "What's going on? Why are you... What's up?"

"Sloane."

I cut to Ares, who'd spoken, and immediately seized up in Dorian's hands.

Dorian noticed, appraising me. Blinking, he glanced over at his friend.

Ares cringed. "Sloane, just let me talk to you. I can explain."

"What the fuck's going on?" Dorian's voice boomed in the room, and not only was my brother up, but Thatcher and Bow were too.

The room silenced but it wasn't as if Dorian hadn't spoken. Everyone was definitely aware, and no one more than Ares.

Ares's gaze flickered around, as if a sheep in the lion's den.

But he was the only predator here.

I reflected back to what I'd seen in his dad's office, and it was hard to deny the connection to previous events. He'd been so helpful, so *unusually* helpful. I thought he'd hated me and was simply jealous of me before that like he'd said, but him hating himself made more sense. Maybe he had been infatuated with me, and that put him between a rock and a hard place.

I mean, Dorian was his friend.

Dorian let go of me, guiding me back. "I'm talking to you, Ares."

He was, but Ares wasn't looking at him. The boy's gaze stopped on me. He swallowed. "Sloane—"

I grabbed Bru. "We're leaving."

I didn't wait for him to fight me on the decision or anyone else trying to come at me about it. I simply left, and since I had the keys, I got right in the car.

"Sloane, hold up. What happened?" Bru trailed on my heels but he wasn't the only party. Ares was once again following me, and how he'd managed to get out of the house before Dorian, I didn't know, but he had.

Once outside, he physically bounded over the Audi's hood. I'd seen him manage a feat before. He only had to use a hand since he was so tall, and though my cardio sucked, *I managed* to get outside and into the car before he could stop me.

I locked the door, and he started to tug, but Dorian's voice once again boomed the air.

Dorian was making his way out of the house. Instinctually, Ares blinked that way, and it was enough time for me to start the car.

And Bru to get inside.

My brother must have seen I was serious, because after I started the car, he basically leaped inside. He snapped the door shut, yelling at me to talk to him, but he wasn't the only one.

Ares's fist pounded against the door, and Dorian was running. It took me a second to realize the dark prince was trying to get in front of my car, but even with all his speed, the quarterback couldn't outrun my brother's Audi.

Dorian had been only quick enough to get hands on the hood before I sped around him.

He called after me, getting smaller and smaller in the rearview mirror, but I couldn't hear or see anything else besides my own thoughts in the moment. I just kept seeing pictures, images and sketches of me that'd been done without my permission.

And how I'd somehow mistaken his friend's attention for simple kindness.

CHAPTER
THIRTY-NINE

Dorian

I drove around for over two hours looking for Sloane.

She never went back home.

I knew because I waited outside her house after I went after her. I'd been quick, but by the time I'd gotten into my car, she'd already peeled off into Wolf's neighborhood.

And I hadn't been the only one to go after her.

Wolf had taken *Wells's* car. Probably because we'd all been parked outside of his house. I saw him handling our buddy for his keys through my rearview mirror, and he got them because he wasn't that far behind me. We'd *both* gone after Sloane, my mind straight trippin' about that.

None of this made any fucking sense.

I didn't know the story. Why she'd left, but Wolf clearly had done something. I lost him during the search and never did find Sloane. Like stated, she never came home, and during *my search*, I'd been trying to call my buddy to pick up the goddamn phone.

I blew his phone the fuck up but with no answer, and

when I tracked it, I realized why. The tracking app I had shown his phone was still at his house, which meant he'd left it.

How had the night turned into this?

We were supposed to tell Sloane things tonight. *I* was supposed to tell Sloane things tonight. It was long past due time that she knew about my grandfather, but I'd been hesitant. She'd just been starting to trust me again and...

Wolf had been in my ear for what felt like forever about it. He didn't like keeping her in the dark and thought she could actually help us. She could if she believed us, believed me, but I wasn't nearly as confident as him. She still didn't trust me. Even after everything and me trying to show her every day that she could.

I'd only fucked up everything more by telling her I loved her, and that hadn't been a part of the plan *at all*. I kept blowing up our fucking plans, and if my grandfather had eyes on her, he definitely knew she wasn't just a lay for me. She was my girl, *mine*.

The only thing my friends and I could do now was tell her everything and hope to fucking God she'd be receptive to what was still just theories. We knew my grandfather was moving here, and with Sloane's father working for him in the past, that connected Sloane to my grandfather in a chilling way. My grandfather loved chess, and Sloane and her brother felt like the perfect pieces. He virtually owned them. He could *do* anything he wanted with them, and he was a man who had a propensity for some dark shit. My grandfather and his possibilities were endless, and what was worse, he had an edge over me. He had looked out for Sloane. He had her trust, and I was the guy who'd pushed her away.

It didn't matter that she knew I loved her.

I knew that as well, as I'd been driving around town looking for her tonight. I'd called her too, of course, texted her, but she didn't get back to me. Whatever had happened with her and Wolf had freaked her out, but she hadn't come to me. She hadn't waited for me *to help* when she should have been able to, and if that didn't tell me all I needed to know about her trust in me, I didn't know what did.

I had no time for pride at the present. I just wanted to fucking find her. In our group chat, Wells and Thatcher told me they'd been looking for her. They'd taken Bow, and everyone was out scouring the city. They hit up the school and several parks, and in all this, Wolf remained silent in the chat.

He hadn't texted back, *not fucking once*, so when I finally did hear something, I was goddamn fucking surprised.

Wolf: We need to meet up. Where are you?

It was like I saw red in that moment, my own trust fucking limited. He was making it really hard to hold faith in him, and the only reason I had a semblance of it was because the last time I'd questioned him, I had been in the wrong.

I sat up in my seat, parked outside Sloane's house. I'd come back around to her house after my circulation of her neighborhood. I wanted to stay close in case she came back.

Me: Sloane's.

Wolf: I'll meet you there.

He'd texted back in seconds, and by the time he did get there, I was out in the street. I had my jacket off, pacing, but I wasn't going to handle things like I had in the past. It wouldn't come to blows with my friend, but that had nothing to do with him.

I'd made Sloane a promise. I was *trying* for Sloane. I wouldn't let my anger take hold of me.

But that didn't mean it made it easy to look at him.

When Ares got out of the car, *Wells's car*, he didn't immediately come over. He had his hands to his mouth, his eyes fucking wild, and though I stopped pacing, he started.

He didn't stop.

"I fucked up, D," he started with, working his hands. He

braced them on his arms like that was the only thing he could do to keep from messing with them. "I fucked up so bad, man."

"How?" My fists tightened, my throat the same. "What happened and where were you?"

"I was out looking for her, but I can't find her." He breathed into his hands. "She found it all."

"Found what?"

"It *all*." He glanced my way, shaking his head. "She knows I've been recording her. That *we've* been recording inside her house. She found one of the DVDs from the camera I put in to watch for your grandfather."

I closed my eyes.

"I kept it in my dad's studio since he never goes in there." He swallowed. "She found it all, D. The screenshots from the surveillance. The folder I made for her and her brother. I don't know what all she saw in there, but she's at least seen the photos. She threw them at me before she ran off."

He'd created a docket for them, notes and stuff he'd actually started before I'd come back to town. He really had been trying to get to the bottom of things with Sloane and her brother back then, and anything he found, he'd kept in there.

Of course after I came back, Thatcher had taken over the case. He'd made a digital file, but Wolf still kept the hard copies at his house. He said they'd be safe there.

I put my fists to my mouth.

"But it's not just that."

I panned, my friend coming over after what he said.

"It's so bad, Dorian," he said, his swallow hard. "She found my sketches."

My eyes narrowed. "What?"

"She found my sketches, bro." He raised and dropped his hands. "And now, she thinks I'm stalking her. She thinks I'm a fucking freak—"

"What *sketches*, Ares?" I scanned for his eyes, but they averted. I braced his arms. "Ares."

He stared off, his eyes fucking haunted. "I couldn't help it." He pressed a fist to his mouth. "She was in my thoughts all the time."

What the fuck?

"Ares?" My brow lifted. "Buddy… what are you talking about?"

"I drew her," he confessed, making me blink. He cringed. "I drew her a lot, and she found all that."

"What do you mean she was in your thoughts all the time?" I asked, and he wouldn't look at me again. I made him. "Bro, you better fucking talk to me."

The words cracked, *broken* and goddamn shattered. I honestly didn't even know how I said them without…

I stayed steady. I checked myself. I had to because if I did anything else in that moment, my voice wouldn't have been the only thing to fucking crack.

"I couldn't help it," he rasped. My hands were braced over his shoulders, and he grabbed them. "She was in my thoughts. My only thoughts most days." He shook his head. "I couldn't close my eyes without seeing her, and the drawings became the only way I *could* see her." He raised a hand. "You said I couldn't trust her, and I didn't *know* if I could trust her." He swallowed. "The drawings were all I had. Even if I couldn't trust her, I at least had those. I just found her, bro, and I had to have a way to see her."

Found her?

Ares was breaking down at this point, his hands gripping mine to fucking hell. He dropped to his knees, and I went with him.

"Ares." I made him look at me. "What do you mean *found her*?"

The color had bled from him, like he truly was on the brink of a crash. He faced me, his nostrils flaring. "I have to tell you something *impossible*, and once I do, you have to help me find her. We can't lose her, man. *I* can't lose her. Not again."

I had no words, my buddy squeezing my shoulders.

"It's her," he said, nodding. "It's *her*, and I don't know how. I don't, but it is her. I swear to God it is. I even have proof. DNA."

I gripped his hands. "Who?"

And then he said a name, one I hadn't heard in years. The name had been buried, *gone*, and it had to be because too much hurt surrounded it.

My buddy and I had too many losses in our lives, too much heartache. The loss of Charlie and my grandparents before that had placed me in anguish, but at least, I'd gotten to know them. Ares's hurt was one of the unknown. His was a *what-if*. He'd never gotten to know the person he lost.

He'd never even been graced with a memory.

CHAPTER
FORTY

Sloane

"This is ridiculous," my brother proclaimed. Sitting up on the bed, he picked up his phone. "I'm calling Callum."

Well, if he found him, he needed to let me know.

I'd been trying for the last two hours.

I wanted to know if he'd actually purchased the home he'd talked about, and if so, if the place were in any type of condition we could crash at. I couldn't go back home.

I'd given Ares the codes.

I didn't think Ares would hurt me, but he did have a *problem*, and I didn't feel comfortable going to a place he had access to. He'd basically been blowing up my phone since I'd left his house, saying I needed to call him and shit. His texts all said the same thing. He needed to talk to me and explain, but there was no fucking way he could explain stalker shit. He was fucking crazy, so being at my house tonight wasn't an option.

Contacting Callum would be easier. I didn't currently

know where he was on the globe, but he wasn't in town, so if he had a house, my brother and I could chill out there.

However, this plan went belly up when I couldn't get a hold of him and Plan B had been this—a motel. I found Bru and me the quickest one I could find and used the credit card Callum had given me for food, general necessities, and emergencies. If this wasn't an emergency, I didn't know what was.

My brother tapped on his phone, and by the grace of God, he hadn't fought me much on coming here. I'd told him Ares and I had an argument, and I wasn't going back to the house for him to roll up and get in my face about it. Once Bru heard that, he hadn't been happy and immediately wanted to drive back to Ares's place. He had no choice but to go with me since I'd been behind the wheel at the time, though.

Bru's counter from there was to call Dorian. He wanted to tell him to check his friend, and though I agreed with that, I refused that option too. Dorian himself had called and texted me many times, but I couldn't talk to him. Not about this. This was…

I forced out a breath, watching as my brother's call to Callum must have gone to voicemail. He huffed. "No answer."

Just like me. I scrubbed into my hair. "Well, we're staying here, then."

"Okay, well, what about tomorrow?"

I shrugged, and he groaned.

He gripped the bed. "This is stupid. You and Wolf need to figure this shit out." He tossed a pillow. "I'm not trying to sleep in this roach motel."

He was completely overexaggerating. The place wasn't a roach motel, but it wasn't a five-star hotel either.

"You'll deal with it," I said right as my phone rang *again*. I looked at it hoping it was Callum, but when I saw Dorian's name, I lowered my phone. I let it go to voicemail, and seeing that, my brother frowned.

"Why aren't you talking to him?" He raised a hand. He directed a finger toward the phone. "He needs to talk to his friend if the guy pissed you off."

I wished it were that easy.

I made no moves to do anything, and rolling his eyes, Bru got up. He put his jacket on, going to the door, but I grabbed his arm. "What are you doing?"

He eased his arm out of my hand. "Getting some food. I saw some vending machines when we came in." When I eyed him, he shot it right back. He gripped his arms. "The guys were about to get pizza, remember? I never got to eat it, and I'm fucking starving."

"Well, call a pizza here, then."

"I will, but I need something before it gets here."

I didn't like the sound of him leaving the room, but I didn't think Ares followed us out there. I didn't see anyone following us. I pointed a finger. "You come right back."

"I will." He popped his collar. "And relax. You're acting weird."

If he knew what I'd seen in that office, he wouldn't say that, but since he hadn't, he simply shook his head at me. He left, the door clicking behind him, and I ventured outside too.

I watched him as far as I could before he disappeared around the corner, feeling really that paranoid. Ares was acting completely psycho, and I really didn't want my brother or me around him.

My phone buzzed, a text this time.

Dorian: Look. I talked to Wolf.

My heart raced.

Dorian: Call me please. I don't know why you haven't or why you aren't answering my calls, but you can. You can talk to me. You have me, little fighter. I told you that. I'm in your corner, so if you're running, you don't have to. I got you always.

The thing was he didn't even have to say it.

Because I knew it.

I hadn't wanted to forgive Dorian Prinze. I hadn't wanted to love him, but that feat proved to be as impossible as forgetting him. Even when he'd gone and hurt me so bad, I couldn't will him from my thoughts. He was embedded, a part of me, and because he was, I physically couldn't bring myself to hurt him.

And that news about Ares would.

If his friend truly was conflicted, I could think of nothing more than the hurt that'd cause Dorian himself. Ares wasn't only his best friend, but his *brother*. Something like that would kill Dorian, and he already had too much hurt.

You really do love him.

Dorian: Please, little fighter.

Dorian: We need to talk, and I need you to come back. Wherever you are, just come back to me.

Dorian: I love you.

I loved him too. So much, and if me wanting to protect his heart wasn't that, I didn't know what was. It pained me to even think about coming between him and his friend.

God, I love him so much.

Me: I did run. I'm sorry. I got scared. You said you talked to Ares?

I hoped he had. Like I said, I couldn't do that to him.

My phone rang in the next second, Dorian again. I felt relief like I never had, and that only reaffirmed my previous thoughts. I was completely in love with him. I needed him.

I answered. "Dorian—"

The hands came from behind me, large hands.

They covered my whole face.

I couldn't even scream, the phone slipping from my fingers. I punched at the hands, kicking, and soon, the hand over my mouth was replaced with a cloth.

I breathed in, things getting hazy. I stared down at my phone, the thing shattered but my last thought had been

Dorian's smile. That lazy grin had always made it into my thoughts, and I hated myself that I hadn't told him how it made me feel. That I hadn't told him how *he* made me feel.

I should have told him.

My eyes rolled back as I gave into the darkness. I hoped I got to see that grin again.

CHAPTER
FORTY-ONE

Sloane - age 6

Mommy and Daddy were arguing again.

They thought I was asleep.

I couldn't sleep because my head hurt again. The doctor said it would hurt for a while.

"He's going to be angry," Daddy whispered. Mommy and Daddy's room was on the other side of my wall. "How could you do this? Do this to her?"

"I did what I did *for* her," Mommy said, crying. She didn't speak for a while, sniffling. "I had to *try*, Godfrey. I love her."

Daddy said nothing. Their room was so quiet.

"She'll be worse off," Daddy gasped. "When he finds out, she'll be worse off."

"He won't."

"He will, Marilyn. Doesn't matter where he is. He has ears everywhere. He'll find out what you tried to do."

"How would he?" Mommy's voice was shaking. "You're not going to tell, and *she* can't. Her recall has suffered. You heard the physician."

Mommy was using big words, and I didn't understand.

Daddy huffed. "And thank God for that. Thank God any memory of what you tried to do was left back there, but that won't stop him. He'll still have people question her."

"So we run."

"Run?" Daddy paused. "That's not possible. *You know* him—"

My little brother Bruno's voice caused me to blink, then sit up. He said Daddy's name.

"I can't sleep," Bru whined.

"It's okay, son. Come here."

The room quieted, no more voices.

"I'm going to put him back to bed," Daddy continued. "You've ruined us both."

"Have I?" Mommy said. "At least I tried. At least I admit I have a heart. I do love her, and it doesn't matter what you say, or how you act. You love her too, Godfrey. I've seen you with her."

"I'm putting *our son* to bed. Or have you forgotten what's fact?"

"I wished I could forget," Mommy stated, her voice low. "I wish I could as easily as you."

A door slammed, and I shook, frightened by it. It also hurt my head, and I touched it, the bandage soft under my fingers. The doctor said I'd heal soon, but that my head hurting would happen. He said that was normal, though.

It was normal after a fall.

I didn't remember falling. Mommy and Daddy had told me about it. I'd just woken up with lots of doctors and a hurting head.

I wished it didn't hurt now. I wished Mommy and Daddy didn't fight. They kept fighting since I'd hurt myself.

This is my fault.

If I hadn't fallen, Mommy and Daddy wouldn't argue anymore. It started real bad after the fall.

I hugged my pillow, pinching at my wrist. My bracelet wasn't there when I woke up in the hospital. I wondered if I'd left it there.

I wished I could find it.

CHAPTER
FORTY-TWO

Dorian - present

I heard her voice for all of a second before the call ended, and when I lowered my phone, my friends were staring at me. Wolf and I had gone back to his place, and Wells and Thatcher returned when we called them back. They'd dropped Bow off at Thatch's before they arrived, making up some excuse. I didn't know what they'd ended up telling her, but I wasn't thinking about any of that right now.

"Did she answer?" shot right away in my direction, Wolf on the couch. He sat completely still between Wells and Thatcher, his hands together. He sat up. "Dorian?"

"Yeah," I said because she had. I heard my name, but then the call ended. I shook my head. "I lost her. I don't know if the call dropped or…"

I redialed before I could finish the statement, hoping she just had a bad connection or something. She'd answered me.

She *had* answered.

Pick up, Sloane. Pick up, baby.

She didn't, the call moving right away to voicemail. It didn't even fucking ring.

"Dorian?"

My friends had gathered around me, but only one of them spoke.

Wolf pushed his way through, his head shaking. I found him hard to look at while I restlessly attempted to contact Sloane. He'd wanted to do it.

But it couldn't be him, though. It had to be me. It always had to be me because it was me and her. *I* had to bring her back.

Why hadn't she let me?

I'd tried to talk her down. I'd tried to talk her back, but she'd shut me down. She'd shut me out. I swallowed. "Ares…"

He laced his fingers above his head, spinning out of the huddle. My buddy was on his way to a quick spiral, and I knew what had to be done next.

It was like the record stopped when I lifted my phone, my friends' eyes on me. I spun through contacts, and Wolf pushed his way over again.

"What are you doing?" he asked, his swallow making his throat jump. He was a wreck, visible pain all over his face. I'd only seen him that way one other time, and that was the day I'd told him I was done with him. He looked like he'd died a slow death.

"I'm calling my dad," I said, but upon finding his contact, I paused. I looked at Wolf. "But I don't think it should just be me."

Bringing our parents into this, *all of them*, was well over-due. It had been before, but especially now.

And that went triple for him.

I had no idea why my buddy kept certain things in his life so close to the cuff, but I'd be naive to think I had nothing to do with it. I'd given him reasons to doubt certain things.

I'd given him reasons to doubt *her*.

Wolf stayed silent, Thatcher and Wells too at his sides. The pair knew everything that had occurred tonight, of course, everything Wolf had told me. We'd told them when they got here. Wolf shook his head. "What will this do to them?" he asked, his nostrils flaring. "My mom and dad. What will this do to them, D?"

I had no answers for him, my friend, my brother opening his own Pandora's box tonight. This one couldn't be closed either once it was done.

I decided to do something for my friend in that moment. It was something he'd do for me, and I needed to help my friend for once instead of hindering him. I needed to be his brother like he had me.

I swiped my phone to a different contact, one *he* needed. I dialed after that…

Then handed him my phone.

———

Sloane

I woke to the smell of gasoline. So pungent, I choked on it, my eyes watering. I gagged, and I saw him through watering eyes.

A man in black.

In fact, he wore all black down to his boots, his bulky figure definitely indicating a man. He had a red gasoline container in his hands, and with his hood up and head lowered, I couldn't see his face.

He was pouring gasoline *everywhere*. The container he had seemed to have a never-ending supply, and he worked quickly, surrounding me with it.

Though I was still hazing in and out, I realized where I

was, even if I couldn't identify the exact location. The man
had me in some kind of warehouse. A factory maybe? There
were big machines with the conveyor belts and stuff.

The man wouldn't stop pouring. He continued to slosh
the gas about, and I watched in horror when he made a circle
around me *with gas*. He had me tied to some kind of chair,

The guy's head shot up immediately. The first thing I
noticed was the man's eyes, dark, haunted. He had grease-
paint covering his face, his beard overgrown…

But I still saw him.

I still *recognized* those eyes and pretty much right away.

The man twitched in front of me, and the shock of his
presence rattled me silent. This didn't make sense.

"Dad?" I breathed out, staring at my father. "Dad,

He should be dead. *He was* dead. I'd seen his casket. It'd
been closed, but I'd seen it. After the fire, my brother and I
had been told there was all but nothing left of the man we
knew as our father. The authorities had said he'd been burned
to the point where there wasn't anything to show at the
funeral. At least nothing that wouldn't be disturbing, and I'd
refused to subject Bru to that. Seeing our father in that condition would have killed him.

It would have killed me.

We loved our dad. He'd had his troubles, but we loved
him. Love was never a question, but this, what was
happening now, didn't make sense. He shouldn't be alive. He
shouldn't be doing this… whatever he was doing.

The man shook his head incessantly as if he was trying to
shake something out of it. Ignoring me, Dad continued to
pour gas, and I gasped.

"*Dad,*" I forced out, my mouth so dry and my body achy. I
had no idea how long I'd been out and tied to this chair, but

pangs in my limbs told me it'd been awhile. "Dad, what are you doing? Why are you *here*? What happened—"

He shushed me like a child, but it wasn't a normal shush. His finger shook against his mouth, a vacancy behind his eyes.

"I have to. I have to," he whispered, the words chillingly low. Severing eye contact, he poured more gas. "I need to."

"Dad—" I cried out as he lifted the can and spilled the last of the gas on my jeans, my shoes. The smell violated my lungs, and I shifted in my chair. "Dad, stop."

"No. No. Can't stop." He sounded unhinged, crazy. "I can't stop. It must be done. It *has* to be done."

"Daddy." I hadn't called him that since I'd been a child, my eyes watering. "Daddy, please stop this."

He faced me then, really looked at me.

He looked so sad.

A visible pain rimmed his eyes. Like it hurt just to look at me.

He touched my face then, and where I should have pulled away, I didn't. There was so much care there in his touch, his thumb gentle when it brushed my cheek.

"I did love you." His lips pinching together, he gazed away. "I did, and she did too. Always did. Your mother."

The tears rolled down my face now. Why was he telling me this?

His teeth clamped down on his lip, his hand squeezing his eyes. "I have to, Sloane."

"You don't have to," I gasped, blinking down more tears. "Whatever you're doing, you don't have to do."

He poured gas around me, *on me*, and people only typically used gas for one reason. My father was starting a fire.

And I was at the center.

Swallowing, I gazed around to find many tanks, ones with warning signs all over them. Some of them said *flammable* and other horribly chilly words. None of this meant anything good for me.

Dad left me then, continuing to pour a line from my seat to those very cans. After he finished, he tossed the can, then came back. He hunkered down.

"I have no choice," he said, hanging his head. "I have to protect your brother."

What?

"I did love you," he repeated, nodding. He got up. "Every time I said it, I meant it. I did, and it hurt every time."

But why would it hurt?

Dad's throat jumped. "She was right. Everything your mother said was right." His hands braced his arms. "I tried to honor her. I did, but it was too late. *I* was too late, Sloane..."

"Too late?" The words trembled from my lips, my dad blurry. I could barely see him behind my tears.

He cringed, as if seeing them there hurt him too. His mouth parted. "To save you, sweet girl."

He lifted a match in front of me, and my eyes expanded. I thought he'd throw the flame at me, but he drew back and tossed it behind the barrels.

The flames were immediate, massive. He must have poured gas there too, and I watched in horror as the flames ate the factory's machinery. They hadn't caught up to the barrels yet, and when I looked away, I found my father's eyes, his sight on me.

"Take care of your brother," he said, backing away. He ran through the barrels, his route the opposite way of the flames.

"Dad!"

My cry disappeared within the fire's roar, its smoke billowing up and filling the room. I coughed, large flames eating the big machines.

"Someone help!" I screamed, rocking back and forth in my chair. I tugged at the tie on my wrists.

Pop! Pop! Pop!

The sounds of rapid fire surged the air, initial rounds followed by more. It sounded like *gunshots*, and I jumped so bad, I teetered.

My chair fell to the floor, my face slamming against concrete. I cried out, my shoulder and hip burning.

"Help!" I cried, my wrists tugging weakly at tethers. "Someone help me. Please!"

Nothing but roaring flames surrounded me, my legs kicking. My jeans caught on a part of the chair, and I realized I broke one of its legs in the fall.

Come on, Sloane. Come on.

I kicked at the chair, my own leg coming away free. Working onto my knees, I brought the rest of the chair with me. I might be able to get my hands out if…

"Miss Sloane!"

My head shot up, a man in a billed hat and dark suit coming over to me. I recognized him as Callum's driver Lucas, and he had his gloved hand over his face, smoke completely around him.

"Lucas?" I gasped, the man nodding. "What are—"

"Are you hurt?" He went for my hands firsts, freeing them. Once he got them loose, he kicked the rest of the chair off me. "Can you stand?"

I was so frazzled he had to help me, physically picking me up. Keeping his back to the flames, Lucas shielded me, and he ran us out of the factory so quick the journey itself felt like a blur.

I coughed once outside, both of us. The night had turned to day, and once Lucas put me down, I wasn't standing for long.

The flames blew out of the factory's windows, a large explosion ringing the air. Lucas grabbed me, covering me.

"My dad!" I called out. "My dad's in there."

I didn't know why I said that. After *all that*, I didn't know why. Maybe it was the last things he said. How he'd loved me. How he told me to take care of Bruno. My father had a lot of mental health issues. But even with them all, he hadn't been what he'd shown me inside.

He must have just gone over the edge.

Lucas didn't let me up until the explosion calmed, and I must have still been yelling about my dad. He held my shoulders. "Your father is gone, Miss Sloane," he said, shaking his head. "He fired on me, and I had to act."

Fired on him?

He opened his jacket then, showing me what was inside. He had a gun, *strapped*. He nodded. "I'm Mr. Montgomery's personal security as well as his driver."

"What..." I gasped. "My dad's gone?"

"He is." His head lowered. "I'm sorry, but he didn't survive. I fired a warning shot but..."

He didn't survive.

But how was he *alive*? What happened and why did he come after me?

Lucas closed his jacket. "Are you okay? Can you get up?"

Again, he helped me up, and though my hip and shoulder hurt, it wasn't because of the fall. Physically, I could stand just fine.

I was in a daze, and Lucas had to steady me. He held my shoulders. "Are you injured?"

I didn't think so, shaking my head. Some sirens rang in the distance, and I gazed around.

"I called for assistance," he said. "I was already on my way over. Your father took you in your brother's car, and my employer and I were able to track you via the GPS."

I didn't know that could be done, but I guess that was good.

Especially in this case.

"Bru—"

"Your brother is fine," he said, and must have felt like I was okay because he let go of me. "He managed to get a hold of Mr. Montgomery late last night. My employer was actually already on a flight on his way back into town. He'd wanted to surprise you kids, but didn't get your calls until after he landed."

"Callum's here?"

"Yes, and at not a moment too soon as it seemed." The man nodded. "Your brother found your phone outside that motel room. Then with you and the car missing, he was obviously worried. Like I said, he managed to get a hold of Mr. Montgomery, and my employer contacted the motel. He was able to work with them and get the security footage outside your room."

The firetrucks arrived then. They sped onto the scene with police assistance, and the already heightened situation reached new levels for me.

I teetered in a sea of words, Lucas explaining to me how they'd spotted my father on the footage. How my dad had drugged me and taken me. The words came as firemen flew out of their trucks, and the cops were with them. They all took over the situation entirely, hoses being pulled toward the fire and cops asking if Lucas and I were okay. I couldn't hear anything. I couldn't speak.

"Did he say why he did this, Miss Sloane?"

I faced Lucas after what he said, the only words that had apparently broken through. I'd been in a head fog, cops and fireman yelling around me...

Water spraying flames.

Lucas homed in. "Did he say why he came after you?"

My father hadn't said why, and I didn't know. "No. I don't know why he did."

Since I had no more answers for the man, I gazed away. Looking at the building, I simply watched the dying flames.

I mean, what else could I do?

CHAPTER
FORTY-THREE

Sloane

At the scene, the police asked Lucas if he'd like an escort on the way to the hospital. Callum's driver had wanted me to get checked out after seeing I had some bumps and bruises.

I didn't think that required a police escort, though, but the cops had been adamant about it. They'd even highly advised it, but Lucas let them know he had the situation covered. He took me away from the scene and let me know both Callum and my brother would be there upon arrival. I was relieved to hear that news, and of course, I wanted to see them both, but I also wanted to see someone else. I'd been on the phone with Dorian before all this started.

I needed to see him *badly*. I needed to hear his voice and just be around him. I had no idea when I'd turned into this girl, but possibly being surrounded by flames had turned me into that. I could have died today.

I need to see him.

I started to ask Lucas if I could borrow his phone for all of a second before realizing I didn't have Dorian's number memorized. I would have to wait until I at least saw Bru. He had Dorian's number in his phone.

The hospital was… surrounded. Legit, there was like a ton of people outside, news vans. The scene itself reminded me a lot of the time I'd gone to Dorian's neighborhood and all those news people had been parked outside his gated community.

Lucas eased his sedan through them, tapping his horn, but as soon as he did that, the floodgates opened. People started taking pictures of *our car* and tapping on the windows.

"Is it her?" Some of them questioned, hitting against darkly tinted glass. "Open up. Is it her?"

Is who her?

I whipped around, studying these people through the window. "What's going on?"

I asked the question to Lucas, the man full-on honking this time to get through the traffic of people and cameras. The whole outside of the hospital was a clusterfuck, and when we pulled up to the doors, he turned. "They're here about your story, Miss Sloane, but it will be okay."

My… story?

"Now, I want you to stay put until I open the door for you." He nodded. "I'll get you inside and to your brother. Don't talk to anyone, but if you do, say strictly no comment. Mr. Montgomery is handling the situation."

I had no idea what the fuck that meant, but I could only gather in this nosy-as-fuck town people had heard I was kidnapped.

Shit, word traveled fast.

I guess *I* was the five o'clock news because those shutters went off in rapid fire when Lucas opened the door.

"It's her. It's her!" shouted around me, people snapping my picture, but Lucas was quick. He grabbed me, and we went soaring through the sea of people and cameras.

Holy shit.

My heart was racing by the time we finally got into the hospital, and once we did, everyone was looking at us. Nurses and doctors *stopped*, and every other person milling around was staring at me.

What the fuck?

"Come on, Miss Sloane," Lucas guided, getting us on the first elevator we could get to. He seemed to know where we were going because when they opened, he took us right out. We zipped through halls, the man fast and I noticed no one was around on this floor. I mean, I legitimately saw no doctors or anyone.

At least until my brother.

Bru stood in front of a television screen, his hands clasping his arms. His back to me, he stood in the center of a hospital room with a made bed, and he must have heard us come in because he shifted.

His shoulders visibly sagged, an instant relief flooding his face. Right away, he crossed the room over to me, and I had him in my arms before he could even make the trip halfway.

I hugged the shit out of my brother, actually shaking. The past twenty-four hours had been completely fucked and for so many reasons.

"Holy shit, Sloane. Holy shit," he just kept saying, and I was crying. His swallow sounded in my ear. "Holy shit."

Holy shit was right.

I squeezed him harder, not wanting to let go.

"You two kids stay here," came from behind us, and when I opened my eyes, Lucas was at the door. He had his hat under his arm. "I'm going to let Mr. Montgomery know Sloane's returned safe. He's with the hospital's director about the situation. Texted that on the way over. He informed me this whole floor is secure, but don't leave the room just in case. The press are very hungry for Sloane's story."

This was *crazy*, madness. What kind of fucked-up town

cared this much about someone else's business? I was nobody, no one.

Lucas closed the door behind him, and eventually, my brother let me go. I hadn't been the one to do it, and I only think he did to look at me. He scanned my eyes. "It was Dad? I saw him on the video feed, but…"

I nodded before he could finish, my brother blinking.

"Did you know he was alive?" he asked, eyes wild. "Why did he take you?"

I didn't want to tell my brother what our father did only moments after he confirmed our dad was still around.

I didn't want to tell him Dad was dead even more.

I had no logical answers for my brother. I swallowed. "I didn't know, and I don't know why he took me, but he did."

"Well, where is he?" He looked around like Dad would come through the door, but I shook him back.

"Lucas," I said. "Lucas found me, and Dad was unstable, Bru."

"What do you mean?"

How did I tell my brother that our father had been shot. How did I tell him that Dad died when that was what he already believed. I gripped his arms. "Lucas is Callum's security, and Dad fired on him. He did, and Lucas had to shoot back to save me."

His face fell. "What do you mean save you?"

It was hard for me to finish, and maybe he saw that because he brought me into a hug.

"Sloane?"

"Dad's gone, Bru," I said, holding him tight. "He tried to hurt me, and Lucas saved me. Dad was going to set the whole place he took me to on fire with me inside. He *did* set the place on fire."

I remembered the flames, so big and all that *gas*. I still smelled like it.

My brother was silent, but he definitely heard me. His fingers dug into my back. "Are you sure?"

I nodded. "He was unstable, Bruno."

I broke down, my body racked with emotion. I didn't like to fucking cry, but I couldn't hold any of this in. It was too much.

I came away with my brother's hands on my face. He wiped away the tears. "Maybe you should sit down."

I wanted to, but I knew something I wanted more. "Have you heard from Dorian?"

He blinked. "Dorian?"

"Yeah. He tried to call me yesterday, but that's when Dad grabbed me. I need to talk to him. I need to see him."

He couldn't make this better. He couldn't make these feelings, *this fear* disappear or anything else. He could help though, and *I* needed to tell *him* something. If my last twenty-four hours told me anything, it was that there wasn't time to waste moments.

Every minute means something. Every hour. Every second.

Those were Dorian's words in one of his notes, and it was time I started living too. "Can I use your phone? I need to call him."

My brother let go off me, scanning my eyes. He directed a thumb toward the door. "Dorian... Dorian's here."

I shot back. "What?" How was he here? I mean, how did he even know I was here? I just got here myself. "Did you tell him I was coming here?"

My brother just looked at me, his head cocked. "The whole world knows you're here right now, Sloane. They're following your story, and the only reason that door isn't bursting down is because Callum had the hospital secure the whole floor and parts of the hospital. Dorian and his family showed up not long after that. They came for you with the Ambroses, Reeds, and..." He pocketed his hands. "Well, the Mallicks. At that point, the hospital was already secure, and from what I understand, things got pretty heated when the families found out. The news is saying they're talking to judges and getting the courts involved so they can physically come in here and…"

My brother's words drifted off, my hand up. I raised the other one. "Why would they all come here?"

"Well, for you, of course." My brother's mouth parted, his eyes narrowing. They flashed. "Did Lucas not tell you?"

"Tell me what?"

"We've been informed that Baby Girl Mallick is somewhere in the facility."

I turned toward the television. It was a reporter who'd spoken.

My brother was watching the news. Well, at least he had been, and what I saw on the screen caused my brow to jump.

I was on the screen, the video recording from only moments ago. Lucas was rushing me inside *this* hospital while photographers snapped my photo and reporters stalked me. The footage reported what had just happened outside, and since I was there, the footage didn't surprise me. I mean, Lucas said they were there about my story.

I eased away from my brother and took a seat when I read the caption on the screen. It said *Mallick Baby Girl Found*, and in the right half of the screen, the news put a picture. The image was a little baby in a blanket, and on the blanket was something I hadn't seen in years.

I used to wear a charm bracelet my parents gave me. I'd worn it, but I'd lost it one day, and the sole charm on it was fastened to the blanket.

I reached toward it, as if I could physically touch the charm, but ended up sitting back and refocusing on the whole screen. For some reason, the news was running the image of the baby next to the feed of me racing inside the hospital with Lucas.

"I don't understand," I said because I didn't. Why were

they putting me next to this baby? *Why* were they running that caption?

The seat beside me sunk down, my brother quiet. He put a hand on me. "Sloane—"

"Why are they showing this?" I asked, and the next image I recognized. It was the picture Wells and I had talked about, Ares's parents and the two babies. One of them was him, the other his twin. I blinked. "Why are they showing Ares's twin? That's disrespectful. Why are they showing that?"

The girl was... *gone*. He hadn't said how, but I'd assumed, in the moment, she'd passed. He'd been talking like that was the case, so showing her now was completely disrespectful.

My brother's throat jumped. "You know about her?"

I did, but not really. I mean, I'd just found out.

I faced the screen, and my brother squeezed my shoulder.

"They're saying that's you, sis," he said, my heart pounding. "That girl in the photo? Ares's twin? They're saying that's you, and that you're a missing person."

A missing *person*?

I stared in horror at the TV, that charm on the baby blanket I recognized. It wasn't on my childhood bracelet, but I definitely recognized it.

Ares wore the same one.

He had that day in the garage, the two charms identical.

Twins.

I sat up, images of me flashing on the screen. They were pictures taken from my social media, my picture and this... missing twin's photos put together in a side by side. They had my name, *Noa Sloane*, then her name next to it.

I read that name. Over and over, I read it, and I definitely noticed something.

The name started with a *P*.

"Pilar Mallick," my brother said, reading it as I had. He faced me. "They're saying that's you, Sloane." He leaned forward. "They're saying *that's* your name."

Thank you so much for reading *Savage Little Lies*! You can continue the Court Legacy series with the conclusion to Dorian and Sloane's story in: *Tiny Dark Deeds*! Amazon